KEEPING SECRETS

Sue Gee had a country childhood and an urban working life in book and magazine publishing before going freelance in 1983. She now writes, reviews and is an Associate Lecturer on the Writing and Publishing course at Middlesex University. Her other novels are *Spring Will Be Ours, The Last Guests of the Season, Letters From Prague* and *The Hours of the Night.* She lives in London with her Polish partner and their son.

KEEPING SECRETS

Sue Gee

ARROW

Published by Arrow Books in 1996

3 5 7 9 10 8 6 4 2

First published in 1991 in the United Kingdom by
Random Century Group

First published in paperback in 1992 by
Warner Books

This edition published in 1996 by
Arrow Books Limited
20 Vauxhall Bridge Road, London SW1V 2SA

Random House Australia (Pty) Limited
20 Alfred Street, Milsons Point, Sydney,
New South Wales 2061, Australia

Random House New Zealand Limited
18 Poland Road, Glenfield
Auckland 10, New Zealand

Random House South Africa (Pty) Limited
PO Box 337, Bergvlei, South Africa

RANDOM HOUSE UK Limited Reg. No. 954009

A CIP catalogue record for this book
is available from the British Library

Papers used by Random House UK Limited
are natural, recyclable products made from wood grown in
sustainable forests. The manufacturing processes conform to
the environmental regulations of the country of origin.

ISBN 0 09 966401 1

Printed and bound in Great Britain by
Cox & Wyman Ltd, Reading, Berkshire

1

The street where Alice Sinclair lived was quiet, and lined with lime trees: a north London street of Victorian family houses set between the roaring Holloway Road and a pleasing common, with tennis courts, broad paths, a playground and swimming pool. During the day mothers pushed small children down past parked cars to the library and up to the sandpit and the swings; at night, curtains were drawn and cats sat motionless on the low walls at the front or prowled the creeper-covered fences at the back. From time to time the darkness was disturbed by yowling, but rarely by more than this. The street was enclosed, sealed off from all but local traffic; in its safety and solidity it represented to Alice everything she used to associate only with other people: contentment, security, peace.

At half-past ten on a Friday night she was wandering round the bedroom in her long cotton nightdress, putting things away. The room was warm and untidy, newspapers and journals heaped in piles on the floor by the big double bed, a bookcase still overflowing from when they'd first moved in, meaning to sort it out later. Clothes were strewn over the sofa beneath the window, and a little trail of toys and crisps led out on to the landing. The evidence of family life, run by someone who had never expected it, the hour domestic and respectable, a time when home-loving people might switch off the news and go up to run a bath. Half-past ten is not like eleven, which begins to be dangerous.

There had been a time when Alice's weekends had barely begun by eleven, when she was neither at home nor respectable. She was restless, out on the prowl; taking risks at parties given by people she hardly knew; going home with strangers; waking, late, alone. In those days she had lived in rented rooms – for a while in London, where she was at art school; for a long time in Oxford, where the start of a love affair had taken her and where the end of another – no, much more than that – had put her in the bin. She had no family near her, although her elder sister Hilda, living an organised life in London, used occasionally to come and visit her, and she had few friends, although she knew a lot of people. She was a solitary, beautiful drifter, smiling at everyone, wanting to die.

Those days, in which some terrible things had happened, and nearly happened, seemed now as remote as though someone else had lived them. These days, she tried not to think of them.

On a chair by the wardrobe her husband's suitcase lay open, haphazardly packed with two clean shirts, clean underwear and socks, the grey ribbed sweater Alice had given him for Christmas. She found a handkerchief, roughly stitched with a 'T' by Hettie, and put it on top; she put Lego in a box and picked up Annie's vest and pants, flung down when they raced to the bath, and her own jeans and sweater, stuffing them all in the laundry basket. Outside, along the landing, Tony was still in his cramped study, opening and closing files, looking for something.

'Okay?' she called. 'Can I help?'

'It's all right.' He was sliding open drawers in the filing cabinet, muttering. Tomorrow he was leaving for a conference in Manchester. Most of the journals heaped up in here were his, overspill from the study: *Family Law, New Law Journal, Legal Action.* 'Shan't be long.'

Alice picked up her brush from the chest of drawers and began to run it through her hair – pale, silky, fair, little changed from when she was a child, quite different from her sister's sleek dark bob. Alice was slender, and looked delicate, although she was rarely ill; in her early thirties but looking younger, despite her past. This was partly due to physical qualities – slenderness, fairness, dressing, still, like a student – more to do with the childlike air she had always had, or at least the air of a particular kind of child: frail, self-absorbed, preoccupied. They were the qualities Tony had fallen in love with, looking for what lay beneath that dreamy vulnerability, searching for her secrets. Tenderly and insistently questioning, discovering, as he thought, each one, he had offered her protection, and she had accepted – protection from the world and from herself, sinking gratefully and disbelievingly into a home, a family, a place.

She put down the hairbrush and went to the window, hearing voices. Pulling the curtains a little apart she looked out, seeing in the quiet, tree-lined street, with its window boxes and drawn curtains, a couple walking up from the far end: he, in flapping coat, was wheeling a bike; she, with cropped hair and beret, kept pace beside him. They were talking loudly, deep in discussion: Alice thought they had probably just come out of a meeting, picturing the smoke-filled upper room of a pub. As they drew closer she saw how young they were, and watched them go past, listening to their animated voices and the

6

whirr of the bike, cutting through her side street to the corner, where they could turn down to the main road.

When I was that age I would never have argued like that with a man, she thought. I wouldn't have dared. Slept with, no doubt, but never argued. That was more dangerous than anything. She closed the curtains and went over to the bed, pulling back the duvet, hoping, as every night, that Annie would not wake up.

In the study, Tony slammed shut the filing cabinet. A couple of minutes later he came out, blowing his nose, on the way to the bathroom. Alice lay back on the pillows, half-listening to running water, the murmur of *The World Tonight*. She had her eyes closed when Tony came in, dropping his clothes on the sofa; he came round to her side of the bed and quietly switched off her light, slipping in beside her. He took off his glasses, put them on his bedside table, and gave a long, tired sigh.

'Found it?' she asked sleepily. 'Whatever it was.'

'Press cuttings. Yes. God, it's a mess in there – you don't ever let the girls in, do you?'

'Never,' said Alice, remembering yesterday morning, when she had found Annie underneath his desk, stirring the wastepaper basket.

'Liar.' He moved closer, and put his arm round her. 'God, I'm done for.'

'What time's your train?'

'Eight-fifteen. I suppose I'd better leave by half-seven.' He reached for the alarm clock, flicking up the button. 'You'll be all right, won't you?'

'Fine.' Alice yawned, and rested her head on his chest. Tony had a long, thin body; he was fit, in the sense that he was perfectly well, and did not smoke, but he walked and ran – occasionally across a squash court, more usually trying to catch a bus, or chasing his daughters in the park – rather awkwardly, as if movement were something of a strange, foreign thing. On first introduction there was always a pause, a moment when you wondered if this was going to be a dull man, seeing his very ordinary glasses, and slightly receding, ordinary-coloured hair. But Tony had rare qualities: a true generosity, a genuine interest in other people. He was reserved but secure, a man whose instincts were protective – hence his work, a criminal lawyer in an inter-city firm where the sign for legal aid was prominent; hence his love for Alice, by whom he had been at first bewitched.

When Alice first met him she had barely noticed him – but then, at that time, she was finding it difficult to concentrate for long on

7

anyone except herself. She was still living in Oxford, and not long out of hospital, still taking things. She had gone to the lunch party – a summer Sunday, a dozen people with forks and glasses sitting on rugs beneath the trees, cows flicking flies in the meadows beyond – because Hilda, on the telephone from London, had told her she had to, that it would be good for her. She sat on the edge of a plaid rug, drinking too much, half-listening to the lazy talk around her, hugging her long bare legs in her pale cotton skirt. She was surprised when Tony rang her the next day, and she realized he must have asked particularly for her phone number. She remembered him only as someone listening to a girl in earrings, who laughed a lot.

Standing in the narrow dark hall of the rented house in Jericho she heard herself saying: 'I've had a breakdown, I'm not very good company at the moment.'

'It doesn't matter,' said Tony. 'We don't have to talk.'

'I don't want to go to bed, either. I've been fucked up,' said Alice, astonishing herself.

There was a pause. 'I only go to bed with people I know very well.'

'How sensible,' said Alice. 'I suppose you think I'm a tart. Excuse me, but I'm not myself. I don't know who I am, if you can understand that.'

'I can,' said Tony. 'I was watching you yesterday – you looked very beautiful and lost. I thought we might go for a walk, if you felt like it.'

'You sound like quite a nice person,' Alice said. 'I'm not very nice at all. And I don't want to be patronised and rescued, thank you. I can't even remember what you look like.' She found she was trembling, and fumbled in her shoulder bag, hanging on a hook among the coats, feeling for the small brown bottle of pink and green capsules. She'd already had this morning's; she thought it was incredible, anyway, that they trusted her with anything, considering how she'd gone into the bin in the first place. But then she'd refused to come out unless they gave her something. Perhaps they were sugar. She unscrewed the cap, swallowing just one.

'Hello?' said the telephone. 'Hello?'

Alice picked it up again. 'Sorry. I'm not feeling very well, I didn't mean to be so rude.'

'You're certainly . . . direct.'

'Well, if you don't like it,' Alice heard herself saying in a shaky

8

voice, 'you know what you can do. I never asked you to ring me up in the first place.'

'I only thought we might go for a walk,' Tony said mildly.

Alice, embarrassed and confused, found she was crying.

'I mean – to start with,' he said. 'I mean I didn't want to rush in and upset you . . . Christ, you've got me in knots now, please don't cry.'

Alice put down the phone and wept.

Now, countless conversations later, years later, she rested her head on Tony's rather too thin chest and said: 'Do you know what I was thinking, earlier on?'

'No,' he said, inquiring.

'When the girls were in the bath – for the first time I thought that I'd like to have another.'

'Did you,' he said, flatly.

'Do you think . . .'

'No. No, I really don't.'

'Why?' Alice raised her head and looked at him. 'You said you wanted a large family.'

'Did I?' He put up a hand and stroked her hair. 'Did I say that?'

'You know you did. When Hettie was born we couldn't wait to have another.'

'We've got another. She's a nightmare.'

'No she's not.' Alice made a face. 'Just one more? Please?'

'What *has* got into you? I thought you were tired out.'

'I am, I don't mean necessarily now, I just thought one day . . .'

'One day,' said Tony. 'Ah. I thought for a moment you were expecting to start tonight. Mind you . . .' A hand moved down under the duvet, stroking her bottom. 'Mmm. How about a quick one? Just to see us through the weekend.'

Alice laughed. 'I thought *you* were tired out.'

'I was. Come here.' His hand moved down further, gently tugging up the long cotton nightdress. 'But no babies, not tonight. Are you suitably equipped?'

'No,' said Alice, suppressing another yawn. 'What do you take me for?'

'For my loving wife, who should be always on the *qui vive*.' He sighed. 'Oh, well, I suppose I'll have to resort to primitive practices.' He rolled over, drawing the length of her against him, slipping a warm hand between her legs. 'You do want to?'

'Yes,' said Alice, feeling nothing at all. She reached over him, switching out his light, and gave herself up to his pleasure.

When it was over, she fell asleep at once, woken at some dark indeterminate hour by Annie, crying in her bed, waiting for one of them to go to her. She stumbled out and snuggled in with her, not wanting to wake Tony, who was usually so good about getting up.

When they woke in the morning he had already gone, leaving the duvet flung back, pyjamas on the floor and a half-eaten bowl of cornflakes in the bathroom.

'Where's Daddy?' Hettie asked, coming downstairs in her nightie.

'In Manchester, a long way away. He's got to work this weekend.'

'Oh.' Hettie hitched herself up on to her chair, and reached for the cereal. 'What are we going to do?'

'I haven't thought yet,' said Alice, putting the kettle on. Annie tugged at her. 'Hang on a minute, Annie, I'm just coming, go and sit down.' She looked out of the kitchen window at a sky threatening rain. 'Tomorrow Hilda's coming to lunch. If it's fine we can go to the playground first. Annie – go and sit down!'

From the top of the common, near the tennis courts, church bells sounded: on Sundays it felt as if they were in the country, or living in the eighteenth century, when the houses on the broad paths bordering the common were full of families, not flats. Who went to church here now? It had rained during the night and the air was fresh; hand in hand Alice and the girls walked slowly through the side streets, bringing Hettie's striped umbrella, just in case.

The plane trees round the playground were just in leaf, and after the rain the ground cover of broken bark beneath the swings and climbing frames smelt of damp wood. Hettie and Annie let go of Alice's hands and ran to the gate. The playground was a big one, new, with a twenty-foot slide and a Tarzan contraption where teenage boys swooped, yelling.

'Don't go anywhere I can't see you.'

'We won't!'

There was a large sandpit for little ones, and picnic tables set out at intervals on brick paths. Alice sat down at one, parking Hettie's umbrella, and pulled the newspaper out of her bag. She skimmed the headlines absently and began to read, looking up every now and then to check on the girls. The playground was filling up. Children clambered and swung, shouting; little ones dug in the sandpit, and played shops and homes: there was a small red and blue house in the middle with a pitched roof, open doors and windows.

Parents – a few fathers, but mostly mothers, who had left fathers to lie in with the papers – pushed and helped on and off, and urged discarded coats and jackets on passing offspring, who shook their heads and ran off. 'I don't *need* a coat!'

Hearing a child cry, Alice looked up from the paper, but it wasn't one of hers. Everything looked cold and bright, under a sky with scudding clouds. Some of the parents had brought flasks of coffee, and were sipping from plastic cups. She put her hands in the pockets of her duffle coat, and wished she'd done the same.

In the old days, seeing Alice out and about, you would have thought her in need of no one, choosing to be alone – that was her defence, an air of preoccupation and detachment covering long years of unease. Even now, you would think twice before going to join her at her table in the playground. She did not look as though she were in need of anyone's company, and now it was true: she was watching her daughters, content.

Hettie, the elder, would be six in the summer, a sturdy, square-faced child, with shiny brown hair beneath a dusty pink crocheted hat which she had chosen herself. She was sensible, and had kept her coat on; she sat at the top of the slide with her legs in navy tights stretched neatly out before her, waiting for the child in front to reach the bottom. When the slide was clear she came down with solemn enjoyment, hands in her lap; she got neatly off, and went straight round to the steps, waiting her turn to climb again. If people jostled Hettie, she walked away; if she fell over she picked herself up. She had slept all night since she was six weeks old and usually woke in a good mood; when Alice asked her to take something upstairs, or fetch Annie's beaker from the kitchen, she usually did it without a fuss. From the beginning, it had been as if a space with exactly Hettie's shape had been waiting all along for her to occupy it, and settle in. Now she was here, Alice, who saw nothing of herself in her first-born, marvelled at her, rejoicing in her ordinariness.

Annie was different. Annie was what Alice would have expected, and could cope with only because of Hettie. Annie was a screamer. She clung. From the beginning, where Hettie could be left with almost anyone, Annie cried, and would not be comforted until Alice came back. The second child, now almost three, she was more like a first: loving only Alice, bellowing to be picked up and made a fuss of when she fell, thumping other children when they took her toys or

11

refused to share theirs. And perhaps Alice was, perversely or in response, more like a first-time mother with her – watchful, anxious, protective. Though Annie was exhausting, Alice understood her; from time to time she was a little in awe of her elder daughter, who seemed to need her less. Annie could, in fact, be more sociable than Hettie, who had never hit anyone: where Hettie would happily play by herself for half a morning, Annie needed a friend – she needed her sister, or her mother, or someone from playgroup. Alone, she had a pleading, disconsolate air, and nothing was ever quite right.

Much of the time, Alice coped with Annie by switching off. When she switched on again she had to force herself to be patient. But although she heard herself snapping at least once a day, for much of the time she did manage patience, more than she would ever have thought possible. For the first time in her life she was able to forget herself, a priceless gift for someone who used to be conscious of every passing moment. For much of the time she was tired – from nights broken by Annie, from early mornings, simply from being with two small children. But often, despite all this, she found herself thinking: my children have redeemed me.

Being Alice, when she did so she felt also a wave of guilt: that she should have found peace to be so simple, after all – all those wasted years before; that she should find it by bringing children into the world, instead of in herself, or in her loving husband; should even have dared to bring children into the world, polluted and corrupt and dangerous. Unlike the old Alice, however, she did not allow herself to dwell on such thoughts. She had one particular regret which grew rather than diminished but, this aside, she did at last allow herself to be happy, relishing solitude, privacy behind her own front door.

It was almost eleven o'clock. Annie and another little girl were passing each other cups of sand through the window of the red and blue house. The sun had gone in again and Alice put up her hood. Annie was beside her, wanting something. 'I'm hungry, I'm hungry!' She clambered on to the bench, and pulled at Alice's open bag. 'I'm *hungry!*'

'All right, Annie, don't do that. Would you like an apple?'

'Crisps.'

'Crisps, *please.*' Alice pulled out a packet and looked at her watch. Annie tugged open the packet, spilled crisps everywhere and began to wail. Alice bent down to pick them up, and gave her the packet again. Annie munched, and Alice put her arm round her, watching

Hettie on a swing, and wondering what Hilda was doing now, before she came. Wondering, too, as before most visits, if Hilda, whom she hadn't seen for weeks, who was so different – always working, always knowing what to do – would for ever have the same effect on her, turning her back from grown-up mother, wife, to the little girl who watched, and knocked at doors, and waited.

Hilda was tall and dark, her hair shaped beautifully into a short, sloping pageboy, her features finely cut where Alice's were soft and vague. She wore the same round glasses she had worn since she was twenty, and dressed in dark colours – charcoal, navy, and slate jackets and trousers worn with expensive shirts. She lived at the top of a Victorian house in Hackney, in a square, from where she was able to walk to work.

The houses in the square were tall and narrow, porticoed, with railings and steep steps to the front door; in the late seventies, when they had become faded and rundown, the developers had moved in, knocking through and opening out. There were sanded floors, and picked-out cornices, basements turned into kitchens fitted in country pine; there were burglar alarms, and boxes of geraniums at gleaming windows.

Not everything had been redeveloped. At intervals, on all sides of the square, stood houses which looked as though no one had opened the front door for twenty years; some of them were visited by council meals-on-wheels vans, district nurses and debt collecters. Hilda, walking to and from work through the square, speculated on the dwindling lives of the people inside. Her house, Anya Novakova's house, had been occupied by the same family for decades; unlike them, it had succumbed neither to neglect nor to a developer's chequebook.

Anya and Hilda had met at the choral society they both belonged to, rehearsing once a week in a church hall near Mare Street.

•

In the spring of 1983 Hilda, talking in the coffee break to a pale soprano, saw Anya approach from the altos and wait, smiling, diffident.

'Hello.' Hilda towered over Anya, five-foot-three in low heels, into her sixties, her spectacles clipped on to a chain which hung over a flowery shirt.

'Excuse me.' Anya had bright brown eyes; she brushed back her straying hair with a mottled hand. 'I hope you will not think I am intruding, but I hear you are looking for somewhere to live?'

'I have somewhere to live,' said Hilda, whose manner could be offputting. 'I am looking for somewhere to buy. I've been left some money by my father, and want to use it sensibly.'

The soprano went to put her plastic coffee cup in the bin; Hilda and Anya eyed each other, neither easy women.

'I have a flat at the top of my house,' Anya said carefully. 'We had it converted last year. My husband was an antiquarian bookseller, we were going to let this flat when he retired. He died in January, it was very sudden.' She spread her hands uncertainly. 'Now I am thinking of selling it.'

'I'm sorry about your husband,' said Hilda. From the corner of the hall the piano sounded; people were moving back to their places, scraping chairs on the bare floorboards. 'Perhaps I could come and see the flat? I'm living in a basement at the moment; it was all I could find when I came to London.'

'And where are you from?'

'Northamptonshire. And you?'

'Czechoslovakia,' said Anya, moving back towards the altos. 'But that was a very long time ago.'

Hilda went to see the flat that following Saturday. She followed Anya up the flights of stairs carpeted in a fading Axminster held in place by stair rods. This reminded Hilda of her parents' house: stair rods were something from her childhood, shared in some sense with Alice and her mother, guided mainly by her father. She felt at home, and full of emotion. Ahead of her, Anya was panting a little.

'We bought this house in 1949,' she said. 'Our first married home.'

'How nice,' said Hilda politely; she looked at faded brown photographs hung on the walls along the landing, of parents and grandparents, stiffly arranged in long-ago sitting rooms in Prague.

'Two years we saved for the deposit; in the day we were working in Foyles, all day on our feet, and then in the evenings in Lyons Corner House.' Anya led Hilda up a second, narrower flight of stairs, and unlocked the door at the top. Light fell on to the landing, and a bookcase, standing in the corner.

'This is the apartment. The flat.' She climbed a little stairway, three or four steps, and stood aside, gesturing. 'Please . . .'

Hilda explored two airy rooms, a small kitchen, a dark bathroom. The sitting room overlooked the square, tall sash windows framing plane trees, television aerials, sky. From the bedroom, six steps across a landing to the back of the house, she looked down on to Anya's garden, walled, trellised, well-tended, with a little terrace and an old garden table. At the far end a cat padded across the lawn and leapt through the trellis. Next door was a tangle of bindweed, and what looked like an air-raid shelter; on the right a rusting tin bath lay in a nest of long grass.

'Blacks,' said Anya beside her. 'They don't care.'

Hilda said nothing, thinking that this was not the moment.

Further along she could see gardens like Anya's, where roses clambered and the grass was cut. She turned back into the room, which had been given a pale, pleasing carpet, and walked through it all again, placing her desk at the sitting room window, her pictures on the walls.

'It's very nice,' she said. 'I should like to live here.' Already the rented basement flat in a road off Newington Green was moving into the past. There was a garage on the corner and a late-night kebab shop two doors up, where car doors banged. Here she could be peaceful.

'Yes,' she said, 'I have enough furniture of my own. And anyway I was hoping to buy one or two things.'

'Come downstairs and have a coffee,' said Anya. She closed the flat door behind Hilda, bumping the bookcase. 'I'm sorry – there are too many books, my husband's. I can move them if necessary.'

'No, please. I shouldn't mind at all. I'll be bringing more anyway.'

'And may I ask what work you do?' said Anya, as they went down the stairs.

'I teach,' said Hilda, whose work was her vocation.

'Music?'

'No, no. I teach English in a college of further education. I've just been made head of department.'

'Have you?' Anya was leading her through the hall downstairs to the sitting room. She indicated a high-backed chair by the fireplace. 'Then you will want peace and quiet when you come home. Please, sit down. I will bring the coffee.'

'Thank you.' Hilda sat, and observed the piano, the family photographs. Two cats, one tabby, one marmalade, watched her from the sofa. 'And what about you?' she asked Anya, when she returned with a round grey metal tray. 'You probably want company, don't you? I'm not always very companionable.'

Anya set down the tray. 'But you are honest. It is better to know where one stands.' She poured dark coffee into little gold-rimmed cups. There was milk in a beaten metal jug and a plate of crumbling unEnglish biscuits. 'Please – help yourself.' She sat in her chair and looked across at Hilda, in her dark expensive clothes. 'You are not married?'

'No,' said Hilda in her calm voice, as if: why should I be?

Anya stirred her coffee with a fluted spoon. 'I was married for almost forty-two years,' she said. She nodded to the photograph above the fireplace, where a small bald man with glasses on a medieval nose looked absently at the camera. 'My daughter took that.'

Hilda looked up at it. 'He has an interesting face.'

'He was a good man. He got on my nerves when he retired, I wasn't used to it, having him here all day, and having the builders in – what a business. I used to say to him: "Go back to work, you are driving me crazy." Then he died – just like that. He went out to post some letters, you know, just on the corner here, and he had a heart attack in the street.' Anya's hand, holding the coffee cup, shook, chinking the fluted spoon.

Hilda said: 'How terrible,' thinking: If she is going to go on at me every evening, I shall not be able to live here.

'What I want now,' said Anya, putting the cup on the tray, 'is . . . I do not expect company, but I should like to know that there is someone coming in in the evenings, to know that I am not going to bed in an empty house. This square is getting quite posh now but still – we are in the East End of London. Things happen. I'm nervous by myself.'

'Yes,' said Hilda, 'I can understand that.'

'Then there are the cats. Sometimes I go to visit my daughter in Sussex, I need someone to feed them.'

I suppose that's all right, thought Hilda, nodding. To be in the house and to feed the cats – it's what anyone would want. So long as there is nothing more.

'That's all,' said Anya. 'You would of course be completely independent.' She got to her feet. 'I will give you the address of my solicitor.'

Hilda stood up, feeling brought to her feet by the headmistress. She was used to conducting interviews on her own terms, and felt a need to reassert her position. 'I want to make a wise investment,' she said coolly. 'After all, one doesn't inherit money every day.'

'Certainly not,' said Anya. 'Poor Josef left me almost nothing, only the house. The books, I suppose are worth something, but there is my daughter . . .' They were in the hall, now; she pulled open the glass-panelled door and the tabby cat went out. Children were cycling round the square, shouting.

Anya held out her hand. 'Perhaps you will let me know at the next rehearsal.'

'Or sooner,' said Hilda, and took her telephone number, snapping shut her address book.

When she got back to her basement room, walking the whole way there because she was restless and undecided, and had nothing else to do, she stood looking at the photograph of her parents on her desk, her father tall, grey-haired, a quiet academic who had loved her mother much more than she loved him, and whom Hilda had loved more than anyone. She could imagine him in conversation with Anya, and dead Josef; she could imagine him liking the house in Hackney, with its faded rugs and yellowing antiquarian books. If I were a different kind of person, she thought, putting back the photograph, I might be thinking now that I had been guided to this point. But I am not that kind of person, so I shall simply say that it feels right, and go ahead. For a moment she wondered whether to telephone Alice, and tell her she was moving, and then she decided to leave it. Alice was with Tony now, expecting a baby; Hilda didn't feel like disturbing a married Saturday afternoon. She had been used to spending weekends with her father, catching the train on Friday evenings to Kettering; he waited there with the car to drive her out to the village where she and Alice had grown up. Now he was gone, she was finding weekends difficult.

She moved into Anya's house at half term.

Hilda lived at the top of the house, Anya mostly at the bottom, although her bedroom and bathroom were on the first floor, and Hilda, working late, could hear her call in the cats and climb the stairs. She also had a small spare bedroom, kept for her daughter, Liba, a large, silent woman, who came to stay every few weeks. When Hilda left for work in the mornings she could hear Anya's radio down in the kitchen, the chink of breakfast things, tins of catfood banged on the table top. She went out, closing the door quietly, not wanting to be buttonholed.

Leaving the square she cut through side streets, crossing two main roads and a park until she came to the high walls topped by mesh, and the tall iron gates outside the college. Asian teenagers, her morning students, were going through the gates in twos and threes, the boys in white shirts, turbans and dark Marks & Spencer trousers, the girls in neon blue and pink baggy trousers and shirts, and ankle socks. They were doing A levels in Business Studies and Information Technology; for Hilda, who brushed up their English, they wrote short, effortful essays in Biro: My Favourite Television Programme; A Story from My Childhood; My Ambition. She also taught a GCSE class to Turkish Cypriot, West Indian and disaffected British students, and twice a week she ran a basic English course for Asian women at home. Their afternoons in the college were for some of them the only time they left the house.

If she had no evening classes, Hilda went out for a drink or a meal with a friend, or to a film. If she went straight home, walking along the square in the late afternoon, she could, in fine weather, hear through the open window Anya playing the piano. Sometimes she would come out into the hall and ask Hilda in for a cup of tea.

Once a week they left the house together, to go to choir; on concert weekends they went to rehearsals on Saturday afternoons. Hilda looked forward to these, to walking in at two o'clock on a Saturday afternoon hearing the orchestra tune up; it was for rehearsals that she had, before her father died, spent rare weekends in London. Otherwise, she had spent her time with him, cooking and talking and doing the garden, sleeping in the room of her childhood.

Alice had not come home; Alice had left a long time ago, in every sense, and now she was married. Hilda and her father used occasionally to discuss her: whether she was happy now, whether it would work. They did not discuss whether Hilda might ever marry, or was happy; if her mother had still been alive there would have been a great deal of such talk.

Hilda and her father read the same papers and recommended books to each other. They discussed Labour politics as if in a friendly tutorial, and in the evenings they watched television or listened to concerts; sometimes they invited friends in from the village. On Sunday afternoons, after tea, her father drove her back to the station, and waved her off from the platform. Hilda used to lean out of the carriage window and watch him walk slowly away towards the ticket barrier, already abstracted; she settled into her seat and was carried back to London, where she supposed she belonged now.

But when he died, she was forced to realise that her life here, so full during the week, had at weekends a borderline quality: without her father she could not imagine how else to spend a Saturday or Sunday, wondered who else she could ever find to talk to in the same easy and absorbing way. Certainly there was no one with whom she felt able to be silent, as they had been able to be, companionable and ordinary.

The concert this weekend was one she would not be able, the following weekend, to tell him about; she and Anya came out of the church, still humming, and walked home. In the square they passed windows with curtains undrawn; Hilda glanced at a couple curled up on the sofa watching television; at a dinner party in a candlelit basement kitchen. 'They will all be robbed,' said Anya.

At their own house, the cats were waiting on the balustrade, one on either side of the steps, unmoving. They leapt off as the two women reached the steps and Anya pulled out her keys.

'Come along.' They curled themselves round her legs, mewing. Light shone through the thick glass panels in the door; she always left on the lamp on the walnut table, and the hall, with its browning wallpaper and polished banister, felt as if it were winter. Anya double-locked the door and slid the bolts, grunting.

'Goodnight,' said Hilda, from the bottom of the stairs.

Anya straightened up from the bolt. 'You won't come in for a coffee?'

'Will you think me very rude?'

Anya shrugged. 'Not at all. You work very hard, you must be tired. Come another time.'

'Thank you,' said Hilda, and climbed the stairs. She heard Anya go into the sitting room and close the door, and, a few minutes later, the sound of the piano. Up in her own flat she undressed slowly and got into bed.

She could hear the trains going through Dalston Junction: when it was very late, they carried through nuclear waste containers. Closer, somewhere across the gardens, she could hear people outside, and music, the tail end of a party. Hilda was going to a housewarming party next weekend, invited by Fanny, a friend from university who had married an ambitious accountant. They had recently moved to a penthouse apartment in Camden Town with views across Regent's Park to the zoo; an airy space constructed of glass, gables and conce-aled lighting, with a minstrels' gallery.

The first time Hilda had visited, invited to tea one Sunday not long after her father died, she had felt a mixture of awe and anger that Alan, so unremarkable a being, evading taxes for dubious companies, should inhabit such luxury, and on the train back to Dalston found herself engaging in a long conversation about it with her father who, had he been alive, would have been driving her down through the village to the Kettering road. She recalled all this now, drifting off to sleep, and at some indistinct moment recollection of his smile and easy understanding became the beginning of a dream, in which he was still alive, and she had someone to talk to.

The following Saturday evening Hilda walked from Camden Road station along the main road towards Parkway. It was warm and close, the end of a dusty July day; buses roared past her and pigeons sidestepped the litter, pecking at takeaway cartons and bits of bread. Outside the pubs were one or two tables and chairs; the canal looked scummy and grey. Hilda walked up Parkway and turned with relief into the quiet side streets. Cars were parked all the way along, and every now and then a front door opened and people came hurrying out in pairs, getting into one of the cars and driving off.

Later, Hilda was to find herself thinking of this walk to Fanny and Alan's as the last time she walked as a single woman. This was untrue, because she remained single, but she no longer felt it. Walking now, she was thinking half about work and half about Fanny, humming a bit of Haydn; she was used to going out by herself, and thought that the way she felt was how most people felt – reserved and self-contained, much of the time switched off from much of the world. Only later, looking back, did she realise how lonely she had been, and by then she was experiencing loneliness of a new kind: of absence, separation, someone longed for. She had thought such feelings related only to bereavement.

She walked up the steps of Fanny and Alan's house, and rang the bell. The intercom was a very expensive one which worked perfectly and Hilda could hear laughter in the background, and music, as Fanny said lightly: 'Hello?' and let her in. Inside, she climbed three broad flights of sea-green carpet, finding Fanny at the top holding the door wide.

'Have you had a ghastly journey?' She was wearing white, a short sleeveless little dress that showed off a sunbed tan. Golden bracelets clattered as she pushed back her thin blonde hair. 'Everyone's dying to meet you.'

'Don't be silly,' said Hilda, kissing her, and followed her into the room, which was enormous. The evening sun slanted through the roof terrace doors and through the skylights and tall, cathedral-like windows inset above and below the gallery, lighting the polished beech floor, the shining heads of the other guests, among whom Alan, in a pale cream summer suit, was circulating with a bottle. He lifted it at Hilda, smiling brightly.

'Hi there.'

Hilda flickered back a smile. Alan was getting a paunch from expense-account lunches, and his hair looked manicured. He moved smoothly towards her, still smiling. 'How are you doing, Hilda?'

'How am I doing what?' asked Hilda, taking a glass and watching it foam to the brim. She took a sip and nodded. 'Delicious. Thank you.'

'You look gorgeous,' said Fanny, as Alan moved on with his bottle. She looked at Hilda's black cotton dress, and the curving silver band around her neck. 'How's the new flat?'

'Different from this,' said Hilda. 'You must come and see it. My neighbour is the widow of a Czechoslovakian antiquarian books dealer.'

'She would be,' said Fanny. 'I suppose you disapprove of all this.'

'It's beautiful,' said Hilda truthfully, as the doorbell rang again. 'Fanny, you don't need to look after me. I'm okay.'

But Fanny led Hilda towards a little knot of three, two men and a woman in flowing indigo silk, whose hair was loose and waving.

'Can I interrupt?' she said. 'I'd like you to meet an old friend of mine, Hilda King. Hilda, this is James Gibbon, the architect who designed our place . . .' James, large and dark, with a full face and beard, inclined his head. '. . . and Klara, his wife . . . and Stephen – Knowles? Have I got that right?' The other man nodded. He was lean, greying, with laugh lines; he wore a loose cotton jacket but his outline was, Hilda later recalled, well-cut and spare, and he stood like someone at ease. 'Stephen and James have just gone into partnership,' Fanny told Hilda.

'Really?' Hilda waited to hear about this and was told, by James, as Fanny disappeared, that he'd been looking for a while for someone with connections outside London and recently found Stephen, whose practice was in Norfolk. 'It broadens our scope,' he said. 'We've both found we have clients looking in different directions – a lot of people are commuting from Norfolk now, or thinking about moving out there, now Suffolk's got so expensive. And of course there are plenty of people who just want a pied-à-terre here.'

'Yes,' said Hilda, 'I suppose there are. How enterprising of you.'

James frowned, fleetingly, and held out a hand to his wife. 'All right, sweetie?'

She nodded.

'We had something rather unpleasant happen on the way here,' James explained. 'I was telling Stephen.'

'Oh?'

'Well, Klara's pregnant,' said James momentously, and Klara gave a modest laugh.

'Congratulations,' said Hilda. 'What happened on the way?'

'Oh, it was nothing really,' said Klara. 'Just that a cat ran out into the road and was hit. I mean, normally that sort of thing doesn't really upset me unduly, you know, but since I've been pregnant – well, I suppose it makes you more sensitive, doesn't it?'

'I wouldn't know,' said Hilda. 'Was it killed?'

'Oh, yes, I think so – straight away, thank God. But I was terribly shaken. I mean, I'm not a morbid person . . . not the sort of person to dwell on things at all, not usually.'

Hilda, before she could stop herself, said: 'Does that mean you don't think?'

Klara looked at her in astonishment.

'Forgive me,' said Hilda quickly. 'That was quite unnecessary.'

'Food, everyone,' said Fanny at her elbow. 'Alan's terribly keen on cooking at the moment, he's been in the kitchen all *day*.' She nodded towards a long table set back beneath the gallery, laid with a linen cloth and pale pink china. Dishes were piled high with salads and seafood. 'Just help yourselves.' She went over to another group, and Hilda, without surprise, watched James and Klara move unhesitatingly away. Beside her, Stephen Knowles said calmly: 'Do you make a habit of talking to people like that?'

'No,' said Hilda, 'I don't know what got into me. Perhaps it has something to do with the weather.' She watched the party making its way, talking loudly, towards the food. 'Do you know many of these people?' she asked. 'How did you meet James?'

'At a conference last year,' said Stephen. 'I came down from Norwich this afternoon; I don't know anyone else here at all.'

'Please don't feel you have to stay with me.'

'Why should I feel that?' Stephen drained his glass. 'I'm waiting for the next outburst.' He looked at her inquiringly. 'Speculating on the last.'

'I shouldn't bother,' said Hilda. 'It must have been the wrong chemistry, that's all.'

Stephen raised an eyebrow. 'Which leads one to speculate still further – what do you do when the chemistry is right?'

Hilda found herself unable to give a crisp reply. There was a brief silence, in which she further found herself acknowledging that she was interested in this man, as he appeared to be interested in her. The experience was unfamiliar.

'I'll tell you something,' said Stephen, 'I'm very hungry – I didn't eat before I left home. May I escort you to the supper table, Ms King?'

'You may.'

'Everything all right?' Alan appeared beside them with another bottle; he refilled their glasses. 'How's it going, Hilda?' He gave her a wink. 'Enjoying yourself?'

Hilda smiled at him sweetly. 'I believe,' she said to Stephen as Alan breezed away, 'that although he is vulgar and undeserving, Alan is a very good cook. Why did you not eat before leaving home?'

'If I asked you that question you would tell me to mind my own business,' said Stephen. They moved towards the table, standing in line. 'You are a puritan,' he continued. 'Whoever said people got what they deserved?'

'One is allowed to have one's views,' Hilda said primly.

'And one clearly has plenty,' said Stephen. 'How do you come to be here this evening? It doesn't seem to be quite your scene.'

'It isn't. But I've known Fanny for a long time; she perseveres with her friends, and she wanted me to come.'

'I see. But really you disapprove.'

'Well . . . a little.'

'Of money?'

'Of the wrong people having it.'

'And who are the right people?'

Hilda began to feel over-interrogated. They had reached the table, where Fanny was serving a plump salmon from a bed of lemon slices and fronds of dill. 'I'm not very good at this,' she said, seeing Hilda approach, 'but do have some.' She smiled radiantly at Stephen. 'Have James and Klara deserted you?'

'They deserted me,' said Hilda, 'I was rather rude.'

'Oh, God, Hilda, why?'

'Sorry.' She took back her plate, on which Fanny had deposited a broken slice of fish, and began to help herself to salad. 'Did Alan do the salmon? It looks wonderful.'

'Yes,' said Fanny, serving Stephen. 'I don't think I'll tell him that you've upset the chief guests. He wanted this party to be a sort of thank you to James: he did break a leg to see that the conversion wasn't a nightmare.' She smiled again at Stephen, handing back his plate. 'You know how conversions can be.'

'Indeed. Don't worry, I should think he'll recover.'

Fanny winked at him, turning to the next in the queue. 'Dominic! When did *you* get here?'

Stephen and Hilda carried their plates and glasses across the beechwood floor to a pale grey sofa pushed back against the wall. There were two, facing each other, and large cushions at intervals between them.

'Now,' said Stephen, sitting beside her, 'Where shall we begin?' He took a forkful of salmon. 'Tell me the story of your life.'

Hilda shook her head.

'Come, come. What do you do?'

'I run an English department in an underfunded college in Hackney.'

'And where do you live?'

'In an attic flat in the house of a lonely Czechoslovakian widow.'

'Intriguing. And do you have a family?'

'My father, died last year, last winter,' Hilda said steadily.

'I'm sorry . . .'

'It's all right. I mean, it isn't all right but I don't want to talk about it. My mother died quite a long time ago, when I was at school. I have a sister, who lives in Highbury.' She swallowed a mouthful of mushrooms. 'Will that do you to be going on with?'

'No,' said Stephen. 'Tell me about your sister. Is she like you?'

'Not in the least.' Hilda paused. 'I suppose that when that woman – Klara – said she never dwelt on things I was irritated because it sounded so uncomprehending of people who do. My sister dwells on everything.'

'Are you close?'

She shrugged. 'Not really.'

'But you certainly sprang to her defence.'

'Yes,' she said, considering. 'I don't quite understand why – Alice is so introspective it amounts to neurosis, quite honestly.'

'And you're not. Introspective, I mean.'

'I don't know. I suppose that must mean that I'm not. I prefer to get on with things. Anyway, Alice isn't so much like that any more, I think she's happy now. She's expecting a baby, it seems to have transformed her.' She shrugged again. 'I don't know if it'll last.'

'You're not very keen on babies?'

She shook her head. 'I don't have any feelings one way or the

24

other, I don't know anything about them. Alice says she's always wanted to have children, but I don't feel like that at all. Anyway – I can't remember the last time anyone asked me so many questions.' She bent down, putting her plate carefully on the floor at the side of the sofa. 'I really think that's enough about me,' she said, re-emerging. 'What about your life?'

Stephen leaned back against the sofa, and stretched out his arm along the top and, turning, Hilda for the first time noticed a wedding ring. Well, of course, she thought, does he look as if he lives by himself? And then at once: do I? And as in most encounters with men she felt a shutter, which had begun to lift a little, come down again, keeping her out of harm's way.

'I've worked for myself for years,' said Stephen. 'I specialise in restoration, rather than new buildings; it interests me more than commercial property, though that's where a lot of people work, of course.' He paused. 'I suppose, if I think about it, restoration of private houses is the kind of thing you might disapprove of. I expect I should be working for a housing association, or a local authority.'

'Perhaps you should,' said Hilda. 'I don't think it matters whether or not I disapprove, does it?'

'On the face of it, no.' He finished his glass. 'Can I get you another?'

'No, thanks, I've had plenty.'

'Two glasses.'

'Enough for me. But don't let me stop you getting one.'

'You won't,' said Stephen, and Hilda found herself feeling awkward and ill at ease. Was she really so bossy and prim? She had an image of herself and her father, who at about this time on a summer Saturday evening might have been going round the garden after supper, pulling a few dead heads off the roses as the air grew cool and the bats flickered, squeaking, beneath the trees. Perhaps Alice and I should not have sold the cottage, she thought, but then, as she had done after their father had died, she tried to picture herself living up there without him, in a village full of families, and knew it would have been impossible.

'What are you thinking about?' asked Stephen.

'Oh . . .' She waved the question away. 'Never mind. What about your drink?'

'I don't want one. I'm quite happy sitting here – unless I can get you something else to eat? I did see strawberries and cream. Also trifle. May I . . .'

'No thanks,' said Hilda. 'I'm fine.'

'You don't seem to be *quite* fine,' said Stephen gently, 'if I may say so. Can I ask you what it is?'

'I don't want to talk about it,' said Hilda, looking away. 'I've told you. It doesn't help me. It wouldn't help me. I don't . . .' she spread her hands, with an expression of distaste. 'I don't like all that. Personal talk.'

'I wonder why.'

'You sound like a shrink,' said Hilda. 'Do stop it.'

'I'm not at all like a shrink. My wife would probably say I don't talk about "personal things" enough.'

'Would she?' Hilda felt part curious, part relieved to be talking about someone else. 'Tell me about your wife: why isn't she here?'

'She didn't want to come, she doesn't really like parties. I suppose if I'd insisted . . .' There was another pause. 'If I'd insisted, I wouldn't be sitting on this sofa talking to you.'

Alan and Fanny had turned the music up. As if she hadn't heard him, Hilda said: 'And so you have children?'

'A son. He's eleven.'

'Called?'

'Jonathan.'

Across the room a few people were dancing; Alan, with another bottle, was circulating again, encouraging. He approached Stephen and Hilda, expansively full of booze. 'Come on, you two, don't look so serious. It's a party!'

'It's a very good party,' said Stephen. 'We're enjoying ourselves.'

'But come and dance! Live a little, Hilda, what's the problem?' He bent down, unsteadily offering the bottle. 'Where's your glass, darling?'

Hilda said icily: 'Will you please stop being so offensive?'

Alan straightened up, mock-shaking his hand as if she'd burned it. 'She doesn't like me, she doesn't like me at all.'

Hilda closed her eyes. She heard Stephen say: 'Perhaps we'll come and dance in a minute', and opened her eyes to see Alan weaving away to a little knot of people stretched out on the floor cushions. She said to Stephen: 'I think it's time I was going.'

'What is it about you and Alan?'

'There's absolutely nothing "about" us at all. He's a vacuous fool who thinks I'm a stuck-up little miss and makes me behave like one.'

'Do you always arouse such strong feelings in people?'

'I wouldn't know,' said Hilda. 'Not that I'm aware of.' She looked at her watch: the last train to Dalston left Camden Road in just over an hour; she did not want to be on the last train, travelling alone with Saturday night drunks. If she left now she could catch an earlier, safer one, and be home before eleven. She thought of her attic rooms with longing.

'Please don't go,' said Stephen.

'I have a train to catch.'

'I'll take you home.'

'Don't be silly.'

'Why, where do you live, Prague?'

'Hackney,' said Hilda, smiling in spite of herself.

'I can take you to Hackney.'

'Well . . .'

'Or is there,' Stephen said carefully, 'someone waiting there for you? Perhaps I've misunderstood . . .'

'No,' said Hilda flatly. 'I live by myself.'

There was another silence, as this fact hung in the air, begging questions – why? For how long? Always? Then Stephen said: 'Well . . . You don't want to go this minute, do you?'

'When you're ready,' said Hilda, wishing already that she had simply got up and gone when she wanted. Now she was in someone else's hands, no longer free.

'Will you come and dance with me?' Stephen asked, and put out his hand. The way he spoke made the invitation sound as intimate as: Will you sleep with me? and almost as dangerous. Hilda shook her head. 'No, thanks. But please . . .' She gestured at the dance floor.

'I know,' said Stephen. 'I mustn't let you stop me.'

Hilda flushed.

Out on the roof terrace, the sky was fading into dusk; Fanny was lighting candles. She came inside with a box of matches and lit more, in tall glass candlesticks on the table and in alcoves, climbing the stairs to the minstrels' gallery. Candlelit, the room became full of shadowy corners, places to return to from the dance floor, to linger in. Earlier, Hilda had been able to summon the feeling that she was simply one guest talking to another, casual and in control. Now, it was inescapably more than that: she was sitting with a married man who had asked her to dance, who was going to drive her home. What were they going to talk about, between here and Hackney?

Beside her, Stephen had stretched out his legs and was watching people. Hilda turned to look at him, and looked away. Stephen said: 'We can go if you want.'

'Well . . . yes. All right.' She stood up, looking round for Fanny.'I must say goodbye; I think Fanny's upstairs.'

'And I must find James and Klara,' said Stephen, getting up.'I'm staying with them; I'd better organise a key or something.'

'Really, if it's a problem, perhaps you could just run me to the station – I'd still get my train if we left now.'

Stephen put out a hand and touched her arm, lightly, affectionately, as if touching a cat or someone he knew very well. 'Stop it. I want to take you. Give me a wave when you've found Fanny, all right?'

'All right.' Hilda moved away and climbed the wooden stairs to the gallery. She found Fanny curled up on cushions with two young men in T-shirts, passing a joint. 'I'm just off,' she said, standing over them.

'*Off?*' Fanny looked at her, drawing out the syllable. 'Darling Hilda, you've only just arrived.'

'Hardly,' said Hilda. 'Anyway, thanks for asking me, it's been lovely.'

'Oh, well, it was sweet of you to come,' Fanny said automatically. 'I suppose you're trying to catch a train – Alan'll call a taxi, if you're really desperate to go.'

'I don't think he will,' said Hilda. 'And I'm not desperate. Stephen Knowles is giving me a lift.'

'Stephen Knowles . . .' Fanny frowned, then brightened. 'Oh, yes! James's new chap, isn't he a sweetie?'

'He seems very nice,' Hilda said calmly. 'He wanted to say goodbye to you, I'll see if I can . . .' She leaned over the balustrade, searching. Stephen was on the far side of the room, kissing Klara on the cheek; he turned away, looking up towards the gallery: when he saw her, and raised his hand, Hilda felt a queer little twist of pleasure. He walked across the room to the foot of the stairs and came up, and as he did so she found herself remembering something a colleague at work had said about the man she lived with: 'It sounds such a small thing, but I like the way he occupies space.' I like the way Stephen does, thought Hilda, and I know what she means. It's such a simple thing, but somehow it makes everything else right.

He had reached the top of the staircase, and raised an eyebrow. 'All right?'

'Fine. Here's Fanny.'

Fanny held up a languorous arm. 'Stephen, it's been lovely meeting you.'

'And you. Thanks so much for the party.'

'Pleasure, see you again, I hope. 'Bye now.' She turned back to the young men in T-shirts.

Stephen and Hilda made their way down again, and past the open doors to the terrace, where the candles were beginning to sputter. They went down the broad carpeted stairs to the hall and Stephen said: 'The car's outside James's house.' They walked on, hearing the roar of the traffic from the main road, brakes squealing. The air felt cooler now. 'That's better,' said Stephen. 'London's so much warmer than Norfolk; I really noticed it when I got here this afternoon.'

'Tell me about Norfolk,' said Hilda, as they turned the corner. 'Where do you live?'

'We have a house just outside Saxham – you won't have heard of it, it's tiny, about twenty miles from Norwich. Not far from Woodburgh, if that rings any bells. That's where Miriam's shop is.'

'Shop?'

'She sells fabrics – for curtains and loose covers.'

'Oh.' Hilda didn't know what to say next; it sounded a very county thing to do, and she pictured a window filled with rustic baskets of flowers, and Laura Ashley prints. Country Living. 'Is she – what's she like?' she asked.

'She's . . . well.' Stephen gave a wry smile. 'It's a big question – what can I say?'

'One would imagine everything.'

'Exactly. But I can't tell you everything, not all at once. And if I say that Miriam is a very nice person – well, what does that mean?'

'All right. Leave it. Do you know where we are?'

'I think so. Next on the left . . . yes.'

They entered a square not unlike the square where Hilda lived: solid, porticoed Victorian houses, but here there ran unbroken lines of white, well-kept homes, no cracked stucco or peeling paintwork, no unwashed net. From the brimming window boxes to the polished brass on the front doors there was a sense of order, money well invested years ago. They were the kind of houses from which little girls came out to go to violin lessons.

'The Gibbon residence,' said Stephen, stopping outside one of them. He fished keys out of his pocket, and nodded towards a blue Peugeot. 'The Knowles family car. Please . . .'

For a while they drove in silence, out through the side streets, passing lit-up restaurants and pubs, to Parkway, and down towards the tube. The traffic was heavy and fast. 'Where do I go now?' asked Stephen at the lights.

'Straight ahead, follow the signs for Holloway.'

'The only thing I know about Holloway is the prison. Do we go near it?'

'We drive right past the back in a minute, I'll show you. I taught there once.'

'Did you really?' He shook his head. 'And what were you doing?'

'I ran a basic literacy course, I was organising volunteers as well as teaching. And I taught a creative writing group: that was quite exciting, we produced an anthology at the end of the year. Look – that's it, on the left.'

Stephen slowed to look at the blank redbrick walls of gabled buildings. 'No windows. Presumably they all face inwards.'

'Yes. You can't look out to the world from anywhere.'

Behind them a car was flashing its lights: Stephen put his foot down. 'Didn't you find it frightening? I mean what's it like in there?'

'Not frightening – I mean I wasn't frightened, why should I be? I was going out at the end of the day. For the women – yes, some of them were very scared. And angry. Writing about their lives seemed to help a bit.'

They had reached the traffic lights at the bottom of the hill. 'You can't go right here, can you? Follow the Highbury sign.'

They climbed a leafy hill to a church and a clock tower, sprayed with graffiti. The clock had stopped, and boys on bikes were hanging around it, eating chips. They cut through quiet tree-lined streets and crossed a busy main road, driving alongside park railings. Ahead, on a broad curve in the road, was another church, towering over council flats; they swept round the bend past rows of shabby shops, with here and there a tiny Georgian house squeezed between, and came at last to an empty street market; a couple of minutes later they turned into the square.

'Number 51,' said Hilda, 'just up there past the lamppost.'

There were cars parked all the way along; Stephen drew up outside 59, which had no lights on. He switched off the engine, and said: 'Well . . .'

'Well . . . thank you very much,' said Hilda. 'Will you be able to find your way back all right?'

'Oh, I should think so. I've got an 'A-Z' if I get lost.'

'Good. Thanks again.' She reached for the door handle, and heard a click.

'Central locking,' said Stephen, smiling. 'You can't get out until I choose.'

For a moment Hilda felt a chill of pure terror. 'Please open the door,' she said coldly. Stephen leaned forward and pressed a switch by the gear lever; Hilda heard another click and felt herself tremble in relief. 'Thank you.' She reached for the handle again.

'Hilda? Did I frighten you? I really didn't mean to, I was only joking. We have the central locking for Jonathan.'

'It's all right.'

'It isn't. Please don't rush off. Surely you know it wasn't serious.'

'Actually,' said Hilda, 'I don't. I mean, I do believe you, but I can't know, can I? Women don't like to be put in situations like that, surely you can understand.'

'Of course. Of course I can. And perhaps you, particularly . . . You don't like to lose control, do you?'

'Nobody,' said Hilda, 'likes to lose control of *that* situation.'

'I know. I'm just saying that perhaps . . . never mind.' He felt for his own door handle. 'Let me see you to your house.'

'There's no need.'

'But may I?'

'If you want,' said Hilda ungraciously. She felt that the evening had slipped out of her grasp, that the exchange of the past few minutes had taken away all the enjoyment she had begun to feel. They walked down the street towards Anya's house in a silence that felt colourless and disappointing. But then, what more might she have hoped for?

The marmalade cat was sitting at the top of the steps outside the front door; he made a little sound and got up, stretching, as they reached the bottom.

'Here, puss.' Stephen held out his hand and the cat came forward, rubbing his head against it. 'Sweet puss. Is it Anya's?' he asked, straightening up.

'Yes,' said Hilda, as if: who else's could it be? 'Well – thank you again.'

Stephen said: 'I've enjoyed meeting you. I can see you're not going to invite me up to your attic rooms – quite right too. But may I phone you some time? We're going on holiday in a couple of weeks, but after that I'll be coming down fairly regularly . . .'

Hilda wanted to say: And what about your wife? What would she think of such a phone call? But that seemed to assume too much, to be putting herself forward – and once more this evening to be pronouncing on other people's lives. So she said coolly: 'Well – all right,' and gave him her number. He pulled out a pen and a printed card from his inside pocket, and wrote it down on the back, and she noticed that he did not write her name beside it.

'Good. Thank you.' He slipped the pen and card back in his pocket.'Right, then.' He held out his hand; she hesitated, then took it, and although they shook hands briefly, like two men concluding a meeting, she could not pretend that it felt like a casual handshake.

'Goodbye,' said Stephen. 'I'll be in touch.'

'Goodbye.' She turned and went up the steps, feeling for her keys, and went inside quickly, followed by the cat.

Upstairs, her sitting room felt warm and close; she opened the windows wider, and stood looking up and down the square. Stephen's car had gone; she found herself pressing her hand to her cheek, as if it still held some of the warmth his had held, and heard his voice, which was a pleasing voice, inquiring: 'And what do you do when the chemistry is right?'

Then she turned away from the windows, and went to the kitchen to make herself a cup of coffee, thinking: And now I must get on.

Alice's baby was born in September, just after the start of the new term. Hilda went to see her the next day, bending over the transparent hospital crib by the bed, the scrunched-up face with its damp fringe of dark hair.

'She's . . . oh, Alice.'

'I know.' Beside her baby Alice leaned against the pillows, pale and triumphant. Her face looked swollen, blurred with exhaustion, but happier than she had ever looked in her life, a new and unrecognisable Alice. 'I can't believe it,' she said. 'I feel as if I could fly out of the window.'

'Wasn't it . . . dreadful?'

'It was, but not half as bad as some of the other women here. You see that one in the bed opposite – she had a terrible time, I could hear her. But she's getting over it . . .'

Smiling, she raised her hand to the woman, large and sweating a little in a bright pink nightdress, her baby at the breast. 'How's it going?'

'Not so bad,' said the woman. 'I expect I'll feel better once the stitches are out. How's your baby, all right?'

'Lovely,' said Alice.

She turned back to Hilda, who couldn't remember Alice ever speaking to a stranger with such confidence, and said in an undertone, 'Her baby squawks all night, poor thing. Hettie's good as gold.'

'Hettie?'

'Harriet. After Tony's mother. And her second name's Sonia, after Mummy.'

'The bluestocking and the film-star,' said Hilda. 'I hope she copes with that.'

'Of course she will. Anyway, no one could call a baby Harriet, could they? She looked like a Hettie as soon as I saw her.'

Between them, the baby whimpered, and trembled suddenly; Alice bent over the crib. 'Come on, Hettie.'

'Are you allowed to pick her up?' Hilda asked, and they both laughed. 'What am I saying?'

Gently, but oh, how surely, Alice lifted the baby, dressed in disposable nappy and hospital-issue vest, and cradled her in the crook of her arm. Her face glowed.

'You look as if you've been doing it all your life,' said Hilda.

'I feel as if I have, isn't it extraordinary? For the first time in my entire life I feel I've got it right, as if I know what I'm supposed to be doing and can do it.' She was unbuttoning the front of her nightdress. 'The only thing I'm not much good at yet is this, but they keep saying not to worry, it'll come. Your tits are supposed to get sore, that's what one of the women along there was saying, she's using this spray stuff . . . come on, baby, latch on.' She laughed again. 'That's all anyone in here talks about – latching on.'

Hilda watched her bend over Hettie, trying to plug the gaping little mouth with an enormous rosy nipple, and felt suddenly like someone from another planet. Alice always used to say she was outside everything, she thought, that I was the one who belonged in the world. Now, seeing the two heads so close, long fair hair brushing small pink forehead, she felt excluded and unnecessary.

'Pity Father can't see her,' she said. 'He'd have been so pleased.'

'Mmm.' Alice was still preoccupied. 'Come on, Hettie, in the *mouth* . . . That's it, clever girl. There we are.' She looked up. 'Oh, lovely, there's Tony.'

Hilda turned to see him coming down the ward with an enormous bunch of roses, which he raised in greeting. 'How is everyone? Hello, Hilda . . .' He bent to kiss her cheek, always the kindly host, including putting the visitor first, even today.

'Congratulations,' she said warmly. 'She's simply lovely.'

'Isn't she?' He went round the other side of the bed, putting his arm round Alice, kissing her and his daughter on the head. 'How are we feeling today?'

'Fine,' said Alice happily. 'Much better. Look, she's feeding really well.'

'Very good.' He perched on the bed beside her, and Hilda got up, saying: 'I must get back to work. Come on, Tony, have the chair.'

'It's all right. I'm okay here. Do you have to go?'

'Yes, I really must. Well . . . Goodbye, all.' She patted the baby's warm creased fingers, and blew Alice and Tony a kiss. 'See you soon.'

'See you,' said Alice abstractedly. 'Thanks for coming.'

Hilda went down the ward, walking past all the other women with their cribs, and flowers, and brand-new babies. Outside the hospital the traffic was thundering down the hill from Highgate to the Archway Road, and it was very hot. She crossed over, and stood at the bus stop, finding herself for a few minutes absorbed in a fantasy in which she lay with her own baby beneath the trees in her father's garden, listening to the birds. Then the bus came and she went back to work, telling everyone: 'I've been to see my niece.'

On an evening in October Hilda was correcting essays at her desk. The weather had turned colder; the last of the light was fading behind the trees in the square. Hilda had switched on her desk lamp and felt cocooned and absorbed, at home in a way she realised now she had never quite felt in the summer months.

My father has a successful import business whom I am hoping to join him shortly. My parents are intending to marry me . . . The telephone rang and she picked it up, expecting a call from Lizzie, one of her part-timers. When Stephen Knowles said carefully: 'Hilda?' she was completely taken aback, recognising his voice immediately.

'Hello.' Her tone was less than welcoming.

'I hope I haven't disturbed you.'

'I was working.'

'Have you got a few minutes? I've been thinking about you . . . I just rang to see how you were.'

'I'm very well, thanks,' she said briskly. 'How are you?'

'Fine. I'm down in London, staying with James and Klara; I'm going back to Norfolk tomorrow.'

'Oh.'

'I don't suppose you're free for lunch?'

'I . . .' In that pause Hilda saw, as the drowning were supposed to see the whole of a life flash past, everything that might, and might not happen if she said yes: that she, a woman who so far had lived a quiet, well-ordered, sensible life might find herself caught up in opera – passion, secrecy, suffering and exaltation. Then, as she had thought when they stood on the front doorstep and he had asked her for her telephone number, she thought: but this is absurd, I am assuming far too much, and so she said carefully: 'I think so. But I have a class at three, so . . .'

'I could come over,' said Stephen. 'Is there anywhere nice near you?'

Hilda said: 'Incredible as it may seem, there is. There are several places near the college, on Church Street. I mean . . .' she floundered a little, 'do you mean a pub? Or what?'

'I'd rather thought a what,' said Stephen, and she could tell that he was smiling. 'A wine bar or something?'

'There's a wine bar with a fox outside,' said Hilda. 'I could meet you there. You can't miss it.'

'On Church Street. Fine. About half-past twelve?'

'Let's say one, I teach until half-twelve.'

'I'll look forward to it,' said Stephen. 'We'll talk properly then, shall we?'

'Yes. Yes, all right. Goodbye.'

She put down the receiver and remained sitting on the sofa, unable to suppress not only pleasure but a rare excitement.

Hilda pushed open the door of the wine bar and stepped inside, looking round. Even at one o'clock, only a few of the round marble tables were occupied, and Stephen wasn't here yet. She hesitated, then went to a table not far from the door, where she could look out on to the street. On the opposite wall, behind the bar, the menu was chalked on a blackboard; approached by a boy in earring and striped shirt, she ordered a mineral water, and sat waiting. Outside, the sky was dull grey, threatening rain, and Church Street was clogged with traffic. The wine bar was not far from the post office; old ladies with shopping trolleys and single men in shiny worn suits went slowly past the window, collecting pensions and giros. Above the town hall a red and white notice announced, each month, the number of jobless in Hackney, tens of thousands. Among them, and the mothers and childminders with push-chairs and trailing children, were several of

35

Hilda's students, wandering with bags of chips; seeing them, she turned away, not wanting to be recognised.

When she turned back again she saw Stephen, who must have parked in a side street. He was looking up at the fox sign, then stepping out of the way of a tall black boy with a Walkman. He looked well-dressed, well-heeled, quite out of place, and seeing him Hilda felt a flicker of disappointment: he was an ordinarily attractive man, that was all, he had nothing to do with her. Good, she thought, now I can live in peace, and then he pushed open the door, looking round as she had done, and saw her, and gave a slow, direct smile of recognition. She smiled back, meeting his eyes, and felt both peace and disappointment disappear.

'Hello. Sorry I'm late.' He pulled out a bentwood chair and sat down beside her, moving a small glass vase of flowers. 'Have you been waiting long?'

'Just a few minutes. What was the traffic like?'

'Oh – ' he spread his hands, smiling. 'Traffic, you know. Not a problem.' He looked at her glass, and the half-empty bottle beside it. 'Is there wine in that?'

Hilda shook her head. 'I can't drink in the lunch hour, I'd never manage to do anything afterwards. But please – '

They both laughed. 'I shouldn't be drinking either,' said Stephen, 'not if I have to drive back. How about just a glass each?'

'Okay. Red, please.'

'Good. And food . . . are there menus?'

'Over there, on the wall.'

He turned, looking at the blackboard. 'Right. What do you feel like? Garlic mushrooms? Quiche, surprise, surprise . . . jacket potato and salad . . . I wonder what the soup is.'

The boy in the earring was beside them again, holding a notebook. He flashed a smile at Stephen. 'What can I get you? The soup today is cream of leek and potato.'

'Is it really?' said Stephen with a laugh, and Hilda could see that the boy was enchanted.

They ordered soup and rolls, and a winter salad, and in a moment the boy came back with their glasses of wine. He put them down carefully, flashing another smile that clearly excluded Hilda, and took their order back to the bar.

'Cheers.' Stephen raised his glass.

'Cheers. You've obviously made a conquest.'

'Do you think so?' he said, and meeting his eyes again – warm, interested, quizzical – Hilda felt the rest of the room slip away, leaving them alone. She looked down, quickly, fiddling with her glass, not knowing what to do with such undeniable sense of intimacy, and Stephen said gently: 'How are you, Hilda?'

'I'm very well,' she said matter-of-factly, looking up again, and past him to the window. 'How are you?'

'I'm also well,' said Stephen, 'if you want a bulletin on my health. I'm working hard, and planning things with James, and I keep thinking about . . .'

'Here we are.' The boy waiter was beside them with a tray. He set down bowls of soup, cutlery, a basket of rolls. Steam rose in thin wreaths between them. 'Piping hot, mind you don't burn yourself.'

'You're very solicitous,' said Stephen. 'Thank you.'

'My pleasure.'

'Does this happen to you often?' Hilda asked, when he had gone, 'I mean, that boy . . .' Easier to talk about him, a welcome distraction.

'Not that I'm aware of,' Stephen said, offering her the basket. 'It must be the weather. Have a roll.'

'Thank you.' She took one and began to draw her soup away from the edges of the bowl with great absorption.

'Tell me what you've been doing,' he said. 'Did you go away in the summer?'

'No, not this year. I've spent too much money buying my flat, but I think it was a mistake – I shouldn't have spent the whole time here. Before, I used to go and see my father a lot, and because he was in the country I could cope with London . . . Still.' She could hear herself begin to gabble. 'Next year I'll fix something up. In the meantime my sister's had her baby, a little girl.' She sipped her soup cautiously. 'This is very good. What about you – didn't you say you were going on holiday?'

'We went to Italy,' said Stephen. 'We've got some friends with a house in Tuscany, they go every year, and they asked us to join them. It's a lovely place, looking down into a valley, all stone farmhouses and a winding path and olive trees. Blazing hot.' He began to break his roll into pieces, watching her. 'I found myself wishing you were there.'

Hilda was silent. A flurry of rain pattered suddenly against the window, and she turned to look at it. Outside, people were starting to hurry home, and a few took shelter beneath the wine bar's awning, stepping back quickly as a bus splashed past. She felt as if she were about to open the door to a house she had sometimes imagined, but never visited.

'Hilda?' Stephen reached out, and carefully touched her hand. 'Say something.'

Hilda looked away from the window, and back at him, feeling his touch on her fingers, lightly insistent. Impossible to pretend that rain, or food, was claiming her attention.

'And what about your wife?' she said deliberately, taking her hand away. 'Not to mention your son. How was their holiday?'

Stephen put down his soup spoon and leaned back, running his fingers through his hair. He sat looking past her, at the window and the rain, and then he said slowly: 'What do you want me to say? I don't want to involve you in . . . all that.'

Hilda said nothing, waiting.

'I suppose,' he said, 'I should have realised that a principled person is a principled person. Somehow principles have not been uppermost in my mind. Only feeling.' He looked back at her, studying her face.

'Honesty,' said Hilda, 'is what I would hope for from anyone.' She smiled. 'Which is probably why I have so far managed to avoid emotional entanglement – perhaps I hope for too much.'

'And expect too little,' said Stephen. 'You don't appear to have a very high opinion of the human race.'

'I don't think that's true, it sounds priggish and superior. I hope I'm not like that. I think I'm just . . . reserved, that's all. Cautious.'

'With everyone, or just with men?'

'I think with everyone. Except my father – we got on very well. I suppose in some ways I feel more comfortable with women: not out of choice, I simply haven't found many men sufficiently interesting.' She shrugged. 'Or interested in me.'

'Which I find quite extraordinary,' said Stephen. 'Because I've thought of nothing but you since we met.' He smiled. 'And that, at least, is the truth.'

'Well,' said Hilda. 'Well . . . I . . .'

Stephen reached for her hand, and this time he did not brush it lightly but took it, holding it in his, and this time she let it rest there, feeling his warmth, and a deep, surprising, joyful sense of belonging.

They sat without speaking, she looking across the room at the bar, which had suddenly the radiance of a painting, Stephen at her face. Then he reached out and turned it gently towards him, to that she had to look at him. 'To think,' he said, 'that holding hands should feel like everything.'

'I know,' said Hilda, 'I know.'

'I have to say,' said Stephen at last, after another silence, 'that this feels absolutely right.'

'I know,' said Hilda again, feeling herself to be a different person from the one who had stepped in here less than half an hour ago. 'But not . . . not really. Is it?'

'Do you want me to answer your questions? Because I will, if that's what you want.'

She hesitated. 'I can only assume that things are wrong, or you would not be with me now. I suppose I want to know if they have been wrong for a long time, or just since . . .'

'Not just since,' he said. 'Meeting you confirmed what has been missing always.'

'Always? Is that true? For you or for both of you?'

'I think,' he said carefully, 'for both of us. In different ways.'

And that, thought Hilda, could cover, and mean, anything. And suddenly she didn't want to hear any more, or to know anything – about his wife, his son, their past, their life together. Only –

'What about others?' she said lightly. 'Do you make a habit of this?'

He shook his head. 'There have been one or two . . . diversions? Nothing more.'

'Everything all right?' The waiter was beside them, carrying a tray. He looked at the soup bowls, disappointed. 'Didn't fancy it?'

'It was delicious,' said Stephen. 'We're just not very hungry, that's all.' They waited for him to clear away, leaving plates, and salad. 'Do you want any of this?'

Hilda shook her head. 'I couldn't eat a thing.'

'Shall we go?'

'Go where?' she asked, and looked at her watch. 'My God, I must be getting back to work.'

'Can't I take you home?'

'I'm teaching.'

'I know. Skip it.' He pulled a face. 'Couldn't you?'

'I'm head of department,' said Hilda, laughing. 'I've never done such a thing in my life.'

'Even heads of department must get headaches sometimes, don't they? Or is it – I mean, would you *like* to go home with me? Or am I rushing you? I hardly like to ask this, but has your lack of contact with men meant . . .'

'A life of celibacy? Not entirely. Let us say that such encounters

39

have left me with no particular desire to repeat them.' She found she was shaking. 'Anyway, it's not just that, is it? You have to go home, don't you?'

'But not until tonight.'

Hilda thought about taking Stephen back to Anya's, climbing the stairs to her flat, showing him round, making him coffee, and then . . . And then. And afterwards? She saw herself standing at her darkening sitting room window, watching him drive away, going home. This won't do, she thought. I stop it, now, or I accept from the beginning.

'Hilda? Perhaps I could stay the night . . . I could make a phone call . . .'

'I skip a class,' she said, 'and you make a phone call. And that's two people lied to before we've even begun.'

'And that,' said Stephen, 'will have to be the nature of things. Inevitably.'

Hilda considered. 'I can't be responsible for what you say to anyone, but I am going to teach my class. If you would like to amuse yourself for an hour or so until it's over, I'll be happy to take you home for tea. There's a library just down the road, I'll meet you there.'

When they came out into the street the rain had stopped and puddles shone. Hilda pointed up towards the library.

'Can't I walk with you to your college?' he said, his hand on her shoulder.

'No, thanks. I'll meet you about half-past four, all right?'

'Don't get wet.'

She opened her bag to reveal a black collapsible umbrella. 'I have come prepared, at least for the weather.'

'Very good. *Lés Parapluies de Cherbourg*. Did you ever see that? The most romantic song in the world, do you remember it? "If it takes for ever, I will wait for you . . ."' He raised an eyebrow, humming.

'I must go,' said Hilda, and he bent down and brushed her lips with a kiss.

'Half-past four.'

She nodded, unable to speak, and turned away, waiting on the pavement for a moment to cross. The flower shop on the corner of Albion Road looked, as the bar had done, like a painting: bronze and yellow chrysanthemums, smoky Michaelmas daisies transformed, as if she were seeing them for the first time. At a gap in the traffic she crossed, walking up towards the side street to the college and, watching her from the other side of the road, Stephen raised his hand.

Fallen leaves from the trees in the square blew along the pavement. As Hilda took out her key to the front door of the house it opened, and Anya came out with a basket.

'Oh, Hilda. I am just going to the shop . . .' She hesitated, clearly a little disconcerted, looking from Hilda to Stephen and away again.

Hilda introduced them, and Stephen held out his hand with a smile, open, polite. Hilda had the sense, then and for years afterwards, that he was – like Tony, although she did not make the comparison then – capable of meeting anyone on their own terms, could instantly summon the right, most agreeable manner, knowing what would please people, and put them at their ease. It did not occur to her, then, to wonder how genuine it might be.

Anya looked up at Stephen with her bright brown eyes, assessing, warming a little.

'Is there anything I can get you?' she asked, turning to Hilda.

'No, thanks.' Hilda moved towards the open door and gestured to Stephen. They said their goodbyes and she led him across the hall, with its faded rugs and photographs in brown frames and up the three flights of stairs to her own front door. She unlocked it, standing aside; with a queer feeling she watched him climb the little flight of steps to her hall with his easy, loose-limbed stride. She followed him up, letting the door click to behind her, and he put out an arm without turning to look for her. They went into the sitting room, overlooking the square; into the bedroom, which overlooked the garden. They stood at the tall sash window, looking down on to Anya's quiet terrace, the weatherbeaten table and chairs, at the patchwork of neglected and well-tended gardens. Someone had lit a bonfire, and the smoke was drifting towards the trees.

'So,' said Stephen. 'You like it here.'

'It suits me,' said Hilda simply, leaning against his shoulder and thinking: does there have to be more than this? I should be happy to stay here like this for ever. 'Would you like some tea . . . or anything?'

'Later, perhaps,' said Stephen, stroking her hair. 'Unless you . . .'

She shook her head, feeling suddenly safe. I think it's all right. I think, this time, it will be all right. Stephen turned her face up to his; he bent to kiss her, his mouth warm, soft, enveloping, and Hilda, who had never been held by anyone without feeling a cold little part of her watching, distant and untouched, found herself, at first uncertain and unsure, now longing, lost, the inhabitant of a new, demanding body.

They drew apart, and with tenderness Stephen took off her glasses, folding them, placing them carefully on the table by the window. Then he pulled the curtains, with a rattle of wooden rings which shut out everything.

'Are you all right? Let me look at you.'

She propped herself up on her elbow. 'I'm fine,' she said smiling, leaning over him, and he reached up and pushed her hair back from her forehead.

'Such a lovely face. Do you look different now? Let me see . . . the face beneath the face . . .' His fingers traced each eyebrow, her nose, her lips. 'I could look at you for ever.'

Hilda shook her head, still disbelieving. 'This can't be happening.'

'But it is, it is. I didn't know it was possible to feel like this, to be sure, to know from the beginning.' He pulled her to him. 'Come here, come here, lie on top of me, I want you again, I want you . . .' His hands ran down her back, over her bottom, between her legs, drawing her on to him. 'Come on . . . It's all right, I won't come inside you, you're safe, come on, come on . . .'

Afterwards, they slept, and when Hilda woke the room was quite dark and for a few moments she couldn't work out what was going on or what she was doing here, in bed at a time when she was never in bed. She turned to look at the little luminous clock on the bedside table. Twenty to seven. In the morning? No. Beside her Stephen was breathing deeply. 'Stephen?' she said quietly, yawned and moved a little away from him, feeling sticky and uncomfortable and sore. Carefully she pushed back the bedclothes and made her way in the darkness to the bathroom, closing the door. She stood under the shower for a long time, and when she had finished, and pulled on her towelling dressing gown, she stood rubbing a space in the steam on the mirror and looked at herself, uncertainly, with damp hair and clean skin.

I'll go and get us some coffee, she thought, and suddenly felt happiness well up inside her, and saw the face in the cloudy mirror give an enormous smile.

She went into the kitchen and put the kettle on, and laid a tray, taking from the cupboard a packet of chocolate biscuits Anya had given her one Sunday. She leaned against the fridge, tapping the packet in her hand. She thought: one moment there is someone who looks vaguely interesting, whom you think you might like to get to know, the next you have fallen in love. How can that be so? How can I never have known it could be so? The kettle came to the boil. She made coffee, and put the biscuits on a blue plate, and carried it all through to the bedroom.

'Stephen?' The tea things rattled, and the room was still in darkness, lit only through the open door. She set the tray down carefully beside the bed and took the lamp off the table and put it on the floor, so that it wouldn't be too bright. When she switched it on the room felt deliciously like a room from childhood, warm and secure and softly lit as if she were ill and were being looked after.

'Stephen?' she sat on the edge of the bed and leaned over to him, kissing his forehead. 'I've made some coffee.'

'Mmm.' He rolled towards her, and opened his eyes, smiling. 'Mmm. I dreamt you'd gone.'

'I've come back,' she said, kissing him again.

He stretched, yawning. 'What time is it?'

'Quarter-past seven.'

'Christ. Christ, is it really?' He ran a hand through his hair and sat up, rubbing his face. 'How did that happen?'

'What time should you have left?' Hilda asked carefully, and turned away and began to pour out the coffee. Stephen sat up, and pulled the pillows behind him as she passed him a cup.

'Thank you. It's all right, don't worry about the time, it doesn't matter. I'll . . .'

'You'll what?' Hilda poured out her own cup and sat watching the steam rise and drift out across the top of the lamp.

'I'll sort it all out,' said Stephen. 'I'm sorry, I shouldn't have worried you, it's got nothing to do with you.'

Hilda said nothing.

'I mean . . . oh, God, take this a minute . . .' He passed her his cup and when she had put it down he took her hand. 'You do know the last thing in the world I want to do now is get out of this bed and leave you?'

She shrugged. 'Well, I . . .'

'You do know,' he said. 'You must know.' He put a hand under her chin and she felt her eyes fill with tears. 'Beloved . . . All too much too soon? Is that what it is?'

'Perhaps.' She swallowed. 'I'm sorry.'

'You don't have to be sorry about anything,' he said. 'It's I who

43

should be sorry. Come here.' He pulled her to him, turning her so that she was lying next to him, and tucked the dressing gown up round her, straightening the collar. 'There.' She put her head on his shoulder and he stroked her hair again, no longer urgent and filled with desire but tender and reassuring. 'Better now?'

'Yes.' She raised her head and saw him looking down at her. 'The coffee will be getting cold.'

'So it will. Pass it over, then.'

They sat up against the pillows with their cups. After a while, Hilda said: 'Tomorrow I shall wake up and won't believe any of this. I can hardly believe it now.'

'I know.' He put down his cup and began kissing her again, her hair, her cheeks, her eyes, and she held him close, his long firm body warm against hers beneath the bedclothes, wanting to say to him: Stay. Please. Don't leave me now. Be here tomorrow.

'Hilda?'

'Yes?'

'You will be all right?'

'Of course. I'm used to being alone. I actually rather like it, most of the time.'

'I know, but . . .' He hesitated, looking at her gravely. 'I feel already as if I'm never going to be able to give you enough, be with you enough. You – you know you wanted me to be honest?'

Hilda thought: he's thinking about home, he doesn't want to have to feel guilty about her. Or me. 'Be honest, then,' she said lightly.

'You've gone all on edge again, I can feel it. Only . . .' He frowned. 'You think I'm going to say something horrible, don't you? That I'm going to get up and go out of here and maybe never come back. Or just drop in when I feel like it.'

'Yes.'

'I'm not,' he said, shaking his head. 'What a mistrustful person you are, to be sure; I can see I shall have to spell things out.' He leaned over, and kissed her forehead. 'If anyone had asked me before if I believed in love at first sight I'd have said never. But . . . if I weren't in my situation, I'd be staying here tonight and hope to be staying for a long time.'

'If you were invited,' said Hilda recovering, and he laughed.

'Well, of course. Perhaps I assume too much, I'd better watch my step. All I wanted to say to you was, I'm just so sorry it can't be like that.' He was stroking her hand. 'Do you understand what I'm saying? That I want you to know from the beginning how much I feel for you, how sorry I am that there'll always have to be . . .' He broke off.

'You're trying to tell me,' said Hilda, 'that you are never going to leave your wife.'

There was a silence.

'Because of . . .' she wavered, trying to remember his son's name. 'Because of Jonathan.'

He looked away. 'I just couldn't do it. I know I couldn't. Perhaps when he was little – there were times, then . . . But not now.' He looked back at her. 'Do you understand?'

'Yes,' she said. 'Of course I do. Anyway, I don't think I could feel very much for someone who could do something like that.'

'Dear Hilda, it happens, doesn't it? It happens all the time.'

'I know it does, but it's not my scene. So messy. And I don't know anything about children, I'd hate to be involved in . . . all that.'

Stephen was silent again. Then he said: 'You don't ever want children?'

'I never have.' She kissed him again. 'It's you I seem to have fallen for, not some dreadful screaming baby. I can't think of anything worse.'

'Is Alice's baby dreadful?'

'No, she's sweet, but . . . Come on, that's enough, now. Don't you have a journey to make?'

'One last embrace. I love you. I love you.'

Hilda held him, filled with a hitherto unknown, weightless sense of delight. 'Yes,' she said. 'Me too.'

That was the beginning, that was years ago.

In the beginning, after that first, undreamed-of encounter, Hilda had tried, for a while, to hold back, to regain and maintain her customary caution. Then she gave up, and was taken over. She'd wanted Stephen, Stephen, Stephen: to hear his voice on the phone, his car drawing up outside, his ring at the door. She wanted him all the time, it was like an illness, living from one meeting to the next, wanting to make a moment, an hour, a night, go on for ever, trying to make days and weeks fly past.

On her bedside table stood a photograph in a silver frame: Stephen leaning back against a low wall outside a pub in Highgate, his eyes half-closed against a sharp, winter-morning sun, but smiling at her, as she held up her camera before they went into the pub for Sunday lunch, as if everything were ordinary, and without complication, as if the photograph might be merely one of many taken during their life together. He had wanted one of her, but had never taken one, and in the end she gave him an old passport photograph, in which she looked rather severe, but which was small enough for him to tuck away. He zipped it into the inner pocket of his jacket and kissed her.

'I wish you didn't have to go,' she said, as he put his case into his car.

'So do I,' he said, and closed the boot.

They kissed again, but lightly, quickly, not wishing to be observed by Anya, who was conspicuously silent about Stephen's comings and goings. Hilda watched him drive away through the square, and returned to the house, and the photograph.

Looking at it over the years, knowing it was foolish to do so, she had nonetheless woven any number of lives together round that loving smile. She spent so much time with it that after a while, when he went home to Norfolk, she found that she returned to the photograph as if that were the real Stephen, waiting for her, not the man she had just said goodbye to, and was waiting for again. Sometimes, next time they met, the real Stephen was at first a disappointment, the smile not quite how she remembered it. There were times when she felt as if she were having a love affair with herself – it wasn't Stephen who saw her cry when she came back upstairs again, it wasn't Stephen who saw her write long letters in the small hours and tear them up in the morning; it was Hilda, the old, cool, capable Hilda, bemusedly watching the new one, restless, ecstatic, desolate, distracted.

Meanwhile, Alice's baby was a year old, taking her first steps; one and a half, calling, 'Mummy, Mummy, Mummy!' Alice took to inviting Hilda over more often: for tea in the holidays, sometimes introducing her to other mothers and toddlers who dropped in on their way to the playground.

Have you got any children, Hilda? No? How sensible.

Hilda found most of these women patronising and complacent; she made her excuses and left with a sigh of relief. In washed-out dungarees, Hettie stood at the top of the steps, holding Alice's hand.

'Say goodbye,' said Alice.

Hettie waved. 'Bye.'

'Bye, Hettie, see you soon.' Hilda waved, feeling slightly foolish, and walked down the street, sidestepping other mothers and push-chairs, hearing Alice lead her daughter back inside the house, and close the door. She walked across the wintry common and through the cold streets to Clissold Park and home: it was quite a long walk, enabling her to reclaim some sense of herself as a woman alone, unencumbered, purposeful. Nonetheless, there were times after such visits when her flat felt as empty as it did when Stephen had just left; she reached for the telephone, dialling friends, and made arrangements.

Early in 1985, with a salary rise and her mortgage payments affordable, Hilda bought a car, a neat little silver-grey Polo. This was more because it seemed sensible to do so while she could manage it than because it was really necessary in London, but she had close friends who were moving out to the country, and wanted to be able to visit them. After this, her visits to Alice, and to her friends, were made by car; from time to time Alice invited her over for Sunday lunch. They were seeing more of each other since Hettie was born than they had done for years: Hilda felt that Alice was keen to show herself as a new person now, settled and secure, and a part of her was glad to go along with this. Another part felt a certain dissatisfaction. She enjoyed being Hettie's aunt but that was because Hettie was Hettie, the kind of child to whom, fortunately, she felt able to respond. She did not enjoy the feeling of being on the fringe of Alice's life, cast in the role of onlooker, someone who had, apparently, days less fulfilled and less enjoyable. Alice never asked her what she did when she wasn't working; Hilda, without being asked, did not feel inclined to tell her. After all, what did it matter what Alice knew, or did not know? They had lived apart for so long, their lives not touching; it seemed both impossible and unnecessary to explain to her, if it was not evident, that Hilda, too, was a different person now.

So she went over to Highbury for Sunday lunch, and sat next to Tony, talking about his work, and her work, films seen and books enjoyed, having her glass refilled, while Alice sat next to Hettie, up in her high chair, pushing her bowl about, dropping bits of food.

'Come on, Hettie, eat up.' Alice fed her little pieces of meat and potato; teddy bears held paws round the rim of the bowl. 'One for this bear, and one for this bear . . . Aren't they sweet?'

Hilda mentally raised her eyes to the heavens. 'Are you asking me?' she said, more sharply than she'd intended.

Alice flushed. 'Not really, I was just burbling.' She spooned another morsel of potato into Hettie's mouth. 'Mothers do,' she said.

Hilda turned back to Tony, who was carving second helpings. 'I saw *Letter to Brezhnev* last week.'

'Any good?' Tony slid slices of lamb on to her plate.

'A bit overrated, I thought, quite honestly. Everyone's been raving about it, haven't they?'

'Have they? It seems light years since I saw a film except on the box, and even then I usually fall asleep.' He turned to Alice. 'More for you?'

She shook her head, her hair falling across her face. 'No, thanks.'

'You should let me babysit, Alice,' said Hilda. 'I'd like to. You two could have an evening out, and Hettie and I could have fun, couldn't we, Hettie?'

Alice didn't answer. Hettie watched Hilda raise eyebrows at her over the top of her spectacles and gave a little laugh, dropping her spoon.

Alice picked it up again. 'I'd better go and check on the pudding,' she said, and went out of the room as Tony called after her: 'You okay, Alice? What are we having?'

'Only apple crumble,' said Alice distantly from the corridor.

'What do you mean, only?'

There was no answer. Hilda passed Tony the runner beans and he passed her the gravy; they ate in silence, hearing the oven door bang. In her high chair, Hettie began to squirm, pushing the teddy bear bowl away.

'Come on,' said Hilda, 'you've had enough, haven't you? Want to come out for a bit?' She leaned forward, unstrapping her. 'Up we go.' Hettie, lifted into the air, put her arms round Hilda's neck. 'Come on my lap? There we are.' She sat her down, and Hettie reached up for her glasses. 'No, no,' said Hilda firmly, 'those are not for babies.' She turned her round to face the table and gave her a fork. 'Go on, you have that.' She leaned her chin on Hettie's silky dark head, one arm round her waist, one hand lifting Hettie's, small and round, clasping the fork. They beat a little tune on the table. 'Tap, tap, tap, the crocodile went snap!' Hettie giggled. 'Again? Tap, tap, tap . . .'

'I don't know that one,' said Tony.

'Nor do I. I just made it up, I must be burbling. Aunts do,' she added, kissing the top of Hettie's head. 'Tap, tap, tap, the crocodile went . . .' She paused, enjoying Hettie's eager anticipation. 'Snap!' Hettie burst out laughing.

And Alice, returning, stopped abruptly in the doorway and said: 'Oh. Have you finished your lunch, Hettie?'

Hettie did not look at her; she was wriggling round to look up at Hilda. ''Gain.' She banged on the table with the fork and lifted it high. The edge of the prongs scraped along her cheek, and there was a sudden scream.

Alice ran into the room. 'Baby, baby, it's all right, come here . . .' She lifted her from Hilda's arms. 'How on earth did she get hold of that?'

'I gave it to her,' said Hilda. 'Sorry. I think she's okay, Alice, it's only a scratch.'

Alice ignored her, rocking Hettie close against her. 'Come on, we'd better put something on it, come on, darling, let's go and sort you out . . .' She left the room again; they heard her climbing the stairs to the bathroom, and Hettie, who rarely cried, stopped crying now.

There was another silence.

'Oh, dear,' said Hilda.

'Don't worry about it.' Tony bent down and picked up the fork. 'She's all right.'

'Alice doesn't think so.'

He stood up, and began to clear the table. 'She'll be okay in a minute.' He clearly meant Alice.

'Shall I go up?'

'No, let them calm down.' He had piled up the plates; Hilda rose, too, and picked up the vegetable dishes; they carried everything through to the little kitchen.

'God,' she said. 'It's difficult territory, motherhood. I feel as if I'm treading on a minefield sometimes.'

'Perhaps Alice does too,' said Tony. He put down the plates on the draining board. 'Come on, forget about it. Has she told you we're going to build an extension here? So we can eat in the kitchen?'

'No,' said Hilda. 'That'll be nice.' She leaned against the door frame and listened to him sketch out the plans, gesturing towards the garden; she felt that he was, really, not much more interested in kitchen extensions than she was, and almost said so, but also understood that he was deliberately introducing safety and neutrality. Perhaps he knows Alice and me better than we know ourselves, she thought, and then switched off completely, wondering what Stephen was doing now, picturing him, over Sunday lunch in Norfolk, as impatient with his family there as she felt now – longing, suddenly to get in her car and drive away, wanting only to be with him.

'Oh, God,' she said heavily, aloud, and Tony said: 'What? What are you thinking about?'

'Oh . . . I don't know.' She waved at the air. 'Sorry. I was miles away.'

'Where?'

'It doesn't matter. Nowhere I can tell you about.' She could hear Alice coming downstairs, talking to Hettie: 'There we are, all better now.'

'But not in a larger kitchen,' said Tony drily, and meeting his eyes, interested and perceptive, she laughed, and then looked away again.

'Absolutely not, I'm afraid.'

'Shall we have pudding?' said Alice, coming in. She passed Hettie over to Tony; he reached out and touched Alice's face, gently concerned. 'All right? Hettie all right?'

'We're fine,' said Alice, kissing him.

'Well done.'

Watching them, observing their absorption in each other and the faint red mark on Hettie's cheek, shining with a film of antiseptic cream, Hilda almost said aloud: 'For heaven's sake!' She bit her lip, thinking: How uncharitable I am – why shouldn't they be like this? And then, as Alice moved away, and bent to open the oven door, she shut her eyes, seeing Stephen reach out to kiss and touch her own cheek – and perhaps, suddenly and astonishingly, to take their own child into his arms. She heard herself give a groan.

'Hilda! What is it?'

She opened her eyes again, seeing both sister and brother-in-law looking at her in consternation. She wanted to say: 'I'm in love, I'm in love! *That's* what it is, isn't it written all over me?' She did not trust herself to speak, and years of holding herself back, of keeping cool, made her shake her head, take off her glasses and rub her eyes, saying at last: 'Sorry,' for the third time in ten minutes, and then: 'I'm tired, that's all.'

She knew that neither of them was satisfied with this, but they let it go, and Tony took Hettie back to the lunch table, leaving Alice and Hilda a tactful opportunity for sisterly conversation, which neither of them took up.

Until Hettie's arrival, Hilda had given no thought to questions about children's upbringing. If she had considered it at all, she might vaguely have supposed that all children had a sleep in the afternoons, and Hettie, being a baby of settled disposition, amenable to routine, usually did so. Today, it transpired, she had had a long sleep in the morning, and after lunch, instead of being taken upstairs, she sat playing on the kitchen floor while Alice and Tony washed up.

'Do let me,' said Hilda.

'No, honestly, it's fine,' said Alice, not turning. 'Why don't you go and sit in the garden?'

Hilda wandered out of the door; she sat at the table next to terracotta pots of geraniums and surveyed the patch of lawn, the overgrown Russian vine and Hettie's climbing frame. The garden needed a lot of work; Alice and Tony had bought this house in a rundown state and put all their money and energy into essentials like plastering and rewiring. Then Hettie arrived, and pots of geraniums were as far as they had got out here. Probably just as well, if they were about to start building kitchen extensions. Hilda put her chin in her hands, hearing companionable conversation through the open window; she began to drift off to Norfolk again.

There was a sound beside her and she looked down to see Hettie, who had followed her out and stood gazing at her.

'Hello.' Hilda wanted to take her on her lap, but felt constrained. Perhaps she was supposed to love only from a distance? But this is ridiculous, she thought, I must have it out with Alice, and she bent to pick her up. 'Come and have a chat.' The red mark on Hettie's face had completely faded; Hilda stroked the baby skin with her finger. 'What shall we do?' Hettie sat looking calmly out over the garden. 'You don't need to do anything, do you? You just are. Not like me – God, I'm restless.' It seemed suddenly impossible to sit still a moment longer. If she couldn't be with Stephen she must walk, or swim, or run round the common.

'More coffee?' said Alice, appearing.

'No, thanks.' Hilda looked up at her: she still looked tense and pale. 'I'm sorry if I upset you,' she said carefully. 'With the fork and everything. I really didn't mean to.'

'I know you didn't. Anyway, you're the one who – ' Alice broke off, awkwardly, and stood looking down at Hettie, resting comfortably against Hilda. 'She looks just like you, isn't it funny? Well . . . what shall we do?'

'I feel like a walk – perhaps we could take her up to the common? Or perhaps, if you're tired . . . how would you feel about me taking Hettie up there by myself? You could have a rest.' She hesitated. 'I mean – only if you'd like me to.'

Alice sat down. 'You must think I'm terribly fussy,' she said, looking at the air.

'No, I don't.'

'It's just – ' She gave a sigh. 'I can't explain. Anyway, take her, that's fine. Tony's going to do some work, I'd like a break.'

51

'Really?'

'Really. I'll just go and change her.' She got up again, holding out her arms. 'Come on, darling, let's get you changed. Then you and Hilda can go for a walk, to the playground. Yes? Would you like that?'

A few minutes later she stood at the top of the steps, waving goodbye. 'Have a lovely time. See you soon.'

Hettie, in her pushchair, gazed ahead.

'We shan't be long,' said Hilda. 'Have a nice rest.' She set off up the sloping street, as if at the helm. It felt as if she were wearing outlandish clothes: she realised that she was expecting people to turn and look at her, as if she were someone extraordinary, or famous. Dear me, she thought, I am thirty years old and I do believe this is the first time I have ever pushed a pushchair.

She crossed the road to the common, approaching the playground with caution; she sat among the mothers, self-conscious at first but after a while relaxing a little, enjoying having Hettie beside her, watching everything going on. The afternoon sun was warm; she carefully unstrapped her and put her in the sandpit; Hettie sat patting the sand, while other toddlers made excavations, or threw it into the air. Hilda spoke to no one, and no one spoke to her; she felt curiously both anchored and adrift, as if in strange calm waters, and she sat there thinking of Stephen, but less painfully now, as Hettie patted the sand and watched the drifting clouds. After a while she looked at her watch. It was half-past three; she got up stiffly from the low wall, and made her way over to the sand.

'Come on, Hettie, time to go. I've got work to do.'

Hettie put up her arms; Hilda picked her up and buried her face in her neck. She carried her back to the wall and sat brushing the sand from her dungarees. 'Had a nice time?'

'Isn't she lovely?' said a woman next to her. 'Such a calm little thing, not like mine.'

'Which is yours?' Hilda asked politely.

The woman pointed to a wild-haired child in a red T-shirt, whirling round and round. 'She wears me out.' She smiled at Hettie, waggling her fingers; Hettie looked away. 'I don't suppose she keeps you awake at night, does she?'

'No,' said Hilda, 'she's not mine. Well – she's sort of mine: my niece.' She felt a little rush of pride.

'Your niece? Goodness, aren't you alike, though?'

'Are we? Come on, Hettie.' She put her, unprotesting, back into the pushchair, and wheeled her home again, down the quiet leafy streets, past family houses.

'Had a good time?' asked Alice, coming out to meet them. She bent down to Hettie, kissing the top of her head. 'Hello, darling.'

Hettie smiled, and stretched out her arms. 'Mummy, Mummy!'

'Out you come.' Alice unstrapped her, and held her close. 'Did you miss me?'

'She was fine,' said Hilda, adding quickly: 'But I expect she did. Thanks for letting her come, I really enjoyed it.' Still, now they were back she felt she'd had enough for a bit. She carried the pushchair up the steps. 'How do you fold this thing?'

'Just kick that little red lever,' said Alice, and showed her. 'Will you stay and have some tea?'

'Well . . .' Hilda hesitated, wanting to go; not sure, either, if Alice really wanted her to stay. Perhaps she needed to have Hettie to herself again.

But Alice said: 'Go on, just for a little while. Tony's still working; I'll take him a cup of tea and we can have a chat.'

'All right. Thanks.'

They sat out in the garden, watching Hettie clamber carefully over the small blue climbing frame.

'A woman in the playground went on about how lovely she was,' said Hilda. She did not add that the woman had also thought she was Hettie's mother.

'Did she?' Alice smiled, pouring more tea. 'That's nice.' She put down the teapot and pushed back her hair. 'Hilda . . .'

'Yes?'

'I've been wondering . . . while you were out. You are all right, aren't you?'

'Yes,' said Hilda steadily.

'I mean . . . at lunch, in the kitchen . . .' Alice trailed away, then went on cautiously: 'You know, if there's ever anyone you want to bring over . . . I mean, a man . . .'

Hilda thought: it would have to be a man, in Alice's eyes, wouldn't it? Why else would anyone groan aloud, if not for a man? But then: after all, she's right. And she laughed, and touched her sister's arm. 'Does it seem *so* improbable?'

'No,' said Alice. 'You know what I mean. Is there someone? Do you mind me asking?'

Hilda watched Hettie sit down beneath the climbing frame and pick at bits of grass. She could hear Tony, through the open study window upstairs tapping away on his new word processor, and from a few gardens along the soothing rhythm of a lawnmower, back and forth.

'There is,' she said at last, and felt her stomach turn over at the strangeness of acknowledging it, and particularly to Alice, who had had so many men in her life, while she herself had had so few.

'*Is* there? How exciting. Who is it?'

Hilda drew a breath. To speak of Stephen, when she was so used to keeping him secret – perhaps, indeed, relished the intense emotion of keeping him secret – made her feel as if she might choke.

'He's called Stephen Knowles,' she said slowly. 'I met him last year, last April, at one of Fanny's parties. Do you know who I mean by Fanny?'

Alice shook her head. 'I hardly know of any of your friends, do I? But Hilda – you mean you've been having a love affair all this time? Why didn't you tell us?'

Hilda looked at her directly, feeling a little pulse of irritation at this 'us'. Was Alice only half a couple now? Like Fanny – whenever you asked: 'How are you?' she always said: 'We're fine, thanks.'

'Why didn't you ask?' she said.

'Because it seemed like prying,' said Alice. 'But mostly I suppose because I've been so caught up with Hettie and everything . . .' She rested her elbows on the table. 'Tell me now. Will you?'

'What do you want to know?'

'Well . . . what does he look like?'

Hilda laughed again. 'Just like Mummy. That's the first thing she'd have asked, isn't it?'

Alice's expression clouded. 'I suppose you and Father had the monopoly on higher things. All right, then, tell me something else. What does he do?'

'He's an architect – not a commercial architect, he restores old houses. And . . . to answer your question, he's very beautiful, at least I think so – loose-limbed, and . . . well, and charming, I suppose.'

'He sounds lovely.' Alice had recovered; she was open, interested, warm; she's on familiar ground, thought Hilda.

'Yes.' She swallowed. 'But the main thing about him is that he's married.'

'Oh.' And a shadow fell across Alice's face.

'What do you mean, "Oh"?'

'I'm – I'm just surprised, that's all.' But she sounded more than surprised: she sounded both shocked and disapproving, as if, although

54

in the old days she might have spent the night with any number of married men, she was now, as a wife, completely thrown by the mere idea. 'Is that a very good thing?'

For a moment Hilda wanted to hit her. Then she got up, saying quickly: 'I don't suppose it is. Actually, I don't want to talk about it any more, I really don't. It's time I was going, anyway.' She called across to Hettie: 'Bye!' and turned and walked back through the door to the kitchen, now fresh and clean again, with the flowers she had brought standing in a vase at the open window. A perfect, orderly home. Upstairs, a husband. Out in the garden, a child. I cannot stay here a moment longer, she thought, and called from the bottom of the stairs: 'Goodbye, Tony, see you soon,' and walked fast down the narrow hall, banging her ankle on the folding pushchair.

'Ouch.' Tears smarted; she rubbed them away beneath her glasses.

'Hilda?' Tony was coming down the stairs. 'You off already?'

'Yes,' said Hilda, feeling for her car keys in her jacket pocket, not looking at him. 'Thanks for the lunch.'

'I didn't do a thing,' he said. 'It was Alice.'

'Yes. Well . . .' She pulled open the front door. Sunshine blazed in the street outside, and a little boy on a tricycle pedalled happily past at top speed. It all looked so cosy, so easy. It made her feel ill.

'Hilda . . .' Alice was behind her, Hettie in her arms. 'You don't understand . . . Please don't go.'

'I'm sorry,' said Hilda, sounding not in the least apologetic. 'I just want to be by myself for a bit. That okay?'

And she ran down the steps to her neat little car, and did not look back. I'll never tell her anything again, she thought as she drove away. Never.

At home, upstairs at her desk, she opened her road map and pored over the route to Norwich, imagining forbidden journeys, unexpected arrivals, open arms. She closed the book with a snap.

'What on earth was all that about?' asked Tony, and Alice burst into tears.

After that, Hilda and Alice did not see each other again for quite a while. For a week or so Hilda toyed with the idea of sending her a postcard, but decided against it, and did not receive one. She was so used, anyway, from pre-Hettie days, to seeing Alice only infrequently, that after the first rush of emotion had subsided it seemed quite normal not to see her now. In any case, she had too much else to think about: getting her students through their exams in June, and getting herself through the summer holidays, when Stephen, as always, went to Italy for three weeks with Miriam and Jonathan.

'What will you do?' he asked her, as they lay together in bed on the Saturday morning before his departure. The loose cotton curtains were still drawn, and shadows from a cloudy sky passed over them; down on the terrace the cat flap banged, and then they heard Anya opening the doors.

'What I did last year,' said Hilda, naked against Stephen's naked chest. She turned her head to look at him. 'I'm running a summer school and I shall visit my friends in Wales. Have I told you about them?'

'No,' said Stephen. 'Tell me another time.' His fingers traced the outline of her lips. 'Hilda's summer,' he said. 'All organised.'

'But of course.' She slipped her hand beneath the sheet, flat on his stomach.

'You don't need me at all.'

'That isn't true.'

His hand took hers; he moved it further down beneath the bed-clothes. 'Will you miss me, then?'

'What do you think?'

They made love slowly, lingeringly, coming together and falling asleep again until after eleven, when Stephen had to go. Hilda saw him off with a smile, and spent the rest of the morning in tears.

'You're a fool,' she said aloud, splashing her face with cold water. 'You're a fool, you're a fool, you're a fool.' And she went back to the sitting room and telephoned Fanny, inviting herself over for supper.

'Oh, yes, do come,' said Fanny. 'We're not doing anything, and I'm so pleased you've phoned. Guess what?'

'What?'

'I'm pregnant. With twins!'

'Good heavens,' said Hilda. 'Good God.'

'I know,' said Fanny. 'I've been feeling simply grim, but it's getting better. Anyway, come about seven, and I'll give you a blow-by-blow account of every developmental stage since conception and my reactions thereto.' She sounded warmer and more light-hearted than Hilda had heard her for years. 'And don't bother to bring a bottle, I'm touching nothing but mineral water.'

'What about smoking?'

'Given up! A new and reformed Fanny. I'd better go now, Alan's honking, I can hear him. Bye!'

Slowly Hilda put down the phone. From a frame next to the photograph of her parents Hettie smiled back at her, clear-eyed, smooth-skinned, showing six teeth. Hilda looked at her, and then she got up and went out to do her weekend shopping.

The summer passed. During the weeks of July Hilda found that she missed not only Stephen but Alice – or, more accurately, Hettie. She realised that because of her she was conscious of time passing in a way she had never been before, that she was missing moments which would never come again. Returning from her holiday in Wales in the first week of August, she found amongst the mail on the walnut table a postcard from Alice and Tony, on holiday in the Lakes. It was brief – cottage stayed in, places visited – but it ended with an invitation to come over soon. There was no letter from Stephen. Hilda greeted Anya flatly, picked up her suitcase and climbed the stairs; when she had unpacked she telephoned Alice and was answered by Hettie.

'Hello.'

'Hello, Hettie! This is Hilda. How are you?'

There was a silence, and much breathing. Alice came on the line.

'Doesn't Hettie sound grown-up?' said Hilda. 'Thanks so much for your card.'

'That's all right.' Alice sounded wary. 'How are you?'

'Fine. I've just come back from Wales. I was thinking perhaps we could meet.'

'When would you like to come? We've had the builders in, it's a bit chaotic.'

'I think it's your turn to come here,' said Hilda, unaware that she sounded as if she was issuing not an invitation but a command. 'Why don't you all come over on Sunday? We can take Hettie down to Anya's garden. About one? Good, look forward to it.' And she put down the phone and dutifully read through her mail. Why haven't you written? she asked Stephen. *Why* haven't you? Not even a card. Is that so much to ask?

Alice and Tony and Hettie came to lunch; they all kissed warmly, and no mention was made of their last encounter. Alice sat at the table with Hettie on her lap, looking tranquil and content; Hilda poured wine, and said: 'You're all looking very well, I must say; you must have had wonderful weather.'

'We did,' said Tony. 'How was Wales?'

'Wet, actually.' She raised her glass. 'Cheers.'

'Cheers,' said Alice, and took a sip. 'You haven't got any mineral water, have you?'

Hilda put down her glass and looked at her, and Alice laughed, as beautiful as she had been when she was expecting Hettie: serene, radiant even.

That night Hilda sat at her desk and wrote Stephen a letter. It was ten when she began and after midnight when she finished. She tore it into fierce tiny pieces and went to run a bath.

She lay in it for a long time, swishing the water with her long slim feet. A daughter? she thought. A daughter.

She summoned up a tall grave girl with plaits, and coloured tights, something like Hettie but older, ten or eleven, a clever girl. She pictured them reading together, making things, going to the cinema on wet Saturday afternoons. Stephen would visit them, as he visited Hilda now, but they would manage without him, contained, companionable.

Alice had the new baby, a cross-looking girl who cried a lot. Hilda, like Hettie, found new Annie, and Alice's absorption in her, tiresome – and yet, and yet. From the first steps into fantasy there gradually, to her surprise, came a longing, which grew.

Alice asked her to babysit, while they went out to dinner with one of Tony's partners. 'We can take Annie anywhere at this age,' she said, 'but I don't like dragging Hettie out in the evenings. She's so fond of you, Hilda, I know she'd settle. Would you mind?'

Hilda was aware that this invitation constituted an act of generosity unthinkable before Annie. With one baby Alice's happiness had, it seemed, been precarious, easily threatened; with two she was self-assured, at ease.

'I'd love to,' she said.

She put Hettie to bed after her bath, tucking her up in clean pyjamas; she read her a story about Spot the Dog. 'Goodnight,' she said, kissing her, and went to the door, leaving it open.

'I want Mummy,' said Hettie.

'Mummy will be back soon, you go to sleep now.'

And Hettie did: as easily, it seemed, as when Alice was there. Hilda went downstairs again, and put away the toys. She sat watching television in the comfortable sitting room, and wondered anew that Alice, who used to be so desperate and unhinged, could have found such contentment. After a while she went quietly upstairs again, to check on Hettie. She was fast asleep, mouth a little open, arms flung back on the pillow like a baby. Hilda bent down, and brushed back the thick fringe of dark hair from the round clear forehead; she leaned over and kissed her, once, twice, and went downstairs again.

I thought I was different from everyone else, she said to herself, making coffee in the airy, extended kitchen. It seems I am much the same. She took out milk from the fridge, filled with Munch Bunch yoghurts and fish fingers. Was this what Alice had felt, this longing, this yearning? And Fanny, now basking with fat twin boys and a nanny? She closed the fridge door and took her coffee back to the sitting room, turning the television low, in case it woke Hettie.

Was this what Stephen's wife had felt like, before she had had Jonathan? Sitting in front of *Panorama*, taking in nothing, Hilda began for the first time to wonder why there had been no more babies for Miriam, whose existence, and life with Stephen, she still preferred not to think about. She wondered, too, what Miriam and Jonathan did with themselves, on the rare weekends when Stephen was not with them in Norfolk but here with her in London. And as she had pictured herself with a companionable daughter, she began now to see Miriam and her son, peacefully at home in their house in the country, having supper together, chatting easily about the day's events. Miriam, whatever else, need never be alone with a photograph.

On those rare Sundays when Stephen was down, he and Hilda sometimes went walking on Hampstead Heath and sometimes in Waterlow Park, where you could have lunch in a cramped room overlooking the rose garden. It was always full of families, beautifully dressed north-London parents asking their over-educated children to behave. 'And then you can run about as much as you like.' Hilda and Stephen sat at a table for two by the window, holding hands.

On a late autumn Sunday in 1986, they had paid the bill and were walking outside arm in arm towards the lake. Yellow leaves fell slowly from the willow trees and floated across the shining blackness of the water. At the railings, toddlers and children threw down bread to the ducks; beyond the trees at the edge of the park was the Whittington Hospital, where Hettie and Annie had been born. Hilda pointed it out, casually, and made her tentative proposal.

'No,' said Stephen, and drew his arm away.

'But I can manage by myself,' said Hilda, filled with certainty.

'You know what I'm like, I'll get it all organised – it doesn't have to disrupt your life, I promise.'

Stephen shook his head. 'You don't know what you're talking about.'

She bit her lip, not wanting to quarrel. From words let drop she understood that Miriam and Stephen quarrelled, or used to. He had moved away from her, and was walking beneath the trees on the muddy path round the lake. Coming towards him, a little girl slipped, and fell.

'Whoops.' He bent down to help her up, handing her to her parents as they drew near. They thanked him, smiling, picking her up and letting him walk past. A daughter, thought Hilda again, watching.

'Wouldn't you like a little girl?' she said when she caught up with him.

He frowned, shaking his head. 'I hope you're not serious about this.'

'I am. I think I am.'

It was getting cold; she turned up the collar of her navy coat and walked with her hands in her pockets. Stephen was silent. Then he said: 'It isn't fair on you, it isn't right. You should be with someone else, someone who can give you these things.'

'What things? I only want one thing. And I don't want anyone else, I want you. I want your child. It's the only thing I've ever asked of you.' She spoke these words looking straight ahead, unable to say them to his face in case she started to get shrill, or cry.

'I'm sorry,' said Stephen. 'I'm sorry.'

Over the two years that followed there were more conversations like this – in parks, in restaurants, in bed. I could do it without him knowing, thought Hilda, I could come off the Pill. But she couldn't bring herself to do that – to deceive him, when she had asked for honesty; to present him with it, like a blow in the face. She left it for a couple of months, then asked again. It was June, warm and sunny; next month, as usual, Stephen was going on holiday with his family.

'Please,' she said, 'please.'

Anya was out; they were sitting in her garden, having tea. In an hour, after two days in London, Stephen was going back to Norfolk; it might be September before they saw each other again. Hilda fiddled with a teaspoon, her eyes fixed on the knots in the table. Birds sang in the trees.

Stephen, as had become the way of things, said nothing, letting her talk. There was a silence, which he did not break.

Hilda said: 'If you don't say yes, I'm going to finish it.' She looked at him quickly. 'I mean it. Forgive me.'

'There's nothing to forgive you for,' said Stephen. 'I understand.' He gave a long sigh. 'I'll think about it. I'll write.'

Hilda spent the summer watching for the post. She drew up plans for a community course in the autumn for volunteer literacy teachers, and she visited her friends in Wales. There was no letter from Stephen waiting when she got back. There was no choir, either, and she missed it. She visited Alice and the children, and Fanny and the children, and a colleague from work who was on maternity leave. She went to the theatre with Anya and her daughter, who visited every summer, and sat out in the garden with them when it was fine. She did all this mechanically, her days making an arc of hope and disappointment between the postman's visits, and slept badly, waking in the dead of night and staying awake, tossing between the alternatives of Stephen and no Stephen; Stephen and no child; child and no Stephen; no child, no Stephen, nothing.

The letter came in the last week of August, and she read it sitting at her desk by the open window. He missed her, he thought about her often, he had tried to phone her twice, from the callbox in the village, but couldn't get through.

I wish I could be more help to you, could say more easily the things you want me to say. I wish everything was different. I have thought and thought about what you want, and, now it has happened, how surprised I am. Dearest Hilda, I have always loved what vulnerability you have allowed me to see in you all the more because you have always been so independent, so involved in your work, and aware of worlds outside your own. This is unlike Miriam, and unlike, if I have understood you, your sister. It's what attracted me from the beginning, and it's one of the reasons I've always wanted everything to stay the same between us, for there to be no more complications than there are already.

There are other reasons, which have no place in this letter, which have nothing to do with us, and which I am not going to discuss because I'm sure you would not want me to.

And yet – not just because I don't want to lose you – I want to give you what you want.

I am writing this out on the terrace, overlooking the valley. It's eight o'clock, still very warm, and there are bats squeaking in and out of the barn behind the house. I wish you were here. I love you. I hope I'll always love you.

Dear Hilda, if after reading this, and knowing all my reservations, you still feel sure that you want to go ahead, then: yes.

Hilda put down the letter. She looked out over the square, filled, as usual on summer nights, with children on bicycles, whooping and calling. ʃhe saw them, but saw also the terrace outside an old Italian farmhouse, shaded by olive trees as the sun went down. Somewhere inside, in a hazy, unimagined place, were Miriam and Jonathan, who had not only Stephen, but each other. Outside on the terrace, he was sitting at a table, writing this letter, missing and wanting her.

I'm sure, she thought, picking up the pages again, and holding them to her face. I've never been so sure of anything.

Last night Hilda dreamed she was walking up the path to Stephen's house, where she had never been, although he had described it: long and low, set back from a lane. She walked in her dream down the path to his studio at the end of the garden.

'Stephen?' She knocked on the door. 'Stephen?' She pushed the door open, and saw him at his drawing board. He turned and said: 'Hilda? What are you doing here?' – as if there could be no possible reason why she should be there, interrupting his work.

She woke and lay, breathing shallowly, listening to the first murmurs of sparrows and starlings, trying to stop the dream from fading. What else might Stephen have gone on to say? How could he have been so bemused, speaking as if to a stranger?

The house was quiet. Last night she had fallen asleep listening to the rain pattering lightly on to the window boxes, then falling fast, drenching the garden and tall trees. She turned over, and looked at the thin strip of dull grey light at the top of the curtains. On Sunday mornings, when it was fine, Anya was up early, unbolting the doors to the garden; taking her coffee and the papers outside before going off to Mass.

'I cannot stand to be shut up indoors. It is very bad for you, for the skin, for everything. If you want to use the garden, Hilda, you must come down and tell me.'

Hilda yawned, drifting back to sleep.

When she woke up again, the room was much lighter, and now she could hear Anya's footsteps outside on the terrace below, and her dry cough. And now she had to get up and pee. She went to the bathroom, then made tea and toast, settling herself back against the propped-up pillows, thinking: in four months' time I shall have had breakfast alone for the last time. She sipped her tea from her china cup, in imagination placing a small white crib by the bed, a downy head and tiny fists visible above a snowy coverlet.

The morning brightened, and clouds blew across the sky. Hilda got up and ran a bath. Lying in it she decided to drive over to Waterlow Park before going to see Alice and the girls. Walking alone was different from walking at a child's pace, stopping and looking at everything; I'd better make the most of it, she thought, and trickled water from the sponge on to the mound of her stomach, wondering if it were a fist or foot which bumped beneath.

In Waterlow Park the trees were in bud, a sharp fresh green, and seagulls wheeled above the lake. There weren't many people about yet: dogs raced across the grass, couples walked hand in hand or sat on benches, reading the papers. Ahead of Hilda, a toddler staggered along the path towards the water, clutching a paper bag; he ran jerkily, at top speed, calling out: 'Ducks, Ducks!' and his father followed, walking fast.

'Careful, Hal.'

That's a good name, thought Hilda. I wish Stephen would talk about names. Rachel? Ruth? Rebecca? I think Rachel.

The path sloped sharply to the lakeside, fenced off from the water with loops of iron. Muscovy ducks, their beaks grotesquely encrusted with purple-pink flesh, trod on the slippery mud among the mallards, darting and gobbling as Hal and his father threw down the crusts.

'That's it, good boy. Look at that greedy one there.'

'More bread.' Hal turned to his father.

'All gone. Sorry.' The man shook out the bag and the last crumbs scattered. Hal began to wail.

'Never mind. Let's go and see the parrot.' He took the child's mittened hand and led him down towards the aviary, where cockatiels and ring-collared doves squawked and murmured behind rusty netting. As they passed Hilda the man's eyes briefly met hers, taking in at once her pregnant body and the fact that she had been watching them. And, perhaps, since she was alone, that she was having this baby alone. He bent down to pick up Hal, still protesting, and gave her a flicker of a smile.

Hilda looked away and walked past them, taking the damp path round the lake, taking an imaginary hand in hers.

Before she left, she went into Launderdale House, where there was a craft fair with stalls of pottery, hand-painted cards and silver earrings. She wandered up and down among the stalls, trying on a pair of loop earrings and wondering if Stephen would like them. I wish he were here, she thought, oh God, I wish he were here. She riffled through the hand-painted cards, and came across a few pen-and-ink prints, a series of family scenes from a garden – an old man in a panama hat asleep on a wooden seat; the back view of a woman weeding, kneeling on a mat; a man with thinning hair, not unlike Tony, hosing a flowerbed. They're rather nice, she thought, and stopped when she came to one of a small child in dungarees, disappearing through an arch in the hedge right at the bottom of the garden.

She bought a set and took them outside to one of the benches, to look through them again: at the little girl, independent and secure, walking away through the arch in the hedge, like Hettie, intent on her own pursuits, needing no one.

On impulse, Hilda felt in her shoulder bag for the fountain pen her father had given her, and turned over the card. She hesitated, then wrote simply: To the future. She sealed it in the envelope, addressed it to Stephen and stuck on a stamp from her wallet. Then she got up and walked out of the garden, dropping the card into the letterbox on Highgate Hill.

Annie tripped on the low wall at the edge of the sandpit, and fell head first to the ground, grazing her knee. She picked herself up and ran, screaming.

'Mum-my! Mum-my!'

'Oh dear, let's have a look.' Alice took her on her lap. 'That *was* a bang.'

'Stupid wall. *Stupid* wall.'

'Never mind, be careful next time.' Alice inspected the smeared blood. 'It needs a bit of a clean-up, keep still while I look in my bag.'

'It hurts!'

Alice rummaged with one hand, and found a tissue. She spat, and rubbed.

'Ow, ow!'

'Be brave, Annie, come on. I'll see if I've got a plaster.'

'I want to go home.'

'Ssh. We can't go yet, we're waiting for Hilda.' She produced a plaster from her purse.

'There. Do you want to pull the paper off?'

Annie pulled, and the plaster stuck to her finger; she shook it furiously. 'Get it off, get it *off!*'

'For heaven's sake . . .' Alice took a deep breath, looking round for Hettie. She wasn't on the swings, she wasn't on the slide. 'Hettie? Hettie!' She stood up, searching the playground for a dull pink hat. It was almost midday, and getting crowded; Hilda should have been here half an hour ago.

'Hettie!'

'There's Hilda,' Annie said suddenly. She had pulled the plaster off by herself and was standing on the bench.

'Where?'

'By the gate.'

Alice looked, and saw her sister push open the wooden gate, looking round, searching for her through the mothers and shrieking children.

'Hilda! Over here!' Alice called, and saw Hilda frowning, shading her glasses from the sharp sunlight. And where was Hettie?

There was Hettie. Alice saw her square, sturdy shape, weaving through darting children and pushchairs; she was walking steadily towards her aunt; she reached her, and tapped her on the arm. Hilda looked down, saw her, and smiled. She bent and kissed her, and then Hettie took her hand, and began to lead her through the crowd.

Seeing them draw near, Annie jumped down from the bench and ran towards them, wanting to be a part of it. 'Hello, hello!'

'Hello, Annie. Hello, Alice.' Holding Hettie's hand, Hilda, whom Alice had not seen for a while, looked relaxed and at home. And somehow different.

'I've hurt my knee,' Annie said loudly.

'Oh, dear, poor you, so you have.' Hilda bent and kissed her; Annie threw her arms extravagantly around her neck.

Watching them, Alice, even now, even after all this time, felt discomfited. The new Alice, the person she had become in the past six or seven years, thought: I'm glad Hilda and the children get on so well. The old Alice, who when she was small had longed for her clever, disdainful elder sister to love her, was on guard, uneasy, murmuring warily: she still looks as though she's running the show; those are *my* children.

The new Alice took charge, smiled, and said warmly, 'Hello, Hilda,' and kissed her on the cheek. And realised, with a sudden lurch of shock, that she was pregnant.

'You didn't tell me,' she said, gesturing foolishly, taken aback.

And Hilda smiled, and said in her light cool voice: 'No,' as if: why should I?

*

Annie, recovered, wanted Hilda to make a castle in the sandpit. In the end, they stayed in the playground for another half hour; by then the fitful morning sunshine had disappeared, and it began to rain before they reached the house. Hettie put up her umbrella and held it over Annie, who wanted to hold it too.

'Oh, come on,' said Alice, not wanting Hilda to see Annie behaving badly. 'We're almost there, don't let's have any dramas.'

'I know,' said Hettie, 'you give me the keys and I'll go ahead and open the door.'

'And Annie can have the umbrella? All right then.' Alice felt in her pocket. 'Here you are, the one with the red ring, okay?'

'I know which one it is.' Hettie reached up and took the bunch, and ran down the street through the rain.

Annie began to wail. '*I* want the keys!'

'You've got the umbrella,' said Hilda calmly.

Annie gets on her nerves, thought Alice, I hope we're not in for a difficult lunch. Ahead of them, Hettie was climbing the steps; she fumbled with the key in the lock, and opened the door, turning to wave at them, hurrying along the wet pavement. When they reached the house she was standing inside, graciously holding the door open.

'*Do* come in.'

'Oh, how very kind,' said Hilda, bowing, sweeping through; behind her Annie, trying to close the umbrella, trapped her finger, and began to scream. Alice released the finger, picked her up and carried her into the hall. She found her some Smarties, took everyone's coats and went into the kitchen, where she checked the joint and potatoes, put the water on for the peas and then stood looking out of the window to the garden, where the rain, from inside, looked gentle as a blessing. In the sitting room Annie had found something else to cry about. I wish I was out there in my boots by myself, Alice thought. I wish everyone would go away and leave me.

Behind her, Hilda was saying: 'Can I do anything?'

'You could lay the table,' said Alice, not turning, 'if you don't mind.'

'Of course not.' There was a pause, in which Hilda waited for Alice to turn, and remind her where things were. 'You all right?'

'Fine.'

It rained steadily for almost an hour, steaming the warm kitchen windows. The children drew pictures on them, waiting for pudding.

Hettie watched Hilda lean across to write their names in the steam, and said suddenly: 'Have you got a baby in your tummy?'

'Yes,' said Hilda, and sat down again.

'I didn't know that,' said Hettie, sounding pleased. 'When's it going to come out?'

'At the end of the summer.'

'Will I be six then? I'm six in July.'

'Yes, you will. What a big girl – what do you want for your birthday?'

Hettie considered, and drew breath for a list. 'Well . . .'

Annie said: 'Can I watch it come out?'

Alice said: 'Here we are,' and brought lemon meringue pie to the table.

Hettie said: 'Oooh, lovely,' and Annie said again: 'Can I?'

'No,' said Hilda. 'Sorry.'

'We'll see,' said Alice, watching Annie get ready for a fight. 'Now, then, who wants some of this? Hilda?'

'Please. But do the girls first, I'm fine.'

'Who's the daddy?' Hettie asked, watching Alice spoon fluffy meringue into her bowl.

'Someone called Stephen,' said Hilda.

'Who's Stephen?'

'A friend. Alice, if that's for me, that's plenty.'

'A friend? I thought you said he was the daddy.'

'He is. What do you want for your birthday?'

'I'd like a baby. I wish we could have one.' She turned to Alice who was helping Annie go round the edges.

'Very hot, just take a little.'

'Mummy?' Hettie asked. 'Can we have another baby? Please?'

'We'll see,' said Alice, giving herself some pie and sitting down. 'All right? Everyone okay? After lunch, Annie, you can go up and have a nice nap.'

'I don't want a nap.'

The rain stopped at last, and the sky cleared to a watery paleness. Upstairs, Annie, protesting, had been put to bed, and lay asleep, flushed face pressed into a pillow patterned with clowns, grubby rabbit dropped to the floor from open fist. Downstairs, Hettie was in a cushioned corner of the sitting room, surrounded by bears, paper and crayons.

'Now you sit there, and you there, and you there . . . I'm going to give you each a piece of paper, and I want you to do a drawing before tea. Here you are, here you are, here you are . . . if you want any help, ask me. What's the matter, little bear, there's no need to fuss.'

Alice and Hilda sat on the sofa with their coffee cups, watching her.

'She's wonderful,' said Hilda.

'She's just like you,' said Alice. She had lit the fire, and the room was warm and comfortable. Beside her, Hilda had kicked off her shoes and stretched her legs, in navy tights like Hettie's, towards the hearth.

'I wasn't like that,' she said.

'Yes, you were.' Alice looked at her. Hilda's neat dark hair shone, and her clean pale skin looked luminous, untouched. Behind her round glasses her eyes were clear and calm. She still looks intimidating, Alice thought, she still has that air of everything being right in her world, but now it's more than that. 'You were always very together, and capable,' she said.

Hilda pulled a face. 'That doesn't sound very interesting. Hettie's so warm, she's a kind child.'

There was a pause, in which an unspoken exchange hung in the air:

Yes, and you weren't kind, Hilda. Not to me.

You got on my nerves. Following me about.

I suppose everything was fine until I came along.

Yes, it probably was.

Then Hilda yawned, and leaned back against the cushions. 'That was such a good lunch. Why can't I cook like that?'

Alice shrugged. 'I used to be hopeless.'

'But not any more,' said Hilda. 'You've made a lovely home, it's always so nice here.' She paused. 'Alice? You are pleased about the baby?'

'Yes,' said Alice, looking at the carpet. 'Of course.'

'Sure?'

'I've just said so.' She raised her head. 'Anyway, what does it matter whether I'm pleased or not?'

Hilda frowned. 'Of course it matters.'

'Why?'

'Alice . . .'

'What matters,' said Alice, 'is that *you're* pleased. I take it you are.'

'Naturally. I wouldn't be having one otherwise.'

Oh, no, thought Alice, of course not. Of course you wouldn't. She said: 'It was planned, then?'

'Yes.' Hilda raised an eyebrow, self-mocking. 'Can you imagine me doing anything I hadn't planned?'

'No,' said Alice truthfully, 'I can't. And – does Stephen . . . does he manage to get to London at the moment?'

'When he can.' And then Hilda's luminous expression changed, the shutters coming down, and Alice was silent again. She looked at her sister, long navy legs stretched out before her, and thought: I've been in your shadow all my life, and having babies was the one thing that made me human, the one thing I thought you'd never do. Or even want to do. I shouldn't be upset but I am, I'm devastated. You're on my territory – more than that: it feels as if you're taking away from me the only thing that has made me real. I never felt real before. She saw Hilda's hand move as the baby inside her moved, and thought, as she had been thinking for weeks, but with real fervour now: I *must* have another one, just one more. Is that wanting too much?

Hilda said: 'Do you disapprove so deeply, Alice? You really shouldn't.' She looked round at the familiar room, at the boxes of toys, the blue jug of daffodils on the mantelpiece, and at Hettie, down in her corner with her bears. 'After all,' she said lightly, 'You've got everything now.'

Have I? thought Alice. Almost everything.

'I suppose it must seem like that. I expect you think I've got too much.'

'Of course I don't,' said Hilda, although, in truth, it was hard sometimes not to feel that Tony had handed it all to Alice on a plate. But even so – why shouldn't she have it all?

'It used to be you,' said Alice, 'disapproving of me.' That's why I never told you anything, you would never have understood. I was mad long before they took me into hospital, mad like Blanche Dubois: brittle, on edge, in pieces, using men like a drug, hating all of it. All of it!

'Well . . . I was worried about you. You were so . . .' Hilda looked down at her sister, who was gazing, again, at the carpet, and said carefully: 'But now it's better, isn't it? Alice? Are you happy now?'

Alice took a deep breath. 'Yes. Yes, of course.'

'But what?'

'But . . . I suppose sometimes I feel I'm not good enough for Tony . . .'

'Oh, don't be ridiculous!' And Hilda was suddenly as tart as she had been in the old days, when Alice had made weeping telephone calls from Oxford, and was told to pull herself together. There'll always be something, she thought now, feeling a rising exasperation. It's never quite right, is it? Here you are, with the nicest man you could wish for as your husband, two lovely children, a beautiful home – and *still* there has to be something to gnaw away at. 'What on earth do you mean?'

Alice's pale face was scarlet. 'Forget it.'

And I've done it again, thought Hilda: Alice over-reacts, and it's all my fault. I can hear Mother now: 'Leave her, poor little thing!' God, she's a pain. But then she moved, and the baby kicked inside her again, an insistent fluttering beneath her ribs, and she was suddenly filled with tenderness and remorse. Perhaps I am too hard on her, she thought. Perhaps I always was.

'I'm sorry,' she said, trying to sound warm again. 'Tell me what you were going to say. If you want to. I promise I'll try to understand.'

Alice floundered. 'I mean bed,' she said, blurting it out as if she had been standing for a long time on the edge of a precipice, and now could no longer stop herself from leaping. 'I mean sex.'

Hilda looked at her, but Alice would not meet her eyes. 'What about it?'

'I mean, if you must know, that I don't enjoy it. I never have.'

Hilda, with images of an endless stream of Alice's lovers floating up from the past, said slowly: 'Are you serious?'

'Yes,' said Alice. 'It leaves me completely cold. It always has.'

'You mean – even with Tony?'

'Even with Tony.' She was hugging her knees, her face buried.

'But . . .' And now Hilda was floundering. 'But why don't you tell him? I mean, Tony, of all men – he's not exactly insensitive, is he?'

'No. Of course he isn't.'

'Then why . . .'

Alice looked up, and gave an unconvincing smile. 'It seems a bit late, somehow, after all these years.'

'But . . .' said Hilda once more, and from upstairs there came a cry.

'Mum-my! *Mummy!*'

From her corner Hettie said: 'What does Annie want now?'

Alice scrambled to her feet. 'I think perhaps she's sickening for something.' She looked flushed, tearful, uncomfortable, pushing back her hair.

Hilda said gently, quietly, mindful of Hettie, who was looking up at them: 'Alice . . . you don't *have* to like it . . .'

'Don't you like it, with Stephen?'

'Yes, but . . .'

'Well, then.'

'*Mum-my!*'

Alice shook her head blindly. 'I must go up to her. Anyway, it doesn't matter, Hilda, I don't want to talk about it any more, and please, just forget it. I don't even know why I said it . . .'

And she was gone, calling up the stairs: 'Coming!'

Hilda and Hettie looked at one another.

'Come over here,' said Hilda.

Upstairs, Alice found Annie sitting up in bed, scrunching the duvet cover. She looked as Alice felt – hot, flushed, miserable, damp fair hair clinging to her head. Alice sat down beside her.

'What's the matter, darling?' She drew a breath, steadying herself. 'Not very well?'

Annie shook her head crossly. 'I want a drink.'

'All right, come on.' Alice pulled back the duvet, and found the bed was soaking. 'Oh, dear, poor Annie.' She picked her up and took her along to the bathroom; she took off her wet clothes and found a last pair of clean pyjamas in the airing cupboard.

'I'm *shivering*!'

'Sorry, darling.' Alice pulled on the pyjamas quickly, sponged Annie's face and gave her a drink. 'Now, you sit there while I go and deal with the bed. I'll be back in a minute.'

She left her in her dressing gown on the bathroom chair, while she stripped the bed. Back in the bathroom, she put wet sheet and duvet cover in the machine. Annie watched her, swinging her feet.

'All right now? Let's go downstairs, and see Hilda.'

Annie scowled.

'D'you want to stay in bed? You can pop into Hettie's bed, if you like.'

'Your bed. Your bed, and you read me a story.'

'Annie, I can't stay upstairs, Hilda's visiting us. Come down, and we'll have a story by the fire.' Alice held out her hand.

Annie put up her arms. 'Carry me. You carry me.'

'You're such a heavy girl.'

'Please.'

'Oh, all right.' Alice picked her up and they went slowly downstairs, Annie's arms round her neck. In the hall, Alice saw an envelope on the front door mat.

'Look, there's a letter.'

'For me!'

But when they went along the hall and picked it up, Alice saw a child's uneven letters: 'HETTIE'.

'It's for Hettie, darling, I think it's a party invitation.'

'*I* want to go to a party.' Annie reached for the envelope.

'I know, never mind. Your turn next, perhaps. Soon be *your* birthday, Annie. Come on now.'

They went back along the corridor, towards the warmth and light of the sitting room. At the doorway, Alice stopped, hearing Hilda's voice. Hettie was not in her corner – when she looked round the door she saw her on the sofa, leaning against Hilda, a bear on her lap. Hilda had her arm round her, and was reading a story aloud.

They look absolutely right together, thought Alice, who had seen Hettie being read to by different people many times. With Hilda she looked as if she belonged: two dark heads, two pairs of navy tights. But it was more than that: Hilda's measured voice, her calm assurance, matched Hettie's own small-scale containment and self-possession. And again, as in the playground, a part of Alice was pleased and a part, even with Annie in her arms, felt uneasy – not only because of the exchange she'd just had with Hilda, but more than that: as if she were watching a scene which no one needed her to join, but which she wanted desperately to join.

Annie was wriggling, and Alice put her down: she ran to the fireside, plopping down on a cushion with her thumb in her mouth, wanting, now she was downstairs, to hear the story, no matter who was reading. Hilda and Hettie looked up, and Hettie smiled.

'Hello, Mummy.'

'Hello, darling.' Alice felt a rush of relief and tenderness – *my* daughter, *my* beloved – and then Hettie had turned back into the crook of Hilda's arm, listening again.

Alice came slowly into the room; she sat on the cushion on the other side of the fire, watching her sister and daughter, close and absorbed. It's just like when we were little, she thought. Still. Hilda and Father, always reading, looking up when I came in, wondering what I wanted.

'Sit on your lap,' Annie commanded. She had got up from the

other cushion and sat down on Alice, still flushed, and Alice wrapped her arms round her, resting her chin on the tousled hair. I thought I was cured, she said to herself in apprehension, almost in despair, watching the street beyond the firelit window begin to grow dark. I thought having the children had cured me of everything. I can remember lying in bed on Christmas night, after they'd gone to sleep, and I felt so peaceful and contented. I thought: this is who I am, and who I'll be for ever. How could I have imagined that?

Hilda turned the page and paused for a moment; she looked across the room at Alice, but Alice did not look back. And Hilda gave an inward shrug and went on reading, her arm round Hettie's small firm body, feeling with pleasure her unborn baby stir again.

Thus Alice, unsteady still. Thus Hilda, full of hope. And meanwhile Miriam, in her house in Norfolk, making her discoveries.

2

Nine-fifteen on a Monday morning; a long, tiled house set back from a winding lane. To the left the lane ran past farmland, to the right towards the road to Saxham, a village of flint and whitewashed cottages with pantiled roofs, a line of fifties council houses, a shop, a pub. The road meandered out of the village, bordered with hedges, reaching the long straight run to busier Woodburgh, where Miriam had her shop. On Mondays the shop was closed and Miriam had a day off, to make up for Saturdays, when she would rather have been at home. With the men gone, banging the front door – "Bye, Miriam!' "Bye, Mum!' – she had the house to herself.

She came downstairs a little unsteadily, her hand on the dark banister. A tall, once striking-looking woman in her late forties; with something of a blurred, vague air now, thick deep chestnut hair hennaed so the streaks of silver didn't show, dark brown eyes puffy first thing in the morning, soft freckled skin getting looser, slacker. Still beautiful – '*I* think you're beautiful, Mum,' – coming down the stairs in her silk kimono and flapping cotton slippers, and charming, always: to her customers, to Stephen's clients, whom she entertained for dinner when she had to, and to Jonathan's friends, who roared along the lane on motorbikes and came into the house in creaking black leather, barricading themselves upstairs in his bedroom, with his tapes.

But the charm did not quite conceal the vagueness, and the vagueness could not quite be accounted for, even by Miriam herself. Had she grown absent-minded and blurry because of the drink, or had she begun to drink because she felt out of touch with Stephen, and from there with everything? Had she been out of touch because she wasn't happy, or if she had been more in touch would she have been able to be happy? Such reflections were often to be found at the bottom of a glass, prompting her to pour another. She drank, always, alone, and made sure – she was sure she made sure – that Jonathan was among those who would be surprised to know she ever had anything more than a sociable glass or two at the dinner table.

There was a postcard for Jonathan, from Amsterdam, lying on the mat. Miriam bent to pick it up, with the letters for Stephen. The hall was broad and airy, running the width of the house, always cool – the sun rose at the front but there were tall woods across the lane, and it was the garden behind, where Stephen had built himself a studio, which soaked up the midday and afternoon sun. Miriam opened the front door because she believed in airing a place, and it calmed her to let in the fresh morning air and see the sun filtering through the trees, full of birdsong. Jonathan had already taken Tess out for a run, he did every morning; she came padding through from the kitchen now and flopped on to the mat.

'Good girl. You stay there.'

She checked to see that the front gates were shut, for the road at the end of the lane was a potential killer: once the school bus and early traffic from the village to the town had gone, it was empty and sleepy except for the chugging tractors from the farm, but every now and then a car would appear from round the bend, coming much too fast, and no animal stood a chance. When Jonathan was small the gates had had to be padlocked. She worried no less about him now that he was seventeen; in fact, with the motorbike, she worried more.

She carried the letters and postcard into the kitchen, and put the kettle on for coffee; Stephen's letters she would take over to the studio later. She sat down, waiting for the kettle to boil, and turned over Jonathan's postcard. In the Easter holidays he had gone for three days to Amsterdam, with friends, to listen to the music in the clubs. The postcard was a black and white photograph of a spike-haired androgyne sticking out an over-sized tongue, touched in in a lurid pink. Miriam turned it over again. *'Dear Jonathan, I am thinking of you and the good times we had. Perhaps I shall come to England one day? Kisses from Marietta.* It was written in spidery, continental ballpoint, with a telephone number at the top. She propped it up against the cereal packet, tongue side out, then turned it over so that she did not have to look at it – but then it would be obvious that she had read it. Had Marietta spent much time wondering whether to send a casual postcard or sealed letter to Jonathan, who had not mentioned girls when he came back? Miriam drank her coffee, and pushed away images of smoky nightclubs and her sixth-form son, far from home, bedding – had he actually bedded? – large blonde Marietta in the small hours.

The sink was full of washing up from last night; on Sundays she let it go, knowing that on Mondays she was there to put the house in order, make it a home. That above all: whatever else was wrong, she could have one day, at the start of the week, in which to cherish the notion of herself as homemaker, her men needing her to make a haven, welcoming and warm, to come back to. Phrases like well-stocked cupboards, clean dry clothes, freshly swept and dusted had at some long-ago story-book time gone deep into Miriam's psyche, although she rarely brought them consciously to the surface.

She finished her coffee and got up, opening the window over the sink, which looked on to the fields, the long hedges bordering a cart track, and the glass door at the back, which led to the garden. The grass was still wet with dew; she drew in more fresh air, and began her tour of the house, where no one could disturb her.

Miriam had an uneasy relationship with solitude. In moments of unhappiness she craved it as a release from the need to keep up appearances, to be pleasantly convincing as the architect's wife: privileged, interesting, running a lovely home and her own small business, too. She was also afraid of it, feeling solitude slip into loneliness, rarely able to lose herself, or a sense of herself as a woman alone – as if she were being observed, usually by someone critical, walking through the quiet house, picking up Jonathan's scattered clothes, tapes and cricket things, putting them neatly away. Hard to confront exactly what this imaginary observer would wish her to be doing otherwise; she only knew that she sometimes, in fact quite often, inwardly rehearsed the externals of her life as if she'd been asked to give a potted biography to present to the outside world, and needed to make it sound as though she were accomplished and content.

Upstairs, she dressed, then made up the beds with clean linen. There were four bedrooms, two large at the front, two small at the back, on either side of a broad landing; Miriam had put a window seat at the front. They'd moved here on an autumn afternoon fourteen years ago, leaving a cramped Norwich flat so that Stephen could save money on studio rent and build up his practice from home. He had made his studio the large room across the landing from their bedroom. Jonathan had a room at the back, overlooking the garden, and the other small room was, Miriam hoped, soon to be occupied by another baby. In the meantime, they could use it as a boxroom. She'd watched the removal men struggle with Stephen's drawing board and plan chest round the bend in the stairs, and had visions of winter evenings spent sewing by the fire, with Stephen working up here. She would come up later with a cup of coffee for him, and run a bath; she would go to bed and read for a while, and presently he would join her. They would lie together, listening to the owls in the woods, the bark of a fox, while Jonathan slept, and then they would make love. The following year their second child would be born, and they would be a proper family.

The boxroom was still a boxroom, and within six months of their move Stephen had built a new studio out in the garden.

The removals van had gone at about four o'clock, rattling back to Norwich. They stood at the window of the little bedroom which was to be Jonathan's, watching him, down below in the overgrown garden, crouch on the path to examine a snail, then get up to run off again, making for a heap of old grass cuttings. No one had lived in this house for over a year; it needed a lot doing to it, and had been on the market for months before Stephen found it. The room smelt of dust and of being shut up for a long time; Stephen fiddled with the catch on the window frame and pushed up with a jerk. He ran his fingers down the side, examining the sash. 'Rotten,' he said. 'Or on the way. I should think every frame in the house will need replacing.'

Miriam leaned out. It hadn't rained for days and the air was warm and hazy, Indian summer weather, the garden laced with spiders' webs. There was a paved area, where straggling weeds poked through the cracks, before the grass began, and the old brick path ran through a gap in an unkempt hedge to a second, secluded part, planted with apple trees, pale with lichen. She waved to Jonathan who was coming through the gap. 'All right? Having a good time?'

'I found a long, long worm – come and see!'

'In a minute.'

She looked over to the left. There was a path running down the side from the front of the house, and across the ragged hedges bordering their garden a cart track led from the lane to the fields of the neighbouring farm, just ploughed. The farmhouse itself was at the end of the track; she imagined they could get snowed in, in winter. As she watched, a tractor came bumping along from the lane; she saw Jonathan leap up at the sound and run to the hedge, peering through. Perhaps there were children on the farm; he could go and play in the haystacks. In the meantime, there was the donkey, whom they had met in the summer when they went for a walk down the lane after looking at the house. He was standing in a field under the trees, shaking his head to get rid of the flies; across the rough grass was a corrugated iron shelter. They hadn't had anything to give him, but Jonathan had pulled out a few blades of sweeter grass from the verge and thrust them through the gate.

'Remember the donkey?' she said to Stephen, behind her. 'We can go and visit him now, Jonathan will love it.'

'Mmm.' He was pulling at a piece of browning flowered wallpaper, and a little heap of plaster pattered on to the bare boards. 'God, I wonder if it's all this soft.'

Miriam looked out to the right, where a grey church tower rose beyond yellow trees. The village was a quarter of a mile away, with one shop, probably expensive, with postcards on the door advertising rabbits, garden tools and paraffin stoves. Miriam wondered how the people in the village would take to them all, if they'd known the old lady who'd died here for years and would view newcomers with caution. Well, Stephen could charm them, he could charm anybody. He'd charmed her into bed on their second meeting, and Jonathan had been the result. Where was Jonathan? She craned her neck and saw him, still by the hedge, talking to himself.

Stephen put his head out beside her. 'Do you think we should put up safety bars?'

'I suppose we should,' said Miriam. She looked down on to the stone slabs and straggling weeds, and pictured a small, spread-eagled figure, very still. 'Ugh. Yes. And we must remember to keep this shut in the meantime.' She drew back her head. As usual, it had been Stephen, not she, who had made the serious suggestion – practical, sensible, anticipating. She would have worried and done nothing, or not thought until it was too late, hearing that sudden, leaden thump, then silence. She shivered. I'm an idiot, a careless fool; that's what could have happened. Then she thought: If I didn't have that streak in me, Jonathan wouldn't even be here. Other women use contraception, or make sure their partners do; I just closed my eyes and hoped. I suppose, of course, I was hoping for a baby.

Self-deprecating, unsure, even in her thirties, about relationships with men, Miriam did not allow herself to face the thought that perhaps it had been up to Stephen, too, to consider the consequences of nights of passion; that his practical, sensible nature, which when she found she was pregnant had made him ask her to marry him, might have kept them both out of trouble in the first place. Or perhaps his asking her to marry him had more to do with his age, his situation – an architect in a moderately successful partnership set upon becoming very successful in his own right. It surely had more to do with that, with needing a wife, after endless girlfriends, than with feeling. Certainly, it was not enough to do with love, at least not the way Miriam loved Stephen.

There was a part of Miriam which, once she had Jonathan, had settled down, had become secure and purposeful through his need of her. There was another part, vulnerable and uncertain, which motherhood had done nothing to diminish: if Stephen did not love her, and she was sure he did not, what was she worth? What was anything worth? It wasn't good to love anyone like that, it took too much out of you, and a stronger woman would not have allowed it; Miriam was not a stronger woman. And she stood, now, in an empty room in their new house, reproaching herself for a tragedy that had not happened – a little dead boy, lives ruined.

Stephen drew his head in from the window. 'The garden's going to need a lot of work.' He sounded pleased, proprietorial, then saw her face. 'Miriam? What are you thinking about?'

'Nothing,' she said. 'Let's go and have some tea.'

There was a sudden scream from the garden. 'Mummy! Mummy!'

'Oh my God.' She fled from the room, down the uncarpeted stairs, out along the passage to the back door. We left him alone too long, she thought, he's only a baby, typical of me to stand about worrying about nothing when all the time. . . . Outside, she found Jonathan howling his way towards the house, clutching his arm.

'I got stung, I got *stung*!'

'All right, darling, all right, come here.' She led him into the kitchen full of tea chests, trying to prise away the hand from the swollen, reddened arm. She was filled with visions of bee stings and allergies, hospitals too far to get to in time; not like Norwich, cramped but safe, with the doctor two roads away. Her hands were shaking: where was the first aid stuff, something she should have packed last, to make sure she could put her hand straight on it in an emergency. Instead, she hadn't a clue where it might be, had spent a week doing all the packing late at night and was too tired this morning to remember sensible things like that. And anyway, what did you do with stings? If it was a bee, and the sting was left behind, if it had been his eye, his mouth . . .

'Stephen!'

'I'm here, don't flap.'

'*Dad-dy*!' A note, detectable even by Miriam in her panic, a definite note of the theatrical. The pain fading, the crisis past.

'Let's have a look.' Stephen drew Jonathan to him, sat on the garden step with him on his lap. 'Was it a whopper?'

'I didn't see,' said Jonathan. 'It just *came* at me.'

Stephen looked at the fading red. 'I don't think it's a bee, do you?' he said to Miriam. 'Just a nasty old wasp.' He kissed Jonathan's head. 'A whopper of a wops. Shall we put some TCP on it? And a plaster?'

'I don't know where the stuff is,' said Miriam. 'I'm sorry.' A sudden inspiration. 'I think soda bicarb is supposed to do something for stings – perhaps amongst the kitchen cupboard things . . .' She turned to look at the tea chests, the last-minute cardboard boxes. Where to begin? 'If it's only a wasp it'll go down anyway, won't it? I'll put a cold poultice on.' She found a clean tea towel, soaked it under the tap, wrung it out and folded it. 'Here, Jonathan, this'll help, let Daddy hold it on. Good boy.' She stood watching them, heads close together, Stephen making funny faces, Jonathan laughing. 'I'll make some tea,' she said. 'At least I know where that is.'

They sat with their mugs at the kitchen table, eating ginger biscuits, Jonathan still on Stephen's lap, the sting forgotten. Miriam yawned, leaning back in her chair. Outside, the sun was low, and the smell of grass, warmed all afternoon, came drifting through the open doors.

Her doubt and insecurity began to evaporate. If Stephen had sought out a house as large as this, where he would spend most of his time, with her at home, he must, too, be envisaging a settled family life, brothers and sisters for Jonathan, no longer feeling trapped – by a baby, by someone who loved him too much. A decision had been made, a life had to be lived. They'd be all right.

The Indian summer ended; by the middle of October they were building bonfires of the leaves which blew across the garden and down the lane. The tall trees creaked in the wind and it began to rain, heavily, for days at a time. Stephen had a contract with a housing estate on the outskirts of Norwich; he drove off on dark wet mornings to the site and came back on dark evenings. In between times he was making contacts, trying to get his name known in their village and in the others nearby, starting work restoring a barn for a local landowner, wanting it to be a showpiece. He spent evenings and much of the weekends either out or up in the studio, and began to complain that it wasn't light enough, even when the last of the leaves had fallen and the trees stood bare. The light faded early, and it began to get very cold, the wind sweeping across the flat, unprotected fields.

Miriam made occasional excursions to auctions and salerooms,

Jonathan in tow, but mostly she was confined to the house. She stripped wallpaper, painted woodwork and waited for Stephen to have enough time to help. He found a local builder, Frank, who came and plastered, watched by Jonathan.

'Can I do some of that?'

'You can have a go if you like.'

When he left in his van Jonathan stood at the window, waving. The plaster was left to dry out but no paper was hung; when Jonathan had his nap Miriam painted the walls with cream emulsion. She listened to Radio Four all day and wondered if he was lonely. He was old enough to join a playgroup, but there was nothing here – until they were five, and bussed into the school beyond Woodburgh, the village children stayed at home with their mothers; they went with them to the shops and came home again to play in the garden or watch television; they all seemed to have brothers or sisters, and plenty of friends. Their mothers nodded to Miriam in the shops where Stephen had put up his card in the window, beside the rabbits and logs and paraffin stoves. Jonathan at first did not speak to the children, overcome by so many, in such a confined space, after the rambling emptiness of the house. After a while he began to say hello, and they said hello back, but nothing ever came of these exchanges – they stood munching crisps until their mothers took them out again, running down the wet lane in their boots and anoraks. 'Mind – there's a car coming!' Miriam and Jonathan walked home under their umbrella, and when it cleared up went to visit the donkey.

He spent a lot of time now in his rusting corrugated iron shelter, where the rain drummed on the roof. When he came towards them over the wet grass, Jonathan held out small green apples, no longer alarmed by the puckering hairy lips and yellow teeth.

'Doesn't he get lonely, all by himself? Poor donkey.'

'Poor donkey. Never mind, at least he's got us.'

'*That's* not very much.'

In the evenings, when Jonathan had gone to bed, Miriam sat in the kitchen making curtains, spreading yards of cotton across the table, whirring along the hems with the machine. In the warm room with the cat asleep on the rug in front of the Rayburn, she began to feel the house grow into a home, closed in on itself, shut up, secure. Evenings were easier than the long wet days; no one expected to be able to go out and do things on winter evenings. She listened to plays and concerts and wondered, sometimes, if she could go back to work in the spring.

When Miriam had met Stephen she'd been working as a secretary to a firm of solicitors in Norwich: over-qualified, with an arts degree, and under-confident, knowing she should be doing more than typing other people's letters, not knowing what more to do. She knew now that there were women everywhere fretting at being at home with small children, longing to get out, get a job, get away from the housework, fish fingers and playdough. Miriam felt out of tune, knowing she really wanted only to be here.

She packed away her sewing, put out the cat, who hunted all night along the hedgerows, and climbed the stairs: she ran a bath and went to look at Jonathan, who had kicked the bedclothes off. His cheek was pale and cold; she covered him up and tucked him in, and went to have her bath, passing the other small bedroom, piled high with bits and pieces, including Jonathan's old cot, and carrycot, and a box of baby clothes. She lay in the hot water, making calculations, and went into Stephen's room in her dressing gown.

'Have you nearly finished?'

'Still a bit to do.'

He was sitting in his high swivel chair, tapping his pen in his hand, long legs wound round the base. The red anglepoise lamp shone on to drawings of open-plan living rooms, long narrow kitchens with rows of units, neat squares of garden. An electric fire burned near his feet; the rest of the room felt very cold.

'Come to bed,' said Miriam. 'It's freezing up here.'

'In a minute.' He tapped the pen against his teeth, thinking. Stephen had beautiful teeth, sloping slightly backwards, and his smile was revealing, inviting. He was a good-looking man whose regular features and curly hair might have made for blandness if he hadn't also been clever and, usually, charming. He was the kind of man women fell for, and Miriam had fallen. What was he thinking about?

'Have you really got much more?'

'I said – just a bit. Go on, darling. Have you checked on Jonathan?'

'Yes, he'd kicked all the clothes off.'

'Okay – I'll have another look at him before I come.' He squinted again at the board. 'See you in a little while.'

Such ordinary conversations, the day-to-day talk of married life; hearing them one might think they came out of an easy domesticity, a deep steady love kept alive by passion. But Miriam and Stephen's bed was becoming a battleground. She went out, leaving the door ajar.

'Shut it,' said Stephen lightly. 'I'll keep you awake.'

'No you won't,' said Miriam, uneasy. If not tonight, then tomorrow? If not tomorrow, when? Tonight, please tonight.

'Go on,' said Stephen, not so lightly. 'I prefer it shut.'

Miriam closed the door and crossed the landing to their bedroom. She took off her dressing gown and climbed into bed, reaching for her book.

In the days when Miriam had slept alone, she had read late into the night, sleeping in the next morning. Even then, as a student, she'd wanted more than anything else to be a mother, hadn't known, really, what else to do with her life. Now she lay sleepily turning the pages, a married woman, mother of one, still wondering. Above her, in the rafters, mice skittered; a car drove past, speeding along the lane, slowing at the bend before the village; a little later, from the woods, came an owl's hoot, breathy and hollow. Miriam's hand dropped from the book and it slid to the floor; she fell asleep with the light on.

And woke to hear Stephen switch it off, very carefully and quietly, not wanting her to wake. He went round the bed in bare feet, pulled back the bedclothes and got in beside her. Only Stephen could go to bed naked in the middle of winter. Did other men get naked into bed and turn away? She moved towards him, hardly daring to breathe.

'Stephen?'

'Mmmm?' he said sleepily, abstracted.

She moved closer, slipping an arm around his bare chest, and yawned, she couldn't help it. Stephen patted her hand and yawned too, elaborately.

'Night, darling.'

Closer still, hearing the owl again, but faintly, hunting further afield, beyond the woods. It seemed suddenly such a lonely cry, and Miriam, her arms around Stephen who so clearly was refusing her, felt her hopes of the house, and her sense of it as a family home, recede into a bleak, unreachable distance. She lay awake for a long time, listening to his breathing grow slower and steadier. Sleepless, she discovered, was quite a different word from awake – awake was alert, interested, alive; sleepless was full of tension and anxiety, restlessness. Miriam's nights became sleepless, wondering: if he doesn't want me, who does he want? She remembered aching lines from Beckett, read years ago:

if you do not love me I shall not be loved

if I do not love you I shall not love

Was that true? Was there only one 'you' in the world?

There were nights which were not like this, nights which followed evenings when they sat at the kitchen table with notebooks and gardening books, making plans for the spring: for bedding plants, a willow, a pond for Jonathan. Through the landowner for whom he was converting the barn, Stephen met other people; his card in the village shop brought phone calls. He asked Miriam to invite these new acquaintances for supper, and since she knew she was a good cook, she in some ways looked forward to these evenings. It didn't matter in the least to anyone else if she didn't talk much – their dinner guests were voluble about life in the country, only too eager to tell her how she should go about things, and to listen to Stephen talk expansively, as he always did at dinner parties, about his work, about local history, and churches, and the guests' own houses, asking all the right questions. Everyone liked him, warming to his easy manner, his way of making sure that they all had what they wanted, and were able to talk about themselves. He was the perfect host, but also – unobtrusively but surely – he was smoothing the path for his own career: inspiring confidence, making introductions. When Miriam got up to make coffee, he would fetch his photographs of earlier projects completed and under way. There were strong, black and white photographs of the derelict barn converted with the best local materials, using the finest craftsmen; of extensions and conservatories and lofts – light, airy homes which looked as if their owners could want nowhere else now.

He took the guests on a tour of the house, gently flirting with the wives, showing them the flagstoned hall, with the rugs Miriam had found in an auction, the sitting room he was going to get Frank to work on, knocking down a wall, exposing beams, ripping out a postwar fireplace to reveal the original chimney breast. If he was in love with anything, Miriam realised, not just at these dinner parties but gradually, over the course of that first winter, it was with the house itself – partly for its own sake, more as a setting for himself and his future.

On nights like this, when she had cooked well, and everyone had eaten and drunk well (she, perhaps, unnoticed, drinking a little more than the others) she and Stephen climbed the stairs together when their guests had gone, and undressed together. The bedroom, too, had long pale rafters beneath the stripped-off layers of paper; Miriam had emulsioned the walls in a washed-out pink, and curtained the low windows with faded tapestry found in an auction. The bed was wide and inviting – as it was every night, but Miriam was, apparently, unable to invite Stephen. Now, when he was aroused – by her, or by the image of someone else at the dinner table? – she lay beneath the soft heap of duvet, warm, open, longing. And Stephen made love to her expertly, as he had done from the beginning – as he would, she felt, have done with anyone. They fell asleep in each other's arms, and she woke next morning filled with hope, to find Jonathan standing by the bed or clambering in between them. 'Hello, darling.' On mornings like this they were the happiest of families, and she absurd to worry. Everything was all right, everything was going to happen.

But by the new year Miriam was not pregnant, and by the end of January Stephen had drawn up plans for a studio out in the garden, where the light was better.

In March, Miriam, as every month, sat at the kitchen table repeatedly counting days on the calendar. Thirty-six, thirty-seven, thirty-eight . . . Thirty-eight! Thirty-eight was hopeful, more than hopeful. Outside, Stephen was talking to Frank, the builder, pacing out an area of ground beyond the hedge that divided the garden. A sharp wind was sweeping across the bare fields, bending the apple trees. She could see the heads of the two men, bobbing along over the top of the hedge, and Stephen's arms, gesturing animatedly. Jonathan, in woolly hat and gumboots, was wheeling his barrow up and down along the path, talking to himself. Sitting in the warm kitchen, watching him, and the men, absorbed in their plans, Miriam found herself thinking: Shouldn't this be enough? He's a contented child, with plenty to do, the country life I wanted for him, following his father about the place, knowing I'm around. Who says he needs a baby to come and disturb all this? Who says Stephen does? It's only me who keeps wanting – can't I be satisfied with what I have? Then she thought: thirty-eight days . . . I really could be, this time. And she felt so excited that she couldn't sit there a minute longer, but got up and pulled on her own gumboots, and went outside, waving and calling: 'How are you getting on?' as if a studio out in the garden, with Stephen working away from the house, and away from her, were of no consequence, indeed an excellent idea. Stephen looked pleased, and Frank nodded to her, touching his hat, a gesture from another age.

'A nice piece of work,' he said.

Jonathan came through the gap, trundling the barrow.

'Can Frank stay to lunch?'

They all smiled, conspirators against the easy world of childhood.

'Will you, Frank?' asked Miriam. 'You're very welcome.'

'That'll be all right, thank you,' he said. 'The wife'll have my lunch waiting.'

Jonathan's face fell. 'Oh.' A high, frustrated note. 'I *want* Frank to stay.'

He does get lonely, Miriam thought, he *does* need someone to play with. Even if it's all right now, it won't be, I know it won't. A boy on his own with his mother, father coming and going – it's not good. 'Perhaps another time,' she said, picking him up. 'Gosh, you're getting heavy.'

'Right, then,' said Stephen, to Frank. 'I think that's about it, isn't it? I'll give you a ring early next week.'

Early next week I'll know for sure, Miriam thought, putting Jonathan down again. They walked up through the garden, the wind cold on their faces. When Frank had gone, taking the path at the side of the house to his old van parked in the lane, they all went indoors. 'Gumboots off,' said Miriam, helping Jonathan. The three pairs stood neatly on the mat, side by side: Father Bear, Mother Bear, Baby Bear, the perfect little family, snug in their house in the woods. What fairy tale was there with a brother or sister who was anything but ugly, or greedy, or jealous? Only Hansel and Gretel, and they were abandoned. Miriam put out the plates and soup bowls, and sliced a loaf of home-baked bread. She pictured a fourth place, a high chair up to the table, with a baby banging a spoon.

By the end of March they were digging the trench for the studio foundations out in the garden, and Miriam had her pregnancy confirmed. She drove back from Norwich down leafless lanes, singing, Jonathan strapped into his seat in the back of the car examining the tipper truck she had bought him to celebrate. 'We're going to have a baby,' she told him, coming out of the surgery. 'You'll have a little brother or sister. Which would you like?' 'A brother,' said Jonathan. 'Can we go to the toy shop?' He didn't mention it again. She looked now into the driving mirror, hearing the tipper truck drop to the floor. 'All right?'

'Mmm.' His head was drooping; the car, as always, sending him off. Dark straight hair, thick soft eyelashes – a beautiful child, unbelievable that anything so perfect should have come from her. She looked back to the lane ahead, feeling the car sway a little. The fields were windswept but the morning was bright, clouds streaming above the trees; the flattened grass along the verges shone. I'm going to have another one, she thought. Thank God, thank God.

At home, she parked the car and left Jonathan asleep in it, walking round the side of the house to see how the men were getting on. Stephen was out on site today, leaving Frank to supervise. 'Everything all right?' she asked them, much as she'd asked Jonathan, feeling now as if everyone could turn to her if things were not all right, because she, at last, was fine, wonderful, over the moon, capable of doing anything for anyone. The men nodded, looking up from their digging. She wanted to tell them, she wanted to tell everyone, and Stephen most of all. Indoors, she made lunch, smiling.

When Stephen came home that evening the men had long gone and it was cold and dark. She was upstairs bathing Jonathan when she heard the key in the lock.

'There's Daddy.'

'Daddy! Come up here!' Jonathan swooshed a wave of water over the side. 'Come *here*!'

'Hey, hey, that's enough, it'll go through the floor.' Miriam found a cloth and mopped at the lake. Behind her, Stephen pushed wide the door.

'Evening all.' He sounded relaxed and cheerful; he sat on the edge of the bath and threw a sponge at Jonathan. 'How's it been?'

'Okay.' He threw it back again, giggling.

Miriam got up, feeling slightly dizzy from the bending. 'Guess what.'

'What? Hey, Jon, that's enough, you'll soak me.'

'What do you think?' Miriam looked at him, long lean body perched on the bathside, perfectly fitting casual clothes: well-cut cords, good cotton collar above a dark crew neck. His foot swung lazily to and fro, like a cat's tail; he looked at her, raising an eyebrow.

'Yes?'

'Yes,' said Miriam, 'Confirmed this morning.' She went across and kissed him, brushing his hair with her lips. There were a few grey hairs, just appearing at the temples; she touched them with her fingertip, lightly. 'All right? Are you pleased?'

'Of course, if you are,' he said, and she frowned, feeling a shiver of anxiety.

He pointed down at Jonathan's wet head, questioningly.

'He knows,' she said, 'I told him straight away. Stephen . . . aren't you pleased?'

'Yes,' he said. 'It's all right, don't look like a frightened rabbit. I am, especially if it's a girl.' He tapped Jonathan on the head. 'What about that, then? Mummy's going to have a baby.'

'I know,' he said. 'She's told me.'

'So now you'll have someone to play with.'

'I want to play with you.'

'Well, here I am. I should think it's about time you got out.'

Miriam passed Stephen a towel. 'Do you want to do him while I get supper ready?'

'Okay.' He took the towel and reached across and kissed her. 'Happy now?'

'Very,' she said. 'Very,' and felt relief sweep over her – they'd done it. She went downstairs humming, hearing him say to Jonathan, 'Come on, monster.'

By the middle of April the trees and hedgerows were hazy with the first green of the year, and the foundations of the studio and several courses of bricks were laid. There was to be a stable door, to let in maximum light when it was warm enough, and windows on all sides.

In the middle of May, in the middle of a morning, Miriam, bending on the garden path to pick up Jonathan's lorries, felt an ache, more than a twinge, and then, please God no, but yes, a light but unmistakable wetness.

Indoors, she stood in the bathroom, shaking. She shook when she sat on the bed and telephoned the house where Stephen was working. A woman answered the phone, a pleasant, light-voiced woman who was terribly sorry but Stephen wasn't there, he'd gone off to another site. Of course she'd tell him, as soon as he came back. Miriam hung up, and lay down, hearing Jonathan coming in from the garden and banging his way upstairs. 'In here, Jon.' She turned her head to look out of the window: birds sang in the woods across the road; thrushes and bluetits and the soft contented coo of wood pigeons. There were bluebells there now, she'd picked some yesterday. A perfect May morning, sunny and fresh. If she lay here all day, all week . . .

'Mum? Where's Batman?'

'What?'

'*Batman*. I left him on the step.'

'Did you? Sorry, I don't remember – I picked up all your lorries and things. Go and have another look, darling.' Go away and let me be all right, please.

'*You* come and look. Why're you lying down?'

'I've got a tummy ache, that's all. Come and lie down with me, if you like.'

'No.' He wandered over to the window, disgruntled. 'Can we go and feed the donkey?'

'Perhaps. A bit later.'

A bit later Miriam was still bleeding. Stephen rang at tea-time, was home by six, complaining about traffic in the city centre, but concerned. By eight, Miriam was in hospital, and bled all night, messily and profusely. The following afternoon she sat in a room full of visibly pregnant women in nightdresses, waiting with a bursting bladder to be scanned.

The woman in charge of the ultrasound was young and thin – well, perhaps no younger than Miriam, but Miriam felt as if she had stepped into the territory of a much older, disappointed woman, light years from the pale white-coated girl who ran her instrument over her stomach, slippery with gel. She turned her head towards the screen, remembering Jonathan, on the same screen in the same room, grow from an animated flicker to a slowly moving bulk, with spinal cord, and beating heart, seeing the blurred face swim into focus, looking like an Easter Island statue, primitive and enormous, calm, with a dreamy smile. Had she really seen all that? Now she heard the girl cough, hesitating, before showing the dark mass of her swollen bladder and the cavity of her womb.

'What a shame.'

She swabbed away the gel with a piece of coarse tissue, and Miriam swung her legs off the couch, pulling the hospital gown around her; she went out, had a pee and then sat waiting for the porter to take her back by wheelchair to the ward, because she'd been told to wait, even though she couldn't see the point. She'd lost it, she'd lost it – where was it now? May as well climb ten flights of stairs.

'What was wrong with your tummy?' Jonathan asked, as they went out with Stephen into the car park. Fool, thought Miriam, fool. Why did I tell him?

They passed a man energetically opening the rear door of a hatch-back; his wife, holding a tiny shawl-wrapped baby, stepped carefully inside, while grandparents hovered, beaming. Miriam turned her head away, saying to Stephen, as if it were the only thing that mattered:

'Where are we parked?'

He nodded towards their car a couple of rows ahead. 'You all right?'

'Not really.' She pointed down at Jonathan, mouthing: 'Have you told him?'

'No.'

'Why?'

'I thought you'd want to. I thought you'd do it better.'

At the car, waiting for Stephen to open up, Jonathan said again, 'What was wrong with you?'

'There was something wrong with the baby,' Miriam said. 'That happens sometimes – it wasn't quite right, and now it's – now it's, well . . . it's gone.' Where? Why? At twelve weeks it – he? she? – had been fully formed, waiting to grow.

'Gone where?' asked Jonathan.

'Come on,' said Stephen, holding open doors. 'Get in, Jon, I've got something for you once you're strapped in.'

'What? What?' He scrambled inside.

They drove out of Norwich eating Smarties. The lanes were bright with buttercups; clumps of cow parsley trembled as they drove past. In the fields beyond the hedges the corn was a sharp, beautiful green; they passed the dairy farm three miles out from the village, where cows swished at the flies and swayed across to the water-trough at the gate. They drove without talking much, and Miriam began to feel soothed: a calm summer evening with her child in the back, her husband beside her, leaving behind the hospital, and everything that had happened there.

Home again, opening windows, pottering about, it felt as if she had been away for weeks. She went upstairs to their bedroom, and stood looking at the cool white bed, seeing herself lie there only two days ago, willing the baby not to drip away. Can I go through this again? she wondered. Can I put them through it again? Downstairs, Stephen was calling: 'I've made some tea, do you want it up there?'

'It's all right,' she called back, 'I'm coming.' She went down the dark narrow stairs, her feet in sandals clicking on the stone floor of the hall. In the kitchen she looked at Stephen, standing with a mug of tea at the garden door, watching Jonathan. He turned as she came in; she wanted him to hold out his arms, to be glad she was back, to have missed her dreadfully. She heard herself saying: 'Do you love me at all?' and then cover it at once, because it was dangerous and desperate to talk like that, with: 'Sorry, I'm still feeling a bit wobbly,' in a high, shaky voice which sounded as if it came from decades ago: as if she wore nylons with seams and was always terribly brave. She sat down at the table as Stephen, still at the garden door, said carefully, 'Poor Miriam,' and put her head on her arms.

That should have been enough. Later, three or four years later,

Miriam thought she should have made sure it was enough, should have begun at once to look for a job, for something outside herself, something more important than herself. Instead, it all began again, but worse this time, because everything was spoken.

Are you coming to bed?

Not yet.

Please.

No!

You make me feel like a cast-off.

Don't be so maudlin.

I need you. I need it. Please!

I cannot, for Christ's sake, do it to order!

But if we don't do it now, that's another month gone . . .

Doors slamming, tears. I'm sorry, I'm sorry. Be grateful for what you have. I try to be, I try.

By the autumn the studio in the garden was finished. Stephen and Frank spent the whole of a Sunday in November carrying out the contents of his room, bumping the plan chest downstairs, staggering along the path with the drawing board. Miriam watched for a while, then took Jonathan for a walk down the lane. They leaned over the rusting gate of the donkey field, holding out their windfalls.

'Come on, boy, come on.'

He had been grazing on the far side, beyond his shelter; now he came slowly towards them, lifting neat hooves over the rough ground, with its straggling sorrel and hard mounds of earth. They stood while he crunched the apples noisily, patting his thick brown coat.

'I wish we could groom him,' said Jonathan. 'Couldn't we groom him?'

'Perhaps.' Miriam felt the word was like a second name, a part of her. She said perhaps to everything now, and thought it, too: perhaps we'll have another child, perhaps we won't; perhaps it doesn't matter; perhaps Stephen and I will be all right in the end. When the last of the apples was gone the donkey began to graze again, staying near them. They moved away, getting chilled standing still, and he raised his head and followed them; when they turned to wave he was hanging over the gate, watching. The light was beginning to fade, and the air smelt damp. 'Let's go,' said Miriam.

Back at the house they stood looking up to where Stephen used to be working, to where there was always a square of light. Now the whole upstairs was dark. They went down the side and into the garden, down to the gap in the hedge. Light from the studio shone out on to the grass. 'It's like a little house!' said Jonathan.

Perhaps I should have bought a housewarming present, Miriam thought, as they walked towards the door over neatly laid stepping stones. Made it a celebration, made it clear I was on his side.

'Daddy!' Jonathan pounded on the white wooden door.

There was a click, and the top half swung open; Stephen leaned out and neighed. Jonathan laughed, and reached up to pat him. 'We've just been feeding the donkey.'

'Have you? Are you going to feed me?'

'No! Come on, Dad, open the door.'

He slid back the lower bolt and they stepped inside. It smelt of wood and fresh plaster, very clean and new. Stephen had been pinning up plans on cork boards all along one wall; there was a large white shelf, running the width of the room, which was to be his desk, and everything was already neatly arranged along it: boxes of cartographers' pens, filing tray, scarlet anglepoise lamp. The telephone was mounted on the wall.

'Where are you going to sleep?' asked Jonathan, looking round.

'In a basket,' said Stephen solemnly.

'A *basket?* Where? Can I see?'

'Actually,' said Stephen, picking him up, 'I'm going to sleep in the house, you goose.'

'With Mummy?'

'Of course. Do sit down.' He placed Jonathan in the swivel chair and spun him round. 'Bye.'

Jonathan shrieked.

'What do you think?' Stephen asked Miriam, still standing by the door. 'Do you approve?'

'It's very nice,' she said. 'You've done it beautifully.' She walked up and down, getting the feel of it. It was an ordered, purposeful place; anyone could work well out here, and for a moment she felt a pang of pure envy: *I'd* like somewhere like this. And at once, mocking: and what would you do in it? Cry? Sew, she thought, I could sew.

'I'll get you some plants,' she said. 'That's all it needs.'

'Thank you. Something exotic, perhaps, like you.' Stephen caught the chair as it spun past, and stopped it.

'Like me?' Miriam looked at him.

'I feel sick,' said Jonathan. 'You shouldn't have done it for so long.'

'Sorry.' Stephen held out his hand. 'Come on. You and Mummy go indoors now, it's almost bedtime.

'And you. You come with us.'

'In a minute. I'm just going to finish unpacking.' He pointed to a pile of cardboard boxes in a corner, full of books. 'You can have those, when I've finished.'

'I could make *my* house!'

'You could. Go on, off you go.'

'I'll call you when supper's ready,' Miriam said. 'Or should I telephone?'

'I know,' said Jonathan, as they walked up the path. 'You could have a *bell*. That's a good idea, isn't it? Then every time we wanted Daddy we could just stand outside and ring it, and he'd come running.'

'A pretty thought,' said Miriam, wondering at exotica.

That night Stephen came upstairs to kiss Jonathan goodnight and afterwards kissed Miriam, too, closing Jonathan's door and pressing her up against the wall on the landing, leaning hard against her. He lifted her long winter skirt and ran his hands between her legs, his fingers teasing, exploring, urgent. He lifted her, wrapping her legs round him, and carried her into the bedroom, closing the door with his foot. Then laid her down gently on the bed, spreading her legs, standing over her as he took off his trousers. Miriam moaned, waiting, wanting him to do it all night, for ever.

'I want you, I want you, I love you, go on, go on, go on . . .'

When they had finished and lay, still half-clothed, sprawled against each other, she thought: This is what married sex should be, perhaps this is what it's like for some people. And perhaps it wasn't. But the truth of their life over the past few months, so loveless and horrible, so bleak and bitter, welled up as she had not allowed it to do before, a nightmare she'd endured without daring to call it nightmare, thinking only: somehow we must get through this.

And here they were, and how had this come about?

'Stephen?'

'Mmm.'

'That was . . .' She drew a long breath. 'What happened?'

Stephen yawned. 'You looked so lovely,' he said. 'In the studio. I looked at you and suddenly I remembered why I wanted to get into bed the moment I set eyes on you. You looked just like you did then – a bit on edge, but very exciting. And being so good about the studio – I know you hate it.'

'No, I don't. Only if you're going to be out there because . . . because everything's so bad between us.'

Stephen yawned again. 'Well, perhaps it'll get better now.'

In the middle of the night, long after they had properly undressed and pulled the bedclothes over them, Miriam woke, without knowing why. It must have been a dream, she thought; what was I dreaming? She lay in the dark, remembering only a boy, running. Away from her? Yes. Had it been Jonathan? She tried to recall the face, but could see only a dark head, bobbing into the distance.

She got up and went to the bathroom, and as she came back again, moving sleepily along the landing, she knew, with sudden certainty, that she had conceived. This time there would be no waiting, and wondering; this time it was only a question of having it confirmed. She went into Jonathan's room and stood looking down at him, imagining, as she had not allowed herself to do for months, his sister in a crib beside him. Or perhaps the baby could be in here, a proper nursery, and Jon could have Stephen's old studio, with more space to play. She bent to kiss him, and went out, wakeful now, and into Stephen's ex-studio. He'd never carpeted it, and never wanted curtains; it was, now, as it had been when they first moved in, empty and waiting. Moonlight filtered through the trees; Miriam, in bare feet, walked up and down, restless and excited.

She started bleeding two days before Christmas, and this time there was no dull ache but a sharp, agonising pain in her side, and no thought of waiting until Stephen came home before she went to hospital. She phoned him, phoned the hospital and went in by ambulance, dropping Jon off with one of the mothers from the village. This time she hadn't told him she was pregnant, but he knew straight away why she was going in, remembering.

'What's wrong with this baby, Mummy?'

'You don't worry your Mum now,' said the woman kindly. 'You come and see what's on telly. D'you like Yogi Bear?'

The ambulance drew away, driving at top speed past bare ploughed fields, frozen hard. Stephen was already at the hospital, waiting outside Casualty. He helped her, doubled up, climb down from the ambulance and into a wheelchair. The pain in her side was like flames.

Inside the entrance to the hospital stood an enormous Christmas tree, with coloured lights and empty boxes wrapped up to look like presents. Miriam was wheeled quickly through the Casualty doors,

Stephen hurrying alongside. A cubicle, a nurse, a doctor, examining – Miriam distantly saw herself go through each step towards the operating theatre, leaving Stephen to go home, and look after Jonathan. In the ante-room, drowsy with pre-med, she felt the nurse squeeze her hand. 'What a shame.'

'Yes.'

'Still – you can always try again.'

'Never.'

Then came the pinprick, and oblivion.

She woke a long time later, dimly registering darkness and a single light, women breathing in rows. She couldn't think where she was, and fell asleep again, waking with the clatter of tea-cups, and carols on the ward kitchen radio. Her side was sore and uncomfortable, but no longer agony. She lay quite still, listening to the words floating tinnily over the banging in the kitchen: *How silently, how silently, the wondrous gift is given . . .*

Miriam pulled the sheet up over her head.

In 1978 Jonathan started school. Miriam drove him each morning through the lanes; he sat in the back seat, fiddling with his straps. He took a few weeks to warm up, clinging to her hand as they went into the classroom, tearful on the first few mornings when she left him. Then he was off, one of the gang. He brought boys home for tea, or to play on Saturdays, but he didn't seem to mind too much when they went: as when he was very small, he always had something on the go, digging a hole, collecting centipedes, building a den. When he was six, they bought Tess, and it was, for a while, as if they'd had another child – only much better, for Jonathan, because a puppy was an instant companion. They went for long walks through the woods and across the open fields, small boy and dog, he whistling and calling when she went out of sight, she running back again, nose to the ground. He never complained about being an only child; he seemed happy at home, and happy at school. But when Miriam dropped him off she came home to an empty house.

She took to calling in at the small supermarket near the school on the way home on Mondays, shopping for a week's after-school teas; one day she found herself adding, on impulse, half a bottle of gin to the basket of apple juice, Wagon Wheels, beefburgers and wholemeal rolls. Why not? They were running low at home anyway, and Stephen, though he didn't drink much himself, liked to have plenty to offer people. When she got back, she let Tess out in the garden, and put away the shopping. She cleared up the house and wondered what to do until half-past twelve, when anyone was allowed, surely, to have a glass of something. She did some weeding, kneeling on an old sack, and piling up dandelions and groundsel. By five to twelve she was sitting in a deckchair with a glass of gin and tonic, wondering why she hadn't thought of this before.

It began, then, quite casually, and from time to time she invited one of two of the women she had got to know through Stephen's dinner parties, or mothers she had met at school, to come over and join her for a drink, a light lunch. On these days she felt a mixture of purposefulness – someone coming, a meal to be made – and discomfort, at least until the first glass, which she generally had before they arrived, waiting for the questions: was Jonathan the only one, did she want more; what was she going to do now he'd started school, what had she done before she met Stephen? Sometimes, trying to answer, or deflect by asking her own questions, Miriam thought it better to have had none than one. How could that be true? At least, if you were childless, you could if you chose avoid children almost completely. Miriam saw children every day, pouring out of the school gate, greeting 'their' babies. Before she met Stephen, she told these other mothers, she had worked as a secretary. All she knew now was that she didn't want to go back to that.

'And I don't blame you,' said Flora, one of the lunchtime visitors, a woman Miriam genuinely liked. Flora was tall, always in jeans, with untidy hair and a loud laugh. She had two noisy boys she was always shouting at, benign and distracted, and a plain, untidy house.

'My God, how I long for order and beauty,' she said, when Miriam showed her round her own house. 'You've got a flair for all this, Miriam, we just live in a heap.' She gazed at the bedroom, with its freshly made bed, flowers, sofa with cushions Miriam had made. 'Even if I didn't work we'd live in a heap, I'm hopeless.'

But happy, thought Miriam, taking her downstairs. Flora taught part-time at the school; at the end of the afternoon she piled her boys and any number of others into the back of the car and drove home to fish and chips and children's television. Her husband was a maths teacher; they had moved out from London five years ago, exchanging a square of garden in Finsbury Park for half an acre and a dilapidated orchard. 'Best thing we ever did,' she said, taking the glass Miriam offered her. 'Gosh, I could do with one of these, thanks.' But she refused a second, and drove off at a quarter to two, to her little group of children with special needs.

When she had gone, Miriam felt like a spare line. She washed up the lunch things, listened to *Woman's Hour*, and had a strong coffee before going to fetch Jonathan. That evening, when Stephen was out in the studio, and Jon asleep, she sat in front of the television with a large gin, and had two more before she went up to bed. Next day, finding the bottle low, she thought she might as well finish it off, and drove to school in the afternoon very slowly.

What had begun as an impulse became a need. She sat with her glass out in the garden when it was fine, indoors at the kitchen table with *The World at One* when it rained. She drank for Stephen, who did not love her and was always working; for Jonathan, who was going to grow up alone and leave her; for the babies she had lost and would never have. She drank for herself, despising her self-pity. She had read that to drink alone was the worst, but she couldn't remember why, and it gave her the most pleasure – no one to watch, or criticise, no one to know. She bought bottles of mouthwash, along with the other bottles, and never, ever, drank herself silly.

On a showery morning just after summer half-term, Stephen came home to fetch some drawings he'd forgotten, and found her at half past ten sitting in the kitchen with the sink full of washing-up and the bottle out on the table.

'What on earth – '

'Sorry,' said Miriam, flushing. 'I was just feeling a bit . . .'

Stephen picked up the bottle, sherry this time, a good third gone. 'Do you make a habit of drinking in the mornings?' he asked, clearly trying to make it sound like a joke, hoping it was.

'Yes,' said Miriam flatly.

'Why?'

She shook her head. 'Because. Because. Sorry.'

Stephen went to the sink and poured the remains of the sherry down it. 'Actually,' he said, 'I don't really want to know why. I don't want to hear about it, or try to understand it, I just want it to stop. Right now.'

Miriam said nothing. He turned round from the sink, threw the bottle in the bin and stood leaning against the draining board, furious. 'What about Jon? What about when you fetch him from school?'

She spread her hands. 'It's okay.'

'It's *not* okay! It is absolutely *not*. You make me sick, moping and mooching about over nothing, letting everything go to pieces – ' He made a gesture to embrace the washing-up, the house, Miriam herself. 'What's the matter with you? What is the *matter*?'

Miriam covered her face. 'I just feel . . . empty. I feel like a black hole.'

'Oh, for Christ's sake. You've got me, you've got Jon, you've got a lovely home.'

'But nobody's in it!' Miriam sobbed through the sherry. 'You're working, he's at school. What am I supposed to do for the rest of my life, walk the dog?'

'*You* should be working,' said Stephen. 'Why the hell aren't you?'

'Because I don't know what to do! Because I'm afraid.'

'Afraid? Of getting a job? Don't be so silly.'

Miriam ran from the room.

In the hall she pulled on her mac, fumbling, and opened the front door. The shower was ending in a fine, intermittent fall and the air was cool; drops hung, shining, all round the bird table. She clicked open the garden gate and began to walk down the lane, her hands in her pockets. Her shoes squeaked in the thick wet grass on the verge when she stepped on to it, hearing a car; beside her, Tess appeared, wagging her tail, sniffing along the ditch. Miriam grabbed her collar – she must have left the gate open, Tess could have got killed. The thought that this might have happened was suddenly overwhelming; as the car drove past she sank down beside the dog, her arms round her neck, stroking her, weeping into the thick damp fur.

'I'm sorry, I'm sorry . . .'

Tess sat patiently, waiting to move on. After a while Miriam got up off the wet grass, and patted her. She found a scrunched-up handkerchief in her pocket, and blew her nose.

'Come on.'

Released, Tess bounded ahead, nosing across the lane to the woods. Miriam crossed with her, walking alongside, hearing twigs break and the clapping of a pigeon, startled into the air. The sherry was wearing off; by the time she reached the donkey field her head was as clear as it had been for a while – she had kept herself so topped-up it was hard to remember what it felt like with nothing inside her. The donkey raised his head and came stepping towards her. Rain dripped from the trees.

'Hello, boy.' He put his head over the gate. 'Nothing for you, sorry. I just came for a chat.' She patted his cheek, and tugged at the rough furry ears. It's the middle of the morning and I'm standing talking to a donkey, she thought, seeing him, disappointed, nosing towards her mac pocket. And I've nothing for him, or anybody else for that matter. What the hell am I going to do?

When she got back to the house, she went down the path at the side, letting Tess in and closing the gate behind her. She went to the studio, and knocked, and hearing no answer tried the door, but it was locked. Back in the kitchen she found Stephen had done the washing-up, leaving it to drain. He hadn't left a note. When she went to the drinks cupboard she found it empty except for a couple of bottles of tonic. Seeing this she felt for a moment so angry she almost smashed them on the floor. Then she thought: but I couldn't have gone on like that, and went upstairs and ran a hot bath and lay in it for a long time. When she went to collect Jonathan she left the car and walked the whole way, taking Tess with her.

'You look better,' said Flora, coming out of the gate with a troop of boys eating crisps.

'Did I look worse?' Miriam asked.

'A bit on the peaky side, I thought. Where's Jon, d'you want to come home for a cuppa?'

'Haven't you got enough?'

'More the merrier. Andrew, *stop* kicking Joshua! Stop it! Now get in the car, all of you, and behave yourselves. We've got Company. Like grown-ups, and manners, okay?'

Miriam and Jonathan squeezed into the front with Tess. 'This is fun,' said Jonathan.

'Have some crisps,' said Flora, easing out into the road. 'I don't know if there's much else in the larder, I seem to be a bit behind.'

In her large, muddled kitchen, she and Miriam sat drinking tea from chipped mugs and eating jam sandwiches. 'Miracle there's any bread left,' said Flora, who had booted the boys out into the garden where a climbing frame stood on scuffed grass. Tess barked, leaping up and down.

'Now,' she said to Miriam. 'I was talking about you to someone the other day, and describing your exquisite home, and she said she needed someone to run up some curtains, being hopeless, like me, on the domestic front, and I thought you might be just the ticket. I mean, is that an awful nerve? You might be sick to death of all that, and yearning to do a computer course. Has Stephen got a computer? Tom longs for one, but I've told him the boys would just take it over with war games, so he's holding off for a bit. Mind you, I suppose they ought to have one one day, we've all got to drag ourselves into the eighties somehow, haven't we? Are you going to let Jon have one?'

Miriam smiled, feeling better. 'Don't know,' she said. 'But curtains, yes. Why not? Who is she?'

That was the past; things were better now. Not right, but better. Running up a couple of curtains for someone Flora knew had grown, over two or three years, to taking the lease of a small shop in Woodburgh, selling and making up fabric of Miriam's choosing, selected on buying trips to factories and wholesalers. The window was hung with Liberty and Sanderson linens and cottons, bold swathes of green, purple and ochre, folds of harlequin, bolts of slubbed silk, soft cotton net woven with birds and flowers. Above the window, in gold on black, was Miriam's name – Stephen had organised that. It had been Stephen who found the shop, and who had encouraged her. Miriam thought he had done so mostly for his own sake, to save him from being saddled with a melancholic wife who drank, but she was pleased, and she enjoyed it.

Inside, the shop had shelves and display stands and a large, flat-topped desk pushed up against the wall. Above it was a cork board, pinned with swatches and price lists; on it were scissors and pinking shears, a telephone, large red diary and a brass measure nailed all along the edge, marked in metres. Here Miriam sat and took orders and measurements, doing some of the sewing herself in a small back room next to a patch of yard where cats slept in the sun. The rest she sent out, to local women with their own machines.

Someone else would have made much of all this. Someone else, more motivated, more ambitious, grown accustomed to running her own show and to being well known in the community, might have begun to speak loudly, authoritatively, to have strong opinions on local issues and hold forth at dinner parties. Another woman might have thought, after seven years, that it was time to open another branch, to break into Norwich. Miriam still disliked dinner parties, and had no desire to open another branch. And although she had an identity, now, to present to the world, and really felt she was, in part, who she appeared to be, she was, still, Miriam – uncertain, unsure of herself. She was confident in her work, she laid out alternatives, and made suggestions, trusting her taste, but she did not, deep down, think of it as proper work – pleasing, yes, to have helped make a house a home, but not really important, or worthwhile, any more than she was.

In a locked drawer of the flat-topped desk was a half-bottle of gin and a medicine glass. There was tonic in the workroom at the back, kept in the little fridge with the milk for tea and coffee. Miriam did not drink every day, at least she tried not to and didn't think she did, but she had to know it was there. Life had been like this for so many years that she had long since stopped remarking on it to herself, or wondering if she were overdoing it. Drinking, was, simply, as much a part of her now as her skin, or her voice, which people used to say was musical, although now, with the gin, it had become lower, sometimes a little hoarse. But no one had remarked on this: as far as she knew no one realised she drank. There were, in any case, plenty of people in the villages whose lives revolved around the pub. Miriam's drinking had nothing to do with pubs. Drinking alone was secret, special, the bottle and the glass the only things in the world to know what she was really like. At home, after the confrontation, Stephen and she had, after a while, had drink in the house again, but that was different – a glass of wine at dinner, nothing more. She had managed to make sure it was nothing more. Only when Stephen was away, down in London where he had a partner, now, James Diffey, and an office in Camden Town.

He was away quite a lot.

Miriam, on a spring morning, tidying up upstairs on her day off, stood looking absently out of the landing window at the woods across the lane. The trees, in late April, were still only just in leaf, and until last week the mornings had been damp and chilly, the tops of the branches threaded with mist. Spring came late here, much later than in London, where Stephen was going again at the end of the week, for a meeting. Occasionally, more than occasionally, Miriam wondered what else was down there for him other than work, and James and Klara's house in Kentish Town, where he stayed, always phoning; she never asked, and she didn't actually want to know. In the end, they had come to an accommodation – no more babies, that was openly agreed, and looked as if it were impossible anyway. No more talk of love – that was something unspoken, that just happened, her slow realisation that the word was never used by either of them. There were no quarrels, little more than irritations, and rarely that. They lived in the same house, eating at the same table, sleeping – rarely more than that – in the same bed. They talked about Stephen's work, and Miriam's work, and about Jonathan, for whom they had stayed together, and who was seventeen now.

Considering everything, he'd turned out all right. He might have been lonely, he might have been spoiled. He might have got into drugs, but as far as they knew he hadn't. Most of the time he was open and direct, an easy companion, and Miriam loved him as she had never been able to love Stephen, because she had not been allowed to. Jonathan was warm, interested in everything, funny. He was studying at the sixth form college for three A levels, wanting, unexpectedly, to read history, but he wasn't bogged down in it, and what he cared about more than anything in the world was his music. He was the one who could have done with a studio out in the garden, away from the house, to make as much noise as he liked. Instead, in summer he and his friends often listened out in the garage, and in winter he was indoors, long since moved from the little room at the back to the large one at the front where Stephen used to work. Miriam, turning now from thoughts of Stephen in London to Jonathan, and the postcard from Amsterdam, wondered what she would do if Marietta took it into her head to arrive here, unannounced. He'd given her his address, it must mean something.

She collected the sheets and pillowcases from his room and carried them downstairs; in the kitchen, she put them into the washing machine and sat down with a recipe book. Tess followed her in from the hall; she sat beside Miriam's chair, waiting for a walk.

'What shall we have for supper, Tess?' She leafed through the pages. Jonathan, on the verge of vegetarianism, complained if they had meat every night. 'Ratatouille?' She stroked Tess's head, mentally going through the shelves of the village shop, which was now a small Spar, run by Patels, and serving the housing development grown up around the outskirts. Fresh vegetables could be a problem on Mondays, but there were a couple of peppers in the fridge. 'Okay, ratatouille and an apple tart. I'll just take these letters down to the studio and we'll be off, all right? Come for a walk to the shop?'

Tess got up stiffly, slowly wagging her tail. She followed Miriam out into the garden, down the path to the gap in the hedge, and round to the side of the studio. The grass was still damp from last night's rain, and the leaves of the honeysuckle and mock orange were wet; the letters in her hand, Miriam opened both halves of the white wooden door and stepped inside. Papers lifted a little with the intake of air; it was quiet as a church in here.

Bringing Stephen's post out was one of the things she always did on Mondays; during the rest of the week she had left for the shop before it arrived. It felt like a ritual, both a wifely thing to do and an acknowledgement that this was almost always the first place he came to at the end of the day, staying out here until supper, a sign that she had accepted this, though she didn't know if he noticed. She walked over to the long white desktop and dropped the letters on to it. And picked them up again, noticing properly for the first time that of the two with London postmarks one was handwritten, in a hand which looked like a woman's.

Miriam stood in the empty studio, tapping the envelope in her hand. She looked at the name and address again, written in a small, sure hand in black ink. It could have been a man, an academic, or a lawyer – there was something that reminded her of letters and signatures in the firm of solicitors where she once worked. The post-mark was Highgate. She went over to the anglepoise and switched it on, tipping up the envelope so that the light shone through. Impossible to make out a word. But somehow she knew that this was not from a man, that although over the years she had seen countless handwritten letters from clients drop on to the mat with the type-written ones from builders and surveyors and county councils, this one was not from someone writing about a house. *Stephen Knowles . . .* How did this woman know Stephen? How well did she know him?

She put the letter back on the desk, with the others, on top. The daffodils in a jug she brought in last week were almost over, the petals dry and papery; she picked them up, and put them down again. She found herself pacing, past the drawing board, the plan chest, the filing cabinet, always locked. Why? From outside, through the open door, she could hear the garden full of birdsong; Tess was sniffing at familiar scents. She came to the doorway and looked in, wanting a walk.

'Go away,' said Miriam, to Tess, and to whoever had written to her husband. Perhaps this woman had written before, perhaps there was a whole bundle of letters somewhere in here. She looked at the filing cabinet, hesitated, went over and tried it. Locked. The plan chest, which had no locks, contained plans. She stood behind Stephen's swivel chair, running her eye over the desk again. The phone, his typewriter, his diary, a box of pens, a dusting of pencil lead and shavings, an overflowing filing tray. Miriam sat on the chair and pulled the tray towards her.

She riffled uneasily through planning applications, letters from the district surveyor, builders' quotes and bills. There was months of correspondence here; what Stephen needed was a secretary. James had one in London. Who did Stephen have in London? She put the heap of papers back in the tray, and pushed it back against the wall, beneath the photographs of work in progress or completed: bare interiors, building sites. Stephen's diary, large and black, lay open by the phone; she leaned forward and went quickly through the pages: four months of meetings, on and off site, with nothing to indicate that he ever did anything but work. Perhaps it was true. She snapped it shut, remembered it had been open and pulled it quickly towards her, feeling ashamed and shaky. The diary fell, and a little piece of paper fluttered out; there was a bang as the diary hit the floor. Miriam bent down and picked it up.

The little piece of paper lay near; she picked that up, too, finding only a till receipt: £35.60. For what? It was dated six weeks ago: had Stephen been in London then? She looked again through the diary: yes. He'd gone down for two days in February but the entry just said London, with a pencilled line – no note of a meeting, no client's name. Had he spent £35.60 on a meal? Who with? When he rang home, had he rung from James and Klara's, as he said, or from someone else's house? The receipt he would have kept for the tax man; he must have forgotten to file it. Miriam slipped it back between the pages and left the diary on the desk. She swung round slowly in the swivel chair, thinking: I am being a fool. There is probably nothing to know, and if there is it's better I don't know it. I am going to take the dog for a walk and make a meal and wait until Jonathan and Stephen come home. We are all going to have supper together, and I am going to say nothing.

She got up, seeing for the first time Stephen's jacket, left hanging on the back of the door. He'd worn it yesterday when they all went walking over the fields to the pub in the next village, which did Sunday lunches. When they came back he'd come out here, to finish a drawing for a meeting in Norwich this morning.

I have been through my husband's papers and now I am going to go through his pockets, thought Miriam. The image was not a pretty one. She walked over the sunlit wooden floor, saying to herself: if there is something in there then at least I shall know. But there will be nothing, and I shall make myself forget this morning.

She felt in the left pocket, then the right, finding a handkerchief, money, keys. There was another receipt but that was from Spar, for £3.47. She pulled the jacket open, feeling in the inside pocket. Two pens, a book of stamps, another, inner pocket, with a zip. From inside it, Miriam brought out a little brown envelope, very worn, and tipped into her hand a photograph. She turned it over and found herself looking at the face of a woman with a sleek bob of dark hair, small, neat features, granny specs. She was unsmiling, as if she felt no need to ingratiate herself with the world; she looked clever and competent and calm and Miriam knew at once that she would write in exactly the small, black, academic hand she had seen on the envelope from Highgate. She took the photograph to the open doorway and looked at it again in the light, as if she could learn more about this woman there. She felt her knees trembling. Was this who Stephen wanted?

Miriam put the little photograph back in the envelope, back in the pocket, zipping it up again. She pressed her face against the jacket, which Stephen had had for years; then she went out of the studio, closing the stable doors very carefully, shutting everything away behind them, and walked up the path to the house.

'Mum? Mum!'

Outside in the darkening lane, Jonathan's lift had dropped him off, and the car was driving away. Inside, the front door had banged; he was coming through the hall into the kitchen, dropping things. It was after five.

'Mum? You okay?'

'Fine,' said Miriam steadily. The bottle was under the table, with the glass. Did it smell in here? 'Had a good day?'

'All right. Hi, Tess.' He bent down and rubbed the dog's head, patting Miriam absently on the shoulder as he straightened up. 'What are you doing in here with the lights off?' He went to the door and flicked the switches; Stephen's spotlights came on, tastefully illuminating corners. 'Any tea?'

'I've got rather a bad head,' said Miriam truthfully. 'You couldn't put the kettle on, could you?' She heard herself speaking slowly, flatly, as if she had been in an accident, and were trying to keep everyone calm.

'Sure.' He went over to the Rayburn, picking up the kettle, and filled it from the tap. 'God, I'm hungry.' He put the kettle back again, and went into the larder. She could hear him banging tins, opening lids in search of biscuits.

'Sorry,' she said, still motionless at the table, not daring to rise. 'I was going to go to the shop, but – '

'Doesn't matter, I'll make a sandwich. Do you want anything?'

'No thanks, darling, just tea.' She pointed to the tabletop. 'There's a postcard. For you, I mean.'

'Oh?' He came over, and picked it up, turning it over. 'Oh.' He slipped the card into his back pocket, and went to the breadbin. 'Did you read it?'

'Yes,' said Miriam. 'Do you mind?'

'It doesn't matter.' He sliced off the end of a loaf.

'Is she nice?'

'She's all right. Was there anything else in the post?'

'No,' said Miriam. 'Nothing.' She hesitated, wondering. 'Why? Should there be?'

'Only a catalogue.' He was spreading the bread with butter, getting honey out of the cupboard over the breadbin. The kettle came to the boil and he made the tea with one hand, eating with the other. 'Not for dirty books,' he added. 'Only tapes. Has Tess had a walk?'

'No,' said Miriam again. 'I was going to, but – '

'I'll take her out in a bit.' Jonathan set down the teapot before her, with two mugs and a milk bottle. 'Are you really okay?'

'Just my head.'

He patted her shoulder again, and poured out the tea. 'You'll feel better when you've had this,' he said, and she smiled, looking up at him for the first time.

'Sorry,' she said again.

'What for? You can't help having a headache, can you?' He picked up his mug and the second half of the honey sandwich. 'I'm going to watch *Neighbours*, okay? Why don't you go and lie down till Dad gets back? I'll get supper if you like.'

'You are a darling. It's all right. I'll be fine in a minute.'

'Well – shout if you need anything.' He went out, followed by Tess; she could hear him turn on the television in the sitting room, and the bouncy, happy signature tune begin. She drank the tea he had made her, lacing it defiantly from the bottle beneath the table.

3

Blazing days. The grass in Anya's garden was full of dry brown patches, and the trees at the far end, and in the square, were dusty and still. Hilda had all the windows open at night, and still couldn't sleep; she walked to work in the mornings beneath a hot blue sky, feeling heavy and slow.

Stephen was in Italy, with the family, taking Jonathan out of school for a fortnight because he had too much on later in the summer. They wouldn't be able to do that next year – Jonathan would be taking his A levels. Hilda watched for the post, and read and re-read the single letter that had arrived so far. Stephen was tired, and did not feel up to writing properly, though he missed her, as always. Hilda missed him, too, and couldn't help wondering at this tiredness, this single letter. Her feelings of doubt and anxiety, however, came mostly at night. At college, where the students were sitting exams in a heatwave, and everyone was winding down, she mostly forgot them.

In the last weeks of the term she was enjoying her afternoon classes with the Asian mothers. On Thursdays, when they did no writing and she held an open conversation group, they sat beneath the high open windows on grey plastic chairs in a circle – it reminded her of the hospital ante-natal classes. Many of the women had been with her all year, and what had begun, last autumn, as a halting, high-pitched, faltering class, felt now like a well-knit group of friends, meeting for gossip.

They showed Hilda photographs of their weddings, and gave her recipes; they talked about their children, and overcrowded schools, and the racist taunts and slogans on the estates.

'It is not possible for us to go out at night; it is simply not possible.'

'For Englishwomen, too,' said Hilda, 'it can be very frightening.'

'But even in the daytime, it can also be very unpleasant.'

At home, they watched *Dynasty*, and prepared elaborate meals. In the last few weeks of term, knowing that Hilda was taking maternity leave, and would not be back in September, they had begun to ask her questions: did the baby move a lot, did she hope for a boy, would she bring him in to show them?

'I want a girl,' said Hilda.

'But your husband – he will be wanting a son.'

Hilda hesitated. 'He has a son already.'

'Ah, you have a son? Well, that is very good.'

'No – *he* has a son. My – the father.'

'Ah.' A pause. 'He has been married before. I am sorry, I did not understand.'

Shall I tell them? Hilda wondered, as the class ended and they pushed back their chairs. On her way upstairs to the library she stood at the mesh-covered window on the landing and watched the women leaving through the gates with their children in pushchairs, going to collect the older ones from school. None of them had fewer than three, and several had five or six, as well as looking after an endless assortment of nephews, nieces, young cousins. Hilda had felt, since the baby had begun to move, and she had begun to believe it existed, that in becoming a mother she would have something in common with these women, something they could identify with, and talk about, where before she must have appeared out on a limb, childless at thirty, incomprehensible. Now she thought: if I tell them the truth I might alienate them completely. Nice Asian girls don't. Or if they do it is a tragedy. That's the myth, anyway.

In the last class of the term they gave her a present, a large soft parcel wrapped in silver and pink paper with babies all over it, blue-eyed, with question marks of hair, sucking their thumbs. Inside was an acid-pink nylon pram quilt and matching pillow, and a pink nylon jacket and bootees.

'Of course, we are buying pink not knowing,' said Parveen, smiling. 'If it is a boy you will be having to change it, but it is from a shop in the High Street, and we have kept the receipt.'

'I am sure it will be a girl,' said Laxmi, as Hilda floundered, her lap full of the puffy pink quilt and the paper. 'If it is a boy you are carrying it very high, see . . .' She gestured to her own stomach. 'My sons, they were all up here. You are very low.'

'We wanted to give you what you wanted,' said Veneta.

'You're very kind,' said Hilda. 'I wasn't expecting anything.'

'Except a baby,' said Parveen. 'Of course you are expecting that.'

Everyone laughed, and Hilda got up and put the presents carefully on a table by the open window. From outside they could hear the children in the crèche, playing in their fenced-off bit of the yard. 'Sometimes it still doesn't feel real,' she said, coming back. 'I can't quite believe I shall ever have a baby at the end of all this.'

'It is like that with the first, I can remember. By the time you have your third or fourth – it is all very real then, Hilda. Too real!'

They laughed again, warmer and more open with her than they had been all year. It's true, she thought, all these years when I felt an outsider, I was. I'm part of a circle now, part of the flow. Except, of course . . .

She said: 'But I only want one.'

'Just one?' They were incredulous. 'No, Hilda, you must have more than one, she will be lonely.'

'And besides,' said Laxmi, 'perhaps later your husband will be wanting another son. Is your . . . adopted son, I mean your stepson, that is the right word, is he living with you now?'

Hilda flushed, and Aysha, the Muslim woman whose thick white headscarf was drawn right across her face, up to her glasses, when she arrived, and only taken off inside the classroom, said quickly: 'We are asking Hilda too many questions about her private life.'

But once you're a mother you're out in public, Hilda thought. I shan't actually, be quite private ever again. That's the price.

'It's all right,' she said, and drew a breath. 'Actually, I don't live with my – with the father. I'm having the baby by myself.'

'He has left you? Oh, Hilda . . .' They were all concern. 'How will you manage?'

'He hasn't left me, he was never with me. I wanted to have the baby alone – well, that's not quite true, I had no choice. But I don't mind.' She heard herself give an embarrassed laugh. 'I'm hardly the first single parent in Hackney.'

There was silence. Then:

'But, Hilda, it will be very difficult for you,' said Veneta. 'It is very hard work, looking after a baby.'

A murmur of agreement.

'Do your husbands help you?' she asked directly.

'Not with the babies, no, of course not,' said Parveen. 'What can they do? But when the children are older, naturally the children must have their father with them, to teach them, isn't it? For the discipline. And if it is a boy, a son in particular needs his father . . .'

'And of course there is the financial side,' said Laxmi gently.

'But I'm coming back to work, aren't I?'

'But even so . . .'

There was another pause, in which the tick of the clock on the wall could he heard. It was almost the end of the class. Then Laxmi said hesitantly: 'Hilda – is it that your boyfriend is married?' and Hilda said simply: 'Yes.'

'But his wife, what is she thinking?' said Laxmi, as if unable to stop herself, and Hilda, feeling every eye upon her, flushed deeply.

Outside, one of the nursery children had fallen over, and begun to cry.

'I hope that's not Raji,' said Veneta, and looked at the clock. There was a silence then which did not feel thoughtful or companionable but awkward and uneasy, and then Aysha said: 'After all, what Hilda is doing is her own business. We are talking too much,' and they pushed back their chairs and began to move towards the door.

Hilda got up. 'Thank you all for the lovely present. I'll see you after Christmas.' Even with the windows wide open at the top, the room was far too hot, and Christmas, more than anything, seemed distant and unreal. She felt dizzy, standing up, watching the women in their sandals and baggy trousers, their floating scarves and saris, smile at her uncertainly and leave the room.

'I'll bring the baby in to show you,' she said.

'That will be very nice. Goodbye.'

'Goodbye.'

Out in the corridor she could hear them talking in low voices, their feet flapping unhurriedly towards the swing doors to the yard. She sat down at the table by the window, looking again at the heap of acid-pink baby things, her head swimming, and put her head down, trying to fight off nausea. It's the heat, she thought, I'll go home and rest, but although the sickness ebbed away and her head cleared she felt empty and disappointed. And what did you expect, she asked herself, getting to her feet again. Anya disapproves, even Alice disapproves.

With the weather so hot, Alice and Tony had taken to having breakfast and supper out in the garden, sitting with the girls at the old wooden picnic table which the previous owners of the house had left behind. Alice had strung up wires running from above the kitchen door to the fence beside the table, and was growing vines along them. Even with this shade it was still too hot to be out here at lunchtime, but first thing in the morning, with the table and breakfast things dappled with leafy shadows, it felt like a Greek café, and the children loved it.

'Poor you,' said Alice to Tony, as he came outside in his shirt and trousers, carrying briefcase and jacket. 'How can you work in this heat?'

'I can't,' he said, running a hand through his thinning hair. 'I sit at my desk and sweat drips down past my glasses.'

'Ugh,' said Annie.

Hettie said: 'You should have a fan.'

'There is a fan, but once I turned it too far towards me, and do you know what happened?'

'What?'

'All the papers on my desk lifted into the air and went flying round the room.'

'Did they really?' The girls were fascinated. 'Like this,' said Annie, lifting her arms, and knocked over the milk jug.

'Oh, Annie!' Alice ran into the kitchen and came back with a cloth. 'It's gone *everywhere*. Mind, quick, out of the way, it's going on Daddy's trousers. Here, Tony – '

'And then I'll have a nasty old judge after me,' said Tony, moving along the bench, and wiping the milk away. 'I shall go into court looking all respectable, and the judge will raise his head and start sniffing, like this – sniff, sniff, sniff – and he'll say: "What is that dreadful smell of cheesy old milk? Who is responsible? Remove that man from the court room immediately! Chop his head off!" '

Hettie giggled. 'No he won't.'

'He might. People do funny things in hot weather.'

'I'll come and chop *his* head off,' said Annie.

'Thank you, Annie, you're very loyal.' He looked at his watch, swallowing tea. 'I must go. I'll leave you all to your disgusting chocolate ricey-pops . . .' He got up, kissing the tops of their heads. 'Bye, horrible children. See you this evening.'

'Bye.'

'What time will you be back?' asked Alice, following him through to the kitchen with the dripping cloth.

'Should be in time for supper, I'm only in court this morning. Supposedly. If it goes on till the afternoon and I have to stay late I'll ring.'

'I should think it's awful in court at the moment, isn't it?'

'Unspeakable. I feel as if I'm in Indiah, like something out of Forster, with the fans whirring away, and everyone hot and grumpy.' He pulled on his jacket and kissed her. 'Still – there's always you to come home to. What have you got in store for the day?'

'Swimming,' said Alice, with an ear to raised voices in the garden. 'What else? I'll think of you.'

'Thanks.' He went out past the bikes in the hall to the front door, and Alice returned to the garden, where Annie was crying.

'Now what?'

'She's being silly,' said Hettie. 'Just because I wouldn't let her spread her own marmalade.'

'Well, of course she can spread her own marmalade, why ever not?'

'She might cut herself.'

'Oh, Hettie, don't be such a prig. She's not using a carving knife, is she? Come on, Annie, that's enough, here you are. And later on we're going to have a swim, okay?'

By the time they had dressed, and walked slowly up to the pool with their swimming things, the pavements were already baking.

'Can we go to the playground afterwards?'

'Not if it's like this.'

'Please.'

'We'll see.'

Everyone they knew was in the pool. Hettie and Annie bobbed up and down in their armbands at the shallow end, shouting to friends from school and playgroup. Alice, in her pale blue and white striped swimsuit, sat on the edge, her hair tied up in a knot.

'Watch this, Mummy!'

Hettie clambered out and ran round to the slide. She went headfirst down into the water, fearless, and came up smiling.

'It's lovely!'

'I want to do that,' said Annie, tugging at Alice's leg.

'Well, go on then.'

'You come in and catch me.'

'In a minute.' She swished her feet back and forth through the water, watching the people come and go. Outside, on the terrace beyond glass doors, the oiled bodies of childless sunbathers were flattened on towels beneath the dazzling sky; mothers, and a sprinkling of fathers, sat up with plastic cups of coffee, keeping watch as toddlers in sunhats ran about. Beside Alice, child after child dropped into the water, and the swimming pool attendants, perched loftily on diving boards, or sitting with tanned legs drawn up on the wall at the side, chewed gum, yawning.

Alice watched two pregnant women, clearly expecting their first babies, since no other child was in evidence, swim carefully up and down the length of the pool, dodging the children as they came up here, dodging the big boys diving and yelling down at the deep end. After two or three lengths they stopped, and sat on the side, smoothing the water from their faces, laughing. They looked fit and relaxed, skin glowing, eyes, even after the chlorine, clear and bright. Did I look like that? Alice wondered. I felt like it, at least with Hettie – even with Annie, though I was tired, there was always that glorious sense of having everything settled and in place, of looking forward, without actually having to do anything. The future was mine, I knew what I was about. Before I met Tony – even afterwards, until I was pregnant with Hettie – the future was like a black curtain; I'd do anything to avoid thinking about it. I did do anything, I did too much. I wish –

'Mummy! Come *in*!'

'Sorry, Annie, I was miles away. All right, I'm coming now.'

She slipped into the water and stood at the bottom of the slide, holding out her arms. Annie lay down at the top.

'Come on, then.'

'I'm coming.'

She stretched herself out, arms in orange bands pointing down, but didn't move. Behind her stood Hettie and a line of other children, coming up the steps, who fidgeted and began to push.

'Annie – it's all right, I'm here.'

'I'm scared.'

'Well, turn round, then. Hettie, move back a bit, so she can turn.'

'I can't, there's too many behind me. Oh, go on, Annie, it's *easy*!'

'I can't!'

'Oh, go on, you silly baby.' And Hettie, pushed from behind, leaned forwards and gave Annie a shove, so that she came down with a whoosh, out of control, and plunged into the water, screaming.

'Hettie!' said Alice sharply, and quickly scooped up Annie and hugged her. 'There, sweetie, there you are, you did it.' She moved away from the slide as Hettie shot down with a splash.

'She pushed me,' Anne spluttered. 'She *pushed* me.'

'Someone was pushing *me*,' said Hettie, bobbing up beside them. 'You have to *move*, Annie.'

'Go away,' Annie put her wet head on Alice's shoulder, sulking.

'You shouldn't have done that, Hettie,' Alice said. 'You must never push, it's dangerous.'

'But she was being so *slow*!'

'I know, but even so.'

'Sorry.' And Hettie, who had learned to swim this summer, swam away, towards Rachel, who was in her class and had just arrived.

'Do you want to try again?' Alice asked Annie.

'No.'

'Perhaps in a little while.' She took her to the side and sat with her on her lap, rocking her to and fro. It's just like Hilda and me, she thought. I dithered about, afraid of everything, while Hilda just got on and did it, and grew tired of me. She was my father's child, clever and purposeful; I was my mother's, pretty and useless. When she died I was bereft; when Daddy died I hardly registered – well, I had Tony by then.

'All right now?' she asked Annie, leaning against the wet head.

'Mmm.'

Across the pool the two pregnant women she'd noticed earlier had got up, and were walking slowly towards the changing rooms. Again she thought: how well they look, graceful and steady – not like Hilda, who was looking so tired last week. Hilda, who never wanted children, who when we were young didn't seem to want anyone, and made her career while I made a mess of things – I still can't believe she's doing this. But of course she has gone about it the way she's always done things: planned it, presented it to us as a *fait accompli*, no discussion, no questions, thank you. Who knows if she's given this baby a thought, really, about whether it might mind not having a father around? I suppose she thinks Stephen will leave his wife in the end. Perhaps he will, perhaps she'll organise that, too.

'Hello, Alice.'

'Oh, hello.'

Rachel's mother, brisk and thin in a black swimsuit, came out of the pool and sat down beside her. Alice smiled, because she felt she should, although Yvonne always made her feel uncomfortable.

'How are you?' she asked.

'Oh, fine.' Yvonne was always fine. 'And how's Annie?' She leaned over, and Annie, predictably, turned away, thumb in mouth. 'Not very bright today?'

'She's had a bit of a fright,' said Alice, on the defensive. 'Hettie pushed her on the slide.'

'Oh, dear.' In two syllables Yvonne somehow managed to indicate both that Rachel would never push, and that she never took fright, either. Alice held Annie close, and felt protected.

'You couldn't just keep an eye on Rachel for me?' Yvonne was asking. 'I'm dying for a proper swim.'

'Yes, yes, of course. That's fine.'

'Thanks.' She slipped down into the water again, calling loudly: 'I'm going for a swim, Rachel! Alice is here.'

'Okay.' Rachel, deep in a game with Hettie, gave a half-wave, barely noticing, and Yvonne set off with strong determined strokes towards the deep end.

'Shall we go back in the pool now?' Alice asked Annie. 'We can have a game if you like.'

'All right.' Annie, cheered, slid off her lap. 'You're a whale and I'm a shrimp, and you have to catch me.' She clambered down the steps and began to walk through the water, trying to find a space between the little knots of splashing children.

'Here I come!' said Alice, with half an eye on Rachel and Hettie. 'Look out!'

Annie shrieked.

'I'm-coming-to-get-you!'

'No, no!'

But she was laughing, and begging, when she was caught, to do it again.

'Catch us, too!' shouted Hettie, waving with Rachel. 'Bet you can't.'

'Bet I can.'

But the pool was too full to play properly, and Alice found herself knocking into babies, held in their mothers' arms. 'Sorry.' She pushed towards Annie again. 'Where's that little shrimp?'

'Gosh,' said Yvonne, coming up beside her. 'You are having fun. I usually just leave Rachel to get on with it.' Alice's children were clearly over-indulged. 'Do you want to go and have a swim now? I'll watch them.'

Alice shook her head. 'No, it's all right, thanks.'

'Oh, go on, they'll be fine.'

'It's only Annie . . .'

'She'll be all right! Look at her.'

Hettie and Rachel were towing her through the water, holding an arm each; Annie was obviously loving it.

'Okay, then, thank you,' said Alice. 'I'll just do a couple of lengths – I won't tell Annie I'm going.'

'She's very clingy, isn't she? You stay as long as you like.'

Alice waited until two small boys with floats pushed across in front of her, and began to swim towards the deep end. I'm sorry Annie's so clingy, she rehearsed to Yvonne, it must be my fault.

The water was cool and green and crowded. A length was always sectioned off with rope for learners and serious swimmers, but Alice, who was neither, had never used it. Now, feeling upset and cross – with Yvonne, and with herself, for not being able to laugh her off – she wanted everyone out of the way. She moved over, ducking under the rope, and with a good stretch of water ahead began to swim in a soothing, regular rhythm, reached the far end, turned, and came back again, breathing steadily. By the time she was halfway up the pool she was already feeling calmer, Yvonne's breezy comments on the girls forgotten. She smiled at a woman she knew from playgroup, also swimming alone; she could see the girls ahead of her, Hettie being the whale; she would do two more lengths, then take them home for lunch.

If this were last summer, she thought, reaching the shallow end and turning back, this day would feel quite ordinary: swimming, making lunch, pottering about with the children, taking things slowly, feeling good. This year, ever since I've known about Hilda's baby, nothing has felt quite right. It's opened up the past, it's made me raw again. This is my sister, the woman to whom I might have expected to be closer than any other, whose baby I should be welcoming with love, and all I can do is feel taken over by sadness, and envy, and regret for something she knows nothing about. For when I was living in Oxford, and found myself pregnant by God knows who but probably Tom, who was married, I thought I wasn't fit to have a child, not on my own. And I had *my* baby, my first, darling baby aborted, sucked out and washed down a drain. It was over in half an hour, it happened eight years ago, and now I have two daughters: it makes no difference. It's going to be with me for the rest of my life.

By the time Tony came home in the evening the girls were already in their nightdresses, swinging bare feet under the garden table, eating apples. It was almost eight, still very warm, the sun going down behind the houses which backed on to theirs and the smell of a barbecue drifting over from three or four gardens down.

'Where've you *been*?' asked Hettie. 'We're having our pudding.'

'Lucky you, I haven't had a bite since lunchtime.' Tony flopped on to the seat beside her. 'I am dead.'

'I'm sorry we didn't wait,' said Alice, putting a plate of cold ham in front of him. 'What do you want to drink?'

'Anything. Beer. Is there any beer?'

'I'll get it,' said Annie, slipping off the bench. 'Let me.'

'You'll drop it,' said Hettie.

'No she won't, and anyway, it's just a can, isn't it?' said Alice, sitting down beside Tony. 'Hettie, you must stop being so bossy.'

'I'm not.'

'You are a bit.'

'Here you are, Daddy,' said Annie, coming out again. 'It's very cold.'

'Wonderful. Thanks, Annie.'

'Can I pull the ring off?'

'If you like.'

'But be careful,' said Alice. 'You know what they're like, those cans.'

'I can *do* it.'

'Now you're being bossy,' Hettie said to Alice.

'That's enough.'

'Do you lot go on like this all day?' asked Tony mildly. 'All right, Annie, very good, don't shake it, shall I just – '

'I can *do* it!' Annie pulled the can sharply towards her, and yanked again at the ring. With a hiss it was suddenly off, and then a foaming jet of beer was whooshing everywhere.

'*Annie!*' said Hettie.

'I couldn't help it, I couldn't help it, it was an accident, I'm all *wet!*' Annie howled, as Tony grabbed the can and upended it into his glass.

'Never mind, so am I,' he said, wiping his trousers with the back of his hand, and took a long drink. 'Ah, that's better. I should have known not to wear any clothes at all, shouldn't I? Mealtimes are a hazardous business with you around, Annie. What was it this morning, milk? Or was that yesterday?'

'It was this morning,' said Hettie. 'I told you she'd drop it.'

'I didn't drop it, it was an *accident!*' Annie screamed, and ran into the house, slamming the kitchen door.

'Oh, Hettie!' Alice snapped, getting up and going after her. 'Do leave her alone. All right, Annie, I'm coming, let's find you a clean nightie.'

When she had gone, Tony finished his beer and pulled the salad bowl towards him. 'Well, well,' he said to Hettie, helping himself. 'Isn't family life delightful? Has it been like this all day?'

'I don't think so,' said Hettie. 'I think it was quite a nice day, really. Do you want some bread?'

117

'Yes, but I'll cut it, thanks.' He sliced off a wedge, and began to butter it. ' "And how was your day, Daddy?" "Fine, thanks for asking." '

'I was just going to ask. Did the judge notice the smell?'

'What smell?'

'The milk.'

'Oh, no; no, he didn't, he had too much else to think about.' He took a big bite of the bread. 'Actually, I had a horrible day today, and so did everyone else.'

'Why? Because it was so hot?'

'Yes, but also because the boy I was looking after got sent to prison for a very long time.'

'How long?'

'Five years.'

'That's not very long.'

'It is when you're eighteen.'

'I thought you were going to say about a hundred, or a thousand or something.'

'No.'

Hettie was silent. Then she said: 'What did he do?'

'He stole a lot of things.'

'You mean he was a burglar.'

'Yes.'

'But burglars should go to prison, shouldn't they?'

'It depends. Sometimes punishing people makes them worse, not better. It makes them angry and unhappy. Sometimes it's better to give people something better to do than steal things, or sit in prison.' Tony yawned. 'Anyway, this is a big conversation for a small person. What have you done today?'

'I can't remember.'

'Hettie!' Alice was leaning out of an upstairs window. 'Come and brush your teeth, it's late now.'

'Coming.' She looked at Tony, who had taken off his glasses, and was rubbing his eyes. 'I wish you didn't work all the time.'

'So do I. Never mind – off you go, and I'll come up and read in a few minutes.' He put his glasses back again and patted her as she went past. 'Run, rabbit.'

'I wish we *had* a rabbit.'

When she had gone, Tony finished eating, and pushed his plate away. He stretched, and walked round the garden with his glass of beer, hearing the voices of other families, and the spit of sausages on

118

the barbecue, a few doors down. He saw again the face of Jason Hanwell, black, sweating, expressionless, as he was given his sentence and taken down, and heard the shouts from the gallery, where his parents and brother had been sitting for three days.

'Daddy! We're ready!'

Hettie and Annie were leaning out of their bedroom window, waving a book.

'Okay, I'm just coming.'

Upstairs, he stepped over strewn clothes and toys, finding the girls in bed, Annie already curled up, sucking her thumb. Hettie was propped up against the pillow; Alice was picking up socks and pants.

'Okay? I'll go down and put the coffee on. Goodnight, you two.' She bent over each bed. 'Straight to sleep after the story, all right? See you in the morning.' She went out, and down the stairs, and Tony perched himself on the chair between the beds.

'Right then, what have we got tonight, *War and Peace*?'

'I want this one,' said Annie pushing a worn copy of *Spot's Birthday* at him.

'Again?'

'I like it – I like opening the flaps.'

'I know you do. All right. What about Hettie?'

'The next chapter, of course.' She held up *Charlotte's Web*, taken out of the library last week. 'Wilbur is going to be *killed*, if Charlotte doesn't think of something.'

'How could I have forgotten? Okay, let's have *Spot* first . . .'

When he had finished reading, he got up and drew the curtains. They were the curtains Alice and Hilda had had in their room when they were children, faded blue cotton with a pattern of pandas and bamboo. Drawn, with the summer evening sky still light, they softened the room with shadows, but did not darken it.

'All right now? Everyone happy?' He bent to kiss them in turn. 'Goodnight, Hettie. Goodnight, Annie, and try not to wake us up, there's a good girl.'

'I can't help it.'

'Well, try.'

She put her arms round his neck. 'Will you ask Mummy to come up?'

'No. Mummy's tired. We'll see you in the morning, if not before.' He disentangled himself and went out, leaving the door ajar. 'Sixpence for the first person to go to sleep.'

'There's no such thing as a sixpence,' said Hettie.

'What a world we live in.' He went downstairs, finding Alice in the garden again, the table cleared and the coffee made and waiting.

'You're wonderful.' He slid along the bench beside her. 'What sort of day?'

'All right.' She poured out the coffee. 'You?'

'Not all right. I was telling Hettie – Jason Hanwell got five years.'

'Who?'

'Alice . . .' He sighed. 'The case I've been on all week, remember?'

'Sorry – I just forgot the name, that's all. Did he? Poor Tony, after all that work.'

'Poor Jason.'

'What do you mean, you were telling Hettie?'

'We had a brief discussion on the demerits of the prison sentence. She seems to think he got his just desserts.' He stirred his coffee, to cool it. 'Why is she getting on your nerves?'

'I don't like her being so superior with Annie. I'm not sure I like you treating her like a grown-up, either – discussing your work and all that. She's barely six.'

'And sometimes I think you're letting Annie go on being a baby for too long,' said Tony equably. 'So there we are.' He picked up his coffee cup. 'Do you mind if I take this upstairs? I've got a mountain to do by tomorrow.'

'Oh, Tony . . .'

'Never mind about the washing-up – I'll do it before I come to bed.'

'It's not the washing-up, I can do it. I just wanted to talk, that's all.'

'About?' He took a sip and yawned.

'Anything.' She rested her head against his shoulder. 'We hardly seem to see you these days. We haven't even had a holiday.'

'I know, I'll try. We'll get away before next term, I promise, even if it's only for a few days.'

'We could even go once term has started,' said Alice. 'It's not the end of the world, is it? And you need a holiday more than anyone.'

'Okay, we'll talk about it properly at the weekend.' He drank his coffee and poured another cup. 'Sorry, Alice, I must get on. Was there anything else on the agenda?'

She shook her head. 'Not really.'

'Meaning something in particular.'

'Just – perhaps I baby Annie because I'm still feeling broody, that's all.'

'Oh, God.' He pulled a face so comical that she had to laugh. 'Please, no. It must be Hilda. Is it Hilda? When's it due?'

'Early August. I think she's leaving work this week.'

'And how is she?'

Alice shrugged. 'All right, I think. Organised.'

'And who's going to look after her? Is Stephen going to be with her when it's born?'

'I don't know, do I? It'll probably come in the middle of the night, when he's in Norfolk.'

'Poor Hilda.'

Alice said nothing.

'If it hadn't been for Hilda,' said Tony, getting up, 'we wouldn't even have met. She was the one who made you go to the picnic, remember?' He pushed his glasses up on his nose. 'I'll see you later.'

By the last day of term many of the students had already left, and coming out of the bursar's office into the canteen Hilda found only the pensioners from the Small Gardens class. They sat smoking and drinking tea, plants brought in from home on the tables in front of them, ailing begonias and geranium cuttings. Hilda tucked her papers into her bag and went up to the counter.

'Can I have a large orange juice, please?'

'You can, my love.' The woman behind the counter was greying and motherly, wearing a green overall. She poured Hilda's drink from the machine behind her and passed it across. 'Isn't this weather something else? I should think you'll be glad to stop work. The heat must be killing you.'

'It is,' said Hilda, counting out change. 'There, thank you.'

'When're you due?'

'First week of August.'

'Ah, lovely. Hope it goes all right for you. You'll bring him in to show us, won't you?'

'Oh, yes,' said Hilda ignoring the automatic 'he'. She took the juice and went slowly over to sit by a window. Last night she had been out for a meal with everyone in her department, coming home late with a head unaccustomedly full of wine and an armful of presents for the baby. This morning she still felt tired and unexpectedly flat and, looking through the wire mesh to the car park, she saw two of her students from the Information Technology course wander through, holding hands, and heard herself give a long sigh. This won't do, she thought. In an hour and a half I am meeting Stephen for lunch in Bloomsbury; I must be pleasantly persuasive, not melancholy. Stephen dislikes tears these days, particularly in public.

Since he had returned from Italy, and the summer went on, Hilda had grown increasingly and unwillingly accustomed to meeting him on neutral territory – in cafés and restaurants and pubs near wherever he was working, and then saying goodbye. In the old days, what seemed now like the old carefree days, she might on a free afternoon have met him in a pub overlooking the canal in Camden, waiting until he came out of the office, but they would almost always have gone home together. Recently, he seemed to have little need to be in Camden, and much more in Norfolk; when he did come down he was liable to be summoned by unpredictable clients to far-flung places all over London, where it wasn't always easy to meet. Last night, when he was supposed to be coming over late, he had rung from a phone box near James's house, where he had been staying for two days.

'I wish I could come,' he said, 'but we've got so much on it's hardly worth it. I've got to be up early to meet a contractor on site just near here.'

Hilda yawned. 'Never mind, I'm almost asleep anyway. But you're coming tomorrow?'

There was a pause. 'Darling, I'm really sorry, but I've got to get back tomorrow. Could you come and meet me for lunch? I've got to collect some stuff from the AA in Bedford Square. We could meet in that little place near the British Museum, do you remember it?'

'I remember it,' she said coolly, with a miserable sensation of everything beginning to go wrong. 'But there seems to be hardly any time for us at all these days. I thought things were slack in the summer.'

Not, apparently, this summer. They made their arrangements and said goodbye without affection.

Hilda drank her orange juice, and looked through the maternity leave papers in her bag. The woman covering for her next term had been appointed, with a permanent job in another college to go to after Christmas; Hilda looked forward to coming back in the new year. To stay at home all day with a baby, then a toddler, as Alice had done – she could not imagine it, and remembering the complacency of some of the mothers she had met at Alice's house in the past, their whole world shrunk to the world of a single infant, she did not want to. It was the child she was looking forward to, the daughter and companion.

She finished her orange juice and got up, passing the pensioners on her way out, who nodded and smiled. My child will have no grandparents, she thought, not for the first time. Stephen had a mother, elderly and frail, living in Southwold: it was hardly likely that they would ever meet.

When she went outside the sun was dazzling, and so hot that the uneven tarmac in the forecourt had begun to bubble up in soft lumps. She went out of the gates and turned to walk up towards Church Street, where she was catching the 73 to Bloomsbury – no point in taking the car all the way down there and trying to find somewhere to park, although the heat was already making her feel lightheaded. She walked slowly along the burning pavements, past dusty roses and hollyhocks in small front gardens, and wished she had worn a hat.

At the top of Bloomsbury Street Hilda got off the bus and walked up towards the turning to the British Museum. The street was full of tourists, strolling beneath the plane trees, stopping at ice-cream vans, and for the first time she began to feel as if she were on holiday – more than that, on leave, with five long months before she need even think about work. She pictured herself with the baby in a sling, wandering on autumn days through the rooms of the Hayward and the Tate.

It's going to be lovely, she thought, as she came to the wide open gates of the museum, where visitors and pigeons swarmed at the top of the steps, and she stood at the zebra crossing, waiting for a gap in the traffic. A group of schoolboys, probably sixth-formers, stood on the island, with two middle-aged teachers.

'Everyone here? Where's Baldry?' 'Must be still on the train.' Near the boys was a party of French students, immaculate in pale sports shirts and well-cut cotton trousers; beside them the English boys looked not so much scruffy as unconsidered. The traffic slowed and halted; Hilda crossed, passing them, and went down Museum Street, pausing to browse among the sun-warmed second-hand bookstalls outside the shops. But the heat here, without the shade of the plane trees, was intense, and the words on the yellowing pages began to blur. The little network of streets between here and the restaurant where she was meeting Stephen was filling with office workers coming out in the lunch hour; Hilda made her way carefully through them, hoping that she wasn't going to faint.

The restaurant was in a narrow street shaded by tall buildings;

there were awnings up, and tables set out on the pavement beneath them; she sank gratefully into a chair and asked for a glass of mineral water. It came, chinking with ice and lemon, and she drank without stopping, watched over by a small fat waiter with brilliantined hair and a pink shirt.

'My wife the same,' he told her when she had recovered. 'She is also expecting a baby – very difficult, this heat, for the mamas.'

Hilda smiled. 'I'll have another glass, please.' She picked up the menu, fanning herself, and watched the passers-by for Stephen, and his easy, unhurried walk; waiting for the sudden flip of her stomach which came, always, still, whenever she had been waiting and he at last appeared. And how many times have I sat waiting for him in all these years, she wondered, sipping at her second glass. I have been waiting for him ever since we met.

A little dish of olives in lemon and garlic was put in front of her, with a basket of bread. 'Something to keep you going,' said the waiter paternally. 'You are ready to order now? Or you wait for your husband?'

'We'll order in a few minutes, I hope,' said Hilda, seeing that the other tables were filling up fast. 'Thank you, that looks lovely.' She ate, looking along the street again, reflecting on how far apart her two lives were: to sit on a sunny afternoon outside a good restaurant, to be waited on, as if she were a woman of leisure, supported and secure – it was not what she had expected of her life, and nor, in truth, were her circumstances how they must appear to the waiter: a cherished wife, waiting for her husband. He would not imagine her to be living alone in an attic flat in the East End, a teacher in a run-down college, a woman who had deliberately decided to bring up a child alone.

Stephen was stepping off the pavement on the other side of the street, raising his hand to greet her in the gesture she thought she might carry with her for the rest of her days, which somehow expressed everything in him she had found attractive from the beginning: someone who knew how to conduct himself, who, like her father, like Tony, was thoughtful and unhurried, never extravagant or showy in his dealings with the world. Her father, too, would have raised his hand like that to her mother – I love you, I'm here – whereas her mother would have greeted by waving, calling, running across.

'Hello, darling.'

'Hello.' She smiled up at him as he bent to kiss her cheek, dropping a small portfolio on to a chair.

'Have you been waiting long?'

'All my life,' she said lightly. 'That's what I was thinking.'

Stephen shook his head. 'Never think,' he said, pulling out a chair. 'Especially in hot weather. Have you ordered?'

'Of course not. I didn't know what you wanted.'

'After all these years?'

He reached across, taking her hand, and she said: 'I'm sorry about last night, being so cross, I know you're very busy. It's just – '

'I know. You were right. And, dear Hilda, your version of being cross is hardly most people's. It's one of the reasons I love you – you never get hysterical, or throw things.'

'That's just what I was thinking about you,' she said. 'More or less.' She stroked his hand, still very brown from Italy. 'I do cry sometimes, though, don't I? I cried the last time we met.'

'So you did. Never mind. Don't cry now, will you? Let's have some lunch, I'm starving.'

The small fat waiter, summoned, took an order for pasta and green salad, beaming upon Hilda as he went back inside.

'How have you been?' she asked Stephen when they were eating. 'You seem to be rushing back and forth all the time.'

He twisted a forkful of pasta. 'Things are getting a bit difficult, with the mortgage rate going up again. We'd begun to think we needed a new partner – now we seem to be running out of work. But, of course, what we do do has got to be first class; we really depend on word-of-mouth nowadays.' He took a mouthful of wine. 'Even so, there are still people with money. You'd be surprised at the number of people with second homes in East Anglia. Don't make that face.'

'You'd be surprised at the number of people in Hackney who'd give anything for a first home,' said Hilda.

'Never mind, let's not get into that one now. I only want to know two things.' She hesitated, nervous.

'This sounds ominous.'

'No. Just – it *is* work, isn't it, that's keeping you away? I mean, at home . . . is everything all right?'

'I think so,' said Stephen carefully, and then: 'I don't think you should ever write to me there again.'

'Oh, God. I'm sorry. I knew it was a mistake.'

'It's all right, nothing's been said. But there's been an air of . . . disquiet. I wasn't going to tell you, but since you ask, things at home are not quite right, no.'

Hilda was silent, running through imaginary scenes. At last she said: 'I don't know, now, if I can ask you my next question, but I have to. Will you be able to be with me, do you think, when the baby comes?'

Stephen put down his fork and sighed. 'I'll try,' he said. 'That's all I can say. Tell me again when you're due.'

'August the sixth,' said Hilda. She had carried the date before her, lit up like a motorway signpost, for so long, that it seemed quite extraordinary that Stephen could not remember it.

'That's . . . five weeks, isn't it?' He took out his diary, and carefully pencilled in a ring. 'I shall do everything in my power to have a week-long series of meetings in London,' he said, putting the diary back in his pocket. 'But you – we – must have a contingency plan, mustn't we? First babies are notoriously late. Or early. Or otherwise problematic. Suppose I can't be here, what then?'

'What then?' echoed Hilda bleakly, and thought suddenly: I need my mother. Father would have come, and waited, and brought flowers, but my mother could have been with me, and held my hand. Who else is going to look after me?

'Alice?' asked Stephen, and she shook her head.

'Absolutely not. She's too busy, and anyway . . . I don't know; she isn't pleased about this baby. I find it rather hypocritical. Still – ' She looked away from him, along the narrow street, in deep shadow, and less crowded now. People were going back to work. 'Don't worry,' she said, as much to herself as to Stephen. 'I'll manage. Just – if you don't hear from me, you will telephone, won't you?'

'Of course I will, of course. And I'll come the minute I can.'

'Thanks,' she said, as if he were going to try to make it to a party. 'I suppose this is another thing I should have thought of. Never mind.' Two schoolboys were coming along the street, and she seemed to recognise them from the party on the zebra crossing: one a stocky, mouse-haired lad, the other taller, suntanned, with straight dark hair and an easy, swinging stride. He wore a loosely knotted tie and carried a cotton jacket over his shoulder. As they drew near, Hilda thought vaguely that he was very good-looking; also, that she had seen that walk before.

'Stephen,' she said, disbelieving. 'You see that boy . . .'

He turned, glancing along the street, and the boy stopped, laughed, and waved.

'My God,' said Hilda, and Stephen said quickly, 'It's all right,' and pushed back his chair and got up, smiling, as the boys reached them.

'Hi, Dad.' The tall dark boy pushed back flopping hair and grinned.

'Well, well, what on earth are you doing here?' Stephen turned to Hilda. 'This is my son, Jonathan. Jon, this is a client of mine, Hilda King.'

The boy nodded, and shook hands. 'How do you do.' Another easy person to meet.

'How do you do,' said Hilda distantly.

'You remember Mike, Dad,' said Jonathan, gesturing to his friend, and Stephen nodded. 'Of course. How are you, Mike?'

'Fine, thanks.' Watching them all, Hilda thought: Stephen could be in personnel, or politics, just as well as an architect; he gives the impression he can handle anything, no wonder he has so many clients. And now, apparently, I am one of them. There came into her mind the image of Tony, also able to put anyone at ease, and with it the small, treacherous thought: but Tony is genuine with people, I know he is. Perhaps with Stephen it's all an act, a means to an end. It makes life easier for him.

He was gesturing towards the two other chairs. 'Are you going to join us? We were just finishing . . .'

'No, it's all right, we've got to meet the others in a minute.' Jonathan shook his head. 'You're hopeless, Dad, didn't you remember I was coming down? I told you at the weekend.'

'So you did.' Stephen ran long fingers through greying hair. 'I'm obviously on the way out. Tell me again?'

'End-of-term cultural expedition to the BM? Looking at nineteenth-century manuscripts?'

'Now, how could I forget that? And how are you getting home again?'

'On the train,' said Jonathan patiently. 'You said you weren't sure if you'd be down here or not, so we didn't make any arrangements . . .'

'Well, let's make one now,' said Stephen smoothly. 'I'm coming home after this anyway. I'll meet you at the studio, okay? D'you want a lift, Mike, or will you be going back with the others?'

'Well, I . . .' The stocky boy, clearly less used to social negotiation, rubbed his forehead, looking hot.

'He'll come with us, Dad, for Gawd's sake,' said Jonathan. 'Okay, we'll see you there. About four? Thanks.' He nodded politely to

Hilda, with an expression which bore no hint of speculation. 'Nice meeting you. Goodbye.'

'Goodbye.'

'All right, chaps, see you later.' Stephen sat down again, and gestured to the waiter, who was flicking at crumbs on the next table, just cleared, with a pale pink napkin. 'Two coffees, please.'

Hilda had not drunk coffee for months, but felt unable to remind him of this or, indeed, to say anything at all. The waiter disappeared inside again, and Stephen drew a long breath.

'Phew.'

She looked at him steadily. 'Did you really forget?'

'I really did. I knew there was something: Bedford Square this morning, British Museum nearby, but . . . I must have a loose connection these days.' He rubbed his face. 'Don't look so appalled. Now do you believe me when I say things aren't easy? When I'm in Norfolk I'm worrying about you; when I'm here I feel guilty I'm not there. Meanwhile, James is hoping to save the day by taking on a bloody great office development near the zoo . . .'

Hilda burst out laughing.

'It's not funny.'

'Two cappuccinos.' The waiter set down little white cups, and a bowl of sugared almonds.

'Thank you,' said Stephen. 'And the bill, please.'

'I didn't mean to laugh,' said Hilda. 'It must be the tension. Or relief. Or something . . . My God, he won't say anything, will he?'

'There's nothing for him to say; he meets people all the time – Miriam's customers in the shop, my clients visiting the studio . . .'

'Goodness,' said Hilda, no longer feeling like laughing. 'What very busy lives you all lead, to be sure.' She thought of Stephen and nice-mannered Jonathan and his friend, meeting up in a couple of hours, driving home together to Miriam and a cool country house, and herself, catching the 73 back to Hackney, Anya and the cats, and her hot, empty rooms upstairs, and felt a lump come into her throat which she could not swallow away.

'And so.' The waiter put down the bill with a flourish, and Stephen took out his wallet. 'Thank you.' He gave the waiter a credit card which to Hilda seemed suddenly to say everything: something obtained too easily, to be paid for later, with charges. By whom? She turned away, blowing her nose, as Stephen signed, and thanked again, and put away the bill, leaving a tip.

'Hilda?'

'What?'

'Look at me.'

She looked, giving him a weak smile. 'He's very nice, Jonathan. Lovely.'

'So are you,' said Stephen. He stroked her cheek. 'I'm so sorry – you were wonderful.' He smiled ruefully. 'My best client.'

'*You* were wonderful,' said Hilda. 'I don't know how you did it. I suppose you've got to go now.'

'Not quite yet. Shall we go for a walk? Now it's cooler?'

'Yes.'

They pushed back their chairs and got up, nodding to the waiter. 'You bring the baby for lunch one day?'

They did not answer, and went down the street with their arms round each other, walking slowly, as if they were an ordinary couple, with all the time in the world to be together.

As always on Fridays, the road out of London was clogged with traffic; Stephen and the boys sat sweating in a half-mile queue up to the roundabout at Epping. The windows were wound right down, but let in only still, baking air; every few minutes they inched forward, past long lines of suburban houses where curtains were drawn against the heat and parasols from motorway garages stood on parched grass.

'God, Dad,' said Jonathan, 'this is worse than Italy. Couldn't you have brought something to drink?'

'Sorry.' Stephen turned to look at him, his school shirt open, hair sticking to wet forehead. 'I got a bit rushed – we'll stop the minute we see a shop.'

'There aren't any shops along here.'

'Well, a garage, then.' He glanced in the mirror. 'You okay, Mike?'

'Yes, thanks.' The other boy made Jonathan look cool and collected; his face was red, his manner awkward. 'I just feel a bit sick, that's all.'

'Oh, dear.' Stephen changed gears and moved forward again. 'You'll be all right once we get going, get some fresh air in.'

Mike did not answer; Stephen felt obscurely guilty. He had said goodbye to Hilda at the last minute, among the crowds on Tottenham Court Road, leaving her to wait in the sun for a 73, while he leapt on to a 24, taking him through to Camden, reaching the studio well after four, finding the boys hanging about in the street outside, looking hot and disgruntled.

'Why didn't you go on up?' He unlocked the door of the building and they followed him inside.

'Because no one answered the door, that's why,' said Jonathan.

'James must have left early. Sorry, I forgot, he usually does on Fridays.'

He led them up the narrow flight of stairs to what was usually the dazzling white of the studio, where now the Venetian blinds were closed and the fans switched off. It was airless: James must have left hours ago. The boys went straight to the kitchenette – a sink and a little fridge behind white louvred doors – and gulped down water from paper cups. Except for half a packet of cheese and a limp cucumber the fridge, well-stocked when he'd last looked, was empty.

'Sorry, boys.' He gathered up the stuff from his desk and snapped his case shut. 'Let's go.' And since they'd had a drink there, and he wanted to get moving, and beat the rush hour, he'd taken them straight round to the car and driven away without stopping. Now that seemed like madness – they'd been out in the heat all day, perhaps Mike had really overdone it.

The cars ahead were moving again, sending up clouds of fumes and exhaust. They left the endless rows of houses behind and drove through a stretch of brown common. Jonathan reached forward and turned on the radio; rock music pulsed through the heat.

'Do you have to have that on?' asked Stephen, after a few minutes.

'Just a distraction. Mum never minds it.'

'Well, I do. At the moment, anyway – especially if Mike's not feeling too good.'

Jonathan turned in his seat. 'Mike? D'you mind this?'

'It's okay.'

Stephen checked the mirror again: the boy was drumming his fingers, nodding his head to the beat. He sighed. 'Well, turn it down a bit, anyway.'

'What's the matter, Dad, getting old? You didn't mind on holiday.'

'Well, we're not on holiday here,' snapped Stephen. 'Now, turn the bloody thing down, okay?'

In silence Jonathan reached for the knob. They drove on in fits and starts without speaking, reaching at last a garage, where petrol fumes shimmered off the forecourt. They stocked up with mineral water and cans of Coke from a fridge running low, and went back to the car. Inside, Jonathan switched off the radio; they all drank like men in the desert.

'Everyone okay now?' Stephen eased out on to the road again.

'Yes, thanks.' Jonathan looked at him; he ran his nails along his teeth in mock terror. 'What about the Führer?'

Stephen patted his knee. 'Sorry.'

'It's doesn't matter.'

'You can have it on again if you want.'

'No, it's all right.'

The traffic was moving well now; air streamed in through the open windows. Stephen moved into the fast lane; they swept past dry open fields and dusty trees.

'What're we doing this weekend?' asked Jonathan. 'Have you got people coming?'

'No,' said Stephen. 'I've got to do a bit of work, but other than that I just want to flop. What about you – any plans?'

Jonathan yawned. 'Not really. Might go into Norwich tomorrow night, there's a gig, isn't there, Mike?'

Silence from the back seat; he turned to look, and turned back again, grinning. 'He's out of it.'

'He hasn't got sunstroke, has he?'

''Course he hasn't. Mike's always out of it. Well, a bit, anyway.'

'But you like him?'

''Course I do.'

They slowed, approaching a roundabout. Stephen said: 'Mum okay?'

'Think so. Same as usual. Why?'

'No reason. She's not got anything on this weekend, has she? Apart from the shop.'

Jon shook his head. 'Shouldn't think so – you're the socialite, aren't you, Dad?'

'Mmm. I suppose so.' For a moment Stephen wondered if he were going to ask about Hilda. For a moment, a split second, he considered telling him. But Jon said nothing, yawning again, and the moment passed. They drove on; it grew cooler. After a while, when neither had spoken, Stephen glanced over at him. He had fallen asleep, too, dark head on graceful boyish neck turned to one side. After a day out in the London heat he looked sweaty and grimy, in need of a bath; he also looked very beautiful, and untroubled. Stephen turned his eyes back to the road, and put his foot down.

They came to the ring road outside Norwich just after seven; by a quarter to eight they were dropping Mike off in Woodburgh. He shambled up the path to his front door, looking like someone in need of help, but turned to wave at them, grinning, as the door was opened by a cross-looking sister in shorts.

They drove out of the town, past shut-up shops and tubs of geraniums, past the war memorial, out on to the long straight country road. The sun was not yet down behind the trees on the horizon, but even in this, the hottest July for decades, it was cooler up here than in London, or at least more bearable. It began to feel like a perfect summer evening, warm and still. Across to the left a combine harvester, working late, was throbbing along the edge of a cornfield; when they turned off on to the narrow road to Saxham, they saw rabbits. In the village, children were bicycling up and down; the usual old boys sat outside the Plough with their pints.

Stephen let out a long breath. 'Thank God we're back.'

'Poor Dad. You have a rest this weekend.'

They turned into the lane leading down to the house; it was caked and hard, from weeks of hot weather; they bumped past verges thick with cow parsley, and when they stopped at the gates and Jon got out to open them the air smelt summery and sweet. Miriam's car was in the garage; Stephen pulled up and turned off the engine. Behind him, Jonathan was closing the gates again.

'Hello, Tess, hello, girl!'

Coming out of the garage with his case Stephen saw Jonathan bend down to hug her, kissing her greying head. 'Good girl, good girl.'

The front door was open, the hall was cool and shadowy. They went inside, dropping their things, calling out.

'Miriam?'

'Hi, Mum!'

There was no answer.

'She must be round the back,' said Jonathan.

They went down the passage to the kitchen, where the radio was on, and out through the garden doors. Miriam, in long cotton skirt and sleeveless top, was hosing the flowerbeds. She saw them, and smiled at Jonathan.

'Good trip?'

'Fine. I met Dad, we came back together. God, I think I'll get under that.'

He was pulling off his clothes, dropping shirt, shoes and trousers in a heap, running over the wet grass in his pants. Miriam turned the hose on him and he shrieked, raising his arms. 'Brilliant! Come on, Dad.'

Stephen shook his head. He sank on to the wooden seat outside the kitchen doors and watched them, the fine spray gleaming in the evening sun, the water trickling down his son's long body, soaking his hair. Tess barked, racing round him.

'That's enough,' said Miriam, after a few minutes. 'Why don't you go and have a proper shower now? We can have supper out here.' She left the hose lying on the grass and came slowly up to the house, and the garden tap, turning it off. Water dripped from the shrubs and roses. Jonathan padded past her and Stephen, picking up his clothes, leaving wet footprints on the stones; Tess shook herself, and followed him inside.

'Wipe your feet,' said Stephen. 'And hers.'

'Yes sir.' They could hear him humming in the kitchen, looking for a towel.

'Miriam?'

'Yes?'

'Everything all right?'

'Fine. How was London?'

'Hot.'

'Well, supper's cold. Are you going to have a shower, too?'

'When he's finished. Come and sit down.'

'In a minute. I'll just get Jon a towel.' She brushed past him, up the step to the kitchen; he could hear her opening a drawer, and she and Jon chattering easily together before he went upstairs. She did not come out again, and he went on sitting there, hearing her lay a tray with supper things, looking at the fresh wet garden, listening to the birds. With a part of him he was glad she had not come back, because it freed him from the sense he always had of her: wanting more than he wanted to give, waiting for him to reach out to her, as if he alone could make everything all right. Even so, he was, as always, glad to be back.

The sun slipped down in the endless Norfolk sky, blackbirds and thrushes sang in the apple trees. After supper he would go across to the studio and sort out what he had to do this weekend, perhaps listen to a concert. He yawned and stretched, hearing from the open window upstairs Jonathan in the bathroom, singing under the shower. He got up and began to walk round the garden, stretching his legs. He thought about Hilda, and the lingering kiss they had exchanged beneath the plane trees in Russell Square: between them, the baby had kicked against his ribs, beyond them the traffic roared.

Here it was peaceful and still. Walking round his garden, where

Tess had reappeared and lay soaking up the last of the sun, he tried, as a cautious experiment, to imagine a time when he might not have all this to come back to.

'And who is going to look after you, Hilda?'

Anya, from beneath the garden parasol, looked as if she were sitting for a painting, leaning forward on the uneven slatted table, elbows bare beneath rolled-up cotton shirtsleeves, teapot in front of her, straw hat on the seat beside her, next to a sleeping cat.

'Who, for example, will drive you to the hospital? If Stephen is not in London?'

'I expect I shall call an ambulance,' said Hilda, sipping her tea. 'It's what most people do, isn't it?'

'Most people,' said Anya, 'even if they go into hospital by ambulance, have someone to be with them. You will be in labour . . .' She let the rest of the sentence trail away, leaving Hilda with imagined agony.

She put down her teacup and shrugged. 'I'll be all right.'

'You may not be all right. You may not want to be alone among strange doctors.'

Hilda did not answer. She had been lying on her bed, with the curtains drawn and the windows open, when Anya summoned her down for tea in the garden, as she did most days. In the interminable weeks between leaving work and now, less than a fortnight before the baby was due, she had received visitors – Stephen, two friends from college, Alice and the family back from ten days in Brittany – but had grown less and less able or inclined to leave the house. It was too hot, she was too heavy and tired. To come down here and sit beneath a shady parasol, listening to the sparrows, and to Anya, who until today had talked mostly about herself – her girlhood in Prague; the train which had brought her out of the city in the last days before the gates of the ghetto had closed; her meeting with her husband – it had been restful, a welcome distraction. As she listened, she sewed, feeling unusually domestic, stitching little cotton tops and pillowslips. In the evenings, as it grew cooler, Anya walked round the garden with the hose, sprinkling the drooping lupins and roses, although she left the grass to go brown.

'It will recover, grass always does. One must not be wasteful with water.'

The cats followed, padding after the spray.

'I can remember,' she said now, 'with Liba. Of course, in those days it was unthinkable for the husband to be with you, but still, Josef was in the hospital, in the father's room. And he had come with me . . .' She broke off, shaking her head. 'Birth in those days was terrible, it is different now, I am sure, with all these breathing exercises and injections. But still – ' She tapped on the table with her teaspoon. 'Hilda! How are you going to manage?'

Hilda looked at her. 'I don't know.'

'Your sister . . .'

'No.'

Anya sighed. 'I suppose,' she said, pouring a third cup of tea and dropping in a thin slice of lemon, 'that I shall have to come with you. Would you like me to, Hilda? If Stephen cannot? I should be very happy . . .'

'I can't sleep,' said Alice. She sat up, threw off the sheet to the end of the bed and lay down again. Behind the lace curtains the windows were wide open, but it made no difference: the hot, still air from the street felt like a blanket, thick and dark.

'Tony?'

He had come to bed before her, exhausted, already asleep when she switched off the light and crept in beside him, her hair damp from the shower.

'Tony,' she said again. 'Are you awake?'

There was no answer, and after a few moments he began to snore, lightly but unendurably. Alice kicked him. 'Ssh!' He snorted and stopped, turning over, and Alice moved to the edge of the bed. She tried lying on her side, on her back, on the other side. Beside her the luminous hands of the clock showed midnight, half-past, one o'clock. Her eyes closed, and she felt herself begin to slip towards sleep. From the children's room came a whimper, then a cry.

'Mum-my!'

Alice lay still, hoping, as always, that Annie might not have fully woken, and might drift back to sleep. There was the sound of bare feet padding along the landing; Annie was beside the bed in her nightdress, her face crumpled.

'I had a bad dream.'

'Ssh!'

She began to clamber on to the bed. 'Let me come in.'

'No.'

Annie opened her mouth to cry.

'Stop it! It's too hot, I haven't slept a wink.'

'I want to come *in*.'

'Well, you can't. I'm fed up with you, go back to bed.'

Annie burst into tears.

'Oh, for heaven's sake.' Alice swung her legs off the bed and took her hand. 'Come on. Ssh, now, you'll wake the others. Come and get a drink.'

She led her to the bathroom, yawning. 'Just as I was dropping off.' She ran the tap, gave Annie a beaker, sponged her face and had a long drink herself. 'That's better. Now – back to bed.'

'Your bed.'

'No!'

'Please!'

'No! No, no, no! I've had enough of it, Annie, you're three and a half and this has to stop, do you understand?' She found herself kneeling on the floor in front of her, gripping her small bare arms. 'You've done it every night since you were born, you did it all the time we were on holiday, and I've had *enough*! Now go back to bed.'

Annie burst into tears again, shaking with shock and anger. 'Why're you being so horrible to me?'

Outside, in the garden below, two cats began to yowl, the sound winding through the heat and stillness like an endless length of string. Alice got up, grabbed the plastic jug she used to rinse the children's hair, and ran the tap into it; she flung up the window and leaned out, hurling the water into the darkness. There was a splash, another yowl, snarling and furious, then silence. 'Good.' She withdrew her head, and put the jug back on the side of the basin.

Annie, mesmerised, looked at her and began to laugh. 'What did you *do*?'

'You saw what I did,' said Alice, and gave her a hug. 'Now, no more fuss, all right? I'll see you in the morning.'

She led her, uncomplaining, back to her room, and smoothed down her sheet, turning over the pillow.

'Hettie didn't hear *anything*.' Annie lay down. 'Night, Mummy.'

'Good girl. Night, night.'

Alice went softly back along the landing, and into the bedroom, where Tony had begun to snore again. She lay down, nudging him until he stopped, and smoothed her own pillow, which felt blissfully soft. Perhaps that's done the trick, she thought, hearing no sound from Annie, and then, as she drifted at last into a deep sleep: and how is Hilda going to cope with broken nights? I suppose her baby will be like Hettie, perfect.

Some time after daybreak she was aware of the telephone, ringing and ringing downstairs, and Tony stumbling out of bed to go and answer it. She opened an eye, saw it was only just light, and went back to sleep again. Tony came back to bed, and shook her gently.

'Hilda's had the baby.'

'What?' She felt as though she would never wake up properly again.

'That was Anya – Hilda's had the baby. It's a boy, eight pounds six ounces.' He yawned, and drew her towards him. 'How nice. We must go and see them.'

4

On the third floor of the maternity hospital, Hilda lay stiff and aching in a high white bed, waiting for Stephen. Beside her, the baby, who had been awake for most of the night, slept now as if he would never wake again, flat on his stomach, head to one side, full-lipped mouth open a little, fists clenched. A big baby, born after what seemed to Hilda now like a battle, raging through her, threatening to tear her apart, stringing her up in the end in stirrups, somewhere far away watching it all, thinking helplessly: this can't be happening to me. Now, two days later, lying in his crib, the baby looked like a different creature from the one belonging to the woman in the next bed, a tiny little girl called Daisy, with a thatch of dark hair. Hilda's son had almost no hair, and no name yet, either: she was unable to decide on one. She vaguely supposed that she was in a kind of shock.

The ward was hot and sunny – far too hot, especially in the afternoons, when the mothers were supposed to rest, before visiting time. For the babies' sake the central heating was still on, and the high windows overlooking the main road on one side and the car park on the other opened, as in the college, only at the top. It seemed to Hilda that the long cotton curtains should be drawn in the afternoons, but none of the nurses had ever drawn them, and she didn't feel she could ask. She didn't feel she could do anything, wanting only to sleep, but she couldn't sleep: there was always a baby crying, or a trolley rattling, or the kitchen staff banging things. Beyond the flowers and cards on the table at the end of the bed other mothers shuffled slowly past, to the bathroom and back again to the dayroom, where they watched television and smoked when the nurses weren't looking. They were visited by their husbands, their mothers and sisters, and other children. Hannah, the Jewish woman across the table, had given birth to her fifth child: two girls in plaits and two pale boys in earlocks and skullcaps had come to see their new brother yesterday, sitting in a silent row on a bench at the end of the bed; her husband, bearded, black-coated, had kept on his hat throughout the visit. When they had gone, Hannah asked the nurse for a bottle for the baby, explaining that he did not approve of breastfeeding. Hilda watched all these comings and goings, visited so far only by Anya, who had, in the end, been the one to come with her in the ambulance.

'He is a beautiful boy,' she said yesterday, getting up to go. 'You will soon feel stronger, Hilda, believe me.' She touched the bunch of Interflora roses sent by Stephen. 'When is he coming to see you?'

'When he can,' said Hilda, and turned away.

It was hotter this afternoon than it had been all week, and it seemed quieter: two mothers had gone home this morning, and their beds were still empty. Beside Hilda the baby was motionless; she felt her eyes begin to close, and with difficulty turned over, and pulled the pillows down.

'Mrs King? You've got a visitor, dear.' A staff nurse was at her bedside.

Hilda heaved herself up. 'Please don't call me Mrs King. It's Miss, I've told you.'

'We call everybody Mrs,' said the staff nurse, plumping up her pillows. 'It's the rule.'

'Oh, for God's sake. If you have to call me something call me Hilda, all right?'

'All right,' said the nurse placidly. She looked down at the sleeping baby, and lifted the chart at the end of his crib. 'He's due for another feed in half an hour. How're you managing – is he feeding well now?'

'I don't know,' said Hilda. 'I think so. Can you get my visitor, please?'

'Of course I can, love.' The nurse walked briskly up the ward to the entrance. Looking after her, Hilda could see Stephen, being told he could come in, nodding and smiling, and then making his way down between the rows of beds, searching for her. He was wearing a pale summer jacket, and carrying more flowers; he looked, as always, well-dressed and personable, but also somewhat disconcerted, and to Hilda he seemed all at once like a stranger, someone who knew nothing of the past few days and therefore, since she was changed utterly, nothing about her at all.

'I'm over here,' she said, as he drew near, and raised her hand.

He saw her, and smiled, came over and bent to kiss her, dropping the flowers on the bed.

'How are you?' she asked, offering her cheek.

'I'm all right,' said Stephen, sitting on the edge of the bed. 'More important, how are you? And this one.' He leaned towards the crib. 'God, he's tiny, look at him, I'd forgotten . . .' He leaned over, and with a finger stroked the baby's face. 'Hello. You're a nice-looking little chap.'

'Actually,' said Hilda, 'he looks quite colossal to me. I think he's the biggest baby on the ward. I mean – see that.' She indicated the next bed, where Daisy was being lifted up by her mother and looked, in a tiny white nightgown, like a crumpled fairy.

Stephen glanced at her, then back at the crib. 'But he's wonderful, he's lovely.' He sat down again beside Hilda, taking her hand. 'Well . . . you've done it, you're very clever. Happy now?'

'Oh, yes,' said Hilda tonelessly. 'A bit tired, that's all.'

'Of course you are, it's only natural.' He paused. 'I'm so sorry I didn't make it.'

'Never mind. It doesn't matter. The midwives were good.'

'Midwives? You mean there were several?'

'I think there were three; it was quite a long labour.' She felt she had to edit it, to give a crisp report on the details of this cataclysm, this undreamed-of climax, as if it were the last thing Stephen would want to know about. 'Anyway,' she said, 'it's over now. Tell me how you are – how's work?'

'Dreadful,' said Stephen, and looked at her, stroking her hand. 'I'm sure you don't want to hear about it.'

Hilda smiled. 'That's just what I was thinking – that you wouldn't be interested in the birth.'

'Of course I am,' said Stephen, although his tone was not one of enquiry. 'I should think the outside world must seem a long way away at the moment, doesn't it?'

'What outside world?' asked Hilda, and felt herself, just a little, begin to thaw.

'That's better.' He leaned forward and kissed her. 'You look a bit more like my Hilda now.' She felt her eyes fill with tears, and pressed her face into his shoulder as he put his arms round her. 'There we are. It's all over.'

It's only just beginning, thought Hilda, not trusting herself to speak. Beside them the baby woke, and stirred, making small creaking noises. She drew away, wiping her eyes. 'He's due for a feed, I'd better pull myself together.' She leaned against the pillows again, unbuttoning her nightdress. 'Can you pass him?'

'One baby coming up.' Stephen carefully lifted him from the crib, and kissed the top of his bald head. 'Here we go. Got him? Well done.'

He sounded steady and in charge, more familiar with the baby and his needs after ten minutes acquaintance than Hilda felt after two days.

'Thanks.' She held the baby to her, watching him begin to search for her breast, sore and rock-hard. With difficulty she helped him take hold of the nipple, and remembered, suddenly, watching Alice learn how to feed Hettie, laughing and confident. How had she known what to do? The baby began to suck, strongly, and she winced.

'What's the matter?'

'It hurts. I suppose I'm just not used to it yet. Oh, God . . .' Again, Hilda felt as if she were going to cry, and shut her eyes. 'Perhaps you'd better go. I must be having the blues or something . . . Sorry.'

'I think you've got some more visitors,' said Stephen quietly. 'Can you cope?'

'What?'

She opened her eyes again to see Alice and the girls coming slowly down the ward towards her, waving.

'I . . .' But what could she do, when they'd come all this way? 'It's all right,' she said, and reached for the box of tissues on the cabinet beside her, wincing again as the baby sucked harder. Beside her, Stephen had risen, and stood aside as Alice reached the bed, slender, suntanned and fair. She looked diffident and cautious, but at the sight of the baby she relaxed, softening, on familiar ground.

'Hello, Hilda.' She bent and kissed her with warmth. 'Well done.'

'Thanks.' Hilda smiled wanly up at her, and stretched out a hand to the girls. 'Hello, you two.'

'Hello.' Hettie and Annie, in cotton shorts and sandals, stood like Tweedledum and Tweedledee, awkward and shy, enormous. Beside them, Alice and Stephen were introducing themselves; then Alice bent down to the baby. 'Oh, isn't he beautiful?' She touched a small red ear, and drew the girls towards her. 'Look, here's your new cousin.'

'What's his name?' Hettie gingerly touched his hand and then, like Alice, softened. 'Oh, isn't he sweet? Look at his little *nails*.'

Hilda shifted as the baby, suddenly full, dropped away from her, head lolling, cheeks flushed. 'He hasn't got a name yet,' she said. 'We've got to choose one. What do you think he should be called?' And as soon as she'd said it, knew that was a mistake – the baby's name seemed, suddenly, far too important to entrust to a six-year-old, even Hettie.

From behind the children, Stephen said helpfully: 'I think he looks like a Sam.'

'Do you?' asked Hilda. 'Yes – that's a good strong name.'

Annie turned and looked up at him. 'Are you the Daddy?'

'I am,' said Stephen. 'And you must be Annie.'

'Yes,' said Annie, and turned away, reaching for Alice's hand.

There was a general silence.

Then Alice said: 'Tony's going to join us here, he's coming on straight from work.'

'Oh,' said Hilda. 'That's nice.' She was hot and thirsty, longing for a cool shower; she moved the baby a little away from her, and reached for the jug of water.

'Here,' said Stephen. 'Let me . . .' He came round the bed, and poured her a drink. 'And now I'd better be off.'

'What?' Hilda, barely beginning to rediscover her feeling for him, felt desolate, cut adrift. 'You've only just got here.'

'I know, but you're tired.'

'Perhaps we're in the way,' Alice said quickly, and Hilda wanted to say: 'Well, actually, perhaps today . . .' but Stephen was already, once again, taking charge of the situation.

'It's all right, I have to go anyway.' He touched Hilda's shoulder. 'I'll be back tomorrow, all right?'

'Oh. Good. Yes, all right, then. See you tomorrow.'

'Get some rest tonight, won't you?'

She smiled wryly. 'I'll try. Thanks for coming.'

'My pleasure.' He patted the baby lightly. 'Bye, Sam, look after Mum.' Then he was gone, nodding to Alice and the girls, and walking away down the ward.

Alice and Hilda looked at each other. 'He's nice,' said Alice.

'I know,' said Hilda shakily, feeling as if she were never going to see him again.

Alice touched the bunch of flowers on the bed. 'Did he bring these? Shall I put them in water?'

'You could. I haven't even looked at them, what are they?'

'Chrysanths.' Alice drew the paper aside, revealing tight heads of bronze and yellow. She looked again at the baby, and her face was filled with longing. 'He does look like a Sam. Can I hold him for a minute?'

'Of course.' But as Hilda made to pass him over Annie said loudly: 'I want a pee.'

'Oh. Oh, all right.' Alice picked up the flowers. 'Come on, we'll go to the loo, and we can find a vase at the same time.'

'I think they're at opposite ends of the ward,' said Hilda wearily, as if it were she who were going to have to make the monumental effort of finding both.

'I'll do the flowers,' said Hettie, picking them up. 'Please – can I?'

'Of course.'

Hilda lay watching them all go off, Alice and Annie hand-in-hand towards the lavatories, and Hettie, bearing the flowers, up towards the sluice at the far end. In her arms the baby stirred again, screwing up his face. And now I suppose he wants changing, she thought; when they've gone I'll take him along to the nursery. The nursery, too, felt an unbreachable distance away; she felt as if she would never get off the bed and walk again.

From the kitchen there came the comforting sound of the tea trolley being manoeuvred into the ward by a tiny Filipino woman in green. And there, overtaking it, was Tony, hurrying in his ungainly way towards her, smiling and waving like everyone else – but, unlike everyone else, someone whom Hilda felt, with a wave of relief, that she could trust unaffectedly, unreservedly, with whom there was no need, or reason, to put on any kind of act.

'Hilda.' He kissed her, and sat down beside her. 'How are you?' he asked kindly. 'How was it?'

'Terrible,' said Hilda, and began to cry.

'Oh, dear.' Tony put his arm round her, comforting and understanding, and Alice, leading Annie, came out of the doorway to the bathroom, saw them, and stopped, and stood watching.

Hilda, not seeing her, went on crying, but couldn't explain, not even to Tony, that it wasn't simply because Stephen had gone and she was tired, and uncomfortable, but because, while everyone else was exclaiming over her baby and his perfection; she herself felt nothing for him at all.

'The only thing that's wrong,' said the night sister calmly, 'is a little bit of post-natal depression.'

'I don't feel depressed,' said Hilda. 'I don't feel anything. That's what's so awful.'

The ward was dark and quiet; apart from her own overhead lamp, beyond the curtains pulled around her bed was only the dim light of the nurses' desk, and most of the mothers were sleeping. Up at the far end, the nursery was brightly lit by neon: Sam had been wheeled up there in his crib, to join the other babies, so that Hilda could rest. She couldn't rest. She had been found sitting in her bedside chair looking blankly at the spot on the opposite wall.

'It's not unusual, you know,' said the sister, who had got her into bed, given her a pill and drawn the curtains. 'You had a difficult labour, didn't you – sometimes it does take a while to love the baby after that.' She was a tall, capable-looking woman, who stood at the end of the bed saying all the right things, but it seemed to Hilda as though she were doing only that – reciting the symptoms of a condition to reassure her patient, because that was what you did, not because she was telling the truth. The truth, Hilda felt, was that she would never love her baby, and that the sister knew this, and inwardly condemned her.

'Were you able to talk to your husband about it?'

She wanted to say: 'I haven't got a bloody husband. How many times do I have to tell you all?' But it felt like another enormous effort, to have to explain all that again, and anyway, she knew they knew. It was easier to fall into line.

'No,' she said tiredly, 'I wasn't.'

'Well, perhaps tomorrow . . . Now you try and get some sleep, and don't worry.'

Hilda took off her glasses, and laid them on the bedside cabinet, next to the plastic water jug and a worn copy of *Baby Child* which Alice had left for her. She herself had brought no baby books, packing in her suitcase *Oscar and Lucinda*: she had imagined lying in her hospital bed and reading, while her beautiful daughter slept beside her.

'When am I going home?'

'We'll see how you get on. Probably another couple of days. Now – sleep! Switch that light off!' The sister went out, leaving the curtains drawn, and Hilda lay listening to her rubber-soled footsteps, walking back to the desk, and the soft rustle of pages in a file of notes. A baby in the nursery began to cry, a door was opened and closed, a lavatory flushed. Then it went quiet again, and Hilda, with her lamp still on, began to feel soothed and safe, cocooned in her little square of curtained room. I am a ship far out at sea, she thought, yawning, a single light in the darkness; I am making a voyage in calm waters. With a tiny part of herself she was aware that this new, unworried state of drowsy contentment had been brought about by the pill the sister had given her; she registered it but did not let it trouble her – it was enough to begin to drift peacefully at last, out across this dark and welcoming sea, leaving on a distant shore the figure of Stephen, walking away, and the baby, who had forgiven her.

'Mrs King? Mrs King? Sorry to wake you, dear . . .'

Beside the bed the small Mauritian night nurse was shaking Hilda's shoulder, gentle but insistent. 'Your baby's crying, he needs a feed. Shall I bring him to you, or do you want to come up to the nursery?'

'I . . .' Hilda turned away, craving to be left alone, to drown in sleep.

'Come on, dear. He has to be fed.'

'Okay. Bring him here.'

The little nurse walked away, and Hilda fell instantly asleep again.

Another night. Two later? Three later? Hilda wasn't sure, but she thought three, and she knew it was half-past two in the morning because there was a large clock on the wall of the neon-lit nursery, where Sam, as every night, was refusing to go down, a phrase with which she had only recently become acquainted but which she felt she had been using all her life. She sat with him on her lap, face down as she jiggled her knees, patting his back and yawning.

The over-heated nursery, with its windows on to the ward, its sweetish smell of disposable nappies, had become an entire world, the only world, a place of panic and safety, crisis and resolution. Whatever happened beyond its walls, and certainly beyond the walls of the hospital, was no longer of interest: everything that mattered, or could ever matter, was played out here, where among the 'ordinary' babies lay one waiting for adoption, and another born with a bloodstream full of heroin; another, two months premature, was in a unit downstairs on a life-support machine. His mother was Bengali, a smiling, sweet-faced, deaf-and-dumb woman, who from time to time stood outside the windows of the nursery, and tapped on the glass. She made gestures to the mothers inside: my baby is very ill; soon he will be better; soon I hope he will come up here, with your nice healthy babies. Hilda and the others nodded and smiled. As life outside was no longer important, so the lack of words did not really matter: everyone knew, everyone understood.

It seemed to Hilda as if she had existed before now in a state of perfect ignorance, not realising that the whole meaning and purpose of life was to be found here and only here, this discovery made even though she still felt numb, and without warmth. She was driven by an exhausted sense of duty, all the more powerful for being without emotion: if I cannot love, I must feign love. When I long for sleep I must hold and comfort and feed, because that is what mothers do. Had she been able to love her baby she might have been able to bring her resentment at this martyrdom to the surface, to say bluntly:

I've had enough, take him away, I need a break. As it was, to have said that would have felt like murder: I don't love him, and I won't look after him. Instead, she was going through the motions, and Sam, at least in the daytime, was doing all right.

She yawned again, and felt him peaceful and floppy now, no longer restless. Cautiously she bent over him, touching his cheek, tensing herself in case he woke and began to cry again. But he didn't, and she carefully put him on to her shoulder and got up, walking slowly back to his crib.

'Gone off now?' asked the nursery night nurse, looking round from the cupboard, where she was tidying vests, and Hilda nodded, gently lowering Sam on to the mattress. There. She'd done it. She tucked the white blanket firmly round him, and straightened up, as tiny Daisy, in the crib beside him, stirred and began to cry.

'What's the matter, flowerpot?' The night nurse closed the cupboard door and came over. She was a large, comfortable Scotswoman with wiry hair and glasses; she patted Daisy with a big red hand, and looked at her chart.

'This little girl needs a feed. Don't you worry, petal, I'll be getting your mother in a moment.' She smiled at Hilda. 'Isn't she a sweetheart? And look, Daisy, here she is already. What a good mum.'

Hilda turned to see the glass door being pushed open, and Jane from the next bed came in, bleary-eyed.

'I heard her crying, I knew it was her. Hello, Daisy, it's all right, I'm here.'

She picked her up and sat on a hard grey chair, opening her nightgown. 'Here we are, then, here we go, that's a good girl.' Jane had bare feet, and wore a man's paisley dressing gown; as Daisy settled into her feed she pushed back fine, tousled hair and smiled at Hilda, sleepily.

'Still here?'

'Just off,' said Hilda. 'He's asleep now.'

'Well done.' Jane yawned. 'I don't think Daisy'll be long, she usually goes straight back. Don't you, Daisy?' She bent over her again, tenderly stroking a creased fist. And she means it all, thought Hilda, watching; she doesn't have to put on an act. How do I know? I just do.

'Do either of you ladies want a cup of tea?' asked the nurse.

Hilda shook her head. 'No, thanks, I'm going back to bed.'

Jane looked up again. 'See you in the morning.'

Hilda nodded. 'Goodnight.' She made her way back down the darkened ward, past the rows of sleeping mothers.

In the morning, at breakfast, Jane said: 'I think we're going home today.'

'Are you?' Hilda sipped her tea. 'You must be pleased.'

Jane nodded, reaching across the Formica table for cold toast. 'Can't wait. It'll be confirmed when they do the rounds, but I'm sure it's okay. They were worried about Daisy's weight, but she's gaining now.' She unpeeled a foil-wrapped rectangle of butter. Hilda watched, wondering about her life. I like you, she thought; you interest me.

'What about you?' Jane asked. 'When're you going?'

'I don't know,' she said. 'I think they're keeping an eye.'

Jane looked up from her toast. 'Why? Sam's doing fine, isn't he?'

'Oh, yes. It's just me –' Hilda broke off, not wanting to explain. 'Anyway,' she said, 'Daisy's two days older, isn't she? So you're bound to be going home earlier.' She picked up the teapot, searching for distraction. 'D'you want another cup?'

'No, thanks.'

At the end of the table the two mothers of second babies, who had found each other early on, pushed back their chairs and went off to the dayroom. Jane said: 'You are all right, aren't you?' She had clear skin and a high colour, always, as if she had a temperature, or had been running.

'Oh, yes,' said Hilda, 'fine.' She pushed back her own chair and got up. 'I'm going to have a bath – this is the one time I know Sam'll sleep. See you later – and good luck. I hope they let you go.'

'Thanks.'

Later, bathed and lying on her bed with the paper and a cup of coffee, Hilda realised she was feeling better. Stronger. Mornings were usually a good time, anyway, full of other people's activity. With Sam sleeping beside her, she watched the doctors come down the ward, bed by bed. She saw them stop by the one occupied by the deaf-and-dumb Bengali woman which was empty, because she was downstairs in the special unit, where her baby had grown much worse. They looked at her chart, and moved on, and when they reached Jane's bed they all smiled, seeing Daisy wide awake, sucking her fist. Everyone loved Daisy. Hilda studied the headlines, not wanting to eavesdrop. A pleasure boat had gone down on the Thames, rammed by a dredger, drowning dozens; Thatcher wondered if there were so many disasters these days because people had more money to spend on leisure. Hilda felt a quickening of anger,

147

and thought: I must be feeling better. Two or three days ago I wouldn't even have been reading this.

The doctors were by her bed, clearing throats.

'And how are you feeling today?'

'Fine, thank you.' She put down the paper. 'When am I going home?'

'Getting restless?'

'A bit.'

'And how's the baby doing?'

'All right, I think. He's very wakeful at night, but . . .' She spread her hands: this was her lot, no problem.

One of the doctors, a woman in her thirties, bent over the crib. 'He's a lovely baby, you're doing very well with him.' She straightened up. 'What about home? What about nights at home?'

No 'Mrs King' now, Hilda noted; this was the time for straight talking. 'I'll manage,' she said.

'Sure?' The doctor touched her shoulder, with a hand which wore a diamond solitaire and a wedding ring. 'It can be a little bit tough on your own. Do you really think you're ready to go?'

Hilda flushed, feeling patronised. 'Yes.'

'And the first few days – the rejection . . .'

'I didn't reject him,' she said coldly. 'I just didn't feel . . . how I thought I was going to feel.'

'And now?'

'Now it's all right,' she said flatly. And all at once the safe, enclosed world of the hospital felt like a prison, where she was forced to tell lies to survive, and be released.

'Okay.' The doctor made a note, and moved away to join the others at the end of the bed. 'You can go home on Saturday,' she said. 'But please – don't hesitate to tell us if you're not feeling well enough, will you?'

'No,' said Hilda, pushing her glasses up her nose. 'Thank you.' Saturday, she thought: how is Stephen going to manage to stay down here that long?

In the afternoon she lay watching Jane, dressed for the first time in a week, packing her suitcase. She wore jeans and a loose T-shirt and gymshoes and had brushed her hair; she looked like a happy schoolgirl.

'Where do you live?' asked Hilda.

Jane snapped shut the suitcase. 'I was going to ask you that. Shall we keep in touch?'

'That would be nice.' Hilda felt in her locker, and wrote the address and phone number in her notebook, tearing out the page.

'Thanks.' Jane looked at it. 'Oh, it's not so far, we're in Abney Road – do you know it?' She wrote the address and telephone number on the back of an envelope. 'Ring me, or I'll ring you. Daisy'd like to play with Sam, wouldn't you, Daisy?'

They looked at each other, and laughed. 'I never thought I'd be so soppy,' said Jane, passing the envelope.

'And here's your chap,' said Hilda. 'Have a nice homecoming.'

'And you.' Jane picked up Daisy, and slipped her into a travelling nest as her husband came up beside her, whistling. He was tall and thin, with cropped fair hair and an earring; Hilda waved as they made their way down to the double doors, and the nurses flocked to say goodbye to Daisy. She picked up the paper again, and tried to read.

'And now,' said the sister, stopping by the bed at tea time. 'I hear you're leaving us too.'

'Yes,' said Hilda, manoeuvring Sam into position for his feed.

'And who is going to be with you? Who's going to see you home?'

'Um – I'm not quite sure at the moment.'

'Someone,' said the sister firmly, 'has got to take you out of here and look after you when you get home.'

'Yes,' said Hilda.

'Move forward a bit,' said Tony, from the bottom of the steps. 'I seem to be cutting off your head. That's it, right, now turn him so we can see his face . . . Okay, smile!' Hilda smiled, and the camera clicked; behind her, she was conscious of Anya, holding open the door, discreetly keeping out of the way. 'And one with Anya,' she said to Tony.

'Of course. Come on, Anya, stop hiding in the shadows.'

'And one with us in,' said Hettie, who was stroking the marmalade cat. 'And the cat.'

'The whole caboodle,' said Tony, stepping back and bumping into Alice, who was holding Annie's hand. 'Sorry, Alice. Okay – one with Anya, one with all of you, and that's it.'

'Then there isn't one with you,' said Annie.

'Never mind. Right – Hilda and Anya. Here we go.'

'I am not at all photogenic,' said Anya, squinting into the sun.

'Do you want to hold him?' Hilda asked. 'Go on – take him.'

'You don't mind?'

149

'Of course not.'

Anya carefully took the sleeping baby, and at once relaxed, smiling down at him. 'You are home, now, Sam.' She straightened the striped cotton vest which had once belonged to Annie. Hilda shook her arms, hot and sticky from holding him all the way home in the car, watching Hettie, who was bending to pick up the cat.

'Hilda – look at me, okay, hold it!' And Tony snapped again. 'Right, now, everyone up the steps!'

A week or so later, Hilda pinned these photographs up on the board in her kitchen, reflecting on how a stranger might see them: Sam and his mother, lovingly cradling him; Sam being held by his grandmother, while his mother stood apart; Sam and his mother and grandmother, aunt and cousins, a united, happy family. And where was Sam's father? Ah, yes – the tall, balding man in glasses, standing close to Hilda, who was holding the baby again, smiling at the camera, the photo taken this time by Alice, at the girls' insistence. 'We must have one with Daddy in!'

There isn't one which tells the truth, she thought, pinning up this last, and then went to Sam, who was fretful.

Months afterwards, when everyone's lives had changed – utterly, irrevocably – she was to look at them again, finding it then all the more painful that it should have been Tony, not Stephen, who had been there to bring her and Sam home, and make it a proper event.

The afternoon sun beat down on the square; even in the shade of the portico the girls were too hot, and the marmalade cat, uncomfortable in Hettie's arms, leapt down and into the cool of the hall.

'Come inside,' said Hilda, trying to manage Sam and her suitcase.

'Here,' said Alice, 'I'll take it. Or shall I take Sam?'

'You take Sam and I'll take the case,' said Tony, behind them all. 'Go on, Annie, move, please, never mind about the cat.'

'Perhaps,' said Anya, as they all trooped inside, 'the children would like to play in the garden. They can have a drink out there.'

'Oh, yes,' said Hettie, and Annie turned to Alice.

'You come, too.'

'All right, just for a minute. Then I'm sure Hilda will want Sam upstairs.' They all followed Anya through the door to her sitting room, where the french windows at the far end stood open, on to the terrace. Hilda and Tony, left in the hall with her camera and suitcase, looked at each other.

'Well,' said Hilda, 'come on up. I'll put the kettle on.'

They slowly climbed the stairs to the top of the house, Hilda leading the way, up the old flower-patterned carpet, past the fading brown photographs in dark frames. She looked at it all again with pleasure, feeding, now she was back, on the thought that there was, in reality, a world outside the hospital which did have meaning, and interest, and nothing to do with babies.

'I'm swinging like a yo-yo,' she said aloud. 'I don't know what I think about anything any more.'

They reached the broad landing, both panting a little. 'Glad to be back though?' asked Tony.

'Very.' But when they climbed the narrower stairs to the attic, and she took out her key to unlock the door, she had a flash of recollection: of doing this the first time Stephen had come here, and she was pierced by a longing for him so powerful that she almost wept.

'Okay?'

'Yes.' She turned the key with difficulty, and pushed open the door.

Inside, the flat was hot and stuffy, and looked like a different place from the one she had left in the middle of the night, barely a week ago. She opened the sitting room windows; she filled the kettle.

'Mind if I help myself?' asked Tony, opening the fridge. 'Is there any juice or anything?'

'I don't know,' she said, lighting the gas. 'Is there?'

'No. Never mind.' He straightened up again, and ran a glass of water. 'Ye gods, it's hot.'

Hilda looked round the little kitchen, wondering what she was going to give everyone for tea; what she was going to have for supper. She supposed she should have taken up Anya's offer to shop, but in the confines of the ward she hadn't been able to think about shopping, and Anya was too tactful to do it without a list. I'll have Weetabix, she thought, if someone will get some milk. God, is there any milk for tea?

Tony drained his glass, and put it down on the worktop. 'You look worried.'

'You couldn't organise a pint of milk, could you? Sorry – I'm just not together yet . . .'

'Of course you're not. It's all right, I'll go and get some. Anything else you want?'

'Probably. I can't think what, that's the trouble.' She wandered out, into the bedroom where Sam's white crib – Hettie and Annie's crib – stood beside the double bed, made up with a clean cotton mattress cover and quilt. That, at least, was ready. She went to the window, and opened it wide, looking down to where the girls stood, somewhat at a loss in this grown-up swingless patch of garden; Alice and Anya were sitting at the table, sipping drinks, admiring Sam. Hilda had seen Alice with a baby so often, and she looked now with Sam so at home that for a weird moment she lost all sense of him as her own child. Perhaps everything that had happened in the past week had happened to someone else, and now she could forget about it, and go back to work.

'Hello, you lot,' she called down, casually, as if all were just as it should be, on an ordinary summer afternoon, with the family visiting. They all looked up, and then Sam began to cry. At once, Hilda felt both the familiar tingling in her breasts and a sensation in the pit of her stomach as if a wire ran between them and he was tugging at it, urgent and desperate.

'Okay,' she called, 'I'm coming,' and found herself running to the door.

'What about nappies?' Tony asked, stepping out of her way. 'Do you want – '

'Oh, God, yes,' she said, stopping. 'I hadn't thought of that, I must be mad.' She could hear Sam's cries, louder and closer, rising to a pitch: Alice must be bringing him into the house.

'Calm down,' he said firmly. 'It's all right, you can't think of everything, you've got enough on your plate.'

Hilda opened the flat door. She could hear Hettie's footsteps, steady and slow, climbing the stairs. 'It's all right,' she called up, sounding just like her father, 'Mummy's bringing Sam.' She came round the corner at the bottom. 'I think he wants some tea.'

'I think we could all do with that,' said Tony, as Sam's cries turned to screams. 'Go on,' he said to Hilda, 'you sort Sam out, and I'll sort out everything else.'

'Thanks,' said Hilda again, unbuttoning her shirt as Alice came up the stairs to the door, making soothing noises. Hilda took Sam from her and went to the chair by the window, where she sat feeding him for what felt like the rest of the afternoon, while around her other people did things.

'You are *still* feeding him?' said Anya, passing round slices of sponge cake.

'He seems to want it,' said Hilda.

'Of course he does,' said Alice. 'He's thirsty, isn't he, in this heat?'

'But perhaps some boiled water,' Anya said. 'Otherwise he will get fat.'

'I haven't got a bottle,' said Hilda. 'Anyway, I'm feeding on demand, now I'm home.'

'On demand,' Anya repeated weightily, and unspoken words about spoiling, and starting as you mean to go on hung in the air.

'I fed Hettie and Annie on demand,' said Alice, a touch defensively.

Anya shook her head doubtfully. 'Liba was fed every four hours; she settled down very quickly.'

'Mummy,' said Annie, tugging at Alice's hand. 'When can we *go?*'

'We're going in a minute,' said Tony, finishing his tea. 'Don't whine, there's a good chap.'

'I'm not a chap. Sam's a chap.'

'So he is. Nice to have another one in the family.' He got up, scratching his head. 'All right now?' he asked Hilda. 'Milk, nappies, bread, butter, fruit juice – that'll tide you over, won't it?'

She nodded. 'You've been wonderful. Thanks.'

'Annie!' snapped Alice. 'Will you please *stop* pulling at me! Come on, Tony.'

They trooped out one by one, saying goodbye. No one kissed Hilda, as if, in feeding Sam, she were doing something so intimate that it was not quite decent to come any closer. Except for Hettie, who came over and patted the top of Sam's head. 'Can I change him?'

'Next time. Bye, Hettie, thanks for coming.'

'Bye.'

'Ring me if you need anything, won't you?' said Alice.

'Oh, yes.'

'Don't you worry,' said Anya, piling the tea things on to a tray. 'I will keep an eye.'

When they had all gone, trooping down the stairs, Sam, at last, stopped sucking. His head fell away from Hilda's breast, his cheeks flushed and damp; he lay in the crook of her arm with his hands half-uncurled, absolutely still, like a doll's hands. She drew a long breath, and leaned back in the chair, feeling a great relief that everyone had gone. Outside, down in the dusty square, she could hear the car doors slam, and Tony starting the engine. Even with the windows wide open it was still stifling up here; she closed her eyes, listening to them drive away.

There were footsteps on the stairs, a tap at the door.

'Hilda?'

'Yes?'

'Let me know if you want anything.'

'I will.'

'Can I cook you some supper?'

'No, thanks. I'll be fine.'

'I'll leave you in peace, then.' Reproachful footsteps down the stairs again; the sound of Anya's sitting room door being closed. Slowly Hilda opened her eyes again, and carefully got out of the chair. She carried Sam into the bedroom, and lowered him into the fresh white crib; she stood looking down at him for a moment, willing him not to wake. He didn't even twitch.

'Good,' she said, 'you stay there. I'm going to have a bath now, I shan't be long.'

While the water was running she undressed and unpacked, putting clean baby clothes into the airing cupboard, her nightdresses and his used vests into the washing machine. Then she went and lay in the bath, swishing the water gently up and down, rejoicing in the peace and stillness of being home again, with no one else's babies, no one waiting to use the bathroom, no more hospital meals. With Sam asleep, the taut, urgent sense of connection slackened, and with it some of the shaming numbness and the guilt. Perhaps it'll be better now we're home, she thought, and sat up, reaching for the bottle of shampoo.

Afterwards, she wandered about in her dressing gown, brushing her damp hair. She made a bowl of Weetabix and grated apple, which was somehow just what she felt like, and ate it watching the news, yawning all the way through. I'd better get some sleep, she thought, when it was finished; I'll change Sam and go to bed. But when she got up and switched off the television the flat seemed suddenly much too quiet, and what had before felt peaceful now felt only empty.

It was growing dark. Hilda crossed the room and drew the curtains; she switched on her desk lamp; she picked up the photograph of her parents and found herself kissing it, with tears in her eyes. I wanted everyone to go, she thought, as she put it down again, and now I want someone to be with me. Not someone – Stephen, that's all. I want him to be here, bringing me a drink in bed; to say that he loves us, to tell me I'll get better, that Sam's going to be all right. I want to go to sleep next to him. Surely, on this one night, he could have managed to stay.

She looked at her watch. Twenty to ten. What did Stephen and Miriam do at twenty to ten? If he's working, she thought, I could ring him, out in the studio. If Miriam answers, I'll just hang up. She reached for her address book, and checked the number; she hesitated, then picked up the telephone and began to dial, her heart beginning to race. With each turn of the dial, it felt as if the numbers were sending out little pulses of light, or like Morse, beating down the wire from an attic room in Hackney to a darkening country lane, a shadowy garden, illuminating the only places on the map which mattered. Norfolk, Woodburgh, Saxham. Stephen's house.

From the bedroom, a cry. Hilda slammed down the phone.

'Okay, okay, I'm coming!'

The bedroom was dark, and beginning to grow cold, with the sudden, surprising chill of summer nights, forgotten in the over-heated ward. She went quickly to the window and closed it, switched on her bedside light and hurried over to the crib. Sam, put down hot and sticky in T-shirt and nappy, covered only with a baby sheet, now felt clammy and cold. The sheet was soaking; so was the mattress.

'Baby, baby . . . I'm sorry, I'm sorry . . .'

She picked him up, peeled off the wet bed things and carried him into the bathroom, flicking on the central heating. She pulled out a towel from the airing cupboard and wrapped him in it, holding him close on her lap, tugging at the tapes on the wet nappy with trembling fingers. He screamed and screamed.

'Poor Sam, never mind, soon be better.'

Visions of chills, fever, pneumonia. She cuddled him, rubbing his back through the towel, easing the wet T-shirt over his head.

'There we are.' She carried him over to the airing cupboard, found a vest, and a little blue sleepsuit, got him into the vest and cleaned him up, but had to leave him, still howling, lying on the changing mat while she struggled to tear open the plastic covering of the pack of disposable nappies. She knelt on the floor beside him, and tugged at it with her teeth. 'Bloody thing.' She crawled over to him, put it on and fastened it with baby lotion still on her hands, so that the tape would not stick down. '*Hell!*' She threw it across the room and tugged out another. In the sitting room the phone began to ring.

With all her visitors seen for the day, who else could it be but Stephen?

'Wait!' called Hilda. '*Wait!*'

She wiped her hands, and did up the second nappy. Sam's feet still felt cold; she eased them into the legs of the sleepsuit and picked him up, fastening poppers as she carried him into the sitting room. If she could get him on the breast and stop him screaming before the phone stopped ringing . . . She pulled open her dressing gown,

155

and Sam's head, his desperate little face almost purple, turned towards her, seeking, yelling.

'Come on, there it is, come on . . .' She was standing in the middle of the room, cradling him, easing his open mouth towards her. Drops of milk splashed on to his face; his lips closed on her nipple and the telephone stopped ringing.

'Oh, no!' Hilda wailed. 'No, no, no!' She stood there weeping, the tears dripping on to her collar as Sam fed greedily, making small sucking noises, undisturbed. After a while, she went to the bathroom, and tore off a piece of toilet paper; she blew her nose, and saw the face of a red-eyed creature, distraught, look back at her from the mirror over the basin.

'Dear me,' she said to Sam, who had fallen off the breast and was drowsy. 'What a sight. Come on, let's call it a day. Stephen will phone tomorrow.'

She carried him out, and switched off all the lights. Back in the bedroom she laid him on the bed while she put clean sheet and coverings into his crib, and then she climbed in and took him in her arms again, to give him the other side. Propped up against the pillows, with the lamp beside her, she found herself, sleepily, begin to feel better. There had been a panic, and she had got through. Her baby was warm, well-fed, soft head nestled in the crook of her arm, the dolls' fingers, so clenched and tense, now limp, relaxed, unfurling. 'All right?' she murmured, and found she was stroking his cheek. 'Better now?' She could feel her eyes begin to close, and reached out to switch off the lamp. I'll put him back in a minute, she thought, and lay down with him close to her, like a lover, and fell asleep.

The weather broke ten days later. Alice and the girls stood out in the garden when the first fat raindrops fell from a bilious sky, spattering the wooden table and the path.

'Come on!' Hettie shouted, tugging off her T-shirt. 'More, more!'

'I'm going to *pull* it down,' said Annie, and clambered on to the table. She stood with her arms upraised like a prophet, hands outstretched towards the grey and yellow clouds. 'Rain! Rain!' But the shower was over in a few minutes, and they went indoors again with damp hair, dispirited. The real downpour did not come for days, and when it did, at tea time, they all jumped up and raced outside.

'Yippee!' Annie yelled. She struggled to pull her cotton dress over her head. 'Get it off!'

Hettie was already out of her shorts and top. She danced down the garden, waving her arms. Alice helped Annie out of her dress, then ran inside, carrying the clothes; she stood at the kitchen window, watching them get soaked, standing on tiptoe with open mouths upturned.

'You come out, too!'

She shook her head. The rain fell faster, beating on to the peonies and drooping roses, bouncing off the parched patch of lawn. Hettie's and Annie's hair clung to their cheeks in thick wet strands. 'That's enough now!' she called. 'Come on in.' They came, bare wet feet leaving prints all over the kitchen floor. 'It's brilliant! It's wicked!'

'I think you'd better have a bath,' said Alice.

Soon after that, the autumn term began. On picture-book mornings, golden and warm, the three of them left the house and walked up the road to school. Hettie had gone up a class; in the corridors they passed new children, searching for their cloakroom pegs, clinging to their mothers as they went in to the nursery or reception class. Beside these little ones Hettie seemed poised and organised, greeting her friends, taking her lunchbox from Alice, calmly kissing her good-bye. She went off without a backward glance. Alice and Annie made their way out again, weaving their way through the boys who came running in from the playground, minutes after the bell, pushing and shoving.

Outside, knots of mothers stood at the gate in the sunshine, with their younger children in prams and pushchairs, discussing the holidays. Among them were au pairs and childminders; the working mothers appeared in the school on open evenings, or at fund-raising meetings, many of them more active in the running of the school than those who, like Alice, brought and collected their children every day. Some of the working mothers managed to do this, too, but they didn't hang around afterwards: down the road, beyond what Alice called the home group, they could be seen walking briskly towards the common, and the tube. There were some, like Yvonne, last encountered in the swimming pool, whose week was a juggling act: dropping off and picking up Rachel and another child two days, swapping with the other mother two days, using a childminder one day. Yvonne did a job-share in a housing association, interviewing and assessing desperate families in bed-and-breakfasts; she was also an active parent-governor and a tireless organiser of weekend outings for Rachel and her friends. She had had only one child out of choice, and had split up with her partner almost at once.

'How was Brittany?' she asked Alice, on the first morning, looking at her watch as they came out of the gate.

'Lovely, thanks. What about you – did you get away?'

'No, but Rachel went down to my parents for a few days, and I had a break, thank God. I must say, I'm glad to be getting back to my own routine, aren't you?'

'Well . . . it's a bit different, with Annie home at lunchtime.'

'Oh, of course, I was thinking she'd started nursery, I suppose it's not till after Christmas.'

'Not till this time next year,' said Alice, shielding her eyes against the sun. On the pavement, Annie was chasing another little girl up and down; traffic approaching the main road slowed for the lollipop lady, then moved off fast.

'Careful, Annie!' Alice called. 'Come away from the kerb.'

'Next *year*,' Yvonne was saying. 'God, it goes on for ever, doesn't it? Of course, Rachel was at day nursery from when she was two. Anyway, I must run. See you.'

'Bye. Come on, Annie.'

Hand in hand they walked up to the common, and across. The first dry leaves from the plane trees swirled gently down to the grass; dogs let off their leads raced up and down or sniffed at and clambered up on each other, panting.

'Why do they do that?' Annie asked.

'They're just getting to know each other. Come on.' Alice, as usual, felt out of sorts after her encounter with Yvonne. She reminds me of Hilda, she thought. I want to admire her – I do admire her, in some ways, for being out there, for caring about issues, for getting things done. But I can't bear her sweeping dismissal of . . . well, of me. She makes me feel as Hilda made me feel, in the old days, before Tony, before the girls: that my life was worthless. In a different way, of course. Then it was because I didn't know what to do with myself, and was afraid of everything. But Yvonne makes me feel it's still worthless. Perhaps it is. Maybe I should have things more important than my children, I expect she thinks I use them to hide away. Perhaps I do. I shouldn't care what she thinks, but I do.

They had reached the other side of the common, and crossed the road to join the other mothers and children, going through the open door of the church hall, where the playgroup met.

'I don't want to go,' said Annie, pulling back.

'It's only because you haven't been for a while. You'll be fine –

158

look, there's Katie.' She waved to a small girl with thick dark hair in a fringe, going through the door with her mother.

'You stay with me.'

'Oh, come on, Annie,' Alice heard herself say, and heard her father saying just the same things, years and years ago. 'Look at Hettie, she went straight back to school without all this fuss.'

There was a silence. Then Annie said: 'I'm not like Hettie.'

'No, I know you're not,' Alice said quickly. 'And you're lovely as you are.' She bent down and gave her a hug. 'But still – you know it's all right really, don't you?'

Annie nodded.

'Good girl. I'll be back at lunchtime, just like last term, remember?'

Annie didn't answer. She let Alice lead her in through the door, and then very deliberately took her hand away, and went to hang her jacket on her old peg, with the picture of an owl above it. Ahead, through the open double doors, Alice could see the playgroup workers waving, and the first arrivals begin to swarm over the climbing frame.

'Right, I'm off,' she said to Annie, and she nodded, and ran into the room.

Trying to be like Hettie? Alice wondered, as she turned and went out again, smiling at the other women coming through the door. Or simply, once she saw it, pleased to be back? She crossed the road again, and walked slowly home over the common.

The weather grew colder, the mornings mistier. Alice dropped off the children and came home again. She cleared up, and made a cup of coffee and took it out into the garden, where she stood surveying the trailing vines, turning a deep, beautiful crimson, the ragged borders and recovering grass. The first garden spiders, speckled and fat, were weaving elaborately from shrub to shrub, and across the shaggy clematis, dropping leaves. Alice got out the leaf rake and the lawnmower and the pruning shears; she swept and mowed and cut back, and piled up a bonfire; she bought bulbs and knelt on an old sack, whole mornings on her knees with a trowel, planting daffodils, crocus, tulips, narcissi. She took out the summer's geraniums from the window boxes and put bulbs in them, too, and carried them all down to the cellar. It began to rain at night, and in the mornings the air smelt fresh; Alice stood looking with satisfaction at the damp earth, freshly planted. She bought bunches of wallflowers and spent hours putting them in along the borders, behind the bulbs.

She did all this partly because it was the first autumn since Hettie was born that she had had a clear run of mornings to herself: this time last year Annie would have been taking all the bulbs out of their bags and muddling them up, pulling leaves off the wallflowers or having a fit if the pruning shears were put out of reach. When Alice and Tony had moved here they'd had no time for the garden; now, with Tony so busy he barely had time to cut the grass, Alice felt as though she were reclaiming it for both of them, after years given to the girls. But it was also more than this. To give the garden new life was both a distraction from and a substitute for what she really wanted: to feel again the new life of a baby inside her, growing, beginning to kick.

And as she snipped and dug and planted, wearing an extra sweater against the mist, she thought about her nephew, out in Anya's garden, soft warm head against her bare arm, the perfect newborn curve of his cheek, the tiny feet in striped socks. His face had begun to screw up with hunger; she had carried him, crying, up the stairs to Hilda, who looked so harassed and drawn and who held him so awkwardly – not like me, thought Alice, I was never like that with Hettie. Thinking this she realised: I do still have an edge; why am I so ungenerous? I thought Hilda as mother would make me feel miserable and inadequate but I think it's she who feels like that. She's in my territory, but I don't need to protect it. It's she who needs protection.

To think of Hilda in this way was so unfamiliar that at first Alice did nothing about it. From time to time she thought of phoning, to see how she and Sam, cocooned in their attic flat, were getting on; each time, she decided against it. Hilda would probably feel she was interfering, patronising, even; also, Alice was afraid of showing too much of the love for Sam which had engulfed her as soon as she bent over his hospital crib. Hilda might find it overwhelming; she herself might find it overwhelming.

Walking up and down her garden, watching the spiders labour in the thinning autumn sun, she found herself wondering: Was my first baby a boy? Was it? Will I ever be able to know? She pictured herself in the surgery, asking the doctor to look through her notes, and seeing him draw across the desk a thick wad of folded papers, all the details of her breakdown, her overdose, the weeks in hospital. She imagined his frown, his unspoken questions: why was this woman resurrecting all this now? Was she building up to something else? No, she thought, I don't think I'll ask.

But the question wouldn't go away. Alice picked up Annie from playgroup; they had lunch together in the kitchen, and afterwards planted a little patch of earth with bulbs just for her. They went to get Hettie from school, and stood at the gate with all the other mothers, with babies in prams. When Hettie came out, swinging her lunchbox and reading folder, often ignoring Annie completely, Alice wondered: wouldn't it do Annie good to have someone smaller? Wouldn't that build up her confidence? She watched her trailing after Hettie as they walked down their road, always following, usually left behind. Hettie doesn't need her, she thought, she's a natural only child. But Annie needs someone, she always has, just as I did. I knew I could never be Hilda, no matter how much I loved her.

At home, the girls watched children's television, sitting on their floor cushions with jam sandwiches and milk. Sometimes Alice watched with them; sometimes, if Tony was due home early, she cooked supper, switching on the lights in the kitchen earlier and earlier as the evenings drew in. From time to time Tony was away, speaking at conferences, a visiting lecturer in law schools all over the country. The rest of the time he was home late, looking weary. Alice could not bring herself to ask, again, about a baby.

Hilda sent copies of the photographs of Sam which Tony had taken the day they came out of hospital. Pinning them up on the board in the kitchen that evening, Alice's thoughts took a new direction, remembering the way she had seen Hilda, in hospital, weep on Tony's shoulder, how he had gone rushing out to the shops for her, carried her case, settled her into her home. No, she thought, standing back and looking at them all again, now I really am being absurd. Tony's like that with everyone. She reached out a finger and touched the picture of Sam, held in her own arms, out in the garden. Hettie had taken that. All I want, she thought, going out of the kitchen, switching off the lights, is one more chance to hold my own baby again. She could hear Tony upstairs in the study, turning pages, dropping files to the floor with a thud; she went into the sitting room, to phone Hilda at last, and thank her for the photographs.

'There we are,' said Hilda. 'In you go. How's that?'

Strapped into his new bouncing chair, Sam looked at her and smiled.

'Like it? Is that fun?'

She pulled him a little closer to the chair by the window and sat down, jiggling him with her foot. Sam smiled again. 'You do like it, don't you? Well, thank God for that. Whole vistas open up before us.' Hilda leaned back in her own chair and stopped jiggling; the corners of Sam's mouth turned down. 'Hey, hey, none of that. You're supposed to be happy in it anyway, not because I'm performing tricks.' She leaned forward and twirled the coloured plastic figures on the bar in front of him. 'There. Have a look at those for a bit. Please, Sam, don't start again now.' Sam's hands flailed at the spinning figures; little bits of plastic rattled inside. He flailed again, intrigued. 'Right, you keep it up. Stephen will be here soon, you can show him.'

She leaned back again, and looked round the room, cleaned and tidied for Stephen's visit, the first for two weeks. The last of the afternoon sun lit her desk, the spines of books, pictures and photographs. She had bought a bunch of hothouse iris this morning, on her daily outing to the shops with Sam; they stood on her desk in a glass vase, and beyond them, through the window, Hilda could see the trees in the square, losing more leaves each day. It's like a piece of haiku, she thought, yawning: 'Winter sun/lights the blue flowers/I am waiting for the sound of the door/my lover's footsteps on the stairs.' She shut her eyes, thinking: That's not right, haiku's much shorter than that. At her feet Sam banged at the little people; they rattled and spun. Outside, down in the square, she could hear women talking on their way to the shops, cars slowing down. Was that Stephen's? She yawned again, feeling herself begin to drift. Sam had woken three times in the night.

A long way away, the sound of a key in a lock, and footsteps. Then, closer, through a thick blanket of cotton wool, Stephen's voice.

'Hello, Sam. Hello. How're you getting on? Mum asleep?'

She opened her eyes to see him squatting beside the bouncing chair, in his long, open raincoat, holding a bunch of flowers, his portfolio on the floor.

'You look like an advertisement for the new man,' she murmured.

Stephen turned to look at her, and at the sight of his steady, smiling eyes, the laugh lines and greying hair she felt a delicious rush of happiness. Usually, after an absence, there were moments, sometimes a disconcerting hour, of unfamiliarity, even coldness, before she could settle into being with him again. Now, she held out her arms. Stephen moved over, the belt of his raincoat brushing the little people on the chair, and she leaned against him, smelling his sweater, the skin on his neck, feeling his hands run through her hair.

'How is my darling?'

'Very well.' She drew away, wanting to look at him again. 'You?'

'Fine. Glad to be here.' Behind him, Sam rattled and bounced. 'How's it going? How is he?'

'He's wonderful,' said Hilda. 'He's wearing me out, but he's wonderful, I feel fine about him now.' She hugged him, kissing his cheek. 'It's so lovely to see you. Would you like some tea?'

'Yes,' said Stephen, 'but I'll get it. You stay there.'

'Oh, what bliss.' She leaned back in the chair again, watching him move about the flat, hanging up his raincoat, putting his overnight bag in the bedroom, putting the kettle on. He came out of the kitchen with his flowers in another vase – more iris, deep, velvety blue. 'Sorry,' he said, putting them on the mantelpiece, seeing hers.

'Not sorry,' she said. 'We like the same things, don't we?'

In his chair, Sam was growing restless, and she bent down and unstrapped him. 'Had enough? Come on, you come on my lap for a bit.' It was growing dark, and she switched on the lamp on her desk. Returning with the tea tray, Stephen put it down and reached up to draw the curtains. 'There,' he said, looking at them both, 'now what could be nicer than this?'

'Nothing,' said Hilda happily. 'Do you want to hold him?'

'In a minute. I'll pour you some tea first. Anyway, I think he's getting hungry, isn't he?'

'He's always hungry,' she said, unbuttoning her shirt. She undid her bra and helped him on to her breast. 'Look at him, what a guzzler. Sometimes I sit here all afternoon.'

'You don't.'

'I do, honestly.' She looked down at Sam, moving his head a little. 'Go on, get comfortable, that's it.' She looked up again. 'Why?' she asked, without thinking. 'Isn't it usual? Didn't – ' and stopped, quickly.

'You must do what's right for you and your baby,' said Stephen easily. 'Isn't that what the books say?' He passed her a blue mug, patterned with birds. 'Can you manage that?'

'Yes, that's fine,' she said, carefully taking it. 'I have terrible visions of scalding tea, but so far – ' She sipped, and the moment, in which the whole of their situation had suddenly entered the room – Stephen's past, Miriam as mother, Jonathan's babyhood – passed, and was not mentioned.

'I've brought the camera,' said Stephen, putting his mug down. 'Stay there, I'll go and get it.'

She watched him go into the bedroom again, thinking: but we'll have to keep all the photos here, he won't be able to have any of us at home, and I'll never be able to send him any.

He was back, unfastening the case. 'Don't pose, just talk to me.' He moved round the room, snapping as she told him about broken nights, outings to the shops, the six-week check.

'I want some of you,' she said, and again thought: but there won't be any of us together. Who's going to take a family snap?

'How's Anya?' Stephen asked, squatting down in front of her.

'Trying not to interfere,' said Hilda. 'Actually, she comes up most days, or I go down sometimes – it keeps me sane. Perhaps I could ask her to take a picture of the three of us.'

'Why not?' The camera flashed again, and Stephen switched it off. 'Good. There should be some nice ones there.' He put it down on the desk. 'Now, what would you like to do tonight?'

'Do?' said Hilda blankly. 'What do you mean?'

He laughed. 'I thought we might ask Anya to babysit. So I could take you out for a meal – would you like that?'

'God,' said Hilda, 'I can't remember the last time I went out at night. It makes me feel quite peculiar.' She thought about leaving Sam with Anya, while she and Stephen set off for a restaurant, and at once pictured him waking, crying, refusing to go back to sleep, needing her. 'I know this sounds very feeble, but I don't think I could. Leave him. I'm sorry.'

'Not even for a couple of hours?'

'Not even for a couple of minutes,' she said ruefully. 'Not yet.' She felt her stomach begin to constrict, feeling nervous and defensive. Was she being silly and fussy? She couldn't help it – the thought of Sam with Anya, refusing to pick him up because it would spoil him, his little face in paroxysms of hunger and despair, made her feel ill. So did the thought of Stephen not understanding, wanting her to be the person she had been before Sam, in that other, long-ago, unrecapturable life.

'Sorry,' she said, and moved Sam on to the other breast.

'Well,' said Stephen, 'we could always take him with us.'

They set out just after seven, Hilda bathed and changed and feeling a mixture of nervousness and excitement. They eased Sam's carrycot into the back of the car, and she sat beside him while Stephen drove them to Church Street. 'How about the Fox?' he asked. 'For old times' sake.'

'It's not called that any more,' said Hilda, 'and it isn't a wine bar, either, it's gone all posh and French.'

'Sam won't mind.' They parked in a side street, and with the baby swinging between them, crossed the road and pushed open the restaurant door. At the sight of the candlelit tables, the air full of the smell of herbs and garlic and hot food, Hilda felt a rush of pleasure. I have been starved, she thought – of good food, of interest, of other people. The world is still here, and one day I shall come back to it. I've come back to it now! She followed Stephen and the waitress to a table at the back of the room, the waitress exclaiming over Sam's downy head on the carrycot pillow.

He slept the whole evening. Stephen and Hilda held hands across the table, and ate and talked, and Hilda felt herself unwind. Everything's all right, she thought contentedly. We love each other, we love Sam – it's going to be fine.

'Is this your first time out?' the waitress asked, pouring their coffee. She nodded. 'It feels wonderful.'

'Must do.' She looked from her to Stephen, clearly seeing him as Hilda's husband, the three of them as a happy little family, and realising this Hilda felt for the first time a flicker of disappointment, the anticipation of Stephen, tomorrow, going again.

'Enjoy it now,' he said, watching her.

'How do you always know what I'm thinking?'

'I just do. It's written all over your face.'

She shook her head. 'I thought I seemed calm and inscrutable.'

'Not any more.'

They paid the bill and left, swinging Sam once more across the road and into the car. It was getting cold; Hilda bent over him, pulling the quilt and blanket up further.

'What a good mother,' said Stephen, unlocking his door. They drove slowly home listening to music on the tape, as people spilled out of the pubs, and babyless cars roared past. Inside the house they passed Anya's closed doors and climbed the stairs, Stephen carrying Sam, Hilda yawning. In bed, with Stephen beside her, holding her, asking nothing of her, being, indeed, everything she could have wished for, she gave a long sigh of contentment.

'Thank you. You're lovely. I love you.'

Stephen drew her closer. 'I love you too. Hilda?'

'Mmm?'

'You wanted a girl. Does it matter now?'

'No,' she said. 'Nothing matters now.'

Beside them, changed and fed once more, Sam slept on. Hilda reached out and switched the light off, and she and Stephen fell asleep in each other's arms, as peacefully as if they did so every night, their baby by their bed, a whole life ahead of them, their future as sealed and assured as the future can ever be.

Next morning, when they had kissed goodbye, Hilda stood at the window, still in her nightdress, with Sam in her arms, as Stephen went down with his bag and portfolio. She watched him wave, and walk along the street to the car, parked several doors along in the only space left last night. She saw him stop dead beside it, and drop his things; craning her neck, she saw a silvery scattering of broken glass on the pavement and Stephen sticking his arm through the gaping hole in the nearside window. He came back, furious.

'They've taken the radio. Bastards! Where's the Yellow Pages? I'm going to have to get someone fast, I'm supposed to be in Regent's Park by ten.'

Hilda found the directory, and watched him run down the columns of windscreen repairers. When he had found one nearby, and slammed down the phone to wait for their arrival, she watched him pace up and down, on edge. Real life, she thought, as Sam began to grizzle, unaccountably restless. Mornings were usually a good time. If she and Stephen were living together, there would be the chance, this evening, of getting over all this, of smoothing things down. As it was, she could only make him coffee and watch him fume, biting back: 'But it's only a radio. And what will happen if you're a bit late for once?' When the repair van at last arrived, hooting down in the square, Stephen picked up his things again and brushed her cheek with his lips.

'Sorry about all this. I'll phone you.'

'When?' she asked quickly, knowing this was not the moment to ask.

'Soon. I must run.'

'Shall I get dressed and come down? Sam might like the air.'

'No, no, don't bother. 'Bye.'

And he was gone, forgetting to kiss the baby, running down the stairs, banging the front door. Hilda stood at the window with Sam on her shoulder, swaying back and forth, while the repair man tapped out the rest of the broken glass and Stephen looked at his watch, and paced, still angry. Months later, she remembered this morning and, recalling the heap of broken glass, evidence of robbery and destruction, wondered if she were being melodramatic in thinking it had been a kind of omen.

*

Nine o'clock. The girls asleep, the curtains drawn hours ago, the house warm and secure. In the sitting room, a fire. In the lamplit kitchen, Alice and Tony, home half an hour ago, finishing supper, about to make coffee, and take it through.

'Do you realise this is the first time we've eaten together all week?'

'It can't be. What's today?' Tony tipped himself back in his chair and rubbed his face.

'Thursday,' said Alice, getting up. She began to clear the table, and put the kettle on. 'You look absolutely exhausted. It's too much for you, all your cases and all these lectures and things.'

Tony yawned, stretching. 'I've got another one next week, in Southampton.'

'Oh, you haven't!' Alice lit the gas and turned to face him. 'That's ridiculous, Tony, it's too much. You'll be ill.'

'No, I won't. Stop getting so indignant and come here.' He stretched out an arm, beckoning. 'Please.'

Alice came and sat on his lap, her arms round his neck, pale silky hair brushing his face. 'Poor Tony. I wish you wouldn't.'

'I'm all right.' He moved his cheek back and forth. 'Mmm.'

'It's not just you, though, is it?' said Alice, drawing away. She looked down at him, pushing his glasses up his nose. 'It's not very fair on us, is it? We miss you.'

'I know. I'm sorry. But that's it till after Christmas – I've said I can't take on any more till January.'

'Good,' said Alice, and got up to switch off the kettle.

'You know,' said Tony, watching her, 'it seems an awfully long time since I heard you say that *you* miss me.'

'I just said it.' She reached up for the coffee jar, and heaped spoonful into the jug.

'No you didn't. You said "we". It's not the same. Sometimes I feel as if Alice has disappeared – she's just part of a "we", with the children.'

'Thanks.'

'But don't you ever feel like that? Lots of women do, don't they? They're afraid of getting lost in their children.'

'Well, I'm not,' said Alice lightly, and put jug and coffee cups on to a tray. 'Shall we go through?'

Tony sighed. 'Okay.'

In the sitting room the fire had gone down; he shovelled on fuel, and poked at it. 'That's better.' He sank into his armchair, stretching

167

his legs before the struggling flames, taking the cup Alice passed him. 'Thanks.'

For a few minutes they sat in silence, as the flames grew stronger, and the fire became a fire again, or as much as it would ever be, with smokeless coal. Then Alice said carefully: 'Tony?'

'Yes?'

'Do you remember what I've been saying?'

'What?'

'About . . . about wanting another baby.'

Tony took off his glasses. He rubbed his eyes, and put the glasses up on the mantelpiece.

'Do you – do you think we could . . .'

He looked at her across the fireside, serious. 'Why? Why, Alice?'

Alice looked away.

'Hilda and Sam?'

'I suppose so. But it started long before he was born, before I even knew she was pregnant. I remember talking about it in the spring, before you went off to Manchester that weekend – remember?'

'No.'

'Well, I did. You know you said just now about losing oneself in one's children – well, I suppose the point is with me that I found myself with mine. Or I lost all the part of myself I didn't like, and couldn't live with. I still feel – as if I'd be nothing without them.'

Tony frowned. 'That's terrible.'

Alice flushed. 'Well, that's how I feel. You know what a mess I was, don't sound so surprised.'

There was another silence. Then Alice said, looking into the fire, 'I thought you knew that. I thought that was the point.'

'What?'

'The point of us . . . being together. That you understood. You're the only one who's ever understood me.'

Across the other side of the fire Tony said quietly: 'Come here.'

'No,' said Alice. 'You come here, if you want.'

He got up, shaking his head. 'She wants a baby and she won't even cross a room for me.' He came over, knelt down in front of her and took her hands. 'Are we growing apart? Is that what you feel? That I'm never here? Do you want a baby to bring us back together?'

Alice looked down at him, at his dear, tired, ordinary face, full of concern for her. 'You're very nice,' she said. 'Too nice. But I want a baby because I want a baby. It's got nothing to do with us.'

'Exactly,' said Tony wryly. 'That's what I thought.'

'You know what I mean.'

'I do. But I don't want another baby, Alice, I want you.' He reached up and turned her face towards him again. 'You. Not Mummy.' He drew her towards him, kneeling up in front of her. 'I want my beautiful Alice, who thinks I have forgotten her in a pile of papers. I haven't, I haven't. I think about you so much, did you know that?' His arms were round her, he was stroking her hair. Beside them, the fire was very warm.

Alice said sadly: 'Don't you love the children?'

'Of course I do. Of course, what do you take me for? But I just don't want any more, is that so terrible? I want us to have time together again. I want to make love to you – just that.' He was drawing her closer, spreading her legs. 'Not for a baby, for itself. For us.'

Alice put her arms round him, her head on his shoulder, burying her face in her hair. Shall I tell him? she asked herself. Shall I tell him, now, what I blurted out to Hilda in the spring? Why on earth did I do that? She could hear Hilda's voice, sensible, reasonable: 'But why don't you explain to him, Alice? It's not as if he's insensitive . . .' Was that what she'd said?

'Yes?' Tony's hands were beneath her sweater, loving and warm. 'What are you thinking about?'

'Nothing,' said Alice, wondering: What am I so afraid of? Do I really trust him so little, after all these years? Do I really believe that if I say to him: Tony, I love you in my way, and I need you, but actually you leave me cold, then he will stop loving me, and go? Yes, she thought, I suppose that's exactly what I believe. And, after all, I've lived with this for so long, I've grown so used to it – what does it matter, now?

'Look at me,' said Tony, kissing her hair.

Alice drew away from his shoulder and looked, meeting his gentle, tender eyes, and looked away again. She said: 'I want to tell you something, but I daren't.'

'Sounds just like the old days,' said Tony, and then: 'It's all right, I'm teasing. Tell me. Please.'

'It's just – ' said Alice, and the phone began to ring. She made to move towards it, quickly. 'I'll get it.'

He shook his head, releasing her, getting to his feet. 'I'd better, it might be Robin, he's in court tomorrow. I said he could ring if he wanted.'

'Robin?' said Alice, pulling down her sweater.

'The new articled clerk, I thought I'd told you about him.' He reached for the phone, shaking his head at her. 'I did tell you, I know I did. Hello? Oh, hello, Hilda, how nice to hear you.'

Tony would say it was nice to hear the bailiffs, thought Alice, and picked up her coffee again. It was almost cold. She sipped at it absently, listening to Tony's kind enquiries about Sam's progress, answering Hilda's questions about his work as calmly and straight-forwardly as if she had simply interrupted him doing the crossword, and nothing mattered more than that he should give her his attention. He must be like this with his clients, no wonder he was so much in demand.

He reached for his coffee and sat down. Alice thought: this could go on all night, and then, hearing him describe the lecture on the new Children Act he was preparing for Southampton: it really could. He's not just talking to any old fool, being polite, they genuinely have something to say to each other. Hilda likes hearing about his work, much more than I do; she probably understands it all much better, too.

She had a sudden image of Hilda in a classroom, Sam on her lap, running a seminar. She was perfectly capable of it. And at once there came unbidden memories: Hilda and their father, heads close together over homework after school, sitting at his big desk in the study, talking quietly, absorbed. And another: ten-year-old Alice, struggling with maths, the note of impatience in her father's voice as he tried to explain; her tears, her bolt from the room to the stairs, banging doors. 'I'll never be clever! I'll never be clever! I *hate* school!' And fourteen-year-old Hilda, coming out on to the landing, coolly annoyed. 'What's all this fuss? I'm trying to work.' There had been many such scenes, and remembering them now, horribly vivid, Alice felt just the same misery, and sense of uselessness – compounded, not helped, by her mother, who had so clearly felt it a waste of time for her father to bother. 'She'll be a nurse or something, darling, why don't you leave her alone?' She hadn't wanted to be a nurse or something; she'd wanted to be bright, like Hilda.

Tony was laughing; she came back to the room with a jolt. Hilda had, presumably, rung in the first place to speak to her, for baby talk. Or had she? Perhaps the last thing she wanted to talk about was babies, perhaps she was only too glad to find Tony on the other end of the phone, and talk about something quite different. Possibly Tony, too, found it a relief to talk to a woman who wanted nothing from him. She got up, and went out to the kitchen, and again, as

170

when she had stood looking at the photographs of Sam's homecoming, she felt the sharp slivers of doubt, and speculation, and mistrust.

The telephone pinged; Tony was calling her. 'Hilda sends her love. Are you coming back?'

'In a minute.' But she didn't go back, she began to do the washing-up, and after a few minutes he appeared in the doorway.

'You were going to tell me something.'

'It doesn't matter, it wasn't important.'

'I don't believe you,' said Tony, but he didn't ask again.

The last leaves were falling in the square. The milk came late, the post came later, and then the clocks went back. Hilda wrapped Sam up in double layers on their daily outings. She tucked him into the pram in the hall, and bumped him down the front steps, watched by Anya.

'It is very cold now, Hilda, I hope he has enough things on.'

'He has, don't worry. Can I get you anything from the shops?'

Sometimes Anya said no; sometimes she said that she would like a breath of air too, and had quite a few things on her list – if Hilda would wait just a moment, she would come with her. Then they would set off together, Anya in brown coat and gloves, lined boots and knitted hat, cooing to Sam in grandmotherly fashion. Hilda suspected her of lying in wait, coat and boots at the ready, and there were mornings when she dreaded coming downstairs, in case this were a day when Anya would decide to accompany her. She felt ungrateful – after all, it was kind to let the pram stand in the hall; nonetheless, she simply did not want always to feel a sense of obligation, to have to listen to Anya's views on bringing up a baby as they made their way down the cracked pavements and up to the High Street. If I had Stephen with me all the time I probably wouldn't even notice it, she thought; it was the fact that Anya, not he, was her daily companion that irked. But Stephen came only once a week, sometimes not even that, and did not always stay. Occasionally Anya asked questions, and made remarks.

'When is he coming to see you again? I am sure he must be very proud of his little boy.' Once, unforgivably, she leaned into the pram and said: 'Do you like it when your Daddy comes? He is a lucky chap to have such a good little son.'

'I hope,' Hilda said coldly, 'that you won't talk to Sam like this when he gets older.'

Anya flushed, and apologised. 'You must understand, Hilda, that it is very pleasing to me to have a baby in the house again. Sometimes I say things without thinking.' She sighed. 'Of course, I should love to have a grandchild of my own, but . . .'

Hilda said nothing. From time to time Anya's daughter came to stay for the weekend; more rarely, Anya went to stay with her, in Brighton, where she taught science in a private girls' school. Liba was a large, uncompromising-looking woman in brown-rimmed spectacles that made Hilda's look almost frivolous. She had shown no interest in Hilda when she moved in, and now showed even less in Sam. She spoke brusquely to her mother, as if Anya were deaf, or not quite all there; she did, however, seem to like the cats. It seemed unlikely that she would ever give Anya a grandchild.

They were approaching the chemist, where Hilda had to buy nappies and baby lotion. She said to Anya: 'If you don't mind, I think I'll leave you here. I'll see you later.'

'Please, Hilda, don't take offence. I didn't mean – '

'I know. I just feel like being by myself for a little while, that's all.'

'You are by yourself too much,' said Anya, and bit her lip. 'I am making things even worse. Forgive me.'

'It's all right,' said Hilda, feeling sorry for her. 'Forget it. Come up and have tea with us this afternoon.'

'Thank you,' said Anya, with dignity. 'I will look forward to it.' She patted the pram and walked away, a small, hedgehog-like figure making her way slowly through the shoppers. Hilda turned with relief to the chemist, parking the pram at the door.

Afterwards, she walked Sam to the park. It was getting colder, and damp, and there was nothing for either of them, really, to do there. I expect next year we'll be here all the time, she thought, hearing cries from the playground, and pushed the pram over to the animal enclosure, propping Sam up so that he could see the rabbits, and the deer. Bantams scratched at the bare earth, disdaining cabbage stalks pushed by toddlers through the rusty netting; a peacock strutted and shrieked, suddenly spreading his tail.

'Look, Sam, isn't that wonderful?'

But Sam was too young to look, the rabbits and guinea pigs were lost on him, and Hilda began to feel bleak, standing in the cold, talking to an unresponsive baby. Next year they might be feeding the ducks, pushing bread and lettuce through the netting for the animals, having a little go on the swings. But next year seemed like a century away, and what were they going to do now? God, thought

Hilda, turning up her collar, how am I going to get through this winter?

A couple was approaching from the other side of the bridge on the stream, also with a pram, old and roomy. He was tall, wearing a long knitted scarf and Doc Martens, she was thin and fair, her cheeks red in the cold, pushing the pram with hands in striped woollen gloves. They looked very young, very Hackney; as they drew closer, they also looked familiar. They stopped on the bridge and threw down bread for the ducks from a plastic carrier bag; their breath streamed in the air. Hilda frowned, trying to place them. Then, as they moved on towards her, the woman waved.

'Hello, I thought it was you.' She came up alongside, and bent over Sam. 'Hello, Sam. Gosh, he's enormous!'

Hilda looked into Jane's battered old pram and smiled, seeing tiny Daisy fast asleep beneath a blanket of knitted squares. 'Daisy would make anyone look enormous. Isn't she lovely? How are you?'

'We're fine,' said Jane. 'She's really good, really easy.' Daisy's father came up beside them, smiling, unobtrusive. 'Did you meet Don?' Jane asked. 'Don – Hilda. From hospital. And Sam.'

He smiled 'Hi. Hello, Sam.'

Don was, Hilda saw instantly, the complete new man: helpful and considerate on principle, easygoing, pleased to take a back seat and talk to babies. Stephen, bending over Sam in his expensive raincoat, might look like the advertisement – this was the real thing. And he was different again from Tony, also kind and unselfish: Tony had an edge to him, fought battles where necessary. Don, Hilda felt, had no edge.

'I've been meaning to ring you,' said Jane. 'I've been wondering how you were getting on.'

'Yes,' Hilda said. 'Me, too.' She shook her head, making a face. 'I'm really glad to see you; I was just beginning to feel a bit desperate.' And was amazed at herself: when, ever, before Sam, would she have told someone she barely knew how she was feeling?

'Oh, I know,' said Jane. 'You can get like that, can't you? I mean, Daisy's really good, but even so . . . sometimes Don has to take over, or I'd go mad.'

There was an awkward little pause, in which unspoken questions and answers about who took over when Hilda felt like that hung in the misty air. Don smiled, self-deprecating, understanding. Then Jane said: 'Why don't you come back and have a coffee?'

'Well, I . . .' More words unspoken – being in the way, intruding on a family morning, feeling desperate and in need of rescue.

'Oh, go on. Don's on his way to sign on, that's why we're here, he's got to go down to the Job Centre. So it'll be just us and the babies.'

'Okay,' said Hilda. 'Thanks, I'd love to.' She watched Jane and Don saying their goodbyes; he bent into the pram and waggled his fingers. 'Bye, Daisy, see you later.' He straightened up. 'Bye, Hilda, Sam.' And then he was gone, long legs striding down the path past the bowling green. Hilda and Jane pushed their prams back over the bridge, and out of the park.

'Are you on maternity leave?' asked Jane.

'Yes, I'm going back at the end of January.' Hilda shook her head again, wonderingly. 'Sometimes I really look forward to it – like today, I was just beginning to think I really needed something apart from Sam. But also – it seems years since I was teaching. I feel as if I've forgotten everything.' They had reached the main road, and weaved the prams in and out among the shoppers, and other prams and pushchairs, the wandering unemployed, and unattached. 'What about you?' she asked, as they stood waiting to cross. 'Are you going back to work?'

'Depends what happens to Don,' said Jane. 'He's a gardener, but there's not much private work in the winter. He's trying for a job with the council in the parks.'

She brushed her fine hair off her face in the gesture Hilda had seen many times in hospital. The intensity of those few days seemed also, now, to belong to another age. The traffic slowed, and they hurried across; Sam began to grizzle.

'Not far now,' said Jane, speeding up. 'I expect they're both a bit cold.'

'And hungry,' said Hilda. 'Sam's always hungry.'

Jane laughed. 'Yes, I can remember.' And though it was said with nothing but affection, Hilda felt at once the same prickle of defensiveness which came with Alice, with Anya, with anyone who indicated for even a moment that Sam was anything but perfect. I've never felt like this before in my life, she thought, as Sam's grizzles grew more insistent, and remembered her last class with her group of Asian women. I was right: once you're a mother you're out in public; everyone feels they can put their oar in, and it *matters*. I wouldn't have thought it possible to be so raw.

'Just down here,' said Jane, turning into a side street. They stopped outside a green front door, and she got out her keys. They left the prams outside, and Hilda picked up Sam, in full voice now, and carried him down a narrow hall with a bike in it.

'Sorry about the mess. Come on, we're down here.' Jane led them past the bottom of the stairs and into a cluttered kitchen overlooking a square of garden. She pushed a ginger cat, just like Anya's, off a high-backed chair, and said kindly: 'You go ahead and feed. I'll put the kettle on.'

'Wonderful.' Hilda, still in her coat, sat on a cushion covered in cat hairs, and unbuttoned herself. 'Come on, Sam, here we go.' He plugged in and she sat looking around, watching Jane, Daisy on her arm, fill the kettle and switch on the gas.

'I never thought you could do so much with one hand, did you?'

'Never,' said Jane. 'I made an omelette like this the other night. Come on, Daisy, I expect you're hungry, too.' She hung her jacket on the back of a chair and sat down, pulling up a charity-shop sweater. Daisy began to whimper and pant. 'There you are, there you are, darling.' She eased herself back against the chair, as her daughter began to suck. Used to Sam's ravenous guzzling, Daisy's feeding seemed to Hilda like delicate sips. Had Hettie and Annie been like that? She couldn't remember and, anyway, how could she really have known? Watching them she found herself thinking: Jane reminds me a little of Alice, perhaps that's why I found her interesting in hospital. I suppose it's just the way she looks, fair and a bit delicate; but the atmosphere felt companionable, as if they'd been friends for a long time, and she thought: I never feel like this with Alice. She heard herself saying:

'Tell me the story of your life.'

Jane laughed. 'There's an invitation.' Footsteps sounded, coming down the stairs into the hall. 'That's Phil. He's staying.'

An enormous young man came into the kitchen, looking rumpled and recently asleep. 'Hi.'

'Hi, Phil, this is Hilda and Sam. Make us some coffee, will you?'

'Sure.' He switched off the boiling kettle and spooned instant coffee into mugs from the draining board, leaving the top off the jar. 'How do you like it, Hilda?'

'White, no sugar, please.' Hilda, watching, felt as if she had recently landed from a far-off planet, and was blocking the kitchen. I don't belong here, I'm light years older, she thought, even if the babies are only days apart. I do not belong in a communal house, where people sign on and get up at lunchtime – but then, I never have. And thinking all this, she felt taken back to the old days, before Sam, before Stephen, when Alice had lived a life which was extravagantly dissolute – apparently unhappy but, nonetheless, a life of feeling – while Hilda had done nothing but work and told herself that feelings were not important. Now – they were everything.

'The. ⸱ we go.' Phil put down two red mugs which looked as if they could have done with a second, more rigorous, wash and went to make toast. 'Anyone else want some? I could do you both cheese on toast, if you like. Nursing mothers, and all that.'

'Why not?' said Jane. 'Hilda?'

'Well . . .'

'Oh, go on. And then go away, Phil, all right? We want to talk.'

'I'm going anyway,' he said, putting bread under the grill. The cat wound itself round his legs. 'Anyone fed this poor beast?'

'I did,' said Jane. 'Just because Daisy's here doesn't mean I'd let the cat starve. Have you got a cat?' she asked Hilda.

'No,' said Hilda, 'but Anya has two, they're her babies.'

'Who's Anya?'

Hilda explained, and found herself also describing the conversation they'd had this morning, on the way to the shops, and thus explaining, too, her situation with – or rather, mostly, without – Stephen. Phil put down a large plate of cheese on toast, and left, taking his with him.

'Bye, Hilda, bye Sam.'

'Goodbye,' said Hilda, easing the baby away from her. 'Thanks.' She laid Sam, now fast asleep, in the crook of her arm, and helped herself to toast, suddenly ravenous. 'Well,' she said to Jane, 'I asked you about your life and told you about mine.'

'Good,' said Jane. 'I was wondering. I remember Stephen, from the hospital; he's very good-looking, isn't he?'

'Yes,' said Hilda, trying, and failing, to bring Stephen into this room, this house. Tony would find it interesting, she thought: he comes into contact with all sorts of people, he enjoys it.

'His wife doesn't know?' said Jane.

'Whose wife?'

'How many fathers has Sam got?'

Hilda looked at her. 'I was miles away for a minute, sorry. I was thinking about someone else. No, she doesn't. Of course she doesn't.' She looked away, and beyond the table to the window on to the garden. Bluetits and sparrows were feeding from a bag of nuts hung from the branch of a ragged elder. If you ignored the tower block of

176

flats rising to the damp grey sky behind, it was almost like the country, where Miriam lived with Stephen. 'At least,' she said slowly, 'I'm pretty sure she doesn't. I try not to think about her, to be honest.'

There was a pause, in which she looked back at Jane, still feeding Daisy, whose little sips went on for ever. 'What about you and Don?'

'The story of my life,' said Jane, taking another slice of toast. 'We met at school, can you believe it? We've been together for seven years. But we only got married when I was expecting Daisy, and that was really just for the parents. I don't think we'd have bothered otherwise. Well . . . perhaps we would, I think once we actually saw Daisy we would've, anyway. Everything changes with a baby, doesn't it? Overnight.'

'Yes,' said Hilda, and fell silent again.

'In the hospital,' said Jane, 'I thought you were . . . disappointed. Do you mind me saying that? Everyone else looked fine – you know, tired and weepy, but buoyed up. You looked much more together than anyone else, but there was something missing. I thought you'd got post-natal depression.'

'That's what the nurses said. I suppose I had. I wanted a girl. I couldn't believe it when he wasn't, and I couldn't . . . love him; I couldn't feel anything. Except guilt. Plenty of that.'

'Is it all right now?' Jane asked carefully, and Hilda said: 'Yes. Yes, it's fine now. Only this morning, in the park – I got frightened because I thought it was all coming back. I felt . . . cut-off, I suppose.' She felt a lump rise in her throat and put down the slice of toast.

Jane reached out and touched her arm. 'Listen,' she said, 'if ever you feel low, you can always come over, you know. Or I'll come to you. Just give us a ring.'

'Thank you.' Hilda tried to swallow the lump away. From upstairs music thumped through the ceiling; outside the sky was darkening for the afternoon. Jane leaned over and switched on the table lamp. 'Have another coffee.'

Hilda shook her head. 'No, thanks, I ought to be going.'

'Why?'

'Well . . . I just don't want to linger, that's all.'

'Oh, shut up. Go on, have another. I'll put the kettle on.' She got up, carrying Daisy, asleep now, too. 'Someone told me the other day to make the most of the sleepy stage. I can't imagine them crawling about, can you?'

Hilda shook her head. While Jane went to put Daisy in her cot, she looked again round the kitchen, at the plants on the windowsill and on top of the secondhand fridge, the noticeboard which resembled the board from the concourse at college, full of community care. The cork tiles on the floor were scuffed and worn, like the cat, who sat at the door to the garden, waiting to be let out. 'Come on, then,' said Hilda, getting up with Sam in her arms, needing something to do. She unlocked the door and watched the cat, tail erect, walk down the concrete path at the side of the grass. It was very cold, too cold for Sam. She closed the door again, hearing a lot of noise in the hall. When Jane came back, she said: 'I've put Daisy down upstairs, and brought the prams in. D'you want to change Sam in the bathroom and put him down too?'

Hilda changed Sam on the floor of a large cold bathroom with more scuffed floor tiles and a shelf full of paperbacks on astrology and alternative medicine. Then she went down again, and tucked him into his pram. She hung up her coat in the hall, among a dozen others, and went back to the kitchen, hearing a sudden, welcome leap from the boiler, as the heating came on.

'I've made a pot of tea,' said Jane. 'And I've found some chocolate digestives. Let's forget about the babies and being mothers for a bit.'

Hilda shook her arms, which were almost numb. 'What a treat.'

They sat at the table and talked for the rest of the afternoon. Out in the hall, and upstairs, the babies slept on; beyond the kitchen window the sky grew dark, with a flurry of rain. The throbbing music from upstairs stopped, and Phil went out, banging the front door, but Sam did not wake until much later, when Don came home, pushing through the hall with a bag of shopping. He came into the kitchen and pulled off a wet woollen hat, dumping the bag on the floor.

'My God,' said Hilda, hearing whimpers, 'what time is it?'

'I think it's about five.' He put his hat on the radiator, kissed Jane, and filled the kettle. 'Had a nice afternoon?'

'Lovely,' said Jane.

'But I must go,' Hilda said, getting up. 'I'd no idea it was so late. All right, Sam, I'm coming!'

'Feed him here, before you go,' Jane suggested as Sam's cries grew louder.

So Hilda stayed, feeling both comforted and excluded, watching Don unpack shopping, make himself a cup of tea and sit at the table rolling a joint as Jane went upstairs to fetch Daisy, who had also woken. Don made no attempt at conversation, and Hilda, who could think of nothing to say to him, found the silence between them, bridged by Sam's eager feeding, perfectly acceptable. When she left, she and Jane hugged each other.

'It's been lovely, thanks so much.'

'Come again.' Jane had left Daisy with Don; she stood on the doorstep, watching Hilda click open the gate and wheel the pram through, pulling the hood up. It was very cold, the street lamps shining on to the wet pavement.

'See you.'

'See you,' said Hilda. 'Go back inside! It's freezing.' She turned up her collar again, as Jane closed the door, and began to walk, talking to Sam, peaceful now but wide awake. 'Well, we seem to have made friends. What did you think of Daisy? This time next year you'll be toddling about together in the park.' The dismal morning spent there, out in the cold, seemed already a long time ago, the creeping loneliness banished. It returned almost as soon as she reached home.

'Oh, my God,' she said, stopping at the foot of the steps. 'Anya was supposed to come up this afternoon.' Sitting in Jane's comfortable kitchen she had forgotten all about Anya. She stood for a moment looking up at the darkened house, the curtains drawn, all at once longing for the door to open wide, and Stephen to be there, welcoming her home. Well, he wasn't. She turned and began to pull the pram backwards up the steps, bumping and grunting. 'Sorry, Sam.' Perhaps she should start by taking him out first, but then she'd have to leave him alone upstairs while she came back down to bring the pram in. A wheel banged against her foot and she swore as the pack of nappies slid from the shopping tray and tumbled down the steps. Behind her the door swung open, and a cat shot out.

'Hilda, I've been worried.' Low-watt light spilled out from the hall. 'Let me help you.'

'It's all right, I've done it now.' Hilda dragged the pram back over the last step, and bumped Anya's sturdy body, just behind her. 'Sorry,' she said, and again thought bitterly: why the hell aren't you Stephen? I don't *want* you hovering round me. She pulled the pram into its place in the hall, and put the brake on. 'I'm sorry about this afternoon,' she said to the air, as she went out again, running down the steps for the nappies. 'I met a friend.'

'It's quite all right,' said Anya, as she came back, and closed the front door after her, bending to slide the bolts as Hilda lifted Sam out. 'I was only worried that something might have happened to you.' She straightened up again stiffly. 'Does your friend have a baby, too?'

'Yes,' said Hilda, and added unkindly: 'Why?' as if Anya had no right or reason to ask.

'I . . .' Anya faltered, 'I was just interested, that's all.'

'We met in hospital.' Hilda turned to go up the stairs. 'She was in the next bed, you might remember her.' She could hear herself sound cold and rude. 'Excuse me,' she said, 'I'm tired. Come up another time, all right?'

'Yes,' said Anya. 'Goodnight, Hilda. Goodnight, Sam.' She crossed the faded rug to her sitting room door, and went inside, closing it slowly behind her.

Hilda climbed the stairs with Sam and her bag and the nappies, feeling it all grow heavier and heavier. At the top she fumbled wearily for the keys: how was she going to manage as Sam grew bigger still? She let herself into the dark empty flat, switching on lights, bath taps, the television, drawing the curtains – doing it all quickly, although she was exhausted now, so that the place could come alive again.

She bathed Sam, dressed him for bed and left him to kick on his playmat while she cooked spaghetti and ate it watching *This Week*. She fed him and put him down in his crib and left him to cry there, closing the door and pacing in the sitting room until he fell asleep. Asleep, or dead? As every night, she checked him, kissing his warm wet cheek, listening to the tiny thread of breath, feeling her anxiety subside. Then she ran a bath and lay listening to *The World Tonight*; she got into her pyjamas and switched off the radio, going back into the sitting room to tidy up.

The room was littered with Sam's toys, bought mostly by herself in desperate moments on the High Street. She bent to clear them away, and picked up a red musical rabbit, whose paws clicked back and forth. Stephen had bought that. The string was caught on the edge of the bouncing chair; as she lifted it, it began to wind itself up again, and the room was suddenly filled with the tinkling of *Frère Jacques*. Hilda had heard it a hundred times, a merry little tune; now, standing alone in the middle of the warm room, it sounded plaintive and thin, unbearably sad.

She stood holding the rabbit until the string had wound slowly up to the end, and the tune was over. The room was quiet; the whole house was quiet. Down in the square two youths went by, laughing until they rounded the corner and their voices faded. Hilda went to the rocking chair by the window, and sat there thinking about Jane and Don and Daisy, all together in their worn, untidy house, with Phil coming and going; about Alice and Tony and the girls, especially Hettie, who looked like her, and whom, until Sam, Hilda had loved more than any child. And she thought about Stephen and Miriam, together in their house in Norfolk with their tall, good-looking son, whom Stephen was never going to leave.

What were they all doing now?

Hilda looked at her watch. It was after eleven. She saw herself sitting alone in her rocking chair, falling prey to self-pity, and pictured a winter full of such evenings, alone with Sam, wanting Stephen. She reached for the telephone, dialling his number once again. The line clicked, and her heart began to race; there was a pause, a silence that seemed to go on for ever, and then the ringing tone sounded. Hilda sat absolutely still, the blood pumping in her throat, listening to the two insistent notes ringing repeatedly, two hundred miles away. Where was the phone in Stephen's house? The kitchen? The sitting room? If he was out in the studio, why didn't he answer?

At last, a woman's voice.

'Hello?' Sleepy, rather hoarse.

'Hello?' Puzzled, an edge of nervousness. Was she, also, alone? A dark house in a quiet country lane; an autumn night, windy and cold.

'Hello? Jonathan? Is that you?' Frightened now.

Hilda put down the phone.

5

The evenings had drawn in and the mornings, too, were dark; Miriam, who had slept badly, woke to hear rain falling against the window, pattering on to the leaves which were blocking the gutter. Stephen had been too busy and too often away to get up there and unblock it, but someone was going to have to. Perhaps she and Jon could do it on Sunday. She lay, her head uncomfortably heavy on the pillow, still half-asleep, picturing Jon's tall figure at the top of the ladder, herself at the bottom, holding it on wet grass; she was looking up at Jon, leaning precariously into the gutter, at the mossy tiles and rainwashed morning sky above him, and she shifted her position on the shining grass and slipped, jerking the ladder, hearing – no! – Jon's sudden shout and then his fall, unstoppable, eternal, and silence.

Miriam's body was shot through with one of the spasms she some-times had between sleeping and waking, limbs jerked out, heart missing beats. But she was fully awake now, her hands clammy, mouth dry, remembering the phone call, and the sleepless hour that had followed, lying in wait for the sound of the motorbike, coming back from Woodburgh, where Jon had been visiting Mike Baldry. Well after midnight, the roar up the lane – too fast, too fast! – the single beam of the headlight in the rain, the slowing down, engine off, footsteps up the path, and creak of the garage doors. Thank God. More footsteps, his key in the lock.

'Jon?'

She stood at the top of the stairs, shivering in her kimono, trying to sound ordinary, calm.

'Had a good time?'

'Yes, thanks.' His black leather gear was soaking, his hair plastered down by trickles of rain and his helmet; he had eased it off and was holding it, letting it drip on the mat.

'You should have a hot bath.'

'I'm going to.' He wiped his feet. 'Why're you up? There's no need.'

'I know, but – ' She came down the stairs, pulling the kimono round her, hesitating. 'There was a phone call . . . I thought it was you.'

Jonathan frowned, moving towards the kitchen. 'No. Where's Dad?'

'He's having dinner with the Sadlers.' She followed him down the passage. 'He said he'd be back late.'

'Oh.' He clicked on the light in the kitchen, and bent to pat Tess, old and grey round the muzzle, who had got up stiffly from her basket to greet him. 'Hello, girl, hello.' He moved the kettle on to the hotplate, and began to take off his jacket, snapping open the stud. 'Why didn't you go?'

'I didn't feel like it, they didn't mind – they're talking work anyway, they want Dad to do a conversion of the stable block, I think.' She yawned, shifting on bare feet. 'He'll be home soon, I'm going back to bed.'

'Shall I make you a drink?' Jon had peeled off his jacket, and was sitting down, easing his feet out of his boots. 'A nice cup of Ovaltine?' He waggled his toes and grinned up at her and she smiled back, filled with relief – that he was home, that they were friends.

'No thanks, you make me feel a hundred.' She bent to kiss the dark flattened hair. 'Want me to run your bath?'

'You could do.'

'Don't let it get cold.'

'Cluck, cluck, cluck. I won't.'

'Night, darling.'

'Night, Mum.'

Upstairs, she lay listening to the sounds of the bath filling up, Jon climbing the stairs to turn it off just in time, closing the door. She listened, too, for Stephen, but though one or two other cars swished past the end of the lane, he did not come. Who has he found to entertain him this evening? she wondered, and wondered again, uneasily, about the phone call. Who could it be?

Who else could it be?

On the borderland of sleep Miriam saw again the steady and unsmiling face of the woman in the photograph, gazing coolly out at the world through her wire-rimmed spectacles. A woman in control, capable, competent.

Why start phoning now?

Drifting into a troubled dream she heard, magnified, the sounds of Jon going to his room, and Stephen's car, the garage doors, the front door. By the time he came quietly up the stairs the dream had taken her.

Now, she could not remember any of it. She lay waiting for the panic, the image of Jon, sprawled on the ground by the fallen ladder, to subside and fade. The rain fell steadily, soothing now; beside her the bedclothes had been turned back, and she could hear Stephen coming up the stairs with the tea tray – the perfect husband, easing her into the day. What day was it?

He set the tray down on the bedside table, and crossed the room to the windows, drawing the curtains. She lay watching him in his dressing gown looking out at the falling rain, the slowly lightening sky above the trees. What was he thinking about? What did Stephen ever think about? She could hear Jon downstairs, banging cupboards in the kitchen; it must be getting late.

'Stephen?'

'Mmm?' He turned from the window, solicitous. From somewhere, probably a television play, she heard a Cockney voice say firmly: I don't want no trouble.

'Sleep well?' He came over and poured out the tea, passing her a cup, not touching her.

'Not very. Thanks.' She took the cup and sat up, propping herself against the pillows. 'What time did you come back?'

'Oh, about midnight. You were flat out.' He took off his dressing gown and pyjamas and began to dress, rapidly, a man in a hurry, searching among piles of ironed shirts in his chest of drawers for the right one, and the right tie.

'Stephen?'

'Mmm?'

She was going to say: The gutter's blocked. Instead: 'Someone rang last night.'

'Oh?' He was standing in front of the mirror, doing his tie, his back to her. 'Who?'

'I don't know. It rang, but no one spoke.'

'How odd,' said Stephen steadily, and reached into the wardrobe for his jacket. From downstairs Jonathan called up: 'Dad? You ready?'

'Coming.' He slipped on his jacket and closed the wardrobe door.

'Who do you think it was?'

'No idea.' Stephen brushed his hair in front of the mirror, and flicked at his shoulders with the clothes brush. 'A wrong number, I should think, wouldn't you?' He said it in the tone of one speaking to the very young or slow-witted; reasonable, unanswerable. 'I must go.'

'Are you coming back tonight?'

'Of course I'm coming back tonight.' His voice held an edge of irritation.

'I thought you might be going to London.'

'I've just been to London.'

'I know.'

'Dad!'

'Coming!' Stephen looked at Miriam. 'I'm not going to London again for another two weeks,' he said. 'All right?'

'Fine. I just wondered.' She put down her teacup. 'I must get going, too. See you for supper then.'

'Right.' And he was gone, running down the stairs, calling to Jonathan: 'Got everything? Okay, let's go.'

'Bye, Mum!'

'Bye, darling!'

The front door banged, and they ran down the path through the rain.

Miriam got up, dressed and took two Paracetamol. Downstairs, she let out Tess and let her in again, and washed up the breakfast things. She had no breakfast herself. Then she, too, ran through the rain to the garage, and backed into the lane, driving off to Woodburgh with the windscreen wipers racing.

The shop was busy. With the quiet period of the summer holidays over, everyone wanted the house to look nice for Christmas, and Miriam measured and advised and snipped off fabric samples, in quiet moments telephoning orders to her suppliers. Last week she had done the window for the season: heavy swatches of crimson and wintergreen velvet hung with prints from Liberty and Osborn & Little. Just off-centre, the polished frame of a little chair, found in an auction and reupholstered, gleamed softly beneath concealed lighting; in a corner a Victorian doll – pale china cheeks, chocolate velvet bonnet and cape, buttoned boots – leaned, smiling, against a pile of presents.

The doll was perhaps a bit much, but it was also just what would draw people, and she had enjoyed doing it, the shop closed for the night, a play on the radio, a glass in her hand – though with something to occupy the evening, to absorb her attention, she had, then, drunk less than she might have done at home. In any case, she needed to be careful because of the drive back: her last drink in the shop was usually at lunchtime, allowing a good few hours before she shut up. When Stephen and Jonathan were at home, those lunchtime drinks were the last of the day; when they were not, her drinking sometimes began as soon as she was inside the house, standing with her coat on pouring out the first, finishing the last in front of the television. She replaced the bottle in the cellar, and climb the stairs very slowly; she rinsed her mouth with mouthwash for a long time in front of the bathroom mirror, watching the woman she saw there with a blurrily detached mixture of compassion and dislike.

Yesterday evening, alone, had been spent drinking. This evening she locked the shop door at five past five and walked quickly down the side street to the car park, wanting to be home before Jon was dropped off, not liking him to come back to an unlit house. The air was cold and fresh, the sky emptied of rain, and a light wind rising; she drove through the town, past bright shop windows, and out to the Woodburgh Road. Clusters of council houses and neat rows of Victorian brick cottages began to thin; after a couple of miles there were only the fields, flat and dark, stretching away behind the hedgerows, the occasional lights of a country house in the distance.

It was from houses such as these that Stephen had commissions; Miriam, too, on a smaller scale, advising people like the Sadlers, with whom Stephen had dined last night, on design and decoration, making the perfect home. She supposed that another couple with such complementary skills might have gone into a business partnership – working together, sharing a studio, talking over projects late into the night, arguing, gossiping, laughing.

She supposed, too, that the local people who, in their very separate domains, she and Stephen advised, must see them simply as a couple like themselves: busy, successful, living in yet another lovely country house. And happy? Moderately, as happy as anyone else. They cannot believe that, she thought, turning off to the Saxham road which led home; surely our emptiness, our lack of intimacy, must be visible to anyone. But perhaps not – after all, we have taken such pains, such separate pains, to conceal it. People, particularly clients, did not want to see unhappiness writ large; why should they? Not even Flora, who all those years ago had helped, in her kindly way, to get Miriam on to a new track, could guess what she was really like. And what *was* she really like? After years of secrecy Miriam no longer knew herself.

This road was narrower, the bare trees closer together, their branches almost touching – in summer, she drove through an arch of leafy green. Now, they swayed and creaked in the rising wind, wet leaves blew across in front of her, and one or two clung to the windscreen. Miriam knew each yard ahead, she had made this journey five days a week for ten years; still, she slowed, and turned on the wipers, brushing the leaves away. Years of drinking, far from making her reckless, had made her extra-careful – not for herself, or for Stephen, but for Jonathan, who needed her. Reckless, she might have confronted her husband with a discovered photograph, with accusations; she might have left, after a quarrel, driving off pell-mell into the night, speeding, dangerous. But there had been too many confrontations, too many pleas in the past. They had made their unspoken agreement, and she had stayed, carefully guarding secrets – her own, and the knowledge of Stephen's.

She was through the village and had reached the turn-off to the lane, an entrance which only someone familiar with the road would notice, even in daylight, and braked, indicating right for the car which had appeared behind her, its headlights blazing into the mirror. When she turned the car behind drove straight past, roaring impatiently away – did she really drive so slowly now?

At other times of the year, she was often made to slow still further in the lane by the tractor from the neighbouring farm, bumping home with a trailer of turnips, manure or hay bales; now, with the autumn ploughing completed, the brown fields furrowed and bare, the tractor was rarely out after dark. Mr Innes left the farm early, taking feed to the sheep and cattle grazing a mile away, and came home early, driving into the shed and tramping across the yard for his tea. Miriam missed the tractor, and the slow lifting of the farmer's hand as he acknowledged her, waiting behind him. When Jon was little he had spent happy days in the farmyard, following Mr Innes about, carrying buckets. Now, he never went over.

The house was dark, so he wasn't back yet. But the outside light on the garage was on, so Stephen must be. Yes, she could see lights from the garden studio shining through the gap in the hedge. It was very cold now; Miriam hurried indoors, flicking switches, taking off her coat, brushing her hair in the hall mirror.

'Hello, Tess.' She put down her brush and patted the thick yellow coat. Tess was hungry, she always was at this time – unless Stephen, home first, had fed her. No. The bowl in the kitchen was as clean as it had been this morning, the tin in the cupboard unopened. 'Here you are, girl.' She set down the full bowl, shaking in biscuits on top, and moved the kettle on to the hotplate. What were they going to eat? Miriam did not feel like eating, she rarely did, but it was unthinkable not to cook for her family. She prepared good hot meals and sat with her husband and son at the table, picking at the edges of her plate. It irritated Stephen, she could tell that it did, but he rarely commented: they often ate, the three of them, in what she hoped seemed to Jonathan like an ordinary family silence.

She sat down, waiting for the kettle to boil, and drew towards her the post Stephen had flung on to the table. Whatever had come for him he would have taken out to the studio; Miriam, in her weekly trips out there, had found no other letter for him in that neat black hand from Highgate. Today there were two for Jonathan, one an airmail, the cheap thin envelope addressed in a wavering ballpoint that looked vaguely familiar. The postmark was Amsterdam: Miriam recalled the postcard in the summer, the lurid punk photograph. What was the girl's name? The other letter was in a large brown envelope, from UCCA, university application forms. What was he going to read, where? She supposed they might discuss that over supper, although the subject of Jonathan leaving was something she did not want to think about. And the girl from Amsterdam – presumably they would not be discussing her. Miriam turned over the envelope, looking for a name on the back. M. van Eycken, Vondel Straat. She put it down, face up, on top of the letter from UCCA; in the hall, the phone began to ring.

Miriam jumped. She waited to see if Stephen, out in the studio, would pick up his extension, but he did not and she hurried into the hall.

'Hello?' It was chilly out here, the central heating wouldn't come on till half-past four. Miriam, listening to clicks on the line, and silence, found she was shivering as she had done last night. 'Hello?'

'Hello?' A thin, distant little voice.

'Yes?' said Miriam. 'This is Saxham 738.'

'I am sorry?'

She repeated the number, slowly. Whoever was at the other end sounded young, uncertain, not English. She realized, suddenly, who it was.

'You want to speak to Jonathan?'

'To Jonathan – yes.' The little voice was audibly relieved. 'I am calling from Holland.'

'I'm afraid he's out.' Miriam heard herself speaking loudly, slowly,

188

almost as if she, too, were speaking a foreign language. 'He will be back soon. Can I take a message?'

'Only – I telephoned, this is Marietta, but there was no answer. I want to know, has he received my letter?'

'I – ' Miriam wavered between wanting to reassure her and not wanting to sound as if Jonathan's mother read his mail. 'I think so, yes. Funnily enough, I think it has just arrived.'

'I am coming to England,' the little voice announced. 'I ask him to find me a job.'

'Oh.' She felt herself flounder. 'Well, I . . .'

A rapid series of pips sounded on the line. 'I'll tell him,' she said quickly; there was an abrupt click at the other end, then silence. Miriam put down the receiver and went slowly back to the kitchen, where the lid of the kettle was rattling frantically, wreathed in steam. She took it off absent-mindedly, pouring boiling water into a tea-less pot. The front door banged and she turned, smiling, the empty kettle still in her hand, calling out: 'Darling? News.'

'What's happened to meat in this house?' Stephen finished buttering a baked potato and surveyed his plate of spinach flan and salad.

'Meat?' Miriam drew the salad bowl towards her.

'Yes, meat. Anyone remember it? Sunday lunch, joint and two veg. something *hot*? Remember that?'

'This is hot,' said Jonathan, through a mouthful of flan.

'You know what I mean.' Stephen looked at Miriam.

'Sorry,' she said, automatically. 'I didn't realise you were missing it. I suppose Jon and I've got used to being vegetarians on our own.'

'What do you mean, on your own?'

'I mean when you're in London.'

'London, London. Anyone would think I lived there, and visited here on rare occasions.' He sliced through the flan with his fork.

'That's what it feels like, sometimes,' she said lightly.

'You two,' said Jonathan. 'Have you got any ideas about a job for my Dutch lady?'

Stephen put down his fork. 'What Dutch lady?'

'She's called Marietta,' said Miriam. 'He met her in Amsterdam, at Easter.'

'Can't he tell me himself?' Stephen looked at Jonathan, who said gently: 'Dad. Cool it. What's biting you this evening?'

For a moment there was a silence; then Stephen said: 'Okay, sorry. Too much on my plate, I suppose.'

'But not meat,' said Jonathan, and added amidst the groans: 'You shouldn't be eating it anyway, it's disgusting – full of hormones, robbing the land, robbing the Third World . . .'

'All right, that's enough. Who is Marietta? Is she beautiful?'

'Sexist.'

'Surely I'm allowed to know what she looks like.'

'You wouldn't ask if it was a male, would you? If I said someone called Pieter was coming over looking for a job you'd have just asked what kind of a job he wanted. Wouldn't you?'

Stephen sighed. 'I feel old. All right. What kind of job does she want?'

'Anything. She's coming as soon as I've got something for her.'

'If she's that liberated why can't she find her own job?'

'Could you find a job just like that in another country?'

Stephen looked at Miriam, half laughing, half exasperated. 'Does he go on like this all the time?'

'Only sometimes.'

We have something to talk about, she thought, something new. And Stephen's going to be here for two weeks, he said so this morning. We feel like a family. Aloud she said: 'How long is she coming for?'

Jonathan shrugged. 'She doesn't know, it all depends. I think she's failed some exams and wants a break.'

'I tell you what she could do,' said Stephen, 'come to think of it. She could be an au pair for the Sadlers; the French one's given in her notice. Rather dramatically, I understand.' He opened his hands, made a *moue*. ' "But it ees too hard work here, and all zees children are so spoiled! In France it is not like zees." '

They all laughed.

'But it ees too hard work also for Marietta?' Jonathan asked. 'I can't remember the Sadlers' domestic arrangements.'

'I can,' said Miriam, relaxed now. 'There are three children, all very energetic and interested in themselves. Like their parents.'

'There's nothing wrong with the parents,' said Stephen, and all at once the laughter and warmth had gone from his voice. 'Why are you so critical?'

Miriam flushed. 'Sorry. I didn't mean to be.'

'If you'd come last night you might actually have enjoyed yourself. The food, by the way, was excellent.'

'I thought you didn't want me to come,' said Miriam, swallowing. One false move and it all yawned open again. She looked down at her plate.

'Stop it, you two,' said Jonathan sharply. 'We're talking about me, all right?' He turned to Stephen. 'Mum didn't say anything so dreadful, did she? Now, are you serious about the Sadlers or not? Do you think they really want someone?'

'I'll phone them,' said Stephen. 'And will you kindly stop speaking to me in that tone.'

The meal ended in a silence no one could pretend was ordinary. As she cleared away, Miriam said carefully: 'What about your university forms, Jon? We were going to talk about all that, too, weren't we?'

'Not now,' said Jonathan. 'I don't feel like it, sorry.' He pushed back his chair and went out; they could hear him climb the stairs to his room, and then his music, turned up full blast.

'God Almighty,' said Stephen. 'What is that?'

'I think it's Def Lepard.' Miriam carried the plates over to the sink.

'*Who?*' He pushed back his chair and got up. 'Never mind.' There was a pause. 'Sorry I snapped.'

'It doesn't matter,' said Miriam, not turning. 'By the way, the gutter needs unblocking. At the front.'

'Okay. I'll have a go at it on Sunday. I'd better go and phone now, hadn't I?'

He went out into the hall; while she did the washing-up she could hear him look up the number and dial, and his voice become sociably warm, charming, as always.

'Daphne? Stephen. Thanks so much for last night, I really enjoyed it. Listen, I think we may have solved your problem . . .'

It is, after all, she thought, hanging the tea towel over the rail on the Rayburn, better when he's not here. Or when he is, that we keep cool. 'Ve have come to this? No. It feels as if we have always been like this.

On a cold grey morning in November Jonathan set off on the bike for Norwich to meet Marietta: she was to arrive on the train from Harwich, after a six-hour crossing. At breakfast he had looked out at the windswept sky through the garden doors. 'Not a good day to be at sea.'

'It might be different out there,' said Miriam, pouring tea.

'It isn't.' He came and sat down. 'I've been listening to the forecast.'

'Oh. Well, let's hope she's a good traveller.' Miriam, still without a description of Marietta to go on, pictured, as she had done when the postcard came in the summer, a large blonde young woman who in her mind's eye was at this moment up on deck, enjoying the feel of wind and spray on her large Dutch face. The little voice on the telephone – and she had phoned again, twice – seemed to belie this vision, but she was still unable to substitute anything else for it.

'Are you sure you need to go all that way on the bike?' she said, passing cereal. 'I'm sure the Sadlers would go.'

'I'm sure they would, but I don't want them to.' Jonathan shook out cornflakes.

'If Dad were here he could drive you.'

'I know. But he isn't. When's he coming back?'

'I think he said Wednesday. Perhaps I should drive you.'

'You've got the shop. Anyway, Mum, do stop it, I want to go.'

'Yes,' she said, 'I know.'

'You remember I said I was bringing her back here, don't you? Just for the night. I mean, she doesn't want to get thrown in at the deep end with that lot after a long journey, does she?'

'I shouldn't think so, no. Yes, it's fine. I've made up a bed in the spare room.'

'Why?'

Miriam put down her teacup. 'So she can sleep there.'

'She's sleeping with me,' said Jonathan. 'That okay?'

They looked at each across the table.

Miriam said slowly: 'Would you do it if Dad was here?'

'Probably not.'

'Why?'

'I don't know. I just wouldn't. At least I don't think so. Do you mind?'

Miriam didn't answer, because she didn't know. 'I suppose,' she said at last, 'that I'm pleased you trust me.' And pushed away other feelings which were not pleasurable at all, or even admissible – of loss, and jealousy, and confusion. And then, oh God, terror.

'Good,' said Jonathan. 'That's what I hoped.' He spooned up the last of his cornflakes, quickly, and got up to put on the toast.

'But you will – ' she broke off, suddenly overwhelmed.

'Be careful.' He was watching the toaster. 'Yes, I will.'

'Of everything,' said Miriam, seeing, unstoppably, Jonathan ill, Jonathan wasted, vomiting, struggling for breath. Dying.

'Of babies and of AIDS,' he said kindly. 'I promise.'

Miriam let out a long breath. 'My God. What an age we live in.'

'*I* live in,' said Jonathan, as the toast popped up. 'It's my generation that's going to cop it, isn't it?'

'Is it?' she said faintly. 'Do you think it has nothing to do with us?'

'I hope not,' he said cheerfully, and sat down again, putting the toast in the rack. 'Want some? I don't think I want to continue this conversation. It takes all the fun away somehow.'

When Miriam got back to the house that evening they were already home; she saw the lights as soon as she came down the lane, and when she had put the car in the garage, she opened the front door with a feeling of nervous apprehension.

'Hello?' she called out in the hall, thinking she must announce herself.

'Hi, Mum.' Jonathan's voice came from the kitchen; as she walked down the passage Tess came out, as every day, but slowly, not as if she wanted anything: Jon always fed her if he were first back. He was sitting at the end of the table, in Stephen's chair; beside him, opposite the door, sat a small girl in a baggy camel jumper, rolling a cigarette. She did not raise her head.

'Mum, Marietta,' said Jonathan, with a gesture. 'Marietta – this is my mother, okay?'

'Okay,' said the little voice, between lips moistening the cigarette paper.

'How do you do?' said Miriam, moving to the table. 'We've spoken on the phone.' She held out her hand.

'Yes.' The girl looked up. 'Hello.' She turned to Jonathan.

'Do you have matches?'

'Yes,' he said easily, 'we have matches. I'm not sure if Mum minds about smoking in here.'

'Oh, it's fine,' Miriam said quickly. 'Here . . .' She crossed the room to the Rayburn and took down the box from the mantelpiece, passing it over. What about Jonathan – didn't he mind? He disliked smoking almost as much as meat. She watched him take out a match and strike it, lighting the girl's cigarette.

'Thanks.' She blew it out, and inhaled deeply.

'Well . . .' said Miriam. She was about to offer tea, but Jon had already made a pot; the table was littered with mugs, a milk bottle, teaspoons, cigarette things. 'I hope you had a good journey.'

'It was very bad,' said the girl, not turning.

'She was sick,' said Jonathan helpfully.

'Oh. Poor you,' Miriam said to the thin little shoulders facing her beneath the baggy sweater. 'Perhaps you'd like to have a rest?'

The shoulders shrugged. 'It's better now.'

Miriam poured herself a cup of tea and came to sit down. There was a silence, during which she tried to take in Marietta's appearance, and disconcerting manner, without staring. Beneath the camel sweater, a black polo neck emerged at the top and became black leggings beneath the table, ending in small black ankle boots – this much she had seen as she stood by the Rayburn. The girl's hands were small and blunt, every fingernail bitten to the quick; her face was pale, small-featured, expressionless except for a fleeting, giggling smile directed at intervals at Jonathan. Her hair was brown, nondescript, but in the peculiarly favoured and unflattering style Miriam saw often on teenage girls in the town: short and nibbled round the face, with a spiky fringe, then allowed to stay long at the back, well on to the shoulders. Marietta's little ears were pierced by several silver earrings; there was also a small gold stud in one nostril. Miriam found herself thinking of fictional blonde, strong, healthy Marietta with longing. She sipped her tea, and could think of nothing to say.

The girl turned to Jonathan, exhaling a cloud of smoke. 'Do you have television?'

'Of course.'

'Let's go.' She pushed back her chair and gathered her tobacco tin and papers.

Miriam watched Jonathan lead the way out; she wanted to catch his eye and burst out laughing, but he did not look at her and she heard smothered giggles in the passage and then, from the sitting room, the sound of the television, turned up loud.

In the evening Stephen rang, apparently from James and Klara's. 'What's she like?'

'Appalling,' said Miriam, before she could stop herself, and then, because Stephen did not like her to be critical – why? why ever not? – she went on quickly: 'I expect she's all right really. She's just very young. How are you, Stephen?'

'Not very good. The Regent's Park job is going down the drain, half the builders are on their way back to Ireland for Christmas. I might have to stay a day or two longer – can you cope?' He always asked that.

'Of course.' She had always coped. 'Anyway, Marietta's going to the Sadlers tomorrow.'

'What do you mean? Where's she staying tonight?'

'She's staying here,' said Miriam matter-of-factly, and added: 'She's had a very bad journey,' as if that provided Stephen with all the information he could need. There was another silence in which, quite clearly, she could feel him deciding not to ask any more.

'I'll be back at the weekend, anyway,' he said. 'Friday evening at the latest, all right?'

'All right. Thanks for phoning.' How many conversations had they had like this? She replaced the receiver and went back to the kitchen, putting spaghetti into a pan, wanting a drink.

Supper was difficult, at least for Miriam. She sat at one end of the table, Jon at the other, Marietta between them, picking at her food. For the first time Miriam understood how irritating this might be to an observer, although after the bad crossing it was understandable. She tried to make conversation – how long had Marietta been learning English, did she have brothers and sisters, how long did she hope to stay – and gave up. The girl answered indifferently, in monosyllables, although it was clear she understood English quite well, and she showed no curiosity about Jon's family or about Norfolk, or the family with whom she was to stay – surely an impending disaster – or, indeed, about anything. Jonathan, too, fell silent, although he did not seem embarrassed – he was, Miriam realised, even at his age, capable, like his father, of riding any social situation. Or so it seemed. After a while she gave up listening to her own bright, forced questions, and Marietta's indifferent replies; she sipped at a glass of wine and told herself to make allowances. The meal over, the two of them disappeared again, leaving her to clear up: she heard them return to the television, then, after a suitable while, climb the stairs to bed. Which was where, presumably, they had wanted to be ever since they got back.

Later, a tactful hour later, Miriam lay in her own bed, hearing from along the landing, even through her closed door, Jonathan's muted but relentless tapes. He hardly ever played so late, certainly not when Stephen was here. She flicked through the pages of *Vogue*, usually a reliable distraction, and could not be distracted; she put it back on her bedside table and turned out the lamp. The music stopped, and began again. After a long, sleepless while, she heard the door of Jonathan's room open, and the landing light switched on; footsteps went to the bathroom and came out again; Jonathan's door was closed.

Miriam got up, and went to the window; she drew back the curtains and stood looking out at the woods across the lane. The wind had dropped; the woods were dark and quiet: in that alert, watchful quietness before the foxes and the owls began their hunting. The moon had risen high above the trees and hung in a clear, unclouded sky. Miriam drew a breath, and tried to calm herself. These woods, this silence, had been her companions on sleepless nights ever since they moved here – comforting Jonathan, small and unwell; waiting for Stephen to stop working and come to bed; waiting for another child. Waiting, in more recent years, for Stephen to come back from London, to come back to her.

And now? Jonathan was no longer small and in need of comfort – at least, if he were, he would not, for much longer, look for it from her. There was no question, now, of another child, and those distant longings had long since been locked away. And Stephen?

The heating had gone off, and the room was getting cold. Miriam closed the curtains and went back to bed. She reached into her bedside drawer for a sleeping pill and swallowed it quickly, without water. The music along the landing stopped, and did not begin again. Within a few minutes she had fallen into a deep, almost suffocating sleep.

From within Anya's flat, on the other side of her door in the hall, a new sound: television. Hilda, with Sam, spent most of her evenings upstairs, but if she came down into the hall to fetch something from his pram, or when they came back from afternoon outings, she could hear it: Channel 4 news at seven, the BBC at nine, ITV at ten. Anya was watching other programmes, too, but it was for the news that she had bought it, looking out of the sitting room window the whole of one wet afternoon for the delivery van, combing the Yellow Pages for someone reliable to come and instal an aerial, inviting Hilda to come down and watch.

They were knocking down the Berlin Wall. That, if nothing else had followed, had to be seen. But then came Czechoslovakia. Prague. Anya sat with the cats on the edge of her sofa, watching the thousands stand in the falling snow in Wenceslas Square, cheering, ringing handbells. If it was moving for Hilda to see again the modest, smiling, unforgotten face of Dubček, as he came out on to a balcony, waving, for Anya it was overwhelming.

'The last time Prague was in the news like this was in '68, and we did not have a television, of course. Perhaps for Liba we could have had one, but except for occasions like that I didn't want her wasting her time. She was such a good student.'

'I can remember watching it,' said Hilda. 'Just. In 1968 I was twelve, and Alice was ten. I can remember my father talking about it, and seeing the tanks on the news. I think he was very shaken, most socialists were.'

'Socialists?' asked Anya. 'He was a socialist, your father?' She shook her head, gesturing to the screen. 'This is what is happening to socialism, thank God.'

'Communism,' said Hilda. 'There is a difference, isn't there?' From upstairs, through the open door of her flat, she could hear a cry: Sam must have woken. She got up quickly. 'I'd better go.'

'Bring him down if you like,' said Anya, turning.

'I'll see. Thanks.'

'Hilda?'

'Yes?' She stopped at the door.

'What are you doing for Christmas?'

'I . . . I'm not sure yet. We might be going to my family, to Alice and Tony, I mean.' She hesitated, her hand on the brown door-knob, not wanting to commit herself.

'Well, Liba and I will be here,' said Anya. 'She may be bringing her friend. If you and Sam . . . you are welcome to join us.'

'Thank you,' said Hilda, feeling her heart sink. 'You're very kind.' From upstairs, the cries grew louder. 'I'd better go,' she said again. 'perhaps I could let you know . . .'

'Of course. There is no hurry.'

Anya turned back to the television, and Hilda closed the door and ran up the stairs. Sam was screaming now. 'All right, all right, I'm coming!' She hurried through to her bedroom. 'Here I am.' He had outgrown the crib, no question. 'We'll have to buy you a cot,' she said, carrying him into the sitting room, and sat in the rocking chair, pulling up her sweater. 'Would you like a cot for Christmas?' She sat there hoping, as usual, that after a good feed this would be the night he slept through. So far, even though she had started him on baby rice and banana, he had woken at least twice every night since they got home.

She yawned, leaning back in the chair. Jane and Don were taking it in turns, now, to get up in the night to Daisy – Jane had told her that last week, when she came for lunch. She had put Daisy down on the playmat with Sam and walked round the flat, looking at the pictures, taking books from the shelves. 'It's great,' she said. 'I really like it.'

'It's small,' said Hilda, coming out from the kitchen.

'Are you going to move? When Sam's older, I mean?'

'I don't know. I don't know anything.' She passed her a glass of juice.

'Thanks.' Jane took the glass and wandered over to the window. 'I've always wanted to live in an attic.' She looked at the photographs on the desk, of Hilda's parents, in a silver frame, and of Stephen, the old one, taken all those years ago outside the pub in Highgate. 'That's Sam's father, isn't it?'

'Yes.' Beside Hilda, on the mat, the babies were rolling over, clutching at toys.

Jane put the photograph down again. 'He's very good-looking,' she said, as she had said when they talked about him before. 'I hope he's looking after you.'

Hilda flushed. 'He does what he can. I always knew I'd be doing most of it alone.'

'But it's a lot, isn't it? I think you're very brave.'

She shrugged, waving it all aside. 'There are plenty of us, aren't there? Women on their own with babies.'

'Yes. It's still hard work, though, I should think.' Sam, holding a plastic rattle, banged Daisy in the face. 'Baby!' She went over quickly, as Daisy began to scream. 'It's all right, you're fine . . .'

They hadn't talked about Stephen again. Now, her eyes heavy, Hilda thought: I'd give anything, anything to have him here now, to offer to get up tonight, to let me sleep. How am I going to manage when I go back to work? I'll just have to manage, that's all. I must get a minder sorted out by Christmas.

Christmas was only weeks away: was there any chance at all that Stephen might be with her, even for part of it? They were meeting tomorrow, at the zoo, because it was near the site where he was working. In the old days, in spring and summertime, they used quite often to meet after work and wander through Regent's Park, hearing roars from the lionhouse, the shrieks of birds and monkeys. But Hilda had never, since she came to London, been inside the zoo, and the visit tomorrow was her idea – neutral territory, somewhere to explore as a future treat for Sam. And she was going to drive there, saving Stephen for once the journey across north London; it was time she got used to taking Sam out in the car.

She yawned again. They would talk about Christmas tomorrow.

'Move! Move!'

In the back of the car, Sam was screaming. In front of Hilda, who was frantically drumming on the wheel, a long line of cars crawled down to the traffic lights, where there was a filter off to the right and a road-widening scheme; the road was blocked by diggers and drills, and heaps of broken tarmac, cordoned off with plastic orange ribbon. The cars ahead picked up speed, and for a moment or two Sam's yells diminished. Then the lights changed to red, and everything slowed and stopped; at once, he began again, but louder.

'It's all right, it's all right,' said Hilda. She turned to pat the tense, furious little body, and he cried even harder, wanting to be picked up. 'I can't, Sam, please stop it. Please!' Nothing would stop him. Behind her a car began to hoot, and she realised that the lights were green. 'All right, all *right!*' she shouted to the driver behind, a man waving at her angrily, and turned and started off again. 'There, Sam! We've moving, now stop it.' In this fashion, and for perhaps ten minutes, they crept along, her stomach churning. They shot through across the main road at last as the lights went to amber, and had a clear run down towards Camden, but once there, caught in the one-way system, with the roads clogged, it all began again. In the end, almost screaming herself, Hilda stopped on a double yellow line on the ring road round the park, and took Sam into the front, where she fed him, listening to *Woman's Hour*.

Graceful Regency terraces overlooked her; the sleek limousines of diplomats swept past. Shut in her little car, Hilda felt a mixture of relief – that Sam was quiet at last – and anxiety that she was going to be late. But it was more than that: her situation here said it all – she was out on a limb, alone with her baby while the rest of the world went by. Fanny and Alan and the twins lived near here. Why had she never taken Sam to see them? Because they were too much of a contrast with her own life, she supposed: too pleased with themselves, too rich. I'll feel better as soon as I've gone back to work, she thought, as Sam's face, calm and replete, fell away; even if I'm tired, I need it. She put him back carefully into his car seat, strapped him in and started up again, driving away to the car park.

Even before she reached it Sam was deeply asleep, his angry red face growing pale, little fists unclenched and still. Hilda got out of the car, unfolded the pushchair and gently lifted him into it, tucking a blanket round him. The afternoon was bright and cold, the grass in the park flattened by the wind, fitfully shadowed by large, slow-moving clouds. With the air fresh on her face she felt some of her tiredness ebb away and her spirits rise. 'Come on, baby.' She wheeled the pushchair out of the car park and along the road.

199

A winter afternoon in term time: there were few people going through the entrance to the zoo, where a young man stood just inside, with a bunch of bright foil balloons. He shifted his feet in the cold, and Hilda looked past him, searching for Stephen. He wasn't there. They had arranged to meet near the ticket booth; she paid, and stood waiting for him, her back to a cage of monkeys, watching families come and go. She was almost half an hour late: surely Stephen wouldn't have given up and gone? She pushed Sam slowly back and forth, more to soothe herself; ten cold minutes, then fifteen went by; where was Stephen?

There he was, coming through the entrance with the collar of his loose tweed coat turned up, carrying a briefcase. He raised his hand and waved his fingers, unsmiling. Hilda stood waiting for him as he side-stepped the balloon seller and came up to her.

'I'm late, sorry.' He kissed her briefly, with cold lips, and she touched his cheek.

'All right?'

He shook his head. 'Problems. Shall we go?'

She followed him to the ticket booth, and then they went down the path at the side, showing their tickets to an old boy in uniform. He smiled down at the sleeping baby: 'He's going to miss it all. Never mind – you enjoy yourselves.'

Hilda smiled back, aware, as always with Stephen and Sam in public, of being seen as just one more ordinary family. They went on down the slope. 'Oh, look!' she said, touching Stephen's arm, as a young elephant trundled past them, following his keeper on baggy legs; little tufts of dark hair sprouted on his head, his trunk swayed after the keeper's bucket. Beside them, another family stopped to watch. 'Isn't he lovely? He looks just like Sam.'

'Mmm. Come on.' Stephen turned away, walking quickly.

'Where are we going?' She hurried after him, passing the snake house.

'I don't know, I just don't want to hang about, it's freezing.'

'You haven't said hello to Sam yet.' She wheeled the pushchair up beside him.

'He's asleep.'

Hilda bit her lip, and fell silent. They passed a signpost, pointing to penguins, seals and tigers, and found themselves facing a large cage of orang-utans, clambering along branches, swinging on ropes and tyres. They stopped, and stood gazing at them, leaning on the barrier. The air was full of whoops and grunting: high up towards the back of a group of young males were half-heartedly chasing each other along the ropes, moving quickly from hand to hand, thrusting out long hairy feet, dropping down to scratch themselves or search for overlooked titbits on the floor of the cage. They looked at the visitors, and looked away, incurious. But an enormous female came slowly towards Hilda and Stephen, cradling a baby in one arm, and pressed herself up against the netting. She clung to the wire with long supple fingers, stretching herself upwards, revealing a slack belly and taut grey teats, and her great domed head moved slowly back and forth. Her face was open and freckled, her sharp brown eye looked out at them, and she drew back her lips, grimacing, baring yellow teeth. Hilda watched, fascinated. Tucked against his mother's vast hairy side, the baby peered out at her, warm and bright-eyed, and she felt a wave of tenderness, pure and uncomplicated, wanting to reach out and stroke him.

Beside her, Stephen said wryly: 'They seem to be everywhere, don't they?' She turned to look at him and he smiled down at her, some of the coldness gone. 'Like him?'

'Yes,' she said, and touched his arm cautiously. 'Have I dragged you here? Should you really be working?'

'It doesn't matter.' They stood side by side watching the mother ape, who looked back at them intently, puckering her lips again. Hilda, her hand on the pushchair, felt herself on the verge of saying to her: And this is *our* baby – and then, abruptly, the animal turned away, bored, and sprang across the floor of the cage and up on to one of the branches.

'Oh,' said Hilda, disappointed. 'Just as we were getting to know each other.'

'Never mind, it's too cold to stand about.' Stephen was buttoning his coat. 'Let's move on.'

They walked past chimpanzees and leaping gibbons, little black monkeys and a colony of gorillas; after a while they stopped at the rhinos, huge and disconsolate, pawing at muddy ground.

'Poor beasts,' said Stephen, looking at the concrete moat which surrounded them. 'It can't be much fun.'

'No.' Hilda leaned on the rail. 'Still,' she said after a while, 'we haven't come just to talk about the animals, have we? You still haven't said hello to Sam.'

'Hilda . . .'

'I know he's asleep. I know it's silly, and he probably won't remember you. You could make the gesture.'

'I do, usually.'

'Why not today? We haven't seen you for over two weeks. We had a dreadful time coming.'

Stephen said nothing. In front of them, the rhino hopefully lowered his head to the ground and raised it again, looked round with empty piggy eyes, then lumbered off round the enclosure.

Hilda said slowly: 'I don't mean to nag. I suppose I'm worried – we seem, as they say, to be drifting apart.' She turned to him, seeing his profile in the winter air looking pinched, older. 'Are we?' she said.

'I don't think so.'

'I do.' She hesitated, then said recklessly: 'What about Christmas?'

'What about it?'

'What are you doing?'

Stephen turned to look at her. 'What should I be doing?' he asked heavily. 'I mean – realistically. What did you have in mind?'

Hilda felt her eyes fill with tears. 'Don't.'

'I didn't start it.'

'But we have to talk about it! Don't we? Is it so unreasonable?'

Stephen gave a long sigh. 'No. I just don't know how to manage it.' He turned away again, looking at the rhino coming back, searching his empty patch of ground. 'God, this is depressing, can't we go somewhere else? Come on. Come on!' He gestured impatiently and strode off, swinging his briefcase. Hilda stood for a moment, feeling cut adrift; then she turned the pushchair round and followed him. Ahead were the penguins, comical and endearing, but Stephen didn't stop; when, at last, he did so, and turned to look for her, it was at the end of the path, a damp expanse of grass ahead and the zoo shop beside them. Inside, she saw through a blur small children clutching model elephants and pandas; from somewhere on the far side came cries and whistles. Stephen stood waiting for her; he held out his hand.

'Sorry.'

She shook her head, unable to speak, very cold. What on earth had possessed her to suggest they came here? The slow-moving clouds were thicker now, the sky overcast; she felt a few light drops of rain and lifted the hood of the pushchair. Sam was still fast asleep, but they couldn't stay outside.

'How about the birdhouse?' suggested Stephen. 'It's just over there.'

'All right.' They hurried towards it, hearing the whistles and shrieks grow louder; rain spattered the path. 'Quick!' They wheeled the pushchair inside, and shook themselves. 'God, that's better.'

It was very warm in here, the only other visitors an art student, sketching on a canvas stool on the far side, and a mother and daughter who had clearly been round already, and now stood looking out at the rain. They were both tall and dark, the girl eight or nine, pale-faced: perhaps she was convalescing from something, having time off school. She turned and said something to her mother, companionably, as if they were good friends, and her mother put an arm round her shoulders and smiled. Watching them, Hilda thought, that's just how I'd imagined it: Hettie and me, sufficient unto ourselves, content. Instead – well, perhaps Sam and I will be like that one day, I wouldn't change him for anyone. Even so . . .

'What are you thinking?' Beside her, Stephen put his hand on hers. 'Let's go and sit down.'

They pushed Sam over to a wooden seat and she parked him at the side, out of the way.

'Well?' Stephen put his arm around her. 'I'm sorry,' he said again. 'Were you thinking what a brute I am?'

She shook her head. 'No. Just – I didn't think it would be easy, but . . .'

'Go on.'

'I thought I'd be able to manage it all so well – I *am* managing – but . . . You don't think about things like Christmas, do you? I know he won't notice much, but the thought of being in London without you, and you with your family . . .' She broke off.

Stephen said nothing. Outside, through the open door, they could see the rain, falling fast now; here, the air felt almost tropical. Parrots and cockatoos in single cages gnawed their grey toes or blinked sleepily; most of the cages were much more elaborate, and bright little birds flitted and swooped amongst glossy plants. From somewhere came the sound of running water.

'Well,' said Stephen at last, 'what are we going to do?' He stroked her hair with a warm hand; Hilda leaned against his shoulder.

'How are things at home?' she asked cautiously. 'I mean – has anything happened?' For a moment she was about to tell him that she had tried to telephone, then she stopped, knowing it would disconcert or anger him.

'Nothing's happened,' he said. 'At least not in the way you mean. Jon has a girlfriend, a little Dutch girl . . . Never mind, you don't want to hear about that. Otherwise, what can I say? I'm finding it hard, too, I suppose. Keeping secrets there, trying to keep James happy down here. Sometimes I think I'll have to give up the London end, let him find someone else – if the bloody mortgage rate goes up again there's not going to be enough work anyway.' He gave an irritable sigh. 'For now we're in the midst of two long-term projects – it never seems the right moment to discuss it.'

Hilda looked at him. 'Are Sam and I just one more problem at the London end?'

'No. No, of course not.'

'We hardly got a mention in all that spiel, though did we? We're just a secret you have to keep in the midst of a hectic career. Another bloody long-term project.'

'Don't be silly, you know I didn't mean it like that. I just mean the whole thing's difficult. More than I'd thought, too.'

Hilda said slowly: 'Perhaps it would be better to have it all out in the open, so we all know where we stand. It can't be very nice for your wife, either.' She thought of the voice at the other end of the phone, hoarse and afraid. How much had she guessed?

'You can't be serious.' Stephen looked at her. 'I told you at the beginning, you can't say I ever gave you false hope. I told you I'd never leave.'

'For her sake or yours?' Hilda heard herself sound harsh. We are going to quarrel dreadfully, she thought, and at once: So? I'm sick of being nice and understanding.

'For Jonathan's sake,' said Stephen. 'I told you.'

'He was a little boy, then. He's almost grown up now, isn't he? You just said he'd got a girlfriend.'

'He's still at school! He's taking his A levels next year – I don't want to mess all that up for him, do I?'

'He might cope better than you think. He might have guessed anyway, when he saw us in the summer . . .'

'He didn't.'

'How do you know?'

'Oh, for God's sake!'

A little sound came from the pushchair, and the blanket slipped to the ground. Hilda turned, on edge, waiting for the crying to begin. Instead, in the warm, balmy air, Sam looked at her calmly.

'Hello,' she said enquiringly. 'All right?'

His round face broke into a dazzling smile: she felt her heart turn over.

'Baby . . . Stephen, look. Isn't he beautiful?'

Stephen leaned across, and Sam's expression changed to one of puzzled curiosity, but he did not turn away. 'Wotcher,' said Stephen, wiggling his fingers. He looked at him wryly. 'You timed that nicely, I must say.' Sam kicked enthusiastically, and smiled again.

'Come on.' Hilda unstrapped him, picking up the blanket; she lifted him on to her lap, and kissed the top of his head. 'Had a nice sleep? We're in the zoo, how about that?'

Sam's hands waved about; he looked at Stephen, and gave another gummy smile. Then, at a sudden squawk from a nearby parrot, he burst out laughing.

'Oh, Sam!' Hilda was laughing too. 'Was that funny?'

The squawk came again, even more piercing, and they all laughed; from the doorway Hilda heard the mother say to her little girl: 'What a lovely baby.' Had they overheard the quarrel? Never mind, what did it matter? She got up, saying, 'Let's go and see this bird.'

They found the cage and she held Sam up to look: inside, the parrot cocked his head at them and sidled along his perch.

'Afternoon,' said Stephen.

Sam looked at the cage and looked away, not making the connection between this and the squawk. 'Go on,' said Hilda, 'do it again.' But the parrot wouldn't. He opened his beak and showed them his funny grey tongue, he lifted one foot and scratched the back of his neck, he cocked his head repeatedly, and ran up and down. Squawk he wouldn't, and eventually they gave up and left him.

'After all,' said Stephen, 'he got us here, didn't he?' He turned to Sam, giving him a finger to hold. 'Have a perch.' Sam gripped the finger, looking round. 'Shall I take him?'

'Oh, yes,' Hilda passed him over, and flexed her arms. 'He's really getting quite heavy. The stairs at home are a killer, especially when I've got shopping and stuff.' For a moment she thought of broaching the fact that she would, one day, have to move; then she stopped herself. They had only just recovered themselves – let it be.

They wandered round the cages, listening to the trills and twitters, stopping to admit parakeets and cockateels, the flash of a tropical wing against dark green leaves. Hilda found herself remembering a walk in the park on the way to Alice's, one Sunday, seeing a father and his little boy make their way towards the rusting aviary, hearing the doves coo. She'd been four months pregnant then, just over the worst weeks, full of certainty and hope. I didn't have a clue, she thought now, how could I have done? But her anger and frustration had evaporated – in the laughter, in the heavy warmth of the air;

she felt languid and sleepy in here, as if in a soothing bath; she looked at Stephen and Sam, and held out her hand.

'Stephen?'

'Yes?' He turned to look at her, and took the hand, drawing her close again.

'Kiss me.'

With Sam between them they embraced, mouths meeting in a sudden flare of longing, lips parting, tongues seeking. The calls and murmurs of the birds around them fell away; they drew slowly apart, and stood looking at each other.

'I'd almost forgotten,' Hilda said shakily, and her body felt as if it were about to melt with the rediscovery. 'I really had.'

'Shall we go?' Stephen reached out and traced the outline of her lips. 'Shall we?'

'You mean – you're coming back with me?'

'I think so, don't you?'

'Yes. Yes!' She was filled with happiness. 'I didn't think you'd be able to.'

'Come on.'

In his arms Sam began to wriggle. 'Well,' said Stephen, looking quizzically down at him. 'And what did you think of that, then? What an exhibition.'

They went back for the pushchair, and wheeled him out to the door. The rain had eased off, and the mother and daughter had gone. They ran down the path, the wheels splashing up a fine spray, and reached the entrance panting.

'Like a balloon, Sam?' Stephen looked up at the silvery bunch, and the young man smiled.

''Course he would.'

They bought one with Mickey Mouse on it, and tied the string to the pushchair. Outside, Hilda said: 'What about your car?'

'It's at James's house – I came by taxi.'

'So we can go home together? What about tomorrow?'

He waved tomorrow away. 'I'll manage.'

They set off down the road towards the car park, the balloon bobbing cheerfully in the fading light.

Hours later, in the middle of the night, their arms still around each other, naked bodies warm, Hilda said softly: 'Do you think – *do* you think you might tell her?'

'Ssh.'

'But . . . how can we go on like this?'

'I'll think about it. Go to sleep.'

She yawned. 'What about Christmas?'

'What can I do? I'll come down afterwards as soon as I can.'

'Promise?'

'Promise.'

They fell asleep, curled around each other, woken in the small hours by Sam, who was hungry again.

Dusk fell rapidly; it was dark by a quarter to four. When Miriam drove through the town on her way home she passed windows bordered by fairy lights, lampposts hung with snowy bells and stars. A tall Christmas tree stood on the patch of green by the war memorial, lit up each afternoon by coloured bulbs: on the 20th, as every year, carols would be sung there, with a collection for the Cheshire Homes. Miriam, as Miriam Knowles from the shop, always gave a generous donation; when Jonathan was little she used to bring him to join in the carols, and he still came sometimes, with friends from school – you got to sing all the good tunes without having to go to church. Perhaps this year he would be bringing Marietta: it seemed unlikely. Or perhaps the Sadlers, who never missed, would bring her along to keep an eye on the children. That seemed unlikelier still.

Marietta and the Sadlers, predictably, were not suited: Miriam gathered, from phone calls, that Marietta was much, much worse than the French girl. 'I mean,' said Daphne, torn between bewilderment and outrage, 'she simply won't lift a *finger* unless I tell her. And she doesn't *speak*. Stephen said her English was quite good.'

'I know,' said Miriam. 'I'm sorry.'

'I mean, I'd get rid of her, but we have to have *someone* over Christmas. Anyway, I've given her most afternoons off, and I only want her baby-sitting when I simply can't get anyone local. But she can jolly well look after the children in the mornings – I'm going to get something out of her. I suppose she's spending the rest of the time with your Jonathan.'

'Yes,' said Miriam, 'I'm afraid she is.'

She was growing used, now term had ended, to coming home to find Jonathan and Marietta sitting at the kitchen table, the remains of lunch and beginnings of tea strewn all over it, the air full of cigarette smoke and Marietta's bitten fingers drumming in time to Radio One.

She felt like an intruder, getting her tea, taking it into the sitting room to be out of the way. There were days when she came back to find them already in there, leaving the kitchen full of unwashed plates and saucepans, watching children's television or an afternoon movie, the floor strewn with cups and ashtrays. There were other days when the house was dark, but she knew they were upstairs, the music pounding behind the door of Jonathan's bedroom. She stayed downstairs, clearing away the mess, having tea with the paper. The papers were full of Eastern Europe: Miriam, whose interest in world affairs was intermittent, found herself reading avidly, wondering once if perhaps it was because she could all too readily identify with the victims of oppression, thirsting for liberation. Almost in the same moment she got up and began to get the supper, waiting for Stephen to come home.

On the days when he was out in the studio, Jonathan and Marietta were never upstairs, and the kitchen was fractionally less of a tip. She wondered if Stephen realised quite how much Jonathan had changed in the past few weeks, and wondered, all the time, what on earth it was he saw in Marietta. Stephen seemed to find her less objectionable than she did, probably because when he appeared she noticeably perked up, offering cigarettes, accepting drinks. Perhaps he was enjoying having someone new about the place; she herself, so used to having Jonathan to talk to, at least some of the week, felt the beginnings of a deep depression, compounded by the fact that with him so constantly around she could not drink. At this time of year she often stayed late in the shop to finish orders; she took to doing so more frequently, drinking in the little back sewing room. She knew it was dangerous, with the drive home through the dark and the police hovering in parked cars. But with Jon and Marietta treating the house like a hotel, and without the usual steady level of alcohol to calm her down, she began to feel increasingly on edge, living on her nerves, liable, most unusually, to snap.

'Are you going to London again before Christmas?' she asked Stephen one morning, shaking biscuits into Tess's bowl.

'Don't think so,' he said, finishing his coffee.

'But do you actually know?'

'I might have to, but I doubt it. James will be there, and everything's winding down on site anyway. I told you.'

Miriam straightened up and put the dog biscuits back on the shelf.

'Well,' she said, turning to look at him, 'when you do know, can you put us in the picture?'

Stephen frowned. 'Of course. What's the matter?'

'Nothing.'

'You're up very early.'

'I woke up early.' She cleared the breakfast things, and the cups shook in her hands. Her nights, usually oblivion once she'd taken a pill, were becoming broken, restless. 'Anyway, I'd better go,' she said, putting them carefully into the sink. 'I suppose Jon's still asleep – we'd better do his UCCA forms, hadn't we? How about tonight? Marietta's baby-sitting, I gather.'

'Okay.' He got up from the table. 'I did say I might meet him in the pub.'

'Oh?'

'I think he could do with a change of scene. I thought I'd drop into the Swan on the way back from Norwich.'

'Oh,' she said again. 'Did you?' She couldn't remember the last time they'd all gone out together. 'And what did you think I might do?'

'Miriam . . .' He came over and put his hand on her arm. 'You don't like pubs,' he said reasonably. 'What has got into you?'

For a moment, looking up at his face, which for once seemed genuinely concerned, she almost told him. Then she saw the time on the clock behind him, and said quickly: 'Nothing. I'll be late,' and went out quickly, gathering jacket and bag from the hall, calling: 'Give Tess a run before you go, can you?' She pulled the front door shut and went to the garage, breathing fast. After all, she thought, getting out the car, backing into the lane with extra caution, what is the point of opening it all up now, just before Christmas, with Marietta hanging round, and everything different? Perhaps in the new year, when I'm feeling better.

She drove slowly down the lane, her hands on the wheel still trembling.

They sat at the kitchen table, the forms spread out between them. Tess was asleep, the basket creaking as she twitched and sighed.

'Shouldn't Dad be here?'

'We're not going to fill it all in, are we? I just think we'd better make a start.' Miriam put on her glasses and gazed at the first page. 'You can talk it over with him in the pub, can't you? And we can finish it all off over the weekend.'

'Okay.' Jonathan leaned back in his chair, yawning. 'I'm knackered.'

'I'm not surprised.' It sounded sharper than she'd intended, and he tipped the chair forward again, frowning.

'Meaning what?'

'Nothing,' she said. 'I was joking.'

'You don't like her, do you?'

'Does it matter?'

He shrugged. 'A bit. I know she's not a mother's dream, but she's okay underneath. She's just a bit . . .' He ran a finger up and down a knot in the table. 'I don't know. Anyway, I like her.'

'Well, that's the main thing, isn't it?' Miriam said nicely, and he smiled.

'Good Old Mum.'

'I'll just say one thing,' she said steadily. 'You won't let it all get in the way of your exams, will you?' She gestured at the papers in front of them. 'You'll need to get at least two Bs, I should think, and you've got mocks next term . . .'

He sighed. 'I know, I know.'

'It is important.'

'I *know*. Come on then, let's get it over with.' He turned to the first page. 'Name, age, address – I think I can manage that, should get a B in that, easy.'

Miriam smiled, and then began to laugh.

'It's not that funny.'

'I know. It's just . . .' she pulled herself together. 'I suppose it feels quite a long time since I had a laugh. And I'm a bit . . . under the weather, I suppose.'

'Been hitting the bottle?' Jonathan asked casually.

Miriam looked at him, the laughter gone. 'What did you say?'

'Don't get so serious, I was only joking. As you would say.'

She didn't know whether or not to believe him. Had he known all along? Were the shakes so obvious? After all these years, was she supposed to bring it out into the open, now?

'Far from it,' she said, equally casual, and telling, indeed, the recent truth. Out in the hall the phone began to ring. Jon pushed back his chair.

'I'll get it, it'll be Marietta. I told her I'd go over and keep her company this evening . . .'

So Stephen would be coming back from the Swan alone. She thought again of the look on his face this morning, the way he had touched her arm. Perhaps, with Christmas so near, they could make a truce? But truces followed battles, and they did not have battles.

What could they talk about? The phone pinged, and Jonathan came back down the passage.

'Okay, that's done, now let's get on with it.' She watched him come through the door. 'You are coming back here tonight, though, aren't you?'

'Of course. I shouldn't think the Sadlers would fancy the au pair girl having it off with me under their roof, would you?'

She laughed again. He looked so beautiful, he was so easy to be with.

'I do love you,' she said suddenly.

'That's what all the girls say.' He dropped a kiss on her head. 'Me, too. Come on.'

They ran through the pages. GCSEs passed, A levels to be taken, particular interests, choice of university.

'Where do you want to go?' she asked. 'East Anglia, perhaps?'

He smiled. 'That's what you'd like, isn't it?'

'Well . . . yes, of course I would. But you don't have to take that into account.'

'Don't be a martyr.'

'I'm not. Honestly. You must go where you want . . .'

'Where they'll have me, you mean.'

'There's that, of course. But I do mean it.'

'I know.' He drummed his fingers; there was a pause. 'Of course, if you'd had another after me, it wouldn't matter so much.'

Miriam, as she had done in the past, on the rare occasions when Jon had mentioned a brother or sister, felt herself switch on to automatic. 'You're the nicest son anyone could wish for.'

'That's not the point, though, is it?' He looked at her. 'It's a shame, isn't it?'

Miriam swallowed. Had he missed it all this time and said nothing? 'For you or for me?'

'More for you, I think,' he said slowly. 'Do you mind?'

'I did. I used to mind a lot. Then I got over it.' Another silence. 'More or less.'

'What about Dad?'

'He wasn't so keen, it didn't bother him so much. Anyway – it just didn't happen.' She looked up at the clock. 'If you're going to meet Dad at seven we'd better get on.'

'Why don't you come?'

'I wasn't invited,' she said lightly, adding 'Perhaps he wants to talk to you man to man.'

'Perhaps he wants a drink. I know I do. Okay. Let's say East Anglia; Exeter . . .'

'Exeter!'

'It's got a very good history department. There are trains, you know. Not to mention the bike.'

'You are careful on the bike, aren't you? I mean, even round here . . .'

'Mum! Exeter. York? Why not? Mike's trying for York. And two more . . .'

The phone rang again.

'I'll get it,' she said. 'You carry on thinking.'

Tess had woken up; she followed Miriam out to the hall, her tail thumping against the walls of the narrow passage.

'Hello?'

Silence.

'Hello? Saxham 738.'

Silence. And this time it could not be Marietta. Miriam waited, and the receiver shook in her hand.

'Who is it?'

Again: Who else could it be?

Silence. Someone's breathing, rapid and light. She slammed down the phone.

Back in the kitchen, Jonathan was finishing off with a flourish.

'I've put down Durham and London. King's College. After all, if I went there I could come back some weekends with Dad. Perhaps I'd better move it up the list, have you got a rubber?'

Miriam sank into her chair. 'No.'

'Mum?' He looked up, saw her face. 'Hey . . . what's the matter?'

She shook her head. 'Nothing.'

'It doesn't look like nothing – who was that?'

'I'm not sure.' God, she needed a drink. 'I suppose you could say it was an anonymous caller.'

'He didn't breathe at you, did he?' Jonathan's tone was teasing, trying to make her feel better. 'Mum? Was it horrible? What did he say? Go on – you can tell me, I'm a man of the world.'

She smiled weakly, and did feel better.

'Forget it. Anyway, it's time you went. You've almost finished, haven't you? Well done.'

He pushed the forms away. 'I'll ask Dad what he thinks about London. But Mum – you will be okay? Why don't you come, go on, stuff the man-to-man bit. It'd be nice.'

'Yes. Yes, it would.' But the need for a drink was overpowering; to sip at a glass of wine in a pub would be unbearable. If Jonathan was out . . . if she gargled a lot, and went straight to bed . . . they'd never know. I'm hooked, she thought. Even more than I knew.

'Darling, on second thoughts I think I'll stay here. If you and Dad get something to eat at the Swan I can have a night off cooking, and go to bed early. The shop's been pretty hectic.'

'Okay. If you're sure.' He bent to pat Tess, whose tail was moving slowly, hopefully, to and fro across the stone floor at his feet. 'Poor old girl, we must give you a run at the weekend.' He got up, and went to the hall for his things.

Miriam stood for a moment in the kitchen, still shaken by the phone call. Her bottles were down behind all the old paint tins in the cellar; another few minutes and she'd be down there. She followed Jon out; he was pulling his boots on, sitting on the stairs.

'I'll be back about one, okay? I'll leave when the Sadlers get home.'

'All right.' She stood hovering, waiting for him to go. Looking at the telephone. She heard herself say suddenly, irretrievably, trying to make it sound as if it really didn't matter much:

'Jon? Do you ever think that Dad might have a girlfriend? In London, I mean.'

He pulled on the second boot, and reached for his jacket. 'It's never crossed my mind. Honest. No, I'm sure he hasn't.' He got up stiffly, doing up poppers.

'Why? Why are you so sure?'

'I don't know, I just don't think he would. He's too busy, for a start. Anyway, Mum, you know what Dad's like – he flirts with everyone, look at the way he eyes up Marietta – sometimes I think she fancies him. It doesn't mean a thing.'

'I suppose not.'

'It doesn't,' he said, coming over, and putting his arms around her. 'He's that kind of person, isn't he? He charms people all the time, that's why he has so much work. I remember bumping into him in the summer, when we all went down on that trip to the British Museum. I met him having lunch with this woman, they were chatting away like old buddies, and she was just a client.'

Miriam said carefully, 'What did she look like?'

'I can't remember. Dark? I think she had glasses. Yes, those round ones.'

'And how,' she said faintly, 'do you know she was a client?'

'Mum! Because he *said* so. Anyway, she was married, she was pregnant.'

It was said so reasonably, so innocently, that Miriam, even as the words roared in her ears, realised that in spite of all his kindness, and apparent maturity, Jonathan was no more grown up, or aware of grown-up lives, than Marietta.

'Right.' He picked up his helmet and opened the door. 'See you in the morning, and for God's sake don't wait up for me, you know it drives me mad. Have an early night. Bye!'

He closed the door, and Miriam sank, leaning against it, distantly hearing him wheel the bike out of the garage, kickstart the engine and speed away.

'Hi, Dad.'

'Hello, Jon, sorry I'm late.' Stephen propped his portfolio up against the seat, below Jonathan's helmet and jacket, and looked at his son's almost empty glass.

'Another pint?'

'Better make it a half, with the bike.'

'Good chap – okay, back in a tick.'

Jonathan watched his father make his way to the bar: in the last week before Christmas it was busy, the biggest pub for miles, all lit up round the porch, with a tree in the car park. There were a few old boys among the regulars, but most of them didn't get out this far; they sat over their pints in the Plough, down in the village, where there was a fire, and they still had dominoes. Jonathan actually preferred it there, where they knew people, but the Swan was a good place to meet, on the way home for Stephen and halfway to the Sadlers for him. Here there was a juke box and fruit machine, and the customers were mostly young, Norfolk yuppies and weekenders. Among them, in his casually expensive clothes, with his greying curly hair, Stephen looked distinguished: neither county nor wholly London chic. He had a clever, interesting face, which over the years had seen a lot of fresh air, as well as plans and drawing boards. But watching his father smile and greet the barman Jonathan realised that he was looking older, too – tired, with more lines.

'Had a busy week?' he asked, as Stephen returned with the glasses.

'Alarmingly quiet, to be honest.' He put the glasses on the table and sat down, stretching. 'Bones are getting old. Cheers. How's things? How's Marietta?'

'She's okay, thanks. I'm going over there after this – she's baby-sitting.' He pulled a face. 'It ees a bore. Cheers.'

Stephen said bluntly: 'I hear from Daphne that she's a bit of a disaster.'

Jonathan flushed. 'I don't think that's very fair. It's hard, being over here in a strange house, with all those kids. They've had too many au pairs anyway – she's just one more. I'd hate to be in her shoes.'

'Still . . . she must have had some idea what was expected. It's a pity, when she's come on my recommendation, so to speak.'

'Oh, Dad! Don't start getting heavy, she'll settle down.'

'I hope so, she seems all right when she's with us. Bit quiet.' He took another sip of his beer and said casually: 'Are you sleeping with her?'

'God, what is this? So what if I am? And don't start telling me I mustn't let her distract me from my A levels, because I've already had all that from Mum.'

'Calm down,' said Stephen, not unkindly. 'I didn't mean to upset you.'

'Some things are private, okay? Mum said you might want a man-to-man chat – I suppose you've both been talking about me and decided to put the screws on together.'

'Actually,' said Stephen, 'nothing could be further from the truth. I'm sorry – I didn't mean to pry. It was just . . . never mind.'

'Just what? Curiosity?'

'That's enough. God, you're touchy. I wanted to talk to you about . . . something else.' He broke off. 'On second thoughts, I don't think this is quite the time. Come on, Jon, let's not get in a flap. What do you want to eat?'

They ordered a vegetarian lasagne for Jonathan, steak-and-kidney pie for Stephen. 'Tell me about the UCCA forms,' he said, while they were waiting. 'Where do you want to go?' Discussing this, the atmosphere grew lighter and more neutral; their plates were brought by a young waitress in a pale blue sweatshirt with very short fair hair. Stephen flashed her a smile. 'That looks delicious. Thanks.'

'You can't resist it, can you?' said Jonathan, as they began to eat.

'Resist what?' Stephen asked innocently, and they laughed.

'I told Mum,' said Jonathan, through a mouthful. 'God, this is hot!' He grabbed his glass. 'Bloody microwave.'

'Told Mum what?'

215

'That you turned it on for all the girls. Even Marietta – I think she secretly prefers you, to be honest.'

'Well, you're safe there,' said Stephen. 'It's all right, I'm *teasing*. She's too young for me, that's all.'

'I'm glad to hear it.' Jonathan broke his roll into pieces. 'Mum even seems to think you might have a lady in London.'

'What?' Stephen stopped eating.

'I told her it's all show with you.' He drained his glass. 'I think I'm going to need another with this – d'you think two pints are safe on the bike?'

'No. Here.' Stephen tipped some of his beer into Jonathan's glass; beer slopped on to the table. 'Damn.' He wiped it away with his napkin. 'What on earth made Mum think that?'

Jonathan shrugged. 'I dunno. She's been getting some funny phone calls, though – there was one before I came out. Still, she said it was a breather. I presume you don't associate with women breathers, do you?'

Could that really have been Hilda telephoning?

Stephen said quietly: 'Jon. Be serious for a moment, will you?'

He looked up. 'Why?'

There was a pause, in which Stephen felt his heart begin to thump. What he was about to say – was he really, at last, about to say it? – could never be unsaid: one sentence and everything would be changed for ever, home no longer a retreat but a place of confrontation, even danger. But perhaps it was better – honesty after years of secrecy; involving everyone, for once, instead of living a solitary lie.

'Dad? What is it?'

'I don't know if I can tell you.'

'Course you can. Go on. As I said to Mum, you're looking at a man of the world here.'

He did not smile. His heart thudded as if he were about to go out on stage and tell the world, and he thought: no, I can't. Better, far better, to leave things as they are. But then, with sudden apprehension: when a love affair ends, and you try to pick up the pieces of your old life, perhaps you find they're not there any more. Everything's different, everything's changed – you, and the family you've neglected. And perhaps, if they have known nothing, returning is even more painful. It is one thing to live a routine buoyed up by a secret life, by thoughts and feelings that have nothing to do with your partner, and everything to do with someone else; one thing to keep up appearances when you're inwardly miles away. But to go back, when it's all over, and they notice nothing – my God, keeping up appearances then must feel so bleak, so flat, so empty.

That prospect seemed, indeed, suddenly unbearable, so much so that he said quickly to himself: but what am I thinking of? Who said my life with Hilda is ending? She's probably right – Jon's old enough to know; perhaps he has even guessed. And perhaps, now Sam's here, he even has a right to know.

'Dad! You look dreadful.'

'I'm thinking.'

'Oh, come on, tell me – come on, you're giving me the creeps.'

And as if from a long way away Stephen heard himself say clearly: 'There is someone in London.'

Jonathan slowly put down his fork. 'Oh. Oh. God, I must be thick.'

'What did you think I was going to say?'

'I don't know – perhaps that you'd got some illness, or something. Or something about work. I don't know.' He was turning his fork over and over on the plate. 'Actually, I don't think I want to hear any more.'

But it was begun, and already could not be forgotten. Stephen reached out his hand. 'You know things with Mum and me . . . they haven't been too good for a long time.'

'Haven't they?' Jon said flatly. 'They seem all right to me.'

'Do they really?'

'Well . . . good enough. You seem okay: you don't fight, you're still together. I'm one of the few people at school whose parents' marriage has stayed out of trouble. Mike's parents fight all the time. There were two divorces in my class last year.' He looked at Stephen directly. 'You're not about to tell me you're going to divorce.'

Stephen hesitated. 'I don't think so. But do you think people should stay together when they're unhappy?'

'You're *not* unhappy!' It was said with vehemence.

'How do you know? Do you think Mum's happy?'

Jonathan drew a deep breath. 'I think she's lonely a lot of the time, I think she's a bit sad, but . . . God, I'm sure she doesn't want a divorce.' There was a silence; he pushed his plate away. 'I can't eat any more of this. Go on, then, tell me if you have to. Who is this London woman?'

'She's called Hilda,' Stephen said slowly. 'I've known her a long time, since James and I went into partnership. She's – actually, you've met her. Very briefly.'

'When?'

217

'Last summer. You came down on that school trip and found us having lunch near the British Museum. Remember?'

Jonathan stared. 'Not her. I mentioned her to Mum tonight as reassurance.'

'That's extraordinary.'

'Isn't it?' Jonathan's face was hard, something it had never, ever been. 'You said she was a client.'

'I know.'

'But . . . God Almighty, Dad, she was pregnant.'

Stephen looked steadily back at him. 'Yes.'

There was another, much longer silence.

'I don't believe it,' Jonathan said at last. 'I don't believe it. Jesus!'

'Jon . . .' He leaned across the table. Around them the noise of the crowd grew louder; there was a lot of laughter, and the door banged open and shut.

'Are you telling me,' said Jonathan, screwing his napkin into a tight, hard ball, 'what I think you're telling me?'

'Yes. You've . . . got a baby brother.' Stephen swallowed. 'He was born in August. He's called Sam.'

Jonathan looked away. Then he said slowly: 'I'm going to kill you.'

'Jonathan . . . darling . . .'

'Don't you darling me!' He got up, kicking back his chair, and hurled the napkin across the table. 'I'm going to fucking kill you, got it?'

Heads turned; Stephen said quickly: 'Please! Sit down!'

'I will not. I'm going to see Marietta, and you'd better go back to Mum. And sort it bloody *out*, all right?' He was almost crying, grabbing his things.

'Please,' Stephen said again, and thoughts he'd had earlier of involving everyone in drama whirled away, leaving him gasping, 'Please don't go.'

Jonathan pushed through the crowd, and slammed out of the door.

'Miriam? Miriam!'

There had been no light on outside the garage, and the house itself was dark, except for the kitchen, which was empty. He made his way through the hall again, slowly followed by Tess, checking the sitting room, going upstairs, into every bedroom, flicking switches.

'Miriam!'

No answer. Downstairs again. He stood in the hall; her car was in the garage; she must be here. At his feet, Tess began to whine.

'Stop it!'

He went to the front door again, and pulled it open, peering out into the garden; across the lane the bare trees sighed in the wind.

'Miriam!'

No answer. Beside him, the dog whined again.

'Where is she, Tess? Where is she?'

He went back inside, noticed, suddenly, that the cellar door was ajar.

'Down there?' He walked over, reached inside and switched on the light. Pushed open the door and looked down. Everything was as usual, the saw hung up on the wall, garden tools leaning against it, wine bottles glinting in the rack. The smell of sawn wood from the log pile; the stack of old paint tins. One had fallen over on its side, and a trickle of white ran through the dust. He went down to pick it up, Tess's claws clicking on the wooden steps behind him. He picked up the tin and set it upright, pushing it back against the others, out of the way. As he did so, there was a chink.

His hand on the cool wall, Stephen leaned over the pile of tins, and looked down into the corner. The white tops of whisky and gin bottles, side by side in a small cardboard box, looked back at him.

'Christ.'

Behind him, Tess was nosing among packets of firelighters, boxes of nails. She stepped in the little trickle of paint, and he pushed her out of the way.

'Not there! Come on, girl.'

He climbed the wooden steps again, and closed the door behind them. The dog left a line of white pawmarks all through the hall and down the passage as she followed him into the kitchen; he flung open the garden doors.

'Miriam!'

He ran across the damp grass, the light from the kitchen spilling into the darkness, and down through the gap in the hedge. He hadn't locked the studio door this morning: had she locked it behind her now?

He tried the handle, turned it, lifted the latch. Inside, Miriam was sitting in his swivel chair. Her back was to him, and a glass and a bottle of whisky stood on his desk, among an untidy heap of papers. It had not looked like that this morning.

'Miriam . . .'

'Go away.'

For a moment he did not take in what she had done. Then he saw the drawing board, scrawled over with thick black pen, the plans ripped from the board above his desk, torn and crumpled, the photographs scattered in pieces on the floor.

'Christ Almighty.'

He moved toward her, and the swivel chair spun round. 'Go away!' Her face was terrible. 'Go away, go away, go away!'

Behind him the door was pushed open, and Tess came in from the garden, smelling of earth. She made her way slowly towards Miriam over the mess on the floor, and laid her greying nose in her lap. Miriam bent down and put her arms around her, howling.

He sat with her at the kitchen table, a pot of black coffee between them, the room warm. Back in her basket, Tess slept deeply. The clock ticked; every now and then cinders in the Rayburn shifted and sank, rattling into the ashpan.

They did not touch, sitting next to each other at right angles; their voices rose and fell.

'I didn't mean to do it.'

'I know. I know.'

'Can you save it? Any of it?'

'I expect so, I'll try. It doesn't matter.'

'Of all the things I imagined – somehow I never thought of that.' Her hands clasped the coffee cup, still trembling.

'I was going to tell you – Jonathan first, then you . . .'

'Why?'

'I thought he could take it better. I thought he was growing up, growing away from us . . .'

'Did you? And how did he take it?'

Silence.

'How could you do it? How could you?'

'Only because . . . she wanted it so much.' He hesitated. 'You can probably understand that better than I can.'

She looked at him. 'So this baby has nothing to do with you.'

'I didn't say that.'

'But she's bringing it – him – up by herself.'

'Yes.'

'And how long is she going to do that?'

'I . . .' He shook his head. 'It was her decision, so far she's managing.' Another hesitation. 'She's very strong.'

'She must be,' Miriam said bitterly. 'You have to be strong, bringing up a child alone.'

'Stop it. You haven't been alone.'

'Haven't I?'

'Not like that.'

'Does it matter how?'

Silence.

She said slowly: 'You must have loved her.'

'Yes.'

'And now?'

'Stop it, stop it, please don't cry again.'

'But what about now? You were going to tell us – why? So we could make a decision for you? Or have you made it already?'

'No. I don't know. Jesus.' He put his head in his hands. Nothing he had imagined in trying to prepare for this had even begun to prepare him for it. He thought of his confusion in the pub, barely two hours ago; he remembered, suddenly, the summer evening when he had sat outside on the garden bench, after the long hot drive from London, and watched Jonathan, barefoot, almost naked, stretch out his arms, laughing as Miriam sprayed him with the hose. The water shimmered in the evening sun, the grass shone. He had thought then: to leave all this would be impossible.

And now?

Miriam finished her coffee; she put down the cup and said: 'I'll make a decision. We have Christmas to get through, we have Jonathan to organise into university. If he doesn't fail every single paper.'

'Don't. I know.'

'And then,' she said unsteadily, pushing back her chair, 'I never want to see you again as long as I live.'

London. A tree in every window, Romania on every television. Fallen bodies, mass graves, interrogation, death by firing squad. Rejoicing, jubilation.

Anya and her daughter were glued to the screen. Hilda, who under other circumstances, in earlier days, would have been just the same, had seen the baby, purplish and stiff, in one of the open graves, and now could no longer bear to watch.

And outside Anya's house she carefully lifted Sam from the car and carried him, a bag of presents on the other arm, up the steps to the front door, opened wide by Tony, smiling, holding out his arms, the children behind him shouting: 'Happy Christmas!'

6

Norfolk. In the strange, unmarked, out-of-time days between Christmas and New Year, the shop shut until the January sale, Miriam walked the lanes in her boots and mackintosh, followed by Tess. The weather was ordinary, the sky a pale grey, the air fresh; from time to time wind from the coast blew across the open fields, but it was rarely too cold to go out. The lanes were still muddy from the autumn rain; in occasional gleams of sunshine, puddles shone. Miriam walked and walked.

Stephen was buried in the studio, sticking together pieces of paper, painstakingly redrawing what could not be saved. In a few days he was going down to London, to stay with James and Klara – after years of waiting for his return, Miriam had asked him to go, perhaps for a couple of weeks, perhaps longer. She assumed that during this time he would see Hilda, and come to some arrangement, but she did not know and told herself she did not care.

They had got through Christmas only by drawing a veil; by having people in, by going out, and by watching the Romanian revolution, beside which their own lives seemed, in any case, temporarily unimportant. But Miriam's dreams were full of gunfire, shouting, whirling snow. She dreamed that she was being led through the underground tunnels of Bucharest, blindfolded, hearing water trickle and the scampering of rats, the cry of a baby, quickly smothered. She was being taken to a secret place, but it wasn't clear whether she was to be saved or tried. Then the bandages were taken off her eyes, and she saw Stephen, in uniform – whose? – saying coldly: 'Take her away.' She woke up gasping, in an empty bed, hearing him moving about downstairs.

In the meantime, Jonathan, when he was at home, seemed able to manage the politeness, the knowledge of things unspoken: it was, after all, what he was used to. On the morning after his return from the Sadlers, Miriam had said simply:

'We've had a crisis, but you mustn't worry about it. Dad and I will sort it out.'

He was sitting at the table, in his pyjamas, stroking Tess.

'But are you okay?' he asked, not looking at her.

'Yes. We've had a talk, we'll – we'll sort it out,' she said again, and put packets of cereal on the table.

'Is Dad going to be here for Christmas?'

'Of course.' She looked at him, but he did not meet her eyes. 'Jon? Is that what you want?'

He shrugged. 'I suppose so. Sort of. Where is he now?'

'In the studio.'

'Okay.' He reached for the Weetabix, and neither of them said any more. Later, they finished and posted the UCCA forms, without further discussion.

Miriam was aware, in the days that followed, of Stephen and Jonathan avoiding each other, treading carefully; a lot of the time Jonathan, in any case, went out; when he was there she took to filling in silences at meals by chattering pointlessly about customers in the shop. From time to time they seized on this, and after a while it began to feel, if not normal, then endurable – a means, at least, of enduring.

And now – Jonathan was rarely in the house. From spending all his time there, cloistered with Marietta in his bedroom or cluttering up the kitchen, he took to leaving after breakfast and staying out, returning so late it was obvious he wanted them both to be in bed and out of the way. Stephen was sleeping in the little spare room at the back; Miriam, as always, lay awake until she heard the bike come up the lane. One night Jon rang to say he was staying at the Sadlers.

'They don't seem to mind,' he said, and after that he stayed there quite often.

Miriam did not press him to be at home; in any case, term would be starting soon, and then he'd have to come back. Marietta was obviously staying on after Christmas – perhaps, after a dreadful start, she was settling down; perhaps she was, in her strange little way, cheering up large, red-faced John Sadler. And Daphne had always liked Jonathan. Miriam did not really care – so long as he was coping, in whatever way he had found, she could cope.

But she could not stay in the house. With Tess nosing along paths and ditches she went out day after day – through the woods across the lane, up the long track past the Innes' farm, along to where Jonathan and she had walked so often when they first came here, when he was little, down to the donkey field.

He was still there. He had grown old and stiff; he was greying, and had a sore on his back; one of his eyes was filmy. But he hobbled towards her and put his head on the rusting gate, and she pressed her face against his, stroking his nose. 'Here, boy.' She gave him apples and carrots and listened to him crunching; gusts of wind blew the hay from his shelter in little drifts over the grass. The field was very muddy; he had spent years in here, walking up and down, standing under his leaking iron roof. 'You never see a dead donkey,' someon: had said to her once when she was a child, and she had believed them: surely he would be here for ever.

She walked on, sometimes hearing shots, and the clatter of pigeons some way distant above the trees. Pheasants stalking across the ploughed earth rose in terror to soar over the hedgerows; once, she saw a pair of partridge scuttling into the verge.

But the shooting season was over; it was only a few farmers who brought their guns out now, and although she had Tess's lead in her pocket in case of cars down the lanes there were hardly any cars, either. They had the whole countryside to themselves: she walked farther and farther, through the next quiet village and the next, past lonely old farms where smoke rose from the chimneys into the pale sky, past distant square-towered churches she had never visited. Once, seeing one a bare quarter mile away, the thought crossed her mind that she might go there and pray, but she could not bring herself to pray for Stephen and Hilda and there seemed no point in praying for herself. Perhaps for Jon, for the baby, even – but then, she was no saint, and anyway she had no faith. Not really. She walked on, watching a tractor crawl along the horizon, where field met sky and disappeared into a haze. The light began to fade, she whistled to Tess and turned back.

She was drinking much less, though she knew she could do so openly now; Jonathan wasn't there and Stephen, she felt certain, would not challenge her. But the walks were making her feel better and fitter; after a while she found, when she got back to the house, that she did not want to drink; she went to bed early, knowing that Stephen would not be coming in late, and slept deeply, without a tablet. The restless dreams of Romania began to fade; she could not remember, when she woke, dreaming anything at all. Soon after New Year she went down to the cellar and brought up the bottles of whisky and gin; she took them into the kitchen and stood at the sink, pouring it all away, flushing with the cold tap until all the smell of it was gone.

I am reborn, she thought, closing the door behind her as she set out with Tess, and she opened the garden gate and drew in the clean fresh air.

And yet – and yet. In all this feeling of renewal, a gradual sense of herself growing stronger, there remained an immense, aching sadness. Sometimes when she got back to the house, and found Stephen in from the studio, making tea, she longed, in spite of what she had said to him, to hold out her arms, to be held; to kiss and make up, to start again. If we can come through this, she thought, perhaps we can, at last, begin a proper marriage.

It wasn't possible. Their lives had been changed for ever by something unalterable, that was never going to disappear, and she said nothing. When Stephen asked her, she described her walks, but briefly, giving no hint of their beauty, or sense of revelation, and their conversations became much like the ones they had had for years, with everything unsaid.

Only Tess behaved differently from usual. She loved the long walks, she was leaner, and looked younger. But she did not like the house without Jonathan, Miriam could tell: when they came in she went round looking for him, and if he wasn't there she often fell asleep, muddy and exhausted, not in her basket by the Rayburn but on the front door mat, waiting for him to come home.

'Hilda? Hilda!'

Above Sam's screams, and through her raging headache, Hilda, in bed, could hear Anya banging on the door.

'I'm coming,' she groaned, and tried again to get out of bed and stand up. Across the room, in his cot, Sam was yelling with hunger. 'Stop it,' she said feebly, 'I'm ill.'

'Hilda!'

She crawled down the steps to the door.

'I was just going down again to get my key.' Anya looked at her and shook her head, taking in the situation. 'Go back to bed, go on, you look terrible.'

Hilda clambered up the stairs again, shivering, pains shooting everywhere. 'Help me . . .'

'Tch, tch, tch. You silly girl, you should have called me sooner.' Anya put her capable arm beneath Hilda's. 'Here, now you can do it.' She led her back to the bedroom, where she collapsed on to the rumpled sheets. 'Ssh, Sam, Mummy has the 'flu, we must look after her . . .' She helped Hilda properly into bed, smoothing the sheets, and went over to the cot that was too big to stand by the bed. 'Now, now, everything's all right.' She picked him up – 'There we are, my goodness, what a heavy chap. Have you had your breakfast?' Sam went on screaming. 'No? Here we are.' She passed Sam carefully over; Hilda undid her pyjamas, and lay feeding him with her eyes shut, scarcely hearing Anya leave the room and hurry downstairs. When she came back she was carrying a hot water bottle and a glass.

'Here . . .' She tucked the bottle in at Hilda's feet, and held the glass to her lips. 'Beecham's. Drink it.' Hilda sipped, her face burning. 'Good girl. Now – Sam is on solids, also?'

'Mmm. Kitchen cupboard.'

'Very good. So – I will take him downstairs, with his lunch, and you will rest.'

'I . . . thank you.'

'I have left the door open, so you can call if you need anything, but I think you will probably sleep. Sam will be fine, won't you, Sam? He's finished?'

'Almost.'

'Good. Oh, look, someone else has come up to see how you are.'

'Stephen? Where?' She turned her head.

'No, no, not Stephen. Only Puss.' She patted the duvet, and with a little throaty sound the tabby cat leapt up on to the bed and began to knead out a place to settle, purring loudly. 'There,' said Anya with satisfaction.

Hilda was too weak either to laugh or cry. She let Anya take Sam, and lay back on the pillows, closing her eyes again. At her feet, the tabby cat purred and purred; vaguely comforted, she drifted into a restless doze, which gradually became deep sleep.

She woke when the effects of the powder had worn off, less feverish but still aching, very weak. Getting out of bed to go to the lavatory felt impossible; after a quarter of an hour she managed it, feeling her way along walls, crumpling back to bed again, exhausted. She looked at the clock: twelve-forty-five. What about Sam? She lay listening, hearing from downstairs the sound of the lunchtime news, and beginning to feel bad again. She shifted her feet beneath the sleeping cat; disgruntled, he leapt off, and padded out of the room. Good. That might bring Anya up again.

Anya came, bringing Sam and a fresh glass of Beecham's.

'How is the patient?'

'A bit grim.' She sipped at the fizzing glass. 'Thanks. How's Sam?'

'He's been very good,' Anya said proudly. 'He has had some of his cereal, and some apple purée which I made, haven't you?' Sam smiled round, stretching his arms towards Hilda.

'Hello.' She gave a feeble wave. 'I don't want him to catch it.'

'No, no, of course not. You mustn't worry, I will manage. You just stay there and rest.'

'You mustn't catch it either . . . you'd better keep away.'

Anya waved her hand. 'I am a tough old bird. Also, I have had the injection. Anyway – if I catch it you can look after me, yes?'

Hilda nodded, unable to imagine looking after anyone. 'Nappies.'

'I have found them, while you were asleep. He has been changed. Now – I will put him down, and you can both sleep, and later I will come up and see how you are getting on. All right?'

'You're very kind. I don't know what I'd do . . .'

'I am glad to be able to help.' She was carrying Sam over to his cot. 'Perhaps . . . I would take it downstairs, but I couldn't manage that . . . Perhaps if I take it through to the sitting room? Then we don't have to worry so much about infection.'

'All right.' Hilda lay watching Anya tug the cot towards the door, panting, with Sam on one arm. 'Put him in it,' she suggested.

'Ah! Why didn't I think of that? In you go, Sam, we're going for a little ride.' She laid him down and Sam turned his head to watch Hilda, unruffled, as he was pulled jerkily away, his hanging toys rattling. 'Off we go!'

Hilda turned over and closed her eyes. After a few minutes she jumped, feeling something at her feet: Anya, reaching in for the hot water bottle. She brought it back, refilled, wrapped in a cardigan. 'So it does not burn you,' she whispered, and tiptoed out. Hilda tugged it up the bed and wrapped her arms round it. Her whole body ached, the fever kept at bay but her eyes throbbing. In the midst of this she was aware of a deeper, underlying feeling of total security: she could rest without anxiety – someone, at last, had taken over and was looking after her. She slept again, and did not wake until the evening, finding the curtains drawn and the bedside lamp on the floor, so that it would not hurt her eyes – just as she had arranged the room for Stephen, the very first night he stayed with her, all those years ago.

She was in bed for two days, nursed and later fed by Anya, who came slowly up the stairs with trays of broth – Hilda couldn't remember the last time she'd heard the word – and steamed fish. The cats followed, winding themselves round her legs as she set down the tray. 'Shoo! You can have yours later.' While all this was going on Sam rolled over on his playmat, shrieking with laughter if a cat came near, or dropping toys from his bouncing chair, another thing almost out-grown. He was enormous.

On New Year's Eve Anya brought up a jug of freshly squeezed orange juice, and they raised their glasses to each other while he slept. On New Year's Day Hilda got up, and sat in her rocking chair with a cup of hot chocolate, while Anya stripped her bed and remade it with fresh clean sheets. Sam, breakfasted on milk from her and Weetabix from Anya, lay kicking on his mat beneath a mobile of felt scraps and bottle tops, his Christmas present from Hettie. Alice and Tony had given him a bar with dangling handles and rattles, which hung across his cot, and a pile of soft cubes with bells inside; Hettie and Annie had made him cards, smothered in glitter. Everyone had been kind and welcoming, putting the baby in his chair beneath the tree so that he could enjoy the lights, giving Hilda books and pretty things from the Body Shop. But Alice did not press her to stay, and thinking about the visit as she drove Sam home on Boxing Day evening, Hilda was aware that there had been something of a silence between Alice and Tony, which at the time she had put down to Tony's tiredness but which in retrospect perhaps was more than that.

The other, more apparent silence, was over the whole reason for her being with them at all: Stephen's name was simply never men-tioned. She presumed that this was because they did not want to pry, or upset her, treating her and Sam as a little unit in themselves without pointing up the obvious absence. A part of her was glad to go along with this – if she behaved, as they did, as though nothing were out of the ordinary, she would begin to feel ordinary. Another part found it disturbing and miserable, because she did not feel ordinary, she felt bereft – not just because she and Sam were alone but because, since the week before Christmas, she had heard nothing from Stephen at all.

Now, at the start of a new decade, she sat sipping her hot chocolate and looking down into the empty square. Everyone seemed to have gone away – or perhaps they, too, like much of country, had been struck down by 'flu. Perhaps Stephen had it, and that was why he hadn't phoned. In the past three days he had become somehow sealed away: after the first wild hope that he might have come down to see her, she had felt too ill to dwell on the pain of missing him. And now, weakly convalescent, it was as though he had somehow, like the old year, been left behind on the other side of a door, leaving her empty and numb. She wished she could be taken away, to get prop-erly better in new surroundings, with fresh air and a log fire. I wish, she realised, that I was in my father's house again and, thinking this, was no longer numb but swept by a total sense of loss: of her lover, her father, and a grandfather for Sam, who lay placidly sucking the corner of a soft brick covered in pictures of Peter Rabbit.

'There.' Anya came out of the bedroom with a heap of linen. 'I shall put this in the washing machine.'

'Thank you.' Hilda sat watching her bustle into the little kitchen, hearing the kettle switched on and then the first slow whooshing of the washing machine, filling up. In a minute she would get up and have a bath: the prospect felt like a monumental effort. I haven't been like this since the birth, she thought, and soon I've got to go back to work. How shall I ever do that, I wonder? And the old, childless Hilda, energetic, collected, self-contained, seemed also like another person left behind, lost, un-recapturable.

'So.' Anya was back in the room again, carrying a cup of coffee. She sat herself down at the desk and regarded Hilda kindly. 'How are you feeling?'

'Not brilliant.'

'It takes it out of you, this 'flu. I hope my Liba does not catch it – she looks strong, but she is even worse than you at looking after herself.' Hilda smiled wanly. 'You want to go back to bed? It's all ready for you.'

'I know, you're very good. I was thinking perhaps I'd have a bath first.'

'Not too hot – you could faint, coming out of a hot bath after all this. It can make your head swim.'

Hilda laughed, in spite of herself. 'Whatever would I do without you?'

'I don't know,' said Anya. She looked down at Sam, chewing happily on his brick with toothless gums. 'Is that nice? We must think about your lunch in a little while.'

Hilda put her mug on the desk and got up slowly. 'Tomorrow I'll be back in charge,' she said. 'You won't have to worry about him any more. But I can't thank you enough for everything.'

Anya said: 'Hilda?'

'Yes?'

'You are going back to work soon.'

'Yes.'

'You have found someone to look after Sam?'

'I – ' Hilda leaned weakly on the back of the chair. 'I think so, yes. I interviewed several people before Christmas.'

'I see.' There was a pause. 'Nice people?'

'They seemed all right – I'm seeing one of them again. Anya, I'm sorry, can we talk about this later? I'm still feeling a bit pathetic. Do you mind?'

'No, no, of course not, you go and have your bath. I'll keep an eye on Sam. Yes?'

'Thanks.' She went slowly to the bathroom, hearing an inquiring little sound from one of the cats, coming up through the open door, and Sam's giggle as he caught sight of it. She turned on the taps and poured in Body Shop bubbles, brushing her teeth while the water ran. In the mirror, a thin white face looked back at her.

In the bath she ran through the women she had visited before Christmas, answering notices in the newsagent's window, printed in uncertain capitals. *Registered reliabel childminder availabel with refs.* She had telephoned several, taking Sam up in the graffiti-sprayed lifts of the local estate, along windswept concrete corridors, and down endless streets off the High Street; she was ushered into small hot sitting rooms strewn with toys, where toddlers turned from the television to look at Sam indifferently. Most of the women looked overtired; three of them smoked, and these Hilda ruled out completely. She could not imagine leaving Sam with any of them for longer than half an hour. She knew, from the college noticeboards, that there were good childminders to be had but she could find only one, a sweet-looking woman in her fifties, who looked after her own daughter's children and two others, but whose list was full. Hilda found one more, who lived in a road on the way to college, which was an advantage, and who had only one other child in her care: it was she whom she must ring again.

There was always the créche at college, the obvious choice, but somehow she could not bring herself to leave a baby there. When Sam was older he'd probably enjoy it, toddling about with other children, with a little slide like the one Hettie and Annie used to have, and a guinea pig in a hutch. But to leave a baby there all day . . . she had heard babies crying there, often, left in their chairs without being cuddled while older ones fell, or fought, or needed changing – she didn't want Sam to be left like that. I suppose I'm fussy and over-protective, she thought; and, getting out of the bath, she began, as Anya had predicted, to feel lightheaded and unwell. She sat on the edge, wrapped in her towel with her head between her knees until the giddiness passed, and crept back to bed in clean pyjamas.

'All right?' Anya stood in the doorway, holding Sam.

'Mmm.'

'I'll bring you some lunch, a little chicken. That'll give you strength. I'm taking Sam down now, all right?'

'Okay. Thanks.'

When they had gone, she lay on her side looking out of the window. It was a grey, flat-looking day, with neither wind nor sunshine to usher in the new year. Still, lying on clean sheets on plumped-up pillows, she began to feel a bit better. She thought about Anya's kindness, her unspoken question, and found herself thinking: after all, it would have its advantages. Sam knows her, he feels safe with her now, and the cats make him happy. And anyway, it's not for ever. She could not imagine Sam growing up in this house, but as a baby, with the garden there when it got warmer . . . So long as she lets me pay her, she thought, hearing the now familiar sound of Anya's footsteps, the cutlery chinking on the tray. I don't want to be indebted, that I couldn't stand.

'Here we are.' Anya was in the room, panting; steam rose comfortingly from the tray and the chicken smelt delicious. In her good grey skirt and the grey cardigan Liba had given her for Christmas, she looked capable and correct, ready to take charge of anyone. 'Can you sit up?'

'Yes, yes. Thank you, Anya, you're wonderful.' She took the tray, seeing Anya's smile, warm and uncomplicated. After all, wasn't a baby meant to cheer everyone up? 'I was wondering,' she said, 'How *you* would feel about looking after Sam.'

Thanks to Anya, that first, real crisis was over. And what would I have done if she had not been there? Hilda wondered, feeling stronger, tidying up a bit, opening windows, getting out books and folders of notes she had not looked at since last July. I suppose I should have phoned Alice, or Jane, but they would have had to leave their own children, or bring them too. How do women manage on their own with babies when they're ill? And as in those intense, cloistered days in hospital, she felt as though she had lived before in total ignorance, with only herself to worry about.

In the past few days she had begun to receive mail from the college: timetables, budgets, policy documents, news of further cuts, rumours of a strike. Sitting at her desk, reading through all this while Sam slept, she felt at first completely at sea, as if the papers related to a life and a person who had nothing to do with her, and she was tense, too, waiting for Sam, who slept less and less in the day, to wake up. But gradually, as there was no sound from the bedroom, she began to concentrate, even to get interested and look forward to going back. She had made her arrangements with Anya, who was going to have Sam every day. It was not, Hilda realized, what she had originally envisioned: Sam going off each day to a bright, well-ordered home full of paints and playdough, run by someone young and imaginative, where one or two other, older children played around and with him, but it seemed the best she could do for him at the moment, and Anya was carefully overjoyed.

'We shall enjoy ourselves, shan't we, Sam? And in the holidays you will have your Mummy back again.'

'You make it sound as if I'm leaving him for weeks on end,' said Hilda. 'I'll be back soon after five, I'm not doing any evening classes, so I'll be able to breastfeed him then, as well as in the mornings.'

'Of course,' said Anya placatingly. Hilda knew she was thinking: But soon he will be on solids completely, with no need for all this breastfeeding. And there is always a bottle. She bit back her own reply – that after five months she had grown almost as dependent on it as he was, that she felt it was the least she could do for him, really, going back to work when he was so small. Well, relatively small. He grew and grew.

In all these preparations and discussions, Hilda occasionally allowed herself to envision the other alternative: she and Stephen in their own home together; Stephen, as well as she, coming home at the end of the day to their baby; Stephen sharing nights, and weekends, and walks in the park – not on a flying visit but always. When she succumbed to all this, usually late at night, she wondered if that, really, was what she had always hoped for. She supposed that it was, deep down. She'd thought she was going to be able to handle it all so well; she certainly couldn't handle this silence, this not knowing. Why didn't he get in touch? She looked at the telephone, waiting on the desk like an enemy, refusing to ring. Or, if she picked it up and dialled his number, an accomplice. No. She wasn't going to start all that again. It made her feel like someone sick, unhinged. And perhaps I shall end up unhinged, she thought one night, pacing again, unable to sleep. All the sense of distance that she had felt while she was ill had gone. Although, in the daytime, she was competent, managing, getting through, in the evening, with Sam asleep, she was beginning to feel desperate.

Hilda went back to work on an overcast morning in the second week of January, trying not to hurry Sam over his morning feed, looking at her watch. No more walks to the college any more, at least not in the winter – she wanted to be able to drive home quickly at the end of the day.

She dressed rapidly, eating a piece of toast on the run, carrying her books and stuff out to the car and racing back upstairs again for Sam. She brought him downstairs to where Anya stood waiting in the hall.

'So,' She held out her arms. 'Good morning, Sam, and how are you today?'

'He's fed and changed,' said Hilda briskly, handing him over. 'Well – ' She stood for a moment, hovering, looking at her baby in Anya's cardiganned arms; he was turning to look at her but not in any alarm.

'He will be fine,' said Anya. 'Enjoy yourself.'

'Yes. Yes, all right then. Bye, Sam.' She moved across, and bent to kiss his round warm head. Tears pricked her eyes. She wanted to say to him: 'I love you, I love you, you're my very own.' Instead, she touched his round cheek and said quickly: 'See you soon,' and turned and ran down the steps to the car.

'Hilda?'

'Stephen! Oh, thank God, I've been so worried.' She carried the phone over to the rocking chair. At her feet Sam, just out of the bath and in his night things, began to fret. 'Hang on a minute.' She bent down and picked him up with one arm, putting him on her lap. 'There we are. Say hello to Stephen.'

Sam grabbed at the receiver, then the flex. 'No darling, careful. Sorry, Stephen, just let me sort this out . . . Sam!' She took the receiver from him and he began to cry. 'Look, have this.' She reached to the desk for his musical rabbit, but Sam was bored with his musical rabbit, he wanted the telephone. 'Stop it! Stephen? Sorry . . .' She put Sam down on the floor again and he cried harder than ever. Well, it was just too bad. She stood with her back to him, her finger in one ear, the other pressed to the receiver. 'Can you hear me? Are you all right? I've had 'flu, have you?'

'No . . . no, I haven't. I'm sorry I haven't rung, I did try this afternoon, but you were out.'

'I was at work,' said Hilda. 'I went back this morning.'

'God, I didn't realise it was so soon. How was it?'

'Fine, I think. I can hardly remember with all this noise.'

'What's the matter with him? I thought he'd be asleep by now.'

'Did you?' Hilda felt suddenly cross and defensive. 'He is usually, but we haven't seen each other all day, we've been playing.' There was a pause, in which she struggled to collect herself. 'Where are you?'

'In Camden. I'm staying with James.'

Sam's cries were growing louder. She said quickly: 'Could you come over?'

'What?'

'I said could you come over? Please?'

There was another pause. Then Stephen said: 'I don't think so, not at the moment. Why don't I ring you back?'

'Okay.' She was deflated. 'Give me an hour or so, all right?'

'Fine. Talk to you later, then. I'd better let you get on with it.'

'Yes. Sorry.' Why was she sorry? 'Stephen? Happy New Year.'

But he didn't hear her, and put down the phone. Hilda turned to Sam in exasperation. 'Come here, horror.' She picked him up and he stopped crying. 'I should think so, you'll have to learn better manners than that when I'm on the phone.' She buried her face in his neck; he smelt of talc from the bath and Lenor from his pyjamas. She nuzzled him and he began to laugh. 'That's better. Come on, let's get you off to sleep.'

Feeding him, lying on her bed with the nightlight on, she held him close, stroking his hair. It was growing much thicker, the colour of straw but soft as feathers. 'I do love you,' she said gently, 'and I did miss you. Sorry I was cross.' Sam sucked peacefully, and she yawned, feeling calmer. At least Stephen had phoned, and if he had sounded tense and irritable it was probably because of Sam crying. Well, at least partly. Whatever it was, they would sort it out in a little while. And if he was staying with James he would surely be able to come over soon. Tomorrow? 'Please,' she said aloud, with sudden longing, 'please tomorrow.'

Sam had fallen asleep. She carried him carefully over to his cot and laid him down, avoiding the rattling bar, pulling up his duvet. Then she went quietly out of the room and sat by the telephone, preparing tomorrow's classes.

Stephen did not phone back until almost midnight. By that time Hilda had given up, had a bath and gone to bed in a fury. She was just drifting off, realising, as she pulled down the pillows, how tired she was, when she heard the phone and sprang out of bed, stumbling to answer it before Sam woke up.

'Hello?' She switched on the desk lamp, out of breath.

'Hilda – I'm sorry it's so late. Did I wake you?'

'It's all right.' She pulled her sweater off the back of her desk chair. 'What happened?'

'I was working – I just didn't realise how late it was.'

'Oh.' There was a silence, in which she managed to pull the sweater round her shoulders, keeping the phone to her ear, and sit down.

'How are you? How have you been?'

'I told you – I've had 'flu. Luckily Anya was able to look after us.'

'You sound very fed up.' It was said almost provocatively, inviting another snapping answer, bound to make things worse, and within moments of picking up the phone Hilda could feel a row brewing: she sat willing it not to happen, not after all these weeks apart.

'Hilda?'

'Yes?'

'What's wrong?'

'Nothing,' she said carefully. 'I'm still a bit sleepy. Please tell me how you are, what's been happening. How was your Christmas?'

She could hear him take a breath. 'Actually, not very good, that's why I haven't rung. I – I did what you suggested.'

'What do you mean? You mean you told them?'

'Yes.' A pause. 'It was pretty grim, to say the least.'

'Oh, Stephen . . . I'm so sorry. What happened . . . ?'

'To put it in a nutshell, Jonathan has more or less left home and isn't speaking to me, and Miriam has given me the push. Sort of. I have a suspended sentence, apparently.'

'Oh, Stephen . . .' she said again. 'But if – I mean – can't you come over here? Come here and stay. I'll look after you.' Was that the right thing to say? If everything was over, then surely that was the obvious thing to do? And then they could – then everything . . . 'Stephen?'

'I don't think that's a very good idea. Not at the moment.'

'But – ' Didn't he want to come?

'Please, don't make it worse.'

'I – ' She covered her mouth. Why should offering comfort make it worse? She thought dully: He's going to say he needs time to himself, I can feel it coming. And even if it's true, it feels like the beginning of the end.

'I just feel I'd better have some time on my own. To think things out. Is that reasonable? Do you understand?'

'Yes. Yes, of course.'

From the bedroom, a cry. She covered her ear. 'It's just – you know, Sam. He'd like to see you, too. We're awfully . . .' No. Don't say it; make it sound okay or he'll never come. 'Never mind. He's woken up, I'd better go.'

'Are you . . . managing all right?'

'Yes, fine. Don't worry. You just – sort things out.'

'I'll be in touch, I promise.'

'Okay, thanks. I'd better go, he's starting to yell.'

'Bye, then, Hilda.'

'Bye.'

She put down the phone and sat for a moment without moving, her hand on the receiver. Then she slowly got up and switched off the desk lamp. By the gleam of the nightlight through the open bedroom door she made her way back there, and picked up her baby – *her* baby; it felt just then as if he had nothing to do with Stephen.

After that, the days became full of contrasts. Hilda went back to work a different person, and for about a week was treated as such: there were excited greetings, enquiries, exclamations over photographs. After that, with astonishing speed, she began to feel as though she had never been away. Each morning she parked the car, pushed open the heavy swing doors of the main building and walked through the concourse, past the tubs of trailing house-plants, the heavy clay pots in glass cases, the students with their files and clipboards, looking at the noticeboard, getting drinks and Kit-Kats from the machine. Hilda, who had not had a coffee for months, now automatically stopped to get one, and carried it up the broad stone steps and along the corridor to her cramped little office on the first floor.

At her corner desk beside the filing cabinet she pinned up a photograph of Sam next to her timetable and sat sipping from the plastic cup, looking through the pile of notes and papers left by the woman who had covered for her. She picked up the threads of her classes again, and covered for people off with 'flu; she chaired meetings to discuss curriculum development and cuts. She went to a union meeting about the threatened one-day strike and voted in favour; she interviewed applicants to run a study-skills course on Tuesday afternoons and realised with a mixture of embarrassment and relief that at least one of them found her formidable. Soon, there were moments

236

– having lunch with her colleagues in the canteen, or coming back to her office from a class – when she realised that for an hour or more she had been so absorbed that the past six months might never have happened. There was no baby, no lover, no change – they had all slipped away like a dream, like someone else's dream, and now she was single again, working, in charge, reclaimed.

As soon as she left the building, however, all this changed again. She found herself hurrying across the car park, driving home listening absently to the news headlines on the radio, drumming her fingers on the steering wheel, taut with impatience when the traffic slowed. When she arrived in the square she cursed if there was no parking space left near the house, and ran down the road with her bag of books, panting up the steps to the front door. Was he crying? Did he realise she was late? She unlocked the door with cold fingers, stepping into the dimly lit hall, calling out: 'I'm home!'

But Sam was rarely crying, and sometimes, even before she reached the front door, she could hear Anya on the piano, playing to him as he lay on the rug by the fireguard. 'Jack and Jill went *up* ze hill to *fetch* a pail of *vat*er!' Her accent was heavier in English nursery rhymes than it ever was in speech, but her voice, from all the years in the choir, was strong and clear; it made Hilda want to go back to rehearsals again.

'So. Here is Mummy.' Anya came out into the hall, holding the door to her sitting room wide. 'Come in, sit down, have a cup of tea.'

Down on his rug Sam, chewing a teething ring, turned his head to look up at Hilda curiously.

'Baby . . .' She wanted to swoop him up and smother him in kisses. Instead, hearing him begin to pant and whimper like a Pavlov puppy – half-past five, time for milk – she sat on one of Anya's old armchairs, still in her coat, and picked him up for his feed, kissing him surreptitiously when Anya went out to the kitchen, slipping a finger to be held in his plump little hand, stroking his forehead, his cheek, his ears. He gazed up at her with wide blue eyes – whose eyes? Hers were brown, Stephen's grey, where had he got this deep, glorious blue? From time to time he broke off to watch one of the cats leap softly off the top of the piano, or stretch and yawn on the back of the sofa, and follow Anya out to the kitchen, miaowing.

'They know it's tea time when you come home.' Anya came back, carrying the beaten metal tray, with cups and biscuits.

'Like Sam.' Hilda looked up at her, holding him close. 'How has he been?'

'He has been wonderful. We have been for a walk to the park, and seen the ducks, haven't we, Sam? And he has had a good sleep this afternoon. I think perhaps his teeth are giving him some trouble, sometimes he is fretful . . .'

Hilda felt a little twist of anxiety. How fretful? Did that mean howling, made light of by Anya? 'It is quite normal,' Anya said calmly, and set down a cup of tea on the table next to the armchair. 'How was your day today?'

Hilda yawned. 'Fine. Busy. I can't remember.' She sipped her tea, asking casually: 'Was there any post?'

It was as though a wall had been built between home and work, neatly dividing her day so that each part was lived by two different people, each more or less incomprehensible to the other. Perhaps, if that had been all she now expected of life – to teach and to look after Sam – she would have grown used to switching on and switching off at the beginning and end of each day. But it was not all, even if she had once thought it would be, and she was not a robot. What connected her two lives were the sudden, unexpected, piercing moments of longing for Stephen.

At college, everyone on the staff knew her situation – it wasn't like the moment of discovery in the last class of the summer with her Asian students, who now studiously avoided all mention of a father when they admired the photos of Sam in her arms, or in his bouncing chair. Nor was it like being in hospital, falsely addressed as Mrs King. Still, it was painful to have to field questions, however well-intentioned, over the canteen table or from people dropping into the office: how was Stephen, did he manage to get down often, had he been with her at the birth; was he – asked on Friday afternoons – coming down this weekend? She knew that none of the people asking all this held any moral views about her life – at least, they did not appear to. They asked out of interest, and friendship, and almost certainly did not want to know more, or to think about what her day-to-day life was really like. Perhaps, deep down, one or two did disapprove, those who were married themselves, with children, but she refused to let it worry her – it was, after all none of their business. And answering their kind, interested questions would not have been a problem if she had known, as she seemed to know in the old days, where she and Stephen were going. Now she knew nothing, she was cut off, confused and unhappy.

At times like this, calmly telling people that Stephen hadn't managed to be with her when Sam was born, or wasn't, actually, coming down this weekend, she felt angry and frustrated and tearful, though she hoped that no one would ever have guessed it, and that they barely noticed her smooth change of subject to their own lives, their own preoccupations. At times like this she would have given anything to look up and see him, suddenly, miraculously, framed in a doorway, holding out his hand, his suitcase in the other, coming to stay.

At college, such moments passed quickly: she was too busy to dwell on them. At home, the longing for him was more painful and more acute, particularly so when she took Sam out of Anya's warm sitting room, with its clutter of books and cats and music, and up the stairs to their own little flat at the top. She could hear Anya switch on the television almost as soon as they left – Romania's revelations of misery and brutality were still in the headlines and, anyway, the television news had become an addiction for Anya now, like *Neighbours* and *Brookside*. After a long day, with Sam and her bag to hump up the two floors, Hilda was exhausted when she reached the top. If she had not fed him downstairs, she did so straight away; more often, she plonked her bag on the sofa and him on his playmat and felt, for a few minutes, totally disoriented.

There was no letter from Stephen, and it was, in truth, the hope of one, as well as the longing to see Sam again, that had her racing up the front steps each evening. The telephone sat silent on the desk – why wasn't it ringing when she came in, why wasn't Stephen here, waiting to surprise her? For those first few moments, each homecoming was an endurance. Then she knelt down on the floor beside Sam, and kissed and cuddled and played with him, before she ran his bath – and often one for both of them, with lashings of baby bubbles – and the evening began to take on its own shape and purpose.

When Sam had fallen asleep – and it took longer, these days to get him off – she had supper with the television and afterwards sat at her desk marking papers, preparing classes, yawning. Once upon a time, she thought, I had my books and no man. Then I had a man and my books and no baby; now I have my books and my baby and no man. There was a poem to be written out of this, but she couldn't find the last line.

She supposed it was time she asked Anya to babysit in the evenings occasionally, so she could go out and do something interesting: Lizzie, one of her part-timers, who ran a creative writing workshop on Wednesday afternoons, rang one night and suggested they went to see a film, *When Harry met Sally*, at the Screen on the Green in

Islington. Hilda jumped when the telephone rang and said she was feeling too tired this week but another time she'd love to. Jane invited her over for supper – 'You can bring Sam with you, he and Daisy can have a bath together' – and Hilda said she would, very soon. She knew she should invite Alice and Tony over, to repay all their hospitality at Christmas, but she couldn't quite face doing supper and found she couldn't quite face having them all for Sunday lunch, either. She went to bed earlier and earlier, and was woken, still, by Sam, at unpredictable hours, and sometimes more than once. Afterwards it was difficult to get back to sleep; when she eventually did so it became difficult to get up with the alarm.

'You are looking terrible,' Anya told her one morning, as she handed Sam over in the hall. 'It is too much for you, all this.'

Hilda shrugged. 'What else am I supposed to do? I'll have a rest at the weekend.' Weekends were worse than anything. She dropped a kiss on Sam's head and turned the catch on the front door. A gust of wind blew it in towards her, unsteadying all of them. 'Heavens.' She pushed it to again, leaving just a gap, and looked out cautiously. The trees in the square were swaying, dustbin lids rattled and banged.

'It was on the forecast,' said Anya. 'High winds. I will keep Sam indoors today.'

'All right. Thanks. I think he's got a bit of a cold, anyway.' Hilda made her way down the steps, holding on to her black beret. It began to pour.

By two o'clock the wire mesh guards on the classroom windows were shaking; slates lifted from the roof and smashed on the tarmac below, and a pile of plywood stacked up against an outside wall came crashing down into the car park. The college secretaries were on the telephone, cancelling afternoon classes; Hilda and the other staff made their way out of the building, holding on to each other, laughing to keep their alarm at bay. She drove home slowly, feeling the car buffeted. Mounds of soaking wet cardboard boxes, put out by shop-keepers in the early morning for the dustcart, lifted and blew along the pavements; the whole of Hackney was awash with wet litter. Hilda parked two doors away from home and got out of the car cautiously.

Those houses in the square that had remained untouched by developers, the shut-up ones, the ones with dark windows, peeling front doors and crumbling porticos, where lonely old people took in meals on wheels and lonely young people took drugs, were, she realised now, not just sad but dangerous. Chimney pots lay shattered on the wet pavement, windows rattled. As she pushed her way along the few yards to her own front door, leaning into the wind and rain, the trees in the communal garden creaked menacingly. Hilda ran up the front steps, seeing Anya at the window, Sam in her arms. She came straight out into the hall.

'Thank goodness. Come in, I must lock the door.'

In the sitting room, they stood at the french windows looking out on to the rainswept garden, watching the trellis, heavy with naked tendrils of honeysuckle and clematis, bend back and forth in the wind. Bits of painted wood and a piece of cardboard came sailing over from other, neglected gardens; at the far end the bare trees began to roar. 'The cats have been terrified,' said Anya. They were crouched beneath the sofa, looking out with dark eyes.

'I suppose the roof is all right,' said Hilda, turning Sam in her arms. His little hands banged on the window, against the driving rain.

'The roof is very sound,' said Anya. 'Josef made sure of it.'

There was a sudden, ugly, tearing noise from the end of the garden, and a branch ripped away, crashing down on to the trellis.

'My God. I shall have to get in a man. They did not say it was going to be as bad as this.'

'They never do,' said Hilda. 'Look at '87.'

'It was at night – we didn't feel it so much.'

'No, but . . .' Clissold Park had been ravaged, whole trees uprooted. And she and Stephen, on a rare weekend together out of London, had driven through Surrey and seen decimation, as if the devil had stormed through woodland, bent on destruction. East Anglia had been spared, then – what about now? There were woods across the lane from Stephen's house, there were trees in the garden – he had described it all, in the old days. When we talked to each other, she thought bleakly; when we were friends. Now I don't know where he is. If he's gone back to Norfolk, if he's driving, out in this – people get killed in the country, trees fall on cars . . .

'Hold Sam,' she said suddenly to Anya. 'Please. I've just thought of – I must just make a phone call.'

She raced up the stairs to the telephone. She knew James and Klara's number by heart, although she rarely used it. Klara, without question, disapproved – no hide-out for illicit lovers there. But still. But now. She dialled, and waited, panting.

'Hello?'

'Klara. It's Hilda King.'

'Oh. Hello.' Somewhere in the background, a querulous child.

'I'm sorry to bother you, I just feel rather worried by this storm. I wondered if Stephen was still staying with you – he hasn't been in touch.'

'No,' said Klara, 'no, he isn't. He left here a couple of days ago.'

'Oh.' Hilda felt her heart sink. 'He's – he's in Norfolk, then.'

'Presumably.' Klara's tone was unencouraging.

'Well – ' Hilda refused to be put off. She had to know, she had a right to know, for God's sake, Stephen wasn't just her lover, he was Sam's father. Did Klara know about Sam? 'Well, do you know when he's coming down again?'

'I'm afraid not.' The querulous child was more insistent. 'Stop it! Mummy's on the phone.'

Perhaps Klara was sick of Stephen arriving, staying, announcing his marriage was over. If he couldn't go there, why didn't he come here? What was he thinking of, shifting his stuff about up and down the country?

'Listen,' said Hilda. 'I *have* to speak to him, it's important. I'm sorry if it's a nuisance, but there it is. Please can you ask him to phone me, as soon as you hear from him.'

'Yes,' said Klara coldly. 'I'll tell him you rang.'

'Thank you.' She put down the phone and put her head in her hands.

Later, she and Anya sat watching the news, the scenes of devastation, hearing of school rooftops lifted into the air, children killed, lorries overturned, scaffolding torn away from buildings, people crushed to death in their cars.

'My God,' said Anya again. 'They should sue those weather men.' She got up stiffly. 'I must telephone Liba, she is always driving somewhere.'

Hilda took Sam up to bed. When he had gone to sleep she lay down with the nightlight on, still in her clothes, willing herself not to go to the phone again. She couldn't phone Norfolk now, it was out of the question. Could she pretend to be someone else? Impossible.

Outside the house the wind had died down; it had roared away towards the south coast and left them unharmed. And what if they had been harmed? What if she and Sam had been out there this afternoon, if she had been like the mother in Brixton, crushed with her baby in a pushchair by a falling wall? They'd have been on the news then, and would *that* have made Stephen phone? By then it would be too late. At least she knew that he was safe – there was no one from Norfolk in the news. Just at the moment, torn between anger and relief, it seemed small comfort.

Next morning, Friday morning, Anya said: 'My Liba has 'flu. She is so naughty not to phone me, I only found out last night, she sounded dreadful. I am going down to Brighton to look after her.' She took Sam into her arms and he clutched at her spectacles. 'No, darling, we will find you your toys.' She looked at Hilda, holding his hands away. 'You will manage this weekend? You don't mind feeding the cats?'

'Of course not, I always manage. I hope Liba's all right – I'll come back early if I can.'

She gave Sam a kiss and opened the front door, walking out to the car through a square filled with pieces of cardboard, litter, torn-off branches and twigs, broken glass. This last made her remember the time when Stephen's car window had been smashed. She stepped wearily over the debris, having slept very little last night, and tried not to think about the weekend.

A cry. Somehow, though she was in the depths of sleep, it didn't sound like an ordinary cry. She stumbled out of bed.

'All right, Sam, I'm here.'

The nightlight stood on the chest of drawers by his cot, a little white owl with yellow feet. Even in its dim glow she could see that Sam's face was much too flushed; she lifted him out and he went on crying; she took him back to bed and he sucked at her indifferently, then turned his head away and began to cry again.

'Oh, God. You're really not well, are you?' Hilda looked at the bedside clock: a quarter to two. Now what? She put her hand on his forehead and he twisted out of her reach, hot and damp. She unbuttoned his pyjamas and carried him to the bathroom; she changed him and he cried and cried.

'What is it, Sam? Tummy?' She opened the cabinet, fumbling amongst the plasters and bottles of Savlon and TCP for the Calpol, which was running low. Calpol would bring down his fever and send him back to sleep – anything, so long as he went back to sleep, he'd woken this morning at five. 'Please stop crying, Mummy's looking for the medicine.' God, where was it? She picked up a tube of toothpaste, and a bottle of aspirin crashed down into the basin; she jumped and Sam's screams grew even worse. 'Stop it! Where *is* the bloody stuff?'

It wasn't there. It really wasn't. Then where – she had a sudden memory of Anya, with Sam in her arms: 'He's teething a little, it's perfectly normal.' Of herself saying yesterday morning, 'He's got a bit of a cold.' Anya must have come up here and taken it. Okay, then, she'd have to go downstairs.

'Come on, Sam, we're going to Anya's.'

For a couple of minutes, as they made their way down, he stopped crying, distracted. It was cold, and she hadn't got slippers on; the house felt very empty. At Anya's door she realised she'd left the key upstairs. She carried Sam all the way up again, and he began to cry once more. She took the keys from her desk, went down, unlocked the door, feeling for the light switch. Now where would Anya have put the bottle? Probably the kitchen.

'Prrt?' With a little sound the cats uncurled themselves from sofa and armchair, and followed her out of the room. They wound round her legs as she put on the light in the kitchen and looked round, shivering; they went to their dishes, set down on the worn linoleum.

'Stop it! It's the middle of the night. Now – where's she put it?' There were shelves of yellowing cookbooks, half of them probably Josef's, collector's items. There were cupboards full of cat food, tinned peas and marmalade, a whole shelf for Sam's jars of strained fruit and packets of cereals; another cupboard full of ancient aluminium saucepans. There was no bottle of Calpol. In her arms Sam was yelling, beginning to struggle. 'Please. Please!' She took him back to the sitting room, searching along the mantelpiece. No. Her bathroom? Possibly.

'Wait there, Sam, I'm sorry, wait just a minute . . .' She put him down on the rug and left him screaming as she ran up the stairs again. Anya's bathroom was large and cold, with cracked white tiles and worn towels hanging on a clothes horse. Her medicine cabinet was locked. Hilda began to moan.

'What am I going to do?' From downstairs Sam's cries sounded as if he were in agony. He obviously was. She raced back down to him again, and picked him up. 'I'm sorry, I'm sorry, come on, let's go back up again, let's think.' She switched off the lights and shut the doors, pushing the curious cats back inside with her foot. 'Move!' Perhaps that was a mistake, it might distract Sam if one of them came up too. Well, stuff it, she'd done it. 'All right, all right, Sam. I think we'll have to . . .' Have to what? Call the doctor, what else could she do? Rarely ill herself, the bout of 'flu the first time she'd been in bed for years, Hilda was the last person to think of calling out the doctor in the middle of the night – it felt like the kind of thing you did only when someone was dying. Sam wasn't dying, was he? She suddenly began to feel frightened – she was alone in this house, with no one nearby to call on, a sick baby. She carried Sam over to her desk, and flicked through her address book. 'All right, all right,' she said for the hundredth time. 'We're getting the doctor, you'll soon be better . . .' His screams were piercing. She dialled the number and put him back on the floor so she could hear when the surgery answered. The telephone rang and rang.

At last, an answerphone. Another number. She dialled that, too, and got a curt receptionist.

'Can I help you?'

'I'm sorry to bother you, but my baby's ill . . .'

'Your name and address? Phone number?'

Hilda gave them. 'How long do you think the doctor will be? It's not Dr Hepworth, is it?'

'No, it's a locum, Dr Srivasti. I can't say, but we're having a very busy night. I'll bleep him now.'

'Thank you.' She put down the phone and picked Sam up again. 'There, the doctor's coming. Poor Sam, poor baby, what can I do for you?' Because she didn't know what to do, she carried him, screaming, all round the flat, looking wildly for the Calpol, just in case. It wasn't there, and she knew, suddenly, what had happened: Anya had taken it, finished it, meant to buy more and forgotten. And she hadn't noticed, or checked.

'Fool,' she said aloud, not sure if she was talking to Anya or herself. She paced up and down, rocking Sam back and forth. He sucked at her for comfort, then cried again.

An hour later, the doctor still had not arrived. By now Sam was almost hysterical, and so was she. In a moment of desperation she thought of calling an ambulance, and remembered, going cold, that the ambulance staff were still on strike. Surely someone would come, a police ambulance or something? No, no, she wasn't going to do that; perhaps she should take him to hospital herself. She carried him over to the window and looked out: it was black and cold and raining, she'd have to bundle him up and drive, with him screaming, and probably wait in casualty for an hour. By that time the doctor would be here.

Sam's face was burning – why, why, why had she never bought a baby thermometer? She just hadn't, that's all, he'd always been so well and she'd never thought of it. Why hadn't somebody told her – why hadn't Alice told her? Anyway, she didn't need one to know it was far too high. She took him to the bathroom and sponged his face with a cold flannel, and he screamed. Shouldn't she have done that? What happened to babies with very high fevers – was it really dangerous? As if a red warning light had flashed on, she suddenly thought: convulsions. That's what happens, they have fits. Oh, Christ.

She went back to the sitting room, and dialled Alice's number.

'Hello?' a sleepy croak.

'Tony!' She was almost in tears.

'What . . .'

'It's me, it's Hilda, Sam's terribly ill, I've called the doctor but he hasn't come, and Anya's away, and he's got such a high temperature . . . I'm sorry, I'm sorry, please can Alice come over, I just don't know what to do . . .'

'Ssh, ssh!' Tony sounded as if he were talking to a wounded animal. 'Listen. Hilda? Can you hear me?'

'Hang on.' She put Sam down on the floor and blocked her ear. 'Yes?'

'Alice can't come, she's just getting over 'flu and now Hettie's got it.'

'Oh, no. Oh, no.'

'Ssh! I'll come, all right?'

'Oh, Tony . . . I'm sorry . . . I just didn't know who else to ring, I mean you're my family, aren't you? You're all Sam's family . . .'

'Of course we are, of course. Calm down, I'm coming. Have you tried giving him Calpol?'

She began to shriek, banging the desk with her hand. 'There isn't any Calpol! His temperature's sky high, that's why I'm phoning! For God's sake bring some, all right?'

'Okay, okay. I'm coming now. Sponge him down with tepid water.'

He put down the phone and Hilda picked up Sam. 'Tepid, he said tepid. Come on, let's go back to the bathroom.'

Twenty minutes later, the doorbell. She put Sam in his cot, flew down the stairs, and heaved at the bolts on the door. Tony, in coat and pyjamas, his hair in tousled wisps, stood on the doorstep and held out a bottle of Calpol. She flung herself into his arms.

'Poor Hilda, dear, dear. Come on, there we are.' He pushed up his glasses and shepherded her inside, closing the door behind them. 'Upstairs?'

'Yes, he's in his cot. I don't know what's wrong with him, I thought he might be going to have a fit . . .'

'Come on, then, up we go. Yes, I can hear him, poor old Sam.

246

Still, when they're crying you know they're all right, in a way. It's when it all goes quiet you have to worry.' His arm was round her shoulders as they climbed the stairs.

'You should've been a doctor,' she mumbled.

'I am a doctor, didn't you know?' They had reached her open door and he held it wide for her, she stumbled up the steps to the sitting room and through to Sam, lifting him out of his cot.

'Here we are, here we are, here's your medicine.' She fumbled at the childproof cap, and poured out the sticky sweet syrup into the plastic spoon. Behind her, Tony had taken off his coat and followed her into the room. 'Here, Sam,' she said, 'come on, you have it.' His fist swung up and hit the teaspoon; Calpol flew everywhere. 'Sa-am!' Downstairs, the doorbell rang.

'All right, I'll get it.' Tony went out again, running down the stairs; she sat on the bed with Sam on her lap and Calpol in her hair, his hair, in thick shining droplets all over the duvet, and waited for other people to do things.

'So. This is the patient.'

Dr Srivasti, inches shorter than Tony, came into the room with his black bag, smiling broadly. 'You have been giving him Calpol? Let's have a look at him.' He put down the bag on the bed, snapping it open; Hilda held Sam while he took his temperature, and inspected his ears with a tiny light. 'Keep still, old chap, if Mum can just turn your head . . . lovely. Now I can see all the way through to the other side! Bit of an infection here, yes.' He switched off his instrument and stood up. 'I will give you an antibiotic powder for tonight, and a prescription for tomorrow. And we must bring this fever down – how much of the Calpol are you giving him?'

'Nothing yet.' Hilda held out the spoon, and waved weakly at the bottle on her bedside table, gesturing at the mess. 'Please . . . could you . . . I've had it.'

'Here we are,' said Tony, coming into the room with two cups of tea. He looked at the doctor inquiringly. 'Would you..'

'No, no, it is very kind but I am already awash.' Dr Srivasti spooned Calpol deftly into Sam's protesting mouth and put the bottle back on the table. 'I have been telling your wife, this chap has an ear infection, nothing too serious but it is as well you called me. Now . . .' He gave Hilda a little packet of powder. 'If you just mix this up with water, according to the instructions . . .'

'Thank you.' She passed Sam to Tony and took the packet out to the kitchen, from where she could hear the doctor saying:

'I will write out the prescription, and then we are all done.' A pause. 'What is your son's name again?'

'Er – Sam,' said Tony. 'Sam King. He's not actually my son . . . oh, never mind.'

Hilda mixed up the medicine in a glass; it smelt of synthetic banana. She took it back to the bedroom, where the doctor was shutting his bag again, preparing to leave.

'Thank you so much for coming.'

'It is no trouble. I hope you all have a comfortable night.' He looked at her, standing there in her pyjamas with the glass in her ringless hand. Over his head, holding Sam, Tony winked at her.

'Do you want to take him, and I'll see Dr Srivasti downstairs?'

'No need, it is no problem.' And the doctor was hurrying out, and down the carpeted stairs, banging the front door. They looked at each other and began to laugh.

'He must have thought . . . God knows what he thought . . .'

'I did think about telling him, but it hardly seemed worth it.'

'No, no, of course you shouldn't have, he's only a locum, it's none of his business.' Hilda leaned against the door. 'Do you think you could give Sam his medicine?'

'Sure. Come on, Sam, what a time you're having. Here we go.' He spooned the medicine down him, and kissed the top of his head.

Hilda watched him. 'Did you ever want a son?'

Tony shrugged. 'You love what you have, don't you? It might have been nice, but . . . One thing I do know, I certainly don't want any more.'

'What about Alice?'

'She does, she'd like dozens, it's a bone of contention. Now, then, what are we going to do with this boy?'

'I'll get him off to sleep,' she said, 'it shouldn't take long now.' She took him back, rocking him gently, yawning. 'Oh, Sam. What a night, eh?'

'I'll leave you to it,' said Tony. 'Where did I put my coat?'

'Oh, please,' said Hilda. 'Please don't go. Could you stay just for a bit?' She looked at him pleadingly. 'Just so I can unwind with an adult for five minutes? Is that terribly selfish?'

'No, of course it isn't, it was thoughtless of me. Go on, you get him off, and I'll have a sit down or something. I don't suppose you've got any hot chocolate?'

'I have. Anya bought it, when I had 'flu.'

Fifteen minutes later Sam was deeply asleep in his cot and they were drinking hot chocolate in the sitting room, Hilda on the sofa, Tony in the armchair.

'Thank you so much for coming,' she said. 'I'm really sorry – I wouldn't have rung if I hadn't been desperate.'

'I know.' He stirred his cup slowly. 'Where's Anya this weekend?'

'In Brighton, with her daughter. She's got 'flu. She's a terrible dragon, the daughter, she frightens me to death.'

'Really?' Tony raised an eyebrow. 'That's hard to imagine.'

'Is it? Am I such a dragon myself?'

'Sometimes. Alice thinks so, anyway.'

'Oh, don't be ridiculous, how can she?'

'Just – you're very capable, determined. Aren't you? Look at the way you've gone back to work, running a department, looking after Sam . . .'

'Oh, yes,' she said, gesturing at the room, full of Saturday's untidiness: Sam's toys, baby clothes on the radiators, papers and coffee cups piled on her desk. 'I'm very capable. Look what happened tonight – if you hadn't come I don't know what I'd have done.'

'Yes, but it's different, with babies. Everyone needs a hand then.'

'Yes.' There was a silence, full of things unspoken. 'I don't know what I'd have done without Anya, either,' she said. 'When I had 'flu, I mean. How's Alice? I'm sorry – perhaps I gave it to her over Christmas.'

'It's all over the place, isn't it? Half the office is off. Alice is on the mend, but it's not so easy, having to look after the children before you're properly better – I took time off the first couple of days, but then I had to get back. Hettie's a bit miserable – I expect Annie and I'll be next.'

'I hope not.'

'So do I, I'm up to here.' He stretched, yawning, and put down his mug. 'That was very nice.'

'You made it.'

'So I did.' He smiled, shaking his head. 'I must be worse than I thought.'

'What have you got on at the moment, then?'

'Oh, I don't know, endless human misery. And these lectures, remember? Juveniles and the criminal justice system.' He yawned again. 'I've got two coming up in February: one on police procedure, one on new developments in social security law.'

'You've made quite a name for yourself, haven't you?'

He shrugged. 'I didn't set out to.'

'Perhaps you should come and talk to some of my students one day. Some of them are living rough with the benefit cuts, you know. Quite a few have brushes with the police. Would you come?'

'Okay, perhaps. At least it would be close to home – Alice doesn't like it when I'm away so much. I've got to go to Norwich and York for these two.'

'Norwich. You mean University of East Anglia.'

'The law school, yes.'

'That's where Stephen is,' she said slowly. 'I mean, not Norwich, but about twenty miles outside. How strange.'

'Where do they – sorry, where does he live exactly?'

'Woodburgh. Well, near a village outside, actually, but Woodburgh's the nearest place anyone's ever heard of. That's where his wife has her shop.'

'Shop?'

'She sells curtains or something. Miriam Knowles, Interiors. I don't know what she does exactly, it all sounds terribly twee. She does that, and Stephen does his thing in a studio at the bottom of the garden, and they hate each other. At least, I assume they do. They're supposed to have stayed together for Jonathan, their son. Perhaps all this silence means they're making a go of it, that'd be nice, wouldn't it?' She gave a false little laugh. 'Perhaps you should go and call on him, tell him how I'm getting on in all these crises.' Her eyes filled with tears. 'Oh dear, I'm always weeping all over you.'

'Hilda.'

'What?' She reached for the box of tissues, and blew her nose.

'What's happening? You haven't told us anything for such a long time.'

'You haven't asked.'

'We don't like to pry, that's all.' He hesitated. 'We – I – I do realise it must be tough.'

'Thanks.' She wiped her eyes. 'It wouldn't be so bad if . . . if everything was all right between Stephen and me. But it all seems to have gone haywire. Apparently his wife knows now, since Christmas, and I think she must have given him the push, but he hasn't properly told me, and he doesn't ring me, or write, and half the time I don't even know where he *is*!' She was starting to cry again. '*Shit*! Sorry.' She fumbled for the tissues.

'Poor Hilda, what a mess.' Tony sat watching her, rubbing his face. 'I'd come and give you a hug, but you'd probably cry even more.'

She nodded, unable to speak, and blew her nose again, smiling shakily. 'As you so rightly say, what a mess. What the hell am I going to do?'

He shook his head, considering. 'I don't suppose . . . I don't suppose you'd like me to talk to him?'

'Oh, God, no. Thanks, but no. He'd hate it, I know he would. I think I'll just have to sweat it out.' She sat screwing wet tissues in her hand, looking down at the floor. 'If he doesn't get in touch next week, then I'll . . . what'll I do?' She looked up, and they both began to laugh again. 'This could go on all night.'

'Yes,' said Tony, 'and I should be getting back.' He got up, shaking his head again. 'I'll have a think, okay?'

'Thanks. There's nothing you can do, but thanks.' Hilda looked up at him, such a dear man, so easy to be with, to talk to. You could say anything to Tony.

And now he was going. She sat watching him look round the room for his coat, thinking: I am going to go to bed and wake up feeling half dead, with the whole of Sunday to get through by myself, with Sam miserable and unwell. To while away the time I can go and see Jane and Don, and sit in their kitchen and walk in the park with them while they hold hands, and then I'll come back to an empty house, with no one to talk to until an old woman comes home and tells me about her sick daughter. I'll go mad. If I have too many weekends like this they'll have to put me away. I can't bear it. I can't bear him to go.

'Tony?'

'Yes?' He was putting his coat on; he looked suddenly very tired – perhaps he really was sickening for 'flu.

'Stay.'

'What?'

She got up and went over to him, touching his sleeve. 'Stay. Please. I don't mean – what you think I mean. I'm not going to jump on you or anything. I just can't bear to be by myself.' She shut her eyes. 'Please understand.'

'I do,' he said slowly. 'Of course I do. I'd ask you to come home with me and bring Sam, but I can't, not with 'flu all over the place, it's too much for Alice.' He patted the top of her head. 'Open up.'

She opened her eyes, which were sore from crying and lack of sleep. 'I'm a wreck.'

'I know. I want you to have a hot bath, and go back to bed, and ring us in the morning, all right?'

'No,' she said. 'It's not all right. Please, Tony, I don't often ask for things, I just don't want to wake up in this empty house – suddenly I can't face it. Please stay. Please. You can sleep in my bed, and I'll sleep on the sofa. In the morning I'll cook you breakfast – it'll take the edge off Sunday . . .' She trailed away. 'Please.'

Tony said quietly: 'Hilda, I can't. Alice would never forgive me.'

'What?'

'She'd get in a state. No matter how innocent I told her it was, no matter how innocent it really was – she's too insecure.'

'She has you all the time.'

'I know.'

'And she knows you adore her.'

'I know.'

'And she still doesn't trust you?'

He didn't answer.

Hilda could feel herself about to become very bitter. 'I have to manage by myself all the time. I have to listen to doctors who think you're my husband, and Sam's your son, and actually I don't seem to belong to anyone at the moment.'

'I know. I know, it's horrible. But . . .'

'Don't say I should've seen it coming. Everyone makes mistakes – I just seem to have made a very big one.'

'I wasn't going to say that, I wouldn't dream of it. I was going to say that you're different from Alice, that's all.'

'Oh, yes? How's that?'

'You know you are. Alice is . . . Alice was . . .'

'Alice is selfish,' said Hilda flatly. 'She always has been.'

'Don't.'

'It's true. I love her, but it's true. She lives in her head with God knows what going on in there, thinking everyone's better than she is, thinking she can't cope . . . She's still screwed up, she must be if she doesn't trust you. I just want you to stay as a *friend*, for God's sake! As *family*. Is that so unreasonable?'

'No, but I can't do it.' He had moved away, he was fiddling with his glasses. 'It would upset her too much – she's always felt threatened by you, and it's just not worth it. Full stop.'

She gave a long, defeated sigh. 'All this for Alice.'

'Yes,' he said. 'All this for Alice. She's my wife, Hilda.'

Hilda felt a sudden jealousy and anger so powerful it overcame her. 'And what does she do for you?'

'Everything. Stop it.'

'Are you sure?'

'Hilda . . . for God's sake . . .'

'She lies to you, I can tell you that.'

'What the hell do you mean?'

'I mean,' she said unsteadily, 'that although Alice must have had more men than I've had hot dinners, she doesn't, actually, enjoy sex at all.'

'Stop it! I don't want to hear any more.'

'Not even with you. She doesn't like it even with you.'

Tony visibly flinched. 'That's enough.'

But she was on a ride now, her blood up; she heard herself go on as if she were listening to a stranger, someone cruel, and driven, and appalling, shouting in another room: 'It's true! She told me. Last year, before Sam was born, you were away on one of your lectures, and she told me then. She fakes the whole thing, didn't you know?'

'That's *enough!*' Tony was angry now, Tony who was never angry. 'I'm going now, I'm going to forget all about this, and I hope you will too. You're under too much strain, but even so . . .' He moved to the landing, the little flight of steps leading down to her front door; he opened it and ran down the stairs.

'Tony! Tony!' She ran down after him. 'I'm sorry, I'm sorry.' She was weeping again, filled with shame and remorse. 'I'm not myself, please understand, I didn't want to come between you and Alice.'

At the bottom of the stairs, in Anya's gloomy brown hall, they stood and looked at each other, out of breath, unnerved.

'Forget it,' he said again. 'Let's both get some sleep. Okay?'

'Okay.' She put out her hand. 'Thank you again. For coming.'

He waved it away. 'Ring if you need anything. Goodnight.'

'Goodnight, Tony. Forgive me. Please.' She let him out of the door and closed it quickly behind him, before the cold air came in; she heard him walk down the steps and get into his car, and drive away. Then she slowly climbed the stairs, drained of all feeling.

It wasn't until she was lying in bed again, holding on to her pillow for comfort, as she'd done when her father died, that she found herself saying Tony's name, and realised at last that although she did indeed think of him as family, and as a friend, he had, if she were honest, for a long time meant much more.

*

253

'All right?' asked Alice. 'Have you got everything?'

She stood in the study doorway, watching Tony pile papers into his briefcase.

'Think so,' he said, reaching across the desk for a folder. 'You're very solicitous.'

'I've packed your case.'

'You didn't have to do that.' He dropped in a notepad.

'I was putting clothes away anyway, I thought I might as well. It is only the one night, isn't it?'

'Just the one. I'll be back for supper on Friday.' He closed the briefcase with difficulty, because it was old, and the fastening was half off, and looked up at her, leaning against the door in her jeans and baggy jumper, her hair falling across her face. She'd lost weight with the 'flu and still hadn't put it back; her clothes were falling off her, and her skin was pale. She looked about ten; he wanted to pick her up, carry her along the landing past the sleeping children and put her to bed.

She said: 'I wish you weren't going.'

'Why?'

'What do you mean, why? You know I don't like it when you're away. I hear noises.'

He pushed back his chair and stretched. 'You'll live. I'm going to have a bath, okay?' He got up and went past her, ignoring her sudden look of hurt and surprise, and went along to the bathroom, where he turned on the radio, and the taps on full.

Afterwards, in his dressing gown, he found the bedroom empty. He checked the children's room, but they were both fast asleep, and she wasn't there. He stood at the top of the stairs.

'Alice?'

'I'm doing Hettie's lunchbox. I'll be up in a minute.'

He went back to the bedroom, and got into his pyjamas; he pulled back the duvet and set the alarm, and sank into bed, closing his eyes. Alice did not come up, and after a while he began to drift off, waking when she came quietly into the room and began to undress.

'Alice? You okay?'

'Yes.' She dropped her clothes on to the chair and slipped her hand under the pillows for her nightdress. In other days he might have reached out to kiss her arm, or touch her soft, falling hair as she bent down; he might have reached out to do much more than that. Now he lay still, watching her pull the nightdress over her head, and down over her little breasts and long pale legs.

'I'm just going to do my teeth.' She padded out; he heard her go to the bathroom and then, as always, look into the girls' room before she came back, slipping in beside him. They lay still, not touching.

'Tony?'

'Yes?'

'What's wrong?'

'Nothing.'

'Why're you cross with me?'

'I'm not.'

'You are. Something's wrong, anyway, isn't it? You don't seem yourself.'

He didn't answer. Outside the house they could hear the wind begin to rise, and the television aerial, damaged in the January storms, shudder up on the roof.

'You will be careful, driving, won't you?'

'I'm always careful.'

'Will you phone me from Norwich?'

'Yes. Come on, I'd better get some sleep.' He reached for the light and switched it off, turning away.

'Tony?'

'What?'

'Is it . . . is it because of the baby? Me going on about it so much?'

He shook his head in the darkness; he said slowly: 'It's not just that.'

Wind blew across the campus; the afternoon sun was bright, spring-like, full of racing clouds. As Tony came out of the heavy Jacobean door at the back of the law school his coat flapped open, against his briefcase; beside him, his companion, in sweater and cords, said: 'God, it's bloody freezing.'

'Go back inside,' said Tony. 'You don't have to see me out, I know where I am now.'

'Okay, then, if you're sure.' The lecturer, his host last night, was a small man with greying hair. 'Thanks again for coming, I thought it went well.'

'Glad you thought so. They seem a bright bunch, sensible questions on the whole. Well – that was a very good dinner last night. Regards to Kate – I'll drop a line.'

'Oh, only if you have a moment, I know what it's like. Right then, I'll let you go. You know your way out on to the London road all right, don't you?'

255

'Oh, yes.' They shook hands and the other man turned back inside; Tony made his way towards the car park. His suitcase was already locked in the boot; he slung his briefcase on to the back seat and drove out slowly, passing students coming in for afternoon lectures, scarves and hair blown about in the wind. They all looked like babies.

At the exit to the road he stopped, waiting to pull out, feeling, as always after these occasions, a kind of high exhaustion, not unlike leaving court, but with the added edge of a different setting, new faces, another part of the country. Now, though, there was more than this – an unfamiliar undertone to everything he did: like toothache, he thought, in moments when he was trying to recover himself, experienced by someone whose teeth had never given any trouble. But he had not recovered himself, and he sat now, his hands on the steering wheel, watching the cars on the road in front of him zoom past, and when a gap came in the traffic he went on sitting there.

After a while he pulled out the road map and opened it at the turned-down page for Norwich. To get back to London he had only to leave the ring road for the A11; there was no need to go into the city. He hesitated, looking at his watch; his finger ran over the page, searching among unfamiliar names. Behind him, another car drew up; after a few moments, a few more gaps in the traffic, it hooted at him. Tony looked in the mirror and nodded a vague apology to an anxious-looking woman in earrings. He pulled out, a little too fast, and drove away, but he did not turn right to the ring road and the A11, he turned left, checking the signs for the B road which led north, to Woodburgh.

Heavy white clouds sailed through the wide sky; rooks flapped, cawing, across open fields, alighting in a noisy muddle on the bare trees. Many had been damaged by last month's storms – the broken branches of oak and ash, ripped away, hung from a thin sliver of trunk or lay on the grass, fallen and still unsawn. Tony found his sign and turned left, on to a long straight road bordered by woodland. Here, piles of cut logs stood in clearings and along the verge; he caught sight of a van and trailer moving slowly through the trees, carrying a great heap of branches. He drove on, and dead leaves lifted in the wind, rising again, and blew across the road.

It was a long time since Tony had acted on impulse – perhaps the last time had been when he got in touch with Alice, in Oxford, all those years ago. He had phoned because, although they had barely spoken, he had watched her, sitting beneath the trees on the edge of the picnic rugs, hunched up, silent, wanly beautiful, and known, even then, that she needed him. He had wanted her, almost from the beginning – who wouldn't have, seeing those long pale legs drawn up beneath her cotton skirt, the pale silky hair falling over her face, pushed back with slender fingers; but it was more than wanting, it was understanding, observing bitten fingernails, an air of isolation. He supposed, even then, it had been the beginning of love.

And now – now what?

The road came out of the woods, and he was in farmland again, driving alongside ragged hedges, where catkins shook in the wind. Ploughed fields stretched into the distance, and the clouds were piling more thickly, growing darker. There was almost no traffic, and what there was he barely noticed; he drove fast, as if he knew the road well, overtaking lorries, rattling vans, a roaring motorbike. There was a gust of wind, a sharp flurry of rain; and he turned on the wipers: it no longer felt, as it had done outside the law school, like early spring, but a wintry country afternoon, beginning to close in. He glanced quickly down at the map and up again; another ten miles or so. He looked at his watch; he could have been well on the way to London by now – what did he think he was doing?

He didn't know what he was doing – what he expected, what he might find, why he was looking. He was restless, unsettled, off-course, giving way to a curiosity that in other days would have been brushed aside; he would have wanted too much to get home. Now, chance had brought him up here, and he, a man who had always felt in charge of his life, gave himself over to chance and to the unknown. Why not? What the hell.

He came to a crossroads, with signs to unheard-of villages; an old man with a bicycle stood waiting for him to go over. He drove on, faster, and the car shook. Another five or six miles, another crossroads, a signpost on the verge, announcing Woodburgh. He was on the outskirts of the town – a line of cottages, a green, a war memorial. Then shops, traffic lights, a couple of pubs and a church ahead, right at the end of the main street. He drove through slowly, looking for a place to park. There were yellow lines everywhere, and no meters; he followed the sign to the car park, and paid his twenty pence. It had stopped raining, but it was very cold; he walked back to the main street buttoning his coat as the church clock struck the half hour. The sky was heavy and grey.

People hurried in and out of the shops, mothers and school children, buying sweets, and something for tea. Tony walked past newsagents, a supermarket, a butcher's and an estate agent's, an antique shop. He paused, here, looking up at the name, but he knew it was not what he was looking for. He went on, passing a greengrocer's, a florist, a chemist; he stopped at the zebra crossing and looked across the road, to where a row of converted Tudor red-brick houses stood set back from a broad pavement – they looked discreet, charming, the perfect place for a tasteful little shop. And it was there, with the solicitors, the bookshop and the bank: a black door with brass knob and letterbox, a mullioned window, a hand-painted sign along the top, in black and gold. He waited for the cars to stop and then he crossed over, quickly, suddenly nervous.

For a few moments he stood at the window, hung with greens and yellows. There was a small, polished oak table, standing to one side, bearing a glass jug of early daffodils; looking inside, he could see a long table with pattern books, stands of fabric samples, shelves of material in bolts and rolls. A woman with dark chestnut hair sat at a desk; she was talking on the telephone, making notes. There was no one else in the shop. He pushed open the door and went inside; a small bell rang.

The woman looked up and smiled, gesturing to him to look round. She was ordering fabric, checking delivery dates and prices in a low, rather pleasing voice which nonetheless had something of effort in it, as though she were not a natural talker. He watched her, covertly, lifting the pages of a pattern book on the table in front of him: the chestnut hair was threaded through with silver; she had a soft, freck-led skin, a face which looked as if it had done a lot of crying and had always been massaged with expensive creams to try to cover that up. A woman probably older than he, certainly older than Alice, who had once been beautiful. He turned away, waiting for her to finish.

She put down the receiver and looked up, smiling again. 'Can I help you?' She pushed back the chair and got up, coming towards him.

'Miriam Knowles?'

'Yes?'

'I –' Tony looked down at her. For a moment he considered pretending: asking for samples, leaving quickly. Then he thought, looking at her again: But I want to get to know this woman, and he said, clearing his throat, 'You don't know me, but . . .'

How many lives had been changed by that opening line? Her eyes showed a flicker of anxiety. He coughed, trying again.

'It's all right, nothing's happened, I mean – no accidents or any-thing. My name's Tony Sinclair, I'm a solicitor from London, I've been up here giving a lecture in Norwich . . . Never mind. I have a sister-in-law, Hilda King, I think you know something of her . . .'

Miriam's eyes met his, serious, direct. There was a silence.

'You mean . . . my husband knows her.'

'Yes.'

The door of the shop was pushed open, the small bell sounded, and a woman came in, with a rush of cold air. Miriam looked quickly at her watch. 'If you'll excuse me . . . I close in an hour. Perhaps you could come back?'

'Of course.'

The bookshop had bare floorboards and a secondhand department. He spent nearly the whole hour browsing along the Norfolk and local history shelves, taking down old titles from Faber and Heinemann and little private presses, sniffing the faded pages. They smelt of dust and cellars; he read of parish councils, egg-collecting, pike-fishing, the tombs of knights in medieval churches; he dipped into an old edition of *Swallows and Amazons* and looked at pale photographs of seals, basking in a pre-war sun on the rocks at Blakeney. He almost lost himself in all this until he began to wonder why to be here felt so familiar, when he hardly ever had time these days to idle away in bookshops, once his greatest pleasure. He realised it reminded him of Hilda and Anya's house, the tottering piles of books on the landing, the overflowing shelves. Then he remembered what had brought him here. He looked at his watch: five-fifteen. He'd better buy something.

At the front of the shop the owner was tidying away bills and catalogues. Tony paid for a mildewed *Norfolk Notebook*, published in 1946: it was full of domestic detail – wartime rationing, duck ponds, orchards and fruit bottling – he thought that Alice would like it; then, as the bookseller slipped it into a paper bag, he felt unsure. Perhaps there were other things about her he had not understood.

It was dark when he went outside. He put the book in his pocket and paced about a bit in the cold; should he go back to Miriam's shop on the dot of half-past five or give her time to collect herself? He began to feel apprehensive again – he had not known what his motives were when he made this detour, and now he had met her he knew even less. But it was, now, something other than simple curiosity. He walked back to the shop, and saw that she had turned down most of the lights inside, leaving only the window brightly lit. Were they going to talk there? Shouldn't he take her somewhere?

He went up to the door: she had turned the sign to 'Closed'. He tapped on the glass and, after a moment or two, the latch was lifted.

'Come in.' In the subdued lighting he followed her into the shop again; they stood there awkwardly; she seemed on edge, and he didn't know where to start.

'I was wondering – perhaps I could take you for a drink. There's a nice-looking pub across the road.'

She shook her head. 'I don't drink. At least . . .' She waved her hands. 'I'm not very good in pubs.'

'Okay. Well . . .' It was much too early to suggest a meal, and anyway that didn't feel right. 'Is there a coffee place or something?'

'Not really. There's a tea rooms, but they're closed now.'

'Oh.' He looked down at her, and smiled, as if it were funny, which it almost was. 'What do you suggest?'

'I'm not sure.' She ran a hand over her hair in an uncertain gesture that reminded him suddenly of Alice. Alice would be expecting him home in an hour or two; so would the girls.

'Perhaps we could talk here?'

'I'm not sure if I want to talk.' She turned away, and went to her desk; she stood there holding the back of the chair, looking down at order books, and snippets of fabric. 'Why have you come?'

'I – I don't know,' he said. 'I'm sorry, it must feel like a monstrous intrusion.'

'Is there something you wanted to tell me? Something you think I should know?' She was still not looking at him. 'When people feel you should know something it's usually rather unpleasant. I think I've had enough unpleasantness for a while.'

'Yes.' He hesitated. 'I can imagine. But it's nothing like that.'

'Then why . . . I don't understand.'

'No. Neither do I.' He was standing next to the long table; he fiddled with the cover of a pattern book. 'This is a very pretty shop.'

She did not answer.

'I was up here anyway,' he said. 'It seemed a strange coincidence, and because . . . because I feel rather unsettled, I suppose, I thought I'd follow it up. That's all. But I know it wasn't a good idea. You've had enough, haven't you? You don't want . . .' He tried to lighten it, to let them both off the hook. 'You don't want stray brothers-in-law appearing out of the blue.'

'Not really.' She pulled out her chair and sat down suddenly at the desk, shaking her head. 'Dear God.'

'I'm going.' Tony snapped shut the book.'You must forgive me – I'm really very sorry.'

'It's all right. It doesn't matter.' He had crossed the room, and his hand was on the latch when she said: 'Why are you unsettled?'

He stopped. 'It's just – something that happened. Nothing I can talk about.'

'Then we're in rather the same boat.' She turned round in her chair. 'Aren't we?'

'Not exactly. At least . . .'

'At least you hope not.' She gave a wry smile. They looked at each other, and his hand dropped from the latch. 'Would you like to come and have supper with me?' she asked. 'I feel suddenly reckless.'

He smiled. 'That would be very nice.'

'Good.' She stood up, picking up her keys.

'Where would you like to go?'

'Home.' She reached up to a peg for her jacket and bag.

'But – '

'It's empty,' she said, pulling her jacket on. 'It's been empty for years.' She came over and switched off the last spotlight; now there was only the window, shining out into the street. 'Where are you parked?'

It was raining again when they drove out of the town, Miriam in front, leading the way, checking her mirror after the traffic lights. He followed her with the other end-of-the-day traffic, gathering speed on the long straight road, leaving the green and the rows of terraced cottages behind. A quarter-mile or less and there were no more street lamps, just the lights of distant houses, blurred by the rain. They drove on through the wet darkness, keeping close. Other cars turned off, to other places; they went on for perhaps four or five miles; she indicated right and he saw a sign to Saxham, 1½ miles. This road was tree-lined, narrower, little more than a lane; it needed resurfacing and the car sent up sprays of water – he slowed down, as she had, seeing a cluster of houses ahead, and a pub sign, swinging in the wind, much stronger now, reminding him of the January storms. They drove through the village and she indicated right again, slowing right down. And now they turned into an unmade lane, and the car began to bump. A few minutes later she drew up, outside an unlit house, low, set well back behind a garden hedge; he saw her open her door and run through the rain to unlatch double gates to a garage path.

He got out quickly.

'I'll do that.'

'Don't be silly, I do it all the time. We have to keep them shut because of the dog.' She lifted the hook and started to push them back. 'No point in both of us getting wet.'

But he took the right-hand gate and swung it into the hedge; they ran to their cars and he followed her in, parking on the path as she drove into the garage and switched her lights off. He switched off his own and everything went pitch black; rain drummed on the roof. What a place to come back to by yourself. An outside light on the roof came on; he got out and she came quickly from the garage. It was pouring down.

'Leave the gates, Tess is indoors anyway. Come on.' She was running across to the house, her feet splashing on the path. There was a tiled porch; they stood beneath it as the rain swept across the garden, and she fumbled with her key ring. 'Sorry – there. Come in, please.' She pushed open the studded door, switched on the hall lights and turned to Tony. 'Let me take your coat.'

'Thanks.' He took it off and watched her hang it, with her jacket, among all the other things on the rack by the door. There were several pairs of shoes underneath, and football boots, and a mildewed mirror, where he could see her face, which seemed, now they had got here, to be studiedly turned away; her hair was very wet, and she combed it, quickly, as if embarrassed. There was a sound from across the hall, and he looked round to see a large yellow dog come padding out from a passageway; she thumped a heavy tail against the side of the stand, lifting her head to be patted.

'This is Tess, she's hungry,' said Miriam, bending down to kiss her. 'Poor girl, come on, let's give you something to eat. And you'd better go out.'

He noticed a telephone on a chest at the bottom of the stairs.

'Miriam? Do you mind – I have to make a phone call.'

'Of course. I'll be in the kitchen.' She gestured towards the passage beyond the stairs, leading to the back of the house, and went without looking at him. He picked up the telephone and dialled; he told Alice the truth about the weather and a lie about where he was. Then he went slowly through the hall and down the stone-flagged passage to the warmth of the kitchen, where Miriam was busying herself with saucepans and preparations.

'Would you like a drink?'

'No, thanks.'

'Sure?' She was rummaging in the fridge, taking out eggs, and a china bowl; she put them down on the table. 'There's beer in the fridge. Or would you like a glass of wine?'

'I really won't, thanks. Not if you don't drink.'

'Well . . .' He saw that her hands were trembling as she undid the egg box. 'I used to. I gave up last month, my new year's resolution.' She said it as if it were nothing, but he realised that it wasn't. 'I've felt much better for it, but I must say that just at the moment . . . God, I could do with one.'

She gave a little laugh; it reminded him of Hilda, who had laughed when she wondered if Stephen and his wife were going to get back together again. Hilda, and Alice and the children, and everyone he knew, seemed to belong in another country just at the moment. He pulled out a chair and sat down.

'Do you smoke? Would that help?'

'No, no, I don't. The only person who smokes here is my son's girlfriend. She smokes like a chimney.' She turned away, pouring soup from the china bowl into a saucepan; she set it on the Rayburn.

'Can I do anything?'

'No, thanks. I'm just doing this and omelettes, is that all right?'

'Fine. Lovely.'

There was a silence; she went to the garden doors and let the wet dog in, and gave her a bowl of meat and biscuits.

'Your son – he's, er – he's where, at the moment?' He felt at sea, wanting to anchor himself.

'With the girlfriend. He shouldn't be, it's the middle of the week, he should be here, studying.' She was cracking eggs, beating them, putting rolls in the oven. 'But we – I – let him stay the night there if he wants, just for the moment. Things have been . . . It's not exactly Happy Families here these days. Well . . . it hasn't been for a long time. As you know, presumably.' She put rush mats, china and cutlery on the bare table. 'What about you?' For the first time since they arrived, she looked at him, and then away. 'Are you happy?'

'I . . .' He took off his glasses, and rubbed them with his handkerchief.

'Sorry. I'm not usually so direct, I don't know what's got into me. Perhaps this is what giving up drinking does to you.' She sat down suddenly, as she had done in the shop. 'Sorry,' she said again.

'Please don't be sorry.' He smiled, putting the glasses back. 'We can't both be sorry. Not all evening.'

Their eyes met and she smiled too, cautiously. 'No, no I suppose not.'

On the Rayburn the thick soup began to make plopping noises, heating up.

'That smells delicious.'

'Carrot and coriander, very simple. It's one of Jon's favourites.' She got up again and went to stir it with a wooden spoon. He saw a photograph on the mantelpiece, a dark-haired boy with his arms round the dog.

'Is that him?'

She glanced up at it. 'Yes. It was taken last summer, it's quite a good one.'

'May I look?' He took it down from the mantelpiece, standing next to her. The boy smiled at him, open and happy, leaning against the dog's thick coat. 'He looks very nice.'

'He is, he's lovely.'

'And happy. He looks very okay, if you don't mind my saying so.'

'He was – at least I hope he was. Now – God knows what he thinks about everything. I hardly see him.' She lifted the saucepan, moving away from him, pouring the soup into bowls. 'It's rather early to eat, isn't it?'

'It's fine. I'm hungry, anyway.'

'Good.' She passed him the bowls, and bent to take rolls from the oven. 'What about you?' she said as they sat down. 'Do you have children?'

'Two girls.'

'Who are?'

'Hettie and Annie, six and three.'

'And? Tell me about them.'

'Well . . . they're kids, you know.' He started on the soup: it was hot and very good. 'Annie was a pain, but she's getting a bit better; Hettie's always been easier, she's a born head girl, I suppose. Very together.'

'You do like them?' she asked wryly.

'Of course I like them. I just don't see them as much as I should, I suppose.'

'Because of work. That sounds familiar. You said that you're a solicitor?'

'Yes, in north London. Holloway. I specialise in criminal law, a lot of my clients are young offenders.'

'The solicitors in Woodburgh do nothing but conveyancing and divorce.'

'I can imagine. I noticed their offices – a bit different from ours.' He described the first-floor rooms, the narrow stairs, the thunder of lorries down the main road.

'Doesn't all that get on top of you?'

'Sometimes. It did last summer.'

'And you teach, too; you said you'd just come from Norwich?'

'I do a visiting lecture number every now and then – different law schools.' He had finished his soup; he noticed she had hardly touched hers. 'That was excellent.'

'I'm glad you liked it.' She took a token sip. 'And what about your wife – does she work?'

'She looks after the girls. Perhaps when Annie starts school . . .'

'Then she'll want another one,' said Miriam. She put down her spoon and said abruptly: 'You've seen this baby.'

'What?'

'This baby. *The* baby.'

'Yes, yes, of course.''

'Your nephew.'

'Yes.'

'What's he – what's he like?'

'He's . . . he's like any other baby. Well – not to us, I suppose, but . . .' He shrugged, helplessly. 'I don't think describing babies is my forte. And anyway . . .'

'And anyway this is a difficult situation.' She covered her face with her hands. Tony was silent. He wanted to comfort her, but it wasn't his place, and anyway, what comfort could he give? He sat and waited. After a few moments she said: 'Have you ever met my husband?'

'No. Never.'

'But this – this affair has been going on for rather a long time. Hasn't it?'

'I think so, yes.'

'Is he with her now?'

'I don't know. He . . . wasn't. I mean, not since Christmas.'

'Really? He must be with James, then. His partner.'

'I wouldn't know.' He felt at sea again. 'Are you saying – do you mean he hasn't been here since Christmas?'

'He comes and goes. He's always coming and going, it's how he operates. He was here last weekend . . . Now you see him, now you don't.' She waved her hands impatiently. 'That's enough. I don't want to talk about it any more, I really don't. I was feeling . . . in control. Talking about it churns me up again.'

He said again: 'I shouldn't have come.'

'Actually I'm glad you did, it makes it real. Confirms it all. It'll stop me pretending it hasn't happened. There's been quite enough pretence here.'

He was silent again, waiting for more.

'And what about you?' she asked. 'Aren't you going to tell me anything?'

'I don't know what there is to tell.'

'There's always something to tell. You wouldn't be here if there wasn't. Would you?'

He shrugged.

'*Are* we in the same boat?'

'No. Not in the way you mean. My discovery was rather more . . . subtle? That is to say there is nothing to show for it.'

'Tell me. Why not? What are encounters like this for, if not to tell secrets? After all, we're never going to see each other again.' She was fiddling with pieces of broken roll. 'Are we? Tell me about your wife.'

He spread his hands. 'Where is one supposed to start? In a strange way you remind me of her – you don't look in the least alike, but there's something. She's – how shall I put it? When we met she was recovering from a breakdown – well, a suicide attempt. She's very vulnerable, she doesn't like the world. Or perhaps I should say she's afraid of it.' He stopped, and drew a breath. 'My discovery was that she hates sex. I mistakenly thought I had cured her of that.'

'And how did you find that you hadn't?'

'Hilda told me.'

Miriam began to laugh. 'Hilda sounds quite delightful, I must say.'

'No,' he said quickly. 'I can't let you make her into something evil. She's not, she really isn't. I know you're the wrong person to say this to, but she's having a pretty hard time.'

There was a pause.

'You mean you're in love with her, too.'

'No! Absolutely not. God Almighty – I just mean – she's human. I don't think she ever knew what she was letting herself in for.'

Miriam gave a long sigh. 'I don't know what to think. It's hard to forgive either of them. As for me being like your wife . . . it's true I don't like the world very much, or rather I don't find life very easy, but even in all this I've never considered suicide. In fact, at new year, I felt as if I'd been reborn.' She shook her head. 'Does that sound overblown?'

'No. Not at all.'

'Well – these things don't always last. And as far as sex goes, I have a different problem: it's my husband who doesn't like it. Not with me, I mean. Not any more.' She blushed, and turned away.

Tony sat watching her, looking at her waving silvered hair, at her softly ravaged face, dark beneath the eyes.

He said: 'He must be crazy.'

'Please.'

In her corner across the room Tess got to her feet and went to stand by the garden doors, looking round at them.

'You want to go out again? It's wet out there.' But Miriam, clearly relieved at the distraction, got up and went to open the doors. At the sight of the driving rain Tess hesitated; Miriam gave her a little shove. 'Go on, make a dash for it, you're not a cat. Go on, Tess, perhaps you'd better.' The dog went out slowly, and Miriam looked out after her. The wind was even stronger; they could hear the trees begin to roar.

'We had a lot of damage last month,' she said, shutting the doors. 'The woods across the lane were ripped to bits. It looks as if we're in for another go, doesn't it?' She cleared the bowls from the table, and went over to the Rayburn. 'What was it like in London?'

'Wet,' said Tony. 'A lot of fences down. Do you really want to talk about the weather?'

'Yes,' said Miriam. 'It's been worth talking about, hasn't it? Jon says it's part of the whole change in climate, he joined the Greens last summer, he's very into it all . . .' She was melting butter in the omelette pan, turning it from side to side. 'Would you like plain, or cheese?'

'Neither.'

She lifted the pan from the heat and put it aside; she turned to look at him, leaning against the rail. He took in for the first time how lovely her clothes were, how gracefully they suited her: soft straight skirt, pale shirt, a waistcoat. She looked suddenly much younger, vulnerable and wary. Their eyes met, and held. He wanted to stroke her, touch her, hold her, to show her just how beautiful she was.

He said slowly: 'I want to make love to you.'

She looked away, biting her lip. 'I didn't ask you to come back here for . . . all this.'

'I know.'

'If it wasn't for the weather . . . I can give you the number of a bed-and-breakfast in Woodburgh where you could stay . . .'

'I don't want to stay in a bed-and-breakfast. I want to stay with you.'

There was a long silence. At last she said:

'Because of your wife . . .'

'No. Because of you.' She shut her eyes, and he said gently: 'Wouldn't you like to?'

'That's not the point. It isn't – wouldn't be – a solution.'

'Does it have to be?'

She didn't answer.

'Miriam?' He pushed back his chair, scraping it along the floor. 'Please?' He stood up slowly. 'Open your eyes. Look at me again.'

She did so, biting her lip again. 'It isn't right.'

'Nothing's right,' he said. 'I've tried to do the right thing all my life – now I just want to do this. For us. No one need ever know.'

She shook her head. 'That's what . . . they must have said. That's just how it must have started.'

'Forget them,' he said. 'Just for tonight. This is you and me, no one else.' He moved round the table and went towards her, holding out his arms. 'Please?' He was in front of her; he folded her to him, kissing the top of her head. 'You're beautiful. You're so beautiful.'

'No, I'm not.'

He could feel her fighting back tears. 'You are, of course you are.' He lifted her face and kissed her, her forehead, her eyes, her cheeks, running his hands through her hair. 'I want you, I can't tell you how much I want you . . . Yes? Yes?'

'Yes,' said Miriam, and raised her mouth to his. They stood rocking gently from side to side, like people who have been lovers for a long time, and have no need to hurry. Then she reached up and took off his glasses, clumsily, almost dropping them. 'Sorry.'

'There must be no more sorrys. Here.' He took them from her, and slipped them into his pocket.

'Now you can't see.'

'I can touch,' he said, and wrapped his arms round her again. 'I want to take your clothes off. Where shall we go?'

Outside the house the wind tore at the branches of the trees across

the lane and twigs snapped like gunfire; it lifted tiles from the roof
and smashed them on to the path; rain beat against the windows
and they shook in their frames.

'Hold me, hold me.'

'I'm here, I'm here, don't cry, you're so lovely . . . there . . . is
that . . .'

'Yes. Oh, yes . . . Don't stop, don't stop . . .'

Afterwards, they lay in the dark listening to the wind and the rain
rage round them.

'All right now?'

'Yes.' She laid her head on his chest, took his hand and kissed it,
holding it to her cheek. 'And you?'

'Very all right.' His fingers stroked her face as they lay together
in silence. 'Tell me about rebirth,' he said at last.

'Oh . . . when I stopped drinking. I'd been drinking for years, in
secret.' She shook her head. 'Horrible.'

'Because . . .'

'Because I was lonely. And couldn't have another child, and – oh,
everything. It all came to a head when I found out – I did something
dreadful . . . never mind, I don't want to talk about all that any
more.'

'And how did you stop?'

'I don't know, I wasn't even trying, not really, but I started to go
for long walks, just to get out of the house. It was so fresh, and quiet
and peaceful . . . oh, my God.' She sat up suddenly.

'What?'

'Tess. She came with me, that's what made me think . . .' She was
getting out of bed. 'I'd forgotten all about her, I must get her in.'

'I'll go.'

'No, she doesn't know your voice, she's getting old . . .' She was
moving across the room, he watched her, naked, reach up for a silk
kimono hung on the back of the door. 'Poor Tess.' At the door she
turned and looked at him in the light from the landing, falling into
the room, and smiled. 'Don't go away.'

'I won't.'

'Anything you want from downstairs?'

'Only you.'

She leaned against the door frame. 'I feel weak with happiness.'

'Go and get the dog. I'll be waiting.'

She went along the landing in bare feet. Tony lay listening to her
go down the stairs and open the front door. 'Tess?' She closed it

again, and then she must have gone into the kitchen, because he couldn't hear anything except the roaring trees. He got up and went to the window, but it was too dark and wet to see anything, and he got back into bed, hearing Miriam calling faintly, from the back of the house: 'Tess! Tess!'

He lay back on the pillow – and Alice's pale silky hair and dreamy, enclosed, secretive face came floating up to meet him, as if in water, drowning, and he groaned.

'Tess!'

Tony lay looking at the room in the light from the open door, at the dark chest of drawers, the long wardrobe mirroring the beams above the bed, his clothes and Miriam's heaped on the floor. He began to feel an immeasurably long way from home, a feeling quite different from nights spent in hotels, or other family houses, where he slept in the spare room. This was not a spare room. And this image of Alice, unbidden, was not what he was used to summoning when he stayed away: the children asleep and Alice sitting up in bed, reading, pushing back her hair; he had imagined her switching out the light, curling up long slender legs in her white cotton nightdress, missing him. Now he realised that perhaps she enjoyed those nights alone – perhaps she craved them. Yet even this knowledge, which had changed everything, and even what had happened between him and Miriam – unimaginable until now – could not stop this sense of her reaching out for him, nor his longing, suddenly overwhelming, to be with her. He closed his eyes and saw her again, floating, like Ophelia, lost without him. Or perhaps he had that wrong, too.

'I can't find her.'

'What?' He looked up to see Miriam beside the bed again, slipping in beside him, shivering. 'You're frozen.' He held her close, as he would do a child.

'I called and called. It's terrible out there.' Her teeth were chattering.

'She'll be all right.'

'She might not be – she's been pining for Jon, she might have gone looking for him.'

'In this lot?'

'Who knows? Animals are different, aren't they?'

'Most of them hate rain,' he said, glad to have something ordinary to bring him down to earth. 'She's probably in the garage. Do you want me to go and look?'

'No.' She had stopped shivering, and reached up to kiss him. 'If she's there it's not worth catching a chill for, and if she's not I'll worry even more. I just hope she is.' She kissed him again, and said gently: 'Are you all right?'

'Yes.'

'No, you're not. You've been thinking. Look at me.'

Her dark eyes regarded him gravely; she moved until she was lying on top of him, holding his face in her hands. 'I feel I should be reassuring you now,' she said slowly. 'We've given each other something. Haven't we? That's all, that's enough. You said – didn't you? – that this was just for us. Please don't regret it.'

For a long time they looked at each other, searching, answering. Out in the lane the wind rose higher, and another tile crashed to the ground. He brought her mouth down on his, and no longer thought of anything.

Early morning, barely that. Tony woke wondering where he was; he lay still, taking in the unfamiliar room, looking at a thin crack of light between the curtains. The storm had died away; beside him Miriam slept deeply, her bare arm across his chest. He went on lying there, knowing he had been dreaming of Alice, and that that was what had woken him, although he could remember nothing else. After a while he reached for his watch from the bedside table: just after six. In London, the children would be waking up soon, clambering into bed with Alice, asking where he was. He thought of them all in their nightclothes, still half-asleep, their hair tangled, Annie's thumb in her mouth. If he left now he could almost be home by breakfast.

Slowly, he slid out of bed and went to the window; he lifted one of the curtains aside and looked out. Above the torn and broken trees the sky was a roughly washed grey; water lay deep on the lane's uneven surface and there was mud flung up everywhere. Pieces of smashed roof tiles lay all down the path, and from somewhere up here he could hear dripping water. He let the curtain drop and moved quietly to pick up his clothes, and went out to the landing, looking for the bathroom; when he found it he saw that this was where the water was coming in – a steady drip from the ceiling in the corner; already a large pool lay on the floor. He had a pee, and dressed, and put on his glasses; he looked in the airing cupboard for a bowl to catch the drips, found one and put it carefully beneath the leak. Then he went back along the quiet landing and down the stairs.

In the hall, he felt in his coat pockets for notebook and pen; he leaned on the hall stand, beneath the mirror specked with mildew, and wondered what to say, or if it was right to leave a note at all. Worse, surely, to leave nothing. In the end he wrote simply: Thank you, and then folded it, and went quietly up the stairs again, and along to the bedroom. Miriam had not stirred; her hair was tousled on the ,illow, and for a moment, as he crept across the room, and left the note by her hand, he remembered a Leonard Cohen song, from a very long time ago, when he had been the one to sit in lecture halls: 'I loved you in the morning, Your kisses sweet and warming . . .' Mornings could be the best time, and Miriam was going to wake alone. He bent over and brushed her face with his lips.

Downstairs again, he pulled on his coat and carefully, quietly opened the front door. The sky was lightening, but it was very cold, the wind still blowing, more than he'd realised. He closed the door and walked quickly along the wet path towards the garage, and down to his own car, which must have had a battering last night. He gave it the once over – wipers, wing mirrors – before he got in, and then he started up, with difficulty until the engine cleared of water, and backed down through the open gates. The car bumped as he turned into the lane; he drove off slowly, splashing through deep puddles; fallen branches lay on the verge beside the woods, and the trees dripped.

At the end of the lane he stopped, and turned left into the narrow road leading into Saxham; the village was shut up, asleep; he saw one or two garden gates flung off their hinges, and a shattered chimney pot outside the pub, but there was no one up and about to look at the damage and he drove on and picked up speed, feeling as if he were the last person left alive in the world. The wind blew at the car; he thought of Alice, switching on the radio, hearing news of the storm, and drove faster, wanting to get to her.

Out of the village the road was lined with trees again, he remembered this from last night, and here, too, were torn-off limbs, dangling or flung down. He felt as if he'd been driving through a storm-damaged landscape for ever, as if the sky were always threatening and dark, and there was no real need to pay much attention, the only thing that mattered was to get home. He came up to the junction with the Woodburgh road, and said aloud: 'Alice, Alice,' and then he pulled out, too fast, much too fast, feeling the car slip on the wet road as he turned, and seeing, too late, but in terrible slow motion, the yellow dog, running with her tongue out after a dark figure on a motorbike, turning in towards him. With a shout he wrenched at the wheel, and felt the sickening, unstoppable thump of the dog against the front bumper, hurled horribly into the air and on to the bonnet, as he swerved off the road, and crashed headlong into a twisted, half-uprooted tree.

And Miriam, waking with a jerk, heard from outside the banging on the door, and Jon, shouting, and raced down the stairs, her kimono flying, and flung the door open to see him standing there, the limp and broken body of Tess in his arms, his face wet with tears. He staggered inside, and knelt over her, sobbing uncontrollably: 'There's been an accident, get Dad, get Dad.'

7

'Don't die,' said Alice. 'Please don't die.'

Tony lay on a corner bed beneath a small high window. Drips ran into him, tubes led out of him; beside him the thin green line of a monitor rose and fell. Nurses came to check it, and make notes; they hooked up new bags to the drip stands and took his pulse and temperature; they brought Alice tea and went away, crepe soles squeaking on the vinyl floor.

Beyond the high window were pale, drifting clouds; Alice looked up at them and back at Tony's battered face, white beneath bandages, and the black tube of the ventilator. When she'd arrived he was still in the operating theatre; back in intensive care she had not been allowed to see him at first, but was put in a room to wait for the houseman to come and talk to her. Tony had broken ribs and a punctured lung; he had a fractured skull which might or might not mean brain damage, and might or might not mean that he was going to die.

When Alice had been told these things she was allowed, after another, longer wait, to go and sit by his bed; she held his hand in hers and watched strangers trying to save him. The morning's turmoil – police at the door, telephone calls, summoning Tony's mother to come and look after the children, the taxis and the endless train – it was all like a thick tangle of wool in her head, the details already forgotten. There was only now: this corner, this one bed, the patch of sky.

They buried Tess the following afternoon, under one of the apple trees. The ground was sodden after weeks of rain; she was a big dog and it took Stephen and Jonathan a long time to dig out her grave, breathing hard, piling up earth on the wet grass. Miriam watched, her hands in the pockets of her raincoat, Tess's body lying a few feet away on her blanket, mouth open, eyes glazed, one soft ear bent back. She felt numb, disbelieving, waiting for her to raise her head and get stiffly to her feet, as if she had been simply lying in her basket.

But then everything that had happened in the past forty-eight hours felt like this – unreal, dreamlike, remote: Tony's arrival, his face, his voice, his touch, the night of the storm they had spent together, her waking to find him gone, and Jonathan shouting, weeping about an accident. Surely all this could not have happened, so fast, so cruel. And now, somewhere in Norwich and Norfolk Hospital, Tony apparently lay in a coma. That felt crueller and more unreal than anything.

'Okay,' said Stephen. He stood for a moment looking down at the grave, measuring it out, then he propped his spade up against the damp trunk of the apple tree and touched Jonathan's arm. 'I think that's enough.'

Jonathan looked across at Tess, and then away; he propped up the other spade, borrowed from the Innes' farm, and then they both went over to her, and he bent down and wrapped the blanket over her, once, twice, and kissed her head. Miriam watched them and her eyes filled with tears; she went over and bent down to kiss her, too, stroking the cold, muddy face; she tried to bend the soft ear flap forwards, but it was stiff. Her hand met Stephen's, and she drew it away.

'Okay,' he said again, and he and Jonathan lifted her in the blanket, one at each end, and carried her to the grave, and lowered her into it.

Jonathan covered his mouth; he leaned against Miriam and they cried and cried. Stephen stood apart, looking down into the grave where already the earth, disturbed by the body, had begun to fall and settle on it. After a while he came and put his arms round both of them, briefly; then he turned and began to shovel in earth, gently at first, and then quickly, to get it over with.

Miriam dried her eyes, and gave Jon her handkerchief. She stood looking at the fresh black earth covering the body of what had, after all, been something of a child, and certainly a dear companion. The air was cold and still; birds sang. She said to Jonathan: 'Are you all right?' and he nodded, blowing his nose.

'Just about.'

'I'll make her a cross,' said Stephen. 'Or something, anyway.'

'Thanks.'

They looked at each other, and then away.

On the morning of the third day Alice came out of the hospital canteen and walked slowly along the corridor. She had spent the night sleeping fitfully in the monastic little visitors' room, furnished with bed and chair and basin, waking properly at six, when she was used to being woken, wondering where she was and then remembering; she scrambled out of bed, into her clothes, and ran across to the main hospital buildings, through the swing doors into intensive care.

'How is he?'

'No change, I'm afraid. Did you sleep?'

'Not really.'

'Would you like some breakfast?'

She shook her head.

'You should eat something.'

'Not yet.'

She sat by his bed again, watching dawn break in the square of glass, grey as ash, letting the tea the nurse had brought her go cold. Later she telephoned the children, before they left for school and playgroup.

'How's Daddy?' Hettie asked.

'He's still . . . not very well. Don't worry, darling. How are you, are you all right?'

'Yes. I'm helping Granny find things.'

'Good girl. How's Annie, can I talk to her?'

'When are you coming home?' Annie asked.

'Very soon, as soon as I can.'

'When?'

'Ssh, soon. Annie, please don't cry, you go and have a nice time at playgroup, all right . . . Let me talk to Granny now . . .'

Afterwards she wandered into the dining room because it was true, she'd hardly eaten anything since she got here, and had some toast and coffee; and now she was wandering out again, passing patients in wheelchairs and blankets, being taken off down other corridors for tests and X-rays. Doors swung open, porters laughed, students in white coats hurried past her. Except for Oxford, when she was ill, she had always connected hospitals with babies. Last time she was in a hospital was when Sam was born. Before that, Annie, before that, Hettie – with both of them the days had been charged, filled with excitement, tenderness, purpose. She thought now: no one knows what that felt like – *my* babies, *my* days, high as a kite, in heaven. I must have wanted it all my life without knowing it – thinking it was men, and being loved and wanted by men, when it wasn't at all: I ended up in the bin partly because of men, but mostly because no one was going to be born, and I wanted to die. It was Tony who made me want to live, because I knew I could have babies with him and be safe. And now I'm in a hospital again because of him, because he might be going to die, and I don't know what to do, I just know I love him much more than I thought. What should I do? What can I do?

She had reached the end of the corridor; two young nurses in capes, just on duty, came walking towards her, and went past; she realised that she had lost her bearings. For a moment she felt so disoriented by this that it was almost like being back at the hospital in Oxford, when she had wandered many corridors, sometimes sedated, sometimes weeping, not caring where she was going. Then she saw the chapel, which she realised she'd noticed when she arrived, and knew the intensive care unit was somewhere at the other end of the corridor. She went over to the chapel door, and looked inside.

It was cool, church-like, with pews and stained glass windows, a plain brass cross on an altar. Just inside the door was a board, where people had pinned messages. Alice came in, and looked at them curiously. *Pray for my daughter, Penny; pray for my husband, my wife, my father* . . . She had thought only Catholics went in for this sort of thing. The messages were written on little squares of paper taken from a notebook on a shelf below the board; there was a ballpoint on a string beside it. Alice read all the messages, and then she walked slowly into the chapel and sat down. There was no one in here, and she did not believe, had never believed, that if she were to pray there would be anyone to hear her, but to sit in this silence was what she knew she needed. The restless sense of wandering about, not knowing what to do with herself, began to fade. The silence was peaceful, healing: she closed her eyes and saw what in later life she was to think of as a vision: a sunlit field, warm grass and willow trees, a river. She was sitting on a rug, with Hilda and Tony; they were watching the children, Hettie and Annie and Sam, walking along the riverbank, talking about insects. Their voices were high and clear and happy; she put her arm round Hilda and kissed her; she felt Tony take her hand in his, loving and strong; she turned and smiled at him, and kissed him too.

There was a sound behind her, quiet footsteps, someone sitting down. Alice opened her eyes and saw another woman, someone older than her, in a stone-coloured raincoat, with greying chestnut hair. She put her head in her hands, and Alice looked away, but went on sitting there, stilled. Then she got up, and walked out of the chapel. She did not leave a message on the board because even if she had believed in prayer, it was not her style. Nonetheless, when Tony the next day opened his eyes, and clearly, after a moment, knew who she was, it was hard not to think it a kind of miracle.

'Hilda.'

'Stephen.'

'I – how are you?'

'All right. How are you?'

'We must talk.'

'Yes.'

'Well . . . where?'

'Where are you now?'

'In Camden, in the studio. I'm clearing my desk.'

'Oh. You mean – '

'There's a recession, isn't there, it's not just us. There isn't enough work for two of us at the moment. Look . . . Should we meet on neutral ground? I don't suppose you could leave Sam . . .'

'No,' she said. 'I couldn't. Why should I? You're his father.'

There was a pause. 'Please – don't make it too difficult.'

Hilda put down the phone.

When it rang again, it was Alice. Hilda listened, and asked questions, and then she began to cry.

'It's all right,' said Alice. 'He's going to be all right. They're bringing him down to London soon.'

'You don't understand,' said Hilda, weeping.

'What? What do you mean?'

'I . . .' But how could she tell her? How could she say to her: Alice, I betrayed you. I betrayed you! That's why Tony went where he did. Do you realise, Alice, where he must have been? Why he was driving from Saxham to Woodburgh at dawn, where he must have been staying?

'Hilda? What is it?'

'Nothing,' said Hilda. 'I am not myself. Forgive me.' Forgive me. She blew her nose and said carefully: 'When did you get back?'

'This morning. I had to come, the girls were getting upset, and Tony's mother wanted to go and see him, she left after lunch . . . Hilda, are you all right?'

'Yes. Yes, of course I am.'

'How's Sam?'

'Fine, lovely . . .' She began to cry again.

'Do you want to come over? Come and stay . . .'

'I can't, I'm teaching all day tomorrow. Anya has Sam, it's all set up . . .'

'Come at the weekend, then. Will you? Please – I want to see you. And the children will love having Sam.'

'All right, that would be very nice. Thank you.'

They said goodbye, and she put down the telephone. And sat at her desk for a long time, unmoving, miles away, thinking about Tony, about what must have happened, and what had very nearly happened.

I knew I was right not to get involved with people, she thought. Look what has come of it all. She saw herself in the old days, when her life, which seemed now to be in pieces, had been ordered, when she had gone about things sensibly, keeping her distance, and realised: only I can't think like that any more. I've changed, everything's changed. I used to think that feeling was Alice's territory, something to frown on; I used to dismiss it, to call it dwelling on things. But love is the only thing that matters, that gives meaning – how could I have found it possible, before, to live without it?

She thought of her father, who had for so long been the only person she had ever really loved, and whose death, perhaps, had made it possible for her to love Stephen. She thought of Stephen, of the years they had spent together and not together, of the passion they had shared, two such different people, and its gradual diminution, until only differences remained. And after a while she got up, and went into the kitchen, where the family photographs of her homecoming with Sam were still pinned to the cork board, curling a little at the corners. She looked at Alice, shielding her pale face from the sun, and said again: Forgive me. And then she looked at Tony, standing beside her, and felt not so much passion as peace, and recognition, thinking: love is both discovery and confirmation. I have made a great journey, and come home.

There was a sound from the bedroom, a rattle being dropped. She went out of the kitchen and quietly to the bedroom door. Sam was sprawled on his back in the cot, the duvet kicked off, hands open, head on one side; she had left him two or three toys to play with – he must have moved in his sleep and the rattle fallen through the bars. She picked it up and put it quietly on the chest of drawers, and pulled up the duvet, tucking it round him; she bent to kiss his cheek. It was soft and warm, smooth as only a baby's skin could ever be – impossible, after only six months, to imagine how her life would have been without him, how it could ever be without him. I loved Stephen, she thought, and now it's over. I love Tony, but no one is ever going to know about that. And as for this one – perhaps this is the deepest love of all. I suppose Alice has known that all along.

Aloud she said: 'What are we going to do, Sam?' Asleep, he was beginning to look just like Stephen. My journey is just beginning, she said to herself, and I shall be making it alone.

She went out of the room again, leaving the door ajar and the nightlight glowing. Sitting at her desk, she dialled the Camden studio.

The first days of March, very cold. Bitter. Forsythia in suburban gardens, daffodils bent by the wind, the first dusting of green on the London trees. Stephen and Hilda meet, in the end, on neutral territory, but she doesn't leave Sam with Anya. They walk across the common near where Alice and Tony live, early on a Saturday afternoon. Children whoosh down the slide in the playground, or race on their bikes along the paths; dogs run panting after sticks and balls, and seagulls, blown inland from the Thames, flap and scream round shining puddles. It rained last night, it seems to rain every night, but now it is dry, and so cold that the obvious thing to do is wrap your arms around whoever you're with, or run.

Hilda and Stephen do not wrap their arms around each other, they do not even hold hands. They have met at the top of the common, near the church and the tennis courts; now they are walking nowhere in particular but having to keep walking – because of the cold, because it's easier to talk like this. Between them, in the pushchair, Sam is sleeping, shielded from the wind by a plastic cover, unaware, as he will be for years, that his future is being decided.

In the end, because neither of them, for different reasons, wants to talk about recent events, this is the only thing left. They make tentative arrangements: about money, and visiting, and wills. In later years Hilda will on many occasions remember this day, and feel that such arrangements barely touch on what is needed. But this is now, and for now they are doing the best they can. The wind blows in their faces, there is a sharp spring sun, lighting thick white clouds. A beautiful day. Hilda's hands on the pushchair are in woollen gloves; she puts up one of them to secure her beret in a gust of wind, and falls silent. They walk on.

Stephen says: 'Hilda.'

'Yes?'

'Look at me. Please.'

She stops, and looks. A little white dog runs past. Stephen's face is drawn and strained; for the first time she notices that his eyes are paler than when they met, more like the eyes of a much older man, the colour beginning to fade.

He says slowly: 'I did think it would be all right.'

'Yes,' she says, 'so did I.'

'I – ' he hesitates. 'I'm around whenever you need me.'

'You haven't been before. Even when I needed you terribly.'

Hilda 'it was you who wanted a baby.'

'Yes,' she says. 'I know. Your baby.'

'Well . . .' he shakes his head.

She pushes the pushchair back and forth, not because Sam has woken up but because she has to have something to do, something ordinary, and calming. She looks away, and they walk on again. 'You are going back to her, aren't you?'

'I don't know. I really don't think she wants me to.'

'Then what – '

'Exactly,' Stephen says flatly. 'Then what.' His hands are in his coat pockets, he jingles his keys. They have come back to the top of the common, near where he parked his car. 'Anyway – I'd better go.'

'Yes,' she says. 'Well – goodbye.'

'Goodbye, Hilda.' He touches his lips, and drops a kiss on the pushchair's plastic hood. 'Bye, Sam.' He puts a leather-gloved hand on Hilda's woollen one; she lifts her face to his. They kiss, perhaps for the last time. Then he walks away to the car, and she turns the pushchair round, and walks back down the windy common, towards the road leading to Alice's house.

Norfolk, where spring comes late. Stephen pulls up at the house and sees Miriam's car and Jonathan's bike in the garage; he parks inside the open gates. When he gets out, he is about to close them, then remembers there's no longer any need. He takes his bag and portfolio from the boot, leaving a pile of cardboard boxes on the back seat to fetch later: they are filled with papers and drawings from the studio in Camden. He kicks the door shut and walks along the path at the front of the house, where he finds the door unlocked.

'Hello?' Inside the hall he drops his things and calls again: 'Anyone home?'

There is no answer, and after a moment he goes out, and down the front path to the little gate, also left open; he notices that it's half off its hinges, and the wood, covered in damp lichen, is beginning to rot. He goes out into the lane, and looks up and down.

It is late afternoon, and even colder than London, but it has been a fine day up here as well, and the sky, streaked with dark fingers of cloud, still holds gleams of the sun going down behind the trees. He hesitates, then hears the sound of the farm tractor, turning into the lane from the Saxham road: he stands back as it draws near and raises his hand, and Mr Innes nods to him and rumbles past, turning up the cart track. It is a greeting they have been making to each other for years, no different today from any other. Stephen steps off the verge and begins to walk down the lane, past the wide entrance to the track.

The lane is full of mud; there are still uncleared branches from the storm, and the hedges are as bare as the trees and the empty fields that stretch beyond them. From the farm he can hear the tractor stop, and then the faint bleating of lambs, kept near the house. He cannot remember the last time he walked down here.

Miriam and Jonathan appear in the distance, walking towards him, their hands in their pockets; it feels even sadder than he had thought to see them without the dog. He stops, and waits for them.

'Hello.'

'Hello.'

'Hi, Dad.'

'Had a good walk?'

He can hear himself sound like an acquaintance.

'Well . . . it's not very nice without Tess.'

'No. I know. Have you been far?'

'Not really. We've been to see the donkey, that's all.'

He frowns. 'Which donkey?'

'Oh . . . Never mind.'

They turn and walk back towards the house in silence. Birds are settling in the trees, the fingers of cloud grow longer.

'I remember the donkey now.'

Neither of them answers.

'Jon?'

'Yes?'

'How's Marietta?'

'She's going back at Easter. I was telling Mum . . . I might go back with her. Just for a bit.'

'For the holidays, you mean? Like last year?'

'Well . . . perhaps a bit longer.' Jonathan is looking straight ahead, dropping offhand words.

'But . . .'

'He can do his exams next year,' said Miriam. 'Can't he? If he wants. It's not the end of the world.'

'No. No, of course not. Well . . . That sounds all right.'

They have reached the house; they walk up the path, bordered by tight, unopened daffodils.

Miriam says: 'I'll put the kettle on.'

'I'll get in my things from the car. Before it gets dark.'

'Want any help?' asks Jonathan.

'That would be nice. Thanks.'

They walk across, and heave out boxes.

'What is all this stuff?'

'Hasn't Mum told you?'

'What?'

'I'm not going to work in London any more.'

'Oh.' Jonathan dumps a box on the path. 'Because . . .'

'There's a slump in the housing market, hence the building trade. Hence I don't have as much work as I did.' He reaches into the car for the last box. 'So . . .' He emerges from the car and closes the door. 'I'll be around a bit more.'

Jonathan looks at him, and turns away. He fiddles with the flap of one of the boxes. 'What about this baby?'

Stephen leans against the car, and shuts his eyes. 'Shall we just . . . give it a rest? Just for a while.'

There is a pause. 'Okay.'

'Unless . . .' He opens his eyes again; Jonathan is picking at a bit of loose label. 'Unless of course you want to see him. Is that it? Do you?'

Jonathan shakes his head. 'No. Well . . . perhaps one day.'

'Okay. Come on, then, let's get rid of this lot.' They stack up the boxes and carry them round the back of the house, down the path through the hedge to the studio, passing Tess's grave. Stephen opens the door and turns on the light. They dump all the boxes on the floor. Jonathan looks round. The studio is cold, unheated for weeks. There is dust over everything, and some of the plans pinned up above the long white desk have been torn, and mended with Sellotape.

He says: 'I can remember when you first built this place. I can remember coming in here when you first got it organised.'

'Can you?'

'Yes. You gave me a spin in that chair.'

'Did I? I don't remember.'

'No,' says Jonathan. 'I don't suppose you do.'

They go out again, turning off the light.

In the kitchen, Miriam has made tea, and is buttering toast. The table is laid with plates, and pots of jam.

Jonathan says: 'I'm just going to the loo.' He goes out, walking quickly up the passage. Stephen sees Tess's empty basket and pulls out a chair and sits down. He is very, very tired.

'Here,' says Miriam. She puts the plate of toast on the table, and pours him a cup of tea.

'Thank you.' He pulls it towards him, and they drink their tea in silence; Jonathan does not come back. They hear the ting of the phone as he picks it up.

'Miriam?'

'Yes?'

'Are you all right?'

She puts down her teacup. 'Yes,' she says, 'I am.' She turns to look at him. 'What about you? Are you all right?'

'Not really.' The room is warm and familiar, but he feels like an intruder. 'Do you think – ' He puts out a hand towards her, on the table top. 'What are we going to do?'

'I don't know,' Miriam says slowly. 'Don't let's talk about it yet.'

London, the Easter holidays. Hettie and Annie are out in the garden, where it is cold, but not so cold that they need to have their coats on. They are wearing old jeans and sweaters, Hettie on the swing, and Annie putting Sylvanian animals into their plastic tree house. The sun is out; a light wind blows Hettie's hair across her face; she pushes it away, and swings higher. Annie puts Mr Badger on the ladder and helps him climb the steps. 'Up you go.'

Indoors, upstairs, on the other side of the house, Tony is lying in bed. The windows on to the street are open a little at the bottom, and the lace curtains move in the breeze. Tony's eyes are closed; he has been trying to read the paper and given up. His hand rests on the pages, he is beginning to drop off. Alice comes in with a tray.

'Tony?' She puts it down on the bedside table, two mugs of coffee; he opens his eyes, gives a half-smile, and shuts them again. She lifts the paper from beneath his hand and puts it on the floor, feeling his cheek to make sure he's not cold. Then she picks up the tray and goes quietly out again.

In the kitchen she stands at the sink peeling potatoes and watching the children through the window. Sheets and pillowcases billow on the line. Annie looks up, and wipes mud off her hands; she comes to the door, her hair in a tangle.

'I'm hungry.'

'It'll soon be lunchtime.' But Alice knows Annie; she nods towards the fruitbowl. 'Have a banana, go on, and take one for Hettie.'

'Thanks.' Annie reaches up, and almost knocks the bowl to the floor. 'Whoops.' She pushes it back on to the table.

'You are getting sensible.'

Annie gives her a smile. 'What's for lunch?'

'Chicken. Hilda and Sam are coming over, remember? I've bought Sam a present.'

'What is it?'

'Wait and see, I'll show you when I've finished the potatoes. Go on now.'

Annie is struggling with the banana skin. 'Can I go up and see Daddy?'

'Later. He's sleeping.'

She frowns. 'He's always asleep.'

'He's getting better, though, darling. He needs it.'

Annie goes out into the garden again, leaving the door to bang shut.

On the other side of the common, Hilda is walking slowly beneath the trees. She is pushing Sam, who has been awake since six, but who was taken by Anya at nine, so that Hilda could have a rest.

'Are you sure?'

'Of course I'm sure.' Anya held out her arms. 'Come on, Sam, let's have a look at the garden.'

This can't go on, thought Hilda, as she climbed the stairs, but she slept until almost eleven. And now Sam is asleep, mittens on, hood up, face to one side. Hilda walks down the broad sloping path towards the playground. Someone is calling her.

'Hilda! Hilda!'

She looks up to see Jane, pushing her battered old pram. Hilda smiles, and waves back.

'Hello.'

'Hi.' Jane's cheeks are pink from the fresh air, she looks younger than ever. 'Isn't it a lovely day? You haven't been in touch, I've been wondering how you are. What's been happening?'

'Quite a lot,' says Hilda. She looks into the pram, where Daisy is sucking her covers. 'Hello, Daisy. What about you?' she asks Jane. 'How are you?'

'I'm pregnant,' Jane says happily. 'Can you believe it?'

'Oh.' For a moment Hilda is utterly disconcerted. 'Oh . . . that's wonderful. Well done.'

'Well, it wasn't exactly planned,' says Jane. 'Still, we're really pleased.' She looks at Hilda, and suddenly kisses her. 'I know you won't tell me anything unless I prise it out of you. Will you?'

Hilda shakes her head. 'Not at the moment. I'll ring you, though. I'm going to see my sister now.'

'All right.' Jane looks down at Sam's sleeping face. 'He's beautiful.'

'Thanks.'

They say goodbye and Hilda walks on, crossing the road, making her way through the side streets to Alice's house again. She heaves the pushchair up the steps, and rings the bell.

After lunch, they all go out into the garden. It is surprisingly warm now, more like early summer. Alice and Hilda sit at the garden table with their coffee, watching the children. Sam is sitting on a rug, surrounded by Sylvanians. He picks them up one by one and chews their heads.

'Stop it,' says Annie. 'Stop it!'

Alice laughs. 'Give him something else.'

Annie looks round, floundering. She picks up his teething ring and holds it out. 'Go on, that's yours, you have that.' Sam pushes it away, and picks up Mrs Rabbit. Annie snatches it back. 'No!' Sam begins to cry. Hettie, who has been squatting down in a corner, digging, gets up.

'I know,' she says. 'Let's put him on the swing.' She looks across at Hilda. 'Can we?'

Hilda looks at the narrow seat. 'I suppose so. So long as you hold him tight.'

'No, no,' says Hettie. 'Not *this* swing. We've got a surprise.'

'Oh. How nice.'

Alice gets up and goes into the kitchen. 'I meant to put this up before you came,' she says, coming out with a box. She pulls out a baby's swing-seat, yellow, with a safety bar.

'Isn't it brilliant?' says Hettie. 'Isn't it wicked?'

Hilda laughs, and gets up, dropping a kiss on Hettie's dark head. Then together she and Alice unhook the big swing and clip on this one; she picks up Sam, who has stopped crying and is looking up at things with interest.

'There.' She eases him into the seat, pulling his legs through the gaps. 'What do you think of that, then?' She gives him a little push, and he giggles.

'He likes it,' says Annie.

'He does, doesn't he?' She pushes him again, and he smiles and laughs. 'What a success.' She turns to Alice, and puts her arm round her. 'Thank you. Very clever.'

'Not really,' says Alice. 'Anyway, I'm glad he likes it.'

They go back to the table, and sit down; they drink their coffee in a silence which feels, after all these years, companionable, and watch Hettie and Annie, one behind Sam and one in front, pushing him to and fro.

Hilda tells Alice about Jane. She says cautiously: 'What about you? Do you want another one?'

'No,' says Alice. 'Not any more.'

Inside, upstairs, Tony is making his way to the bathroom, slowly but with more confidence. He no longer feels as though he might collapse every time he gets out of bed; he has rested, and eaten a bit of lunch and can feel himself picking up strength. In the bathroom he has a pee, hearing the voices of the children from the garden below. He slowly washes and slowly shaves; he stands at the window and looks down.

The girls are pushing Sam on the swing, back and forth, back and forth; he is smiling all over his face. Alice and Hilda are out of sight from here, but Alice is suddenly visible, getting up and going across the garden to get the washing off the line. He watches her, her slender arms reaching up to unpeg clean cotton sheets, her soft pale hair brushed by the corner of a pillowcase.

Tony goes out, and carefully along the landing. In the bedroom he looks absently at the overflowing bookshelf, wondering if he is up to reading anything yet. The shelf is full of novels, a muddle of his and Alice's, jammed in when they unpacked from the move and waiting, seven years and two children later, to be sorted out. He runs his eye along them, books he hasn't thought about for ages. He pulls out *Vanity Fair*, and sniffs the pages. He'd read that years and years ago, long before Alice. Standing here now, leafing through it again in his pyjamas, he remembers how it ended, although usually he cannot remember endings. He must be getting better.

Amelia had loved her dashing husband George, who betrayed her with Becky Sharp; she was loved all the time by faithful Dobbin.

When George was killed on the battlefield of Waterloo, Dobbin, at last, was able to marry her.

And what happened then? After all the waiting and longing, something had changed. He went on loving her, oh, yes, but it wasn't quite as he'd always thought it would be.